DEADROLL

DEADROLL

A Cycling
Murder Mystery

GREG MOODY

VELO
press®

BOULDER, COLORADO

Deadroll: A Cycling Murder Mystery
Copyright © 2001 Greg Moody

Printed in the United States of America

Distributed in the United States and Canada by Publishers Group West

International Standard Book Number: 1-884737-92-7

Library of Congress Cataloging-in-Publication Data

Moody, Greg, 1952-
    Deadroll : a cycling murder mystery / Greg Moody.
      p. cm.
    ISBN 1-884737-92-7
    1. Ross, Will (Fictitious character)—Fiction. 2. Television broadcasting of news—Fiction. 3. Bombings—Prevention—Fiction. 4. Bicycle racing—Fiction. 5. Colorado—Fiction. 6. Cyclists—Fiction. I. Title.

PS3563.O5525 D43 2001
813'.54—dc21   00-069338

VELO
press®

VeloPress
1830 North 55th Street
Boulder, Colorado 80301-2700 USA
303/440-0601; Fax 303/444-6788; E-mail velopress@7dogs.com

To purchase additional copies of this book or other VeloPress books, call 800/234-8356 or visit us on the Web at velopress.com.

Cover illustration: Matt Brownson
Cover and interior design: Erin Johnson

Acknowledgments

First and foremost, to Amy Sorrells, Tim Johnson and the dedicated staff of *VeloNews*/VeloPress, who always supported and never questioned. Well, they questioned, but they did it politely.

Second, to the staff of WMAX-AM, WRIT-AM, *The Milwaukee Sentinel*, WITI-TV, KUSA-TV and KCNC-TV, as well as other media outlets in the Milwaukee and Denver markets. Not only have you taught me a great deal about radio, newspaper and television journalism, but you have taught me about life as well—some of it funny, some of it crazy, some of it tragic, all of it magic.

And, finally, to Becky, Devon and Brynn, the three women who fill my life with wonder and keep my slippers safe from Cosmo, the Evil Scottie of song and legend.

To Becky

CONTENTS

PROLOGUE

THOUGH THE SUN HAD SET AN HOUR BEFORE, THE HEAT STILL HUNG IN THE Colorado air, still thick with car exhaust, heat, dust, smoke, and the business of the day.

Within another hour or so it would clear, but he saw his chance and decided it was now or never for today.

He had missed her.

He had grown so busy at work that there had been no time for intimacy, for that special moment when two become one.

When the magic began.

He ran his hand along her spine and felt the cool smooth of her back. So long. Too long. Too long alone. Too long away from that touch.

Too often it seemed that he was continually running in place, and work was slowly sapping him, pulling him away from all that was important to him, all the things that made him love to be alive—riding and sex and her. The worst thing about it was that he worked for a bike company. Bikes had been the centerpiece of his entire life, and in working for a bike company, he sat back helplessly and watched the rest of the company, if not the rest of the world, ride like it all belonged to them. They pedaled in from their homes to start their days, flirted shamelessly with whatever it was they considered work, and pedaled off again at the end of the day back into their real lives.

Jesus, he wanted that back again.

His life, well, what there was of it, was now trapped in suits and loafers and dress chinos that were meant to impress the clients. Know us. Ride us. Buy us.

He chuckled, wondering what that would be in Latin.

Cognitum, emere, ire curru?

Oh, what Mr. Sands would say if he knew that ninety-nine percent of all the Latin he had ever learned had squirted out of his ears within forty-five minutes of learning it?

Veni, vidi, oblivisci.

He took a deep breath and let it out slowly, through his nose, lowering his head and resting it upon her.

Too long.

He stood there for a long time, silent, breathing the scent of her in, feeling the curves and bends and welds of her.

She was obsolete, but she was still gorgeous, one last prize stolen from a final year of professional racing in Europe.

The leather of her seat smelled of rides under a French sun, in Italian rain, Belgian cold, of sweat and oil, and also of him. It was not an unpleasant smell, though he could certainly create his own and that could certainly be unpleasant.

He laughed at himself and felt a shudder run through her frame, unexpected, minute, but there nonetheless.

She was ready.

Long overdue.

A bit dusty, perhaps. But who wasn't?

A bit dusty, but ready.

❖

PHIL CASSELL, OF CASTLE SPECTACULARS, WALKED THE EDGE OF THE FLOATING barge one last time. Something was out of place, he knew, but there was no time to completely check the lines, the fuses, or the connections to the charges. They were set, the sun was just a hint over the western mountains and the crowd was growing restless. This was the highpoint of his year, their year. Each and every year everyone was convinced that this year would be bigger, better and more spectacular than anything these mountains had seen in all the years of watching his shows.

Phil smiled. The party downtown at the Lariat after it was all done would be something, no doubt about that. He always drank for free and to excess after a particularly good show.

He shook his head, closed his eyes and looked again at the set-up. Something, somewhere was ringing a bell in his head. But it couldn't be. There simply couldn't be anything wrong.

He had designed the display, created the computer firing program, placed the charges personally and wired them himself. He had then gone back and looked everything over a second, third and fourth time.

Minutely.

If there was something wrong, it had happened today. And he had been out in the middle of the lake since just after dawn, setting his position and getting ready for the show.

Paranoia. That's what it was. Phillip Cassell came by it honestly. His mother was constantly looking over her shoulder, and forever running back into the house to check if she turned off the gas, the water, the iron, even though she had just done it only seconds before. So, maybe he was simply getting as crazy as his old lady. His sister had done it years ago, completely—her train not only jumping the track, but rattling off hell-for-leather across the neighboring countryside. Maybe it was just his turn to go Cassell-crazy.

He flashed the small MagLite on his watch. 9:26. Four minutes to the show.

He ran the small flashlight back and forth over the rows of mortars and rockets and cannons, admiring the layout and the occasional burst of Chinese lettering on the sides. He ran the light along the edges of the barge and saw nothing out of order.

The wires were still correctly bunched. The connections seemed good. He was ready for the show.

He picked up the firing console and stepped off the barge into the small Zodiac, pulling off about fifty feet from the deck of the barge.

His father had spent his life working right in the middle of the fire.

He saw no point in dying that young.

He looked at his watch one more time and waited for the synchronized music from the local radio station to begin.

✴

MAX DOWER HAD BEEN AS OBNOXIOUS AS HELL ALL DAY, SETTING NEW STANDARDS even for a seven-year-old. He ran, he screamed, he got in his mother's face, his father's face, the face of everyone else at the Crooked Lake Lodge.

"Jesus H. Christ, Max," his father moaned, rubbing his forehead and wishing the gin-induced too-much-sun headache would just throb itself away. Perhaps taking him with it.

"Just turn it down a notch, would you son?"

"What's the *H* stand for dad?"

"What?"

"What's the *H* stand for in Jesus H. Christ?"

"It stands for Herbert. He was named after his uncle. Now sit down and be quiet."

But Max didn't. He couldn't. He was a slave to his own hormones and metabolism and chemical imbalance, but no more so than he was a slave to his own excitement. He bounced away from his father and mother and into another group of families—all waiting anxiously for the show, but no one waiting more anxiously than he. Of all the holidays in the world, only Christmas came close to the Fourth of July. The cool evening air, the dark night sky, the sudden lights bursting over his head. And the closer the better.

He wanted to run down to the shore, at least a mile away, but his father wouldn't hear of it. Get caught in Crooked Lake on the Fourth, he said, and you might as well buy a home there 'cuz it will take you forever to get out.

And Max knew he was right.

So why didn't they buy a home, thought Max, buy a home and actually live there, rather than spend thousands each year to stay in a musty cabin a mile away from the action? Because my father is a cheap bastard, he thought, with a nasty smile for thinking a nasty word. And since my father is a cheap bastard, he thought, here he was a mile away, out of the action and overlooking the lake from the Lodge bluff.

Still—it was fireworks. And Dad said that they'd be great. Different, but great. Not as great as being on the lakeshore, with the effects going off over your head and the lake breeze carrying the stinky ash into your eyes. But great. He said it would be great.

Max Dower couldn't wait for the first streamer to reach up into the night sky. Max ran farther away from his parents and the other families, toward the darkened edge of the bluff in front of the pool, stretching out into the night to get closer, closer, to become a part of the shattering lights themselves.

The music started.

9:29:30 ON THE NUT. HE SLIPPED ON THE GOGGLES AND THE EAR PROTECTION, THEN checked his watch again. It was as if it hadn't moved at all.

Phil Cassell turned his watch down, flipped up the red cap of the main toggle and checked it one last time. He had armed the system, and checked his firing box connection for the twelfth time in the past ten minutes. Show time and actually doing the damned performance would be the only thing in the world that could break that one small note of paranoia running through his head like a hopped-up hamster on a nonstop wheel.

Putting on his performance face, he forced the random thoughts out of his head so he could listen carefully for the opening strains of music to drift across the lake from the huge speakers on the beach. He took a deep breath. It was time to put up and shut up. A tinny symphonic sound, the opening strains of the music rose up in the darkness, supposedly coordinated to the fireworks show.

It was thin, but it was loud. He was loud. It would be close enough. After the first three rounds, no one would notice the music again that night. He fired the opening mortar.

Show time.

Whatever had been bothering him before would have to wait now for nineteen minutes and fifty-five seconds. The show had begun. Phillip Cassell was in his element. He had become Zeus, with thunderbolts flying from his fingertips.

With the exquisite timing and flair of a showman, he fired his charges with a calculated rhythm. One and up and over, and two and up and over, and now a combination, sailing into the night sky. The explosions above him reflected in the black water below, giving him the chance to clearly see the firing system and never look away to confirm if everything was going as planned.

It was. It was gorgeous. He was a star. The black water of the lake told him that it was so.

The pops of the firing charges were dead in his soundproofed ears, but he knew their sounds well enough to realize that he was perfect tonight. Not a short. Not a misfire. Not a dud.

Bingo.

Ten minutes into the performance and he fired the mid-show combination, the false finale; a collection of effects designed to make the audience think, for even a few seconds, that they had been shorted and that all their time spent waiting in the sun and dealing with the kids and shoveling down marginal potato salad had been for nothing more than ten lousy minutes of fireworks.

The launch charges popped on the barge with a staccato roll. All in perfect order. All with a perfect pitch even to his muffled ear.

Pop-pop-pop/pop/pop/pop/pop-pop-pop-pop … pop

All the perfect sounds were followed closely on board by one single sound he dreaded more than any other.

One additional round. Something wired-in that wasn't meant to be there. How could he have miscounted? It wasn't possible. He was a perfectionist.

The false finale had ten charges. And somehow, he had wired in eleven.

Thunk. Shit. Short round. Short launch. Short flight. Destined to fire just above his head. He instinctively crouched down, using the Zodiac as a kind of floating foxhole in the icy water.

Well, he thought, at least he had discovered what had been bothering him all day.

He watched the water in that split second and realized that it might turn out all right. The final charge hadn't been a short round after all, but was rising lazily up into the night sky, surrounding by the balls and sparkles and starbursts of the planned display.

Breaking his own rules, he looked up to see what it would be and how he had managed to surprise himself.

At 9:40:25 P.M. on Tuesday, the Fourth of July, Phillip Cassell saw the sun come out for a second time that day, and then felt a gigantic hand push him and the Zodiac straight down into the icy grip of the mountain lake. As the blackness closed around him, almost a relief after the quickly searing heat of the sun's return, his final thought was that he was going to have a hell of a time topping this one next year.

※

MAX DOWER TOOK IT ALL IN WITH A SHADE OF DISAPPOINTMENT. HE WAS TOO FAR away. He wanted to be back at the Lakeside Lodge, as the fireworks went off over his head, seemingly closer, closer and closer with each and every burst of air, the reports popping his ear drums and making his lips wiggle.

This was nothing. This was too far away. It was like watching them on TV.

They were nothing but little puffs and pops and starbursts way too far away to make anything seem spectacular. Light a sparkler and stick it in the lawn and walk twenty feet away, why don'tcha?

A flurry of starbursts and cascades caught his eye and for a second, just a second, he thought that maybe the show was already coming to an end. But then instinctively, he knew, naw, they did this every year. A big thing in the middle of the show to make you think it was done, teasing you, hooking you in, so that you were relieved when it continued on for another ten or fifteen minutes.

He knew them too well. Whoever did this might be a showman, but he was becoming predictable, even to a boy Max Dower's age.

Then, Max's eye caught the lazy ascent of a single, yellow streamer, which seemed, somehow, out of place. Not because it was spectacular—it wasn't—but simply because it was different. Why, he didn't know, it was just different. Like it was somehow out of place, designed for something else, somewhere else, sometime else.

He barely had time to blink.

The light of the blast was on him in a second, in a double beat, as if someone had just turned on a powerful flash bulb.

Wham-wham.

The world ignited around him. It was as bright as day.

Then the sound. A hard-edged *crack!* that started sharp, then grew into a deep-throated roar, a freight train of sound that grew and grew until he thought his head would explode.

The pressure wave then hit him full in the face with a hot slap. The concussion flapped his lips like those of a dog hanging its head out the window of a Dodge Durango on a downward slope of Interstate 70.

Max was picked up by the change in air pressure and rolled backwards up and against the chain-link fence of the lodge pool. As the boom rolled across the lawn, echoing back and forth, he could hear windows shattering and screams of both women and men tossed ass-over-teakettle across the Lodge lawn.

He slid down the chain link fence to the ground, and stared without seeing toward the lake, which was still foaming and cresting as the noise and light receded.

Whatever the show had been before, it was over with now. Short, but definitely worth it.

Max looked, shook his head and smiled.

"Yeah!" he screamed, pumping his fist in the air.

"Yeah! Yeah! Yeah! Yeah!"

For once in his life, his father had been right.

These seats were better.

✵

THE MAGIC BEGAN.

It rose up out of the tarmac, and through the dry, hard skin of the Continentals, rippling first along the surface and then through the fibered skeleton of the tire until it reached the aero' rims, setting up a growing progression of sound. It hummed along the spokes and through the Mavic hubs, then into the steel front fork of the Colnago.

As he leaned into the ninety-degree turn, it shifted, slightly, to a higher pitch, giving the move its own special sense of danger, its own heightened sense of life.

As he rose up out of the turn, he could feel the power of the road tingle the palms of his hands through the gloves, then rise up into his wrist, his elbows, his shoulders, then to his chest. His heart began to beat faster, his breath grew deeper, his face, slowly, began to flush.

Not long now.

He dug down into himself and picked up the pace, watching his ankling, his rhythm, perfect small circles just inches above the road, three feet below where his eyes focused now.

Ahead, he reminded himself, always ahead.

The magic is always just ahead.

The wind grew in his ears and then slackened, the shift moving it to his back. Tailwind out. Headwind back. The rules of the road. He broke his concentration for a split second to avoid a landscaping rock thrown onto the street, worried for a moment about losing his rhythm, then dropped immediately back into it. Ankle, knee, hip. Ankle, knee, hip. Circles. Perfect circles.

He felt himself slide away, the homes on either side beginning to blur. The scenery dropped away, no longer a part of his world. Ahead, he saw the road, the obstacles, the traffic, three, six, ten, fifteen, twenty feet, his gaze running out to half a mile, then back in, section by section, partitioning the road, his route, his future.

Waiting for the magic.

It grew. He could feel its approach. It sat just behind his heart and moved slowly upwards. It was almost here. He could feel it. One more time, it would be his, one more time, just one more.

The course wound through the foothills west of Denver, past fields of prairie dogs that would soon be evicted to make way for another cookie-cutter development. Homes exactly alike, all six feet apart, one kitchen looking into another, the smells mingling with the conversations among people who didn't know each other and couldn't stand each others' guts if they did. Homes where you could get any color you wanted, as long as it was putty. Homes built by developers who gutted the land, and now enjoyed the sunset from the deck of their multi-million dollar California coastal home, nowhere near the scene of the crime. A bubble of anger rose in his chest as his blood pressure rose to meet the demands of the ride. It grew into a rage, a fury, then, popped, gone as quickly as it had presented itself.

He shook his head. He was close.

Lost in his reverie, he had pushed it away. It was a delicate thing, this magic. It came from the road itself, he felt it slowly, ever so slowly, but then it quickly disappeared if the focus was lost and the connection broken. He chopped the road ahead again with his eyes, breaking it down into smaller sections he could deal with as he reached each and every one: turn, dip, hill, flats.

Look ahead. The magic is ahead.

More quickly than he thought it would happen, the feeling again rose upon him, the scenery began to blur around him and he swept through a corner into the quiet of the foothills, blocked by a natural barrier from the madness of the city now behind him. Despite the climb, he rose up out of the saddle and picked up his pace.

He rode the route, or one close to it, six days a week in the past. Then, he had been in the best aerobic shape of his life. He had let it slip away. Now, the first rise, the first real climb, caught him off guard, wheezing, sweating, phlegm catching in his throat. He hacked and retched and blew something solid toward the side of the road, fertilizing a lawn that was greener than nature ever intended.

He gagged again.

This, too, would pass, but it would push the magic away for another moment as he dealt with the harsh reality of an older body, higher stress, thinner air and the ever-present brown cloud.

Again, he spit a glob of something to the side. This time it was brown. It could have been coffee, it could have been the Denver air, it could have been something he swallowed when he was sixteen. It was gone now. He rose to the false summit of the hill and picked up his pace again.

There was no longer any wind, only moving air he alone created, heavier, warmer, wetter, and somehow tougher to cut through, all of his own making.

Then it came.

Now. Now was the moment.

He crested the hill, took the short straight into the hard right turn, then banked left, tucked and charged ahead. He could feel the hum, the waver, the rise with a momentary hesitation.

He charged ahead. A distant roll of thunder passed him on its way to the Kansas border. Now, now.

Now.

The sound in his ears evaporated. The world around him disappeared. There was no bike. There was no road. There was no world. There was no him. There was only the ride.

And without his realizing it, the magic was upon him again.

The magic was his, for a few minutes, a few miles, a few turns.

And he felt alive again.

Will Ross felt alive again.

The magic had returned.

Once again.

Thank you, Herbert.

CHAPTER ONE:

HERE WE GO AGAIN ...

"WHATCHA DOIN'?"

The voice caught Will off guard. He had been staring out the window, wistfully looking up at the cloudless sky of a gorgeous June day, wishing he was out in it, catching a rhythm on the flats. But he wasn't. He was sitting inside a heavily paneled, musty old LoDo office, which had plenty of personality, but lousy plumbing and not a lick of fresh air. At the turn of the last century, it had been a whorehouse.

It had lost some of its luster.

"Hmm? Oh, nothing," Will nodded, turning to his boss, Hootie Bosco, Chief Operating officer of Bosco Bikes. "I was," he stammered, "I was ..."

"Not working on endorsements, that's for sure," Bosco said, shaking what remained of his Rastafarian dreadlocks, the rest being lost over the past few months to both maniacal barbers and the demands of the corporate world.

"I know you'd rather be riding, so would I, bud, but we've got to get the endorsements set up for the 9000. You've got the contacts. You've got the job. You've got to get on the stick."

Will smiled and nodded, wishing that the Hootie he had first met was still the Hootie he now worked for, the man who looked like he had Slinkys for hair and could adjust a bike at sixty miles-an-hour while hanging out of a Peugeot's back window, not the sudden multi-millionaire who had parlayed a trunk of misplaced mob cash into a high-end bike company in less than fourteen months.

Bosco Bikes. Ridden by the pros. Endorsed by them as well. The endorsements had been gathered up by Will, playing off of favors owed him after too many years of riding the circuit in Europe, in spite of the fact that the bikes were too heavy and everyone in Europe refused to ride the things off the location of the commercial photo shoot.

But Hootie believed they would. It was a graceful, almost childlike faith in the product, the last gasp of a fascinating personality. The past few months had really changed Hootie. He had gone from a loose and amiable guy —"Hey, kids, let's build some bikes in this place I found downtown"—to one who was deeply into marketing, research and beating the other bike builders to the next step.

"You with me?"

"Yeah," Will nodded, knowing that he really hadn't heard a word said since Hootie had walked into his office, as if his brain was playing the theme to "Green Acres" over and over on an endless loop drowning out anything and everything that was said to him. "Yep, caught it all."

"Well, get on it, then, bud. You don't, I'll find someone who can."

Ohhh, thought Will, that was a red flag. That he had heard. Eb and Lisa and Mr. Douglas had quickly retreated to Hooterville while he mulled that thought over. What did he really think about Hootie finding somebody else to do his job?

"Sure," Will said, nodding dumbly, wishing in that moment he had the courage to say, even under his breath, that ol' Hootie should go out and do just that: Find somebody else. But courage fled quickly when you were trapped by circumstance.

Reality sucks when you're in it up to your neck.

His wife was pregnant, they had just bought a little house they could barely afford, and, quite frankly, there were no other prospects. He was a torn-up, burned-out, washed-up rider with a bad knee, no right calf to speak of and a reputation worse than a black widow spider.

His final season on the circuit had been his best ever. A win at Paris-Roubaix and a wild ride in Le Tour, but people had had a nasty habit of dying around him while he was riding that year. Thirteen dead bodies by his last count, although there may have been a few he missed. And you really couldn't blame him for old man Bergalis, that dude was already ancient.

He just died.

You couldn't blame Will for natural causes.

But there were plenty of bombs and bikes and bullets, at least two syringes and one mountain lion. Couldn't take the blame for that, could he? That was Mother Nature's fault, that mountain lion. He had just been nearby to witness it.

Thirteen.

That would make a pretty good plane crash. Lucky thirteen.

He had been the lead story on national news—then. Today, he couldn't even make it below the fold in some suburban shopper's guide. Thank God for small favors.

As he had been mentally counting up the bodies, a persistent buzzing slowly intruded upon his thoughts. He came to realize, through sheer will alone, that his eyes were staring at Hootie Bosco, his ears were hearing the latest marching orders from Hootie Bosco and his brain was someplace else altogether, whistling through the barnyard with Arnold Ziffle.

He nodded.

"Got it."

"Got what?" Hootie asked suspiciously.

"What you just said," Will answered carefully, mentally trying to keep his face from flushing, revealing the truth that he hadn't been listening worth a damn. "But, I wonder if you could have Nance put it on paper for me? I work best when I've got a checklist in front of me that I can just work my way down to make sure I hit all your points."

"All my points ..."

"All your points." Will nodded dumbly.

"Look, Will," Hootie sighed, quietly, running his fingers through what was left of his hair, making it wiggle like a Jello mold gone furry, "the business is changing. The company is changing. We aren't a bunch of goofs who just happened to land in some dough and create a bicycle company. Not at all. Not any more. We're a real, honest-to-God business now. I can't go back to smoking doobies the size of a baby's arm and hair that looks like it was done in a Mix-Master, much as I might want to. I'm the boss. The company lives or dies on my say so. The line lives or dies on my actions. Your career—and those of seventy-four other people—live or die on how I do. We do. You do."

"I know."

"I'm not sure you do, Will. We're in it now. The past is gone. The Hootie Bosco you knew is just an advertising slogan now. An image on paper. That's all.

We are in it up to our eyebrows. We've caught the wave. We're the next big thing. We're popular. We're the name that everyone is riding. From little André in France to Willie Gilligan down the street in Aurora. That's us."

The theme from *Gilligan's Island* suddenly intruded in his head. Will pushed it away.

"You're a part. You signed on. Your career is done. That's a fact. Your job is here now. Either you get with the program, or you move on and I find somebody else with a fire in his belly who is ready to step in and do this."

Will said nothing, but just kept staring at his old friend and present boss. He was right. No doubt about it. It was the hard reality of the world.

But there was a problem here, a problem that had been bothering him for weeks, if not months. Almost from the moment he signed his name to the exclusive, three-year management contract with the two-year noncompete clause at the end.

The problem was that he just didn't want to be a part of it anymore.

It wasn't any fun. The magic, he realized, was not in the bike business, not in the machines, but on the road itself, in what rose up out of the ground and forced itself through his muscles and heart and mind when he rode.

The magic was in the road. It sure as hell wasn't in this office.

Still, in the back of his mind, there were bills, babies and house payments keeping his mouth shut. And there wasn't anything else he could think of to do. He wasn't qualified for anything other than this, shaking hands with old bike riders, reliving the old days and hoping beyond hope that they knew the young riders who were willing to sell out their names to promote a particular bicycle. His bicycles.

There were so few major careers that depended on second-rate riders past their prime with no right side to speak of, not anymore.

Maybe he could block hats. Shine shoes. Dig ditches. No, no ditches. No right side, remember?

He smiled.

"Hootie," he said with as much enthusiasm as he could muster, "I'm with you. I'm with you."

Hootie Bosco nodded, unconvinced.

"Alright," he sighed, "alright. I'll go with that. But make sure that you are,

Will. I've got two people in line right now who want nothing more than to sit in this office and tell you what to do."

"Who?"

"That's not important."

"Sure it is, Hoot, I mean, who is sneakin' up with a meat cleaver? I'd like to know at least which hallway they're takin' to reach me."

"Just people with drive and ambition. They're the future of this business."

"Not old hacks who just happen to be friends, right?"

"There comes a point, Will, where friendship doesn't enter into this—can't enter in."

"What does Nancy think?"

"What?"

"What does your secretary think?"

Hootie was caught off guard by that one. He stumbled for a moment, then shook his head.

"Not a thing. This is a management decision, not a clerical one."

"Okay. Interesting," Will nodded.

"What is that supposed to ... never mind. Just keep in mind what I said, Will. I mean it."

Hootie turned quickly and headed down the hall to the stairway. Will could hear the stair joints creak as Hootie took the steps two at a time in a rush to get away.

Will had his answers.

First, he now knew that Hootie and his secretary, Nancy, had a thing going. The rumor machine was right for once. Now he knew why Hootie's complexion had done such a one-eighty.

And, secondly, Nancy was on Will's side. Who knew why, it had just worked out that way. Yeah. She had told him, on the sly, that this was coming. That his job could be on the bubble. She knew that Lisa Shannon, the chunky number two in sales, was angling for his job, and was running with a bunch of ex-pros in Denver and doing deep knee bends for an America Cycling coach in the Springs in the hopes of gaining the sprint lane to Will's job. Then there was Bobby Francota, a kid in the warehouse, who claimed that he personally knew LeMond and had also been helping Lance Armstrong with his motivational speaking gigs.

Will didn't believe him. Didn't know how anybody could. But you never knew who was saying what, what was being heard and, more than that, what was finally accepted as the truth.

Keep an eye on them. Keep an eye ...

Christ, Will thought, shaking his head. Now he was worried about keeping a job he hated. How did that happen?

He chuckled. The threat of a mortgage payment hanging over his head. He pondered what the world might be like if everybody owned a paid-off house. Would there be a sudden burst of people telling their bosses to stuff it? Or, would everybody just dig themselves deeper into another debt? He sighed, checked the clock, picked up the phone, and tapped out an endless string of numbers, hoping to catch Richard Bourgoin in his Team Haven office in Paris before his traditional afternoon ride. Maybe they could shoot the breeze, air out the laundry and see if there was any way that Haven could pick up more Boscos for the last half of the season, maybe even ride one or two in Le Tour.

Impossible, sure, not about to be done, not in the real world, but this was no longer the real world and Will knew that he wasn't above calling in a favor or two to save his own ass. The ass he didn't necessarily want to be saved.

That was the real world. That was reality.

And after Bourgoin, there was Carl Deeds in Switzerland. And Tony Cacciavillani in Milan. And Winston McReynolds, south of London.

Old friends. Old favors.

In search of new markets.

To save an old and tired ass.

His old and tired ass, to be precise.

He spent the rest of the day dialing and chatting and trying not to plead, but little came of it. The bikes Tony agreed on for low-end riders in practice certainly wouldn't be enough to pay for the calls. But a few here, a few there, maybe a criterium win late in the season and it could snowball from there. A Bosco bike carrying the Yellow Jersey was the dream. Now he just had to set himself and the company up to getting it, to winning the biggest photo op prize in Paris.

Everybody wants to ride the winner—and now you can on a Bosco bike, ridden by the winner of the Tour de France.

Shit. Even his daydreaming was thin, watery and filled with marketing piffle.

Why the hell was he even bothering?

He looked at the clock, spun his feet off the desk, gathered up a few things to take home and read later, though they'd largely be ignored, and walked to the door.

He checked the hall both ways before he stepped out.

It was the end of the work day, but since he hadn't accomplished anything other than boost the daily profits for AT&T International, he still felt guilty about leaving.

But leave he did.

✳

ROGER FLYNN WAS PISSED.

Not merely pissed, but raging pissed.

It was the kind of raging pissed that made the vein in his right temple stand out like the Great Wall of China as seen from ten thousand feet. The kind of rage that took him from the world of being just another sports anchor to Mephisto, King of the Underworld.

The production assistant, another low-paid flunky more than likely just out of J-school, or worse, just hired off the street, had failed—once again—to deliver, to his hand, his scripts. He hustled down the hall toward the studio and realized that he was, again, about to miss the "Supertease," the around-the-horn promotion at the end of the "A" block of the early evening news that he was nightly reminded not to miss, but, somehow, through a mental block, or some deep-seated hatred of having to share face time with the three other boobs on the set—weather knob, old dude and techno bitch—he regularly did miss. The result was more time spent in the news director's office being told how unprofessional he was than in the sports office—his domain—where he could tell everyone else where to get off, from the news director bitch to the coach of the Denver Broncos.

He hustled.

Across the atrium, down the hall, he strode past the gallery of huge studio portraits of former anchors and reporters and beloved weather men, including that one with the sock puppet who always made Flynn laugh. Damn, what were they thinking? Puppets on a newscast? Small town. Big-city small-town news.

Jesus. Amateur night.

7

And the audience loved it.

One of the largest portraits, certainly in the most ornate frame, was of a striking blonde in a frozen pose, her nobility clearly an affectation, her regal gaze pointed at some distant horizon in search of the truth.

Barbara. The anchor woman turned news director.

Without pause, he swung his left fist in a quick, short arc toward the picture, and the glass at her crotch splintered with a muffled pop, a sound unheard within the station that had quickly emptied out ten minutes ago at five P.M. He had moved so quickly that his fist was back at his side before the first muffled echo of the impact returned to his ear.

Flynn smiled. He felt better. He still didn't have his scripts, he was still late, but he most certainly felt better.

He hurried on, and turned the last corner, passed through the sound door, through the second, into Studio A, the main news studio.

The floor director took a quick look at him, keyed his microphone and said, quietly, "He's here."

That was all. No "Saints be praised" or "I'll be damned," just "He's here."

That didn't matter to Flynn. He wanted to kick the guy in the nuts. Another damned flunky who didn't know shit, probably couldn't tie his shoes, and surely didn't go through four interviews at ESPN 2 before losing the job to that twit from Kalamazoo and winding up here in Denver. Four call-backs. At ESPN 2. What did this asshole on the studio floor have to show for anything in his life?

"Fifty seconds," the floor director said to no one in particular.

Flynn stopped mid-stride, balancing on the first and second step of the news set. He turned to the floor director.

"I don't know how many times I've got to remind you of this: Don't talk to me unless I talk to you first."

The kid on the floor took a short, deep breath and said, to no one in particular, "forty-five seconds."

Flynn took his seat beside the ancient male anchor, one of the few people in the country who had stayed on the air in the same city for his entire career, an unheard of achievement in the annals of local TV news, a nomadic existence at best. The man reeked of cigarette smoke and vaguely of a martini. By ten o'clock, the cigarette scent would be stronger, but so would that of the martini. How he got through a newscast without going headfirst into the desk and flipping his toupee into the ether was anybody's guess.

Flynn turned to his camera and waited for part three of African Odyssey to end, a news series based on an afternoon anchor's journey to a small African village with some manufactured tie to one of Denver's suburbs.

How'd she talk them into the money for that, and Jesus, the time, six and one-half minutes per story on the news, when he couldn't convince them to pick up the tab for a dinner at a playoff game in New York?

So what if the bottle of wine tipped the scales at $325?

Didn't he deserve some consideration?

He folded his hands on top of his scripts, placed on his position at the news desk, without noticing them.

The old dude was talking. Roger smiled. The rhyme of the ancient mariner. He always put his teases into a sing-song rhythm. "In Crooked Lake today, investigators were held at bay ..." Shit. So small town. How the hell did this dude survive so goddamned long? Now it was the techno bitch. Swept-back hair, bedroom eyes and a chest that made you want to just reach out and ... weather, jolly weather, yes, tornadoes tomorrow afternoon on the plains, we'll chase them for you.

The tally light glowed red on camera three.

"And I'm Roger Flynn, speaking of sports—the Av's trade hot, the Rocks swing big sticks—and—you won't believe the bike race I've got for you."

He smiled, his piercing one hundred watt, "we're all in this together" smile. The tally light blinked clear. The smile disappeared a milli-second later. He leaned back in his chair and stepped from the set without saying a word.

No one said a word to him until he reached the door.

"Roger," the aging anchorman called quietly from across the studio, "next time you might want to remember to put on your microphone."

He stopped, turned and smiled, about to say "Thank you, Tom, for noticing," in a smarmy tone of voice, when he heard frantic footsteps outside the studio doors.

Two steps away, the doors opened with a crash and the production assistant bounded in. Roger caught the young woman by the left arm and spun her to meet him. Her eyes went from clear and excited to dark and troubled within the instant of his touch.

He squeezed, hard.

Flynn had screwed up. Now it was time for someone else to pay.

"Don't you ever—ever—forget my scripts again. Do you understand me?"

"Yes. Yes, I do."

"Yes I do, what?"

The PA took a deep breath and looked at the floor in despair. She looked at the set for help. The weatherman was gone, Tom Blakely was in another world and Martine was checking her makeup. There was no salvation.

"I understand you ... Mister Flynn."

"Better. Better."

"I left them on the set for you ... your scripts ..."

"I want them in my hand. In my hand. You—are my cue to leave for the studio. I miss another Supertease and you've lost your little career in TV."

"Understand?"

"Yes. Yessir. Yes, Mister ... Flynn."

She tugged at her arm and pulled it away. It hurt like hell, but this was, she figured, the price for being in TV. You just put up with the pricks.

"Great," he smiled, flexing his fingers, "I'll see you during weather with my segment copy."

"Yessir." She nodded, looked at the floor and hated herself for not acting on her gut instinct to kick him in the nuts and turn him into a soprano. Her father would be furious with her for not standing up for herself.

Flynn smiled at his small victory, crossed to the double doors and stepped into the hall, walking quickly through the shortcut that would take him back to his office.

Shit kickers, he thought. Floor directors who let the tally lights do their work for them and anchors who haven't moved from their chairs in forty years. He smirked, that last thought gave a whole new meaning to the word "anchor," like an albatross hanging around the station's neck.

Damn, he thought, he should anchor. He could do it and likely double his salary. And—more, if he could parlay it all into a bigger TV market, Chicago, LA, New York.

Or national. Remember E-S-P-N-2. They loved you.

Roger Flynn could take Bob Costas apart.

What a loser.

He turned down the last hallway toward his office, already beginning to turn the phrases over in his head. The Av's were easy, the trade with Vancouver was hot enough to melt the ice in the Pepsi Center. Dust off the shelf for another Stanley Cup. The Rockies wouldn't be all that tough either, toss in a few thin-air home run jokes and the fans would eat it up.

That bike race, though, that goddamned all-day bike race in the mountains. Shit. He had no idea what the hell he was going to say about that and say about it in such a way that the audience wouldn't bail on him and switch the channel to reruns of *Friends*.

Who the hell cared about cycling? No viewer he knew, even though bikes were hot in Colorado. Riding didn't translate to watching, as far as he was concerned. And to top it all, he was giving up a vacation weekend in July to cover it.

"You're goin' to pay me for it," "no, we ain't goin' to pay you for it," he mocked aloud.

Goddamned station. So goddamned cheap.

He'd have to bring it up with the news director when he sat down with her to explain why he didn't have his microphone on tonight.

He stepped into his office, crossed to his cubicle and sat down in his chair. He glanced at his Far Side calendar and saw the reminder note on it that tomorrow morning would be an early one. Production had set up a site survey for the bicycle course so he could familiarize himself with it.

What the hell. He could sleep in the back of the car.

Turning to the computer screen, he read over the trade story again on the wire and refreshed himself on the afternoon baseball scores.

He still didn't know what to say about the bike race.

He'd make it up on the set.

He did anyway.

He hadn't used a script in years

❋

EVEN THOUGH THE GUY SOUNDED LIKE HE WAS TALKING INTO THE BOTTOM OF A FIFTY-five-gallon drum, Will could still, if barely, make out what he was saying, through his own haze of two beers and a droopy-eyed run up to an early evening nap.

You didn't get much international cycling news from the local TV station, so he hadn't been listening for it.

But just that hollow mention had been enough to make him sit up, pay attention and fumble for the volume control on the remote. He turned it up now for a Dodge commercial from some guy named Dealin' Doug.

He drained his third can of Tecate and wormed his butt back into the seat of the couch. Now he was ready to pay attention, even though he knew it would be a while. He never paid much attention to the nightly news, *Six at Five*, but he knew enough that he would have to sit through more news, weather, some feature thing, and an army of commercials before he would get the chance to find out what the hell that sports guy, Flynn, the one with the jerk-off smile, was saying about a bike race.

Governments could fall, candidates could rise, the price of everything could do a roller-coaster dance across his bank accounts, planes could crash—and always did a day or so before he had to fly anywhere—Fourth of July celebrations could go up in a pillar of fire and anchorwomen could go to Africa, but nothing caught his attention more than two words: *bike race*.

Sad, but true. And despite the bitter social commentary of his realization, Will Ross realized that he was smiling.

He leaned back over the couch and looked up the stairs of his transplanted Milwaukee bungalow.

"Hey, sweetie," he shouted, "you might want to come on down. I think we've got a race coming."

His wife was no better than he was about such news. Two seconds after his call, and her reply, "On my way," Cheryl Cangliosi Ross, seriously pregnant, bounded down the stairs, two at a time, dropped heavily into the seat beside him, curled her arms around his, burrowed into his side and whispered hotly in his ear, "What's up?"

Despite her condition and the problems that this sort of thing had already led to, he realized that he already was.

But that could wait. Right after this story about a small mountain town decimated by a Fourth of July accident, there was the story he wanted to hear.

There was going to be a bike race.

✳

IT WAS A LIVING, BREATHING THING. IT WAS CREATED LIFE, HE THOUGHT, IN THE manner of a demi-god, a creature that existed with the ability to take other lives, while its own would be so very difficult to take.

The machine hummed, very softly. The secondary was set. The lid of the antique Andy of Mayberry lunchbox was closed and latched, the primary trigger now coiled inside of it in a maze of red, blue, green and white wires.

"Figure out my color scheme," he whispered to no one in particular, then gazed at the lid of the box.

Andy of Mayberry.

It was the only antique he had found that had a bicycle theme at all. Gomer Pyle, in the background, riding a huge, old, heavy-framed fat-tired bike.

He shook his head, vaguely wondering if bicycling had been such a great choice. Baseball, now, that would have been something: packed stadiums, rabid fans, lots of media coverage, a wonderful secondary target, a way to truly re-announce his arrival after the spectacular debut at Crooked Lake. But something about this upcoming race through the mountains of Colorado had caught his eye and his mind, and, now, he couldn't quite shake it.

He wasn't sure why. It was as if a hand of destiny was pushing him toward a target he didn't fully realize or understand yet.

He flipped open the brochure and stared at the sponsor logos. The tea company. The TV station. Some on-the-web insurance company. He stared at the corporate insignia to renew his commitment. It was their smugness, their holier than thou attitudes that gnawed at him. This superior attitude of having the money to sponsor something as stupid as a bicycle race when he could use it for something important. Like a new, high-end Mercedes.

Now that would be worth it.

He continued to stare at the brochure and the map of the ride. First this way, then that, until he knew the exact progression of the race course.

This was like a drama. A well-constructed drama. It had to build to a crescendo. A little in the first act, maybe even a prologue. Confusion in the second. The drama then building, building in the third until it reached up and grabbed the audience with the power of its finale, leaving them with nothing but awe for the creator of the production, and, in this case, the miracle of his machines.

It would be perfect. He felt a glow of pride deep within his chest.

He had merely given them the prelude at the lake. One big, spectacular show out of nowhere, there and gone, but this time, this time, he would have to build and do it in such a way that they'd see a formal pattern as he moved on to baseball and basketball and hockey and golf.

The suspense would build, the destruction increase, the ingenuity progress, each and every time, and they'd never be smart enough to catch up with him.

Each moment, each time, with each new machine, he'd grow a little larger, get a little better, and make a bigger statement.

A bigger statement with a bigger payoff at the end, as much in satisfaction as in money, though money would not be a bad plan, either.

He wiped down the metal lunchbox one last time, picked it up carefully in his gloved hands and turned out the garage lights before he stepped out the door and carefully walked in the darkness to his car.

He had a delivery to make.

Not much.

Just a calling card, really.

A small surprise that couldn't kill, most likely, but would certainly surprise the living hell out of somebody. Who knew? Maybe surprise the living right out of them, too.

Maim them the way he had been maimed.

Take notice of me, you bastards.

For Peter the Great has arrived.

He looked at his watch.

The evening news was just ending.

He'd give them a lead story for yet another newscast.

That's for damned sure.

CHAPTER TWO:
THE HUMAN CANNONBALL

THE ROUGH IDEA HAD KEPT HIM UP ALL NIGHT, TOSSING AND TURNING IN his mind just as he was tossing and turning on the Serta. Cheryl would grumble deep within her dreams, roll into a new and very uncomfortable position, and then begin to snore again.

She had never snored before, but the pregnancy was giving her a doozy of a honk, nothing like his Dad, to be sure, but a good, solid, low-grade rumble to keep Will company through the night.

And so he rolled and thought and pondered and decided. This idea would be perfect for Bosco bikes. Not necessarily as big as having a Tour team ride the product, but that was years away—if ever. For that, he'd need an American team that he had contacts within, lots of promises, and, more than anything else, a product that someone could possibly ride to victory. As much as Hootie might believe in his bikes, Bosco bikes were, at this stage of the game, stiff, unresponsive and too heavy.

A good bike needs to feel like a fly rod between your legs, he thought, not a brick wall, smiling at what the cotton between his ears was possible of coming up with in terms of free-form thought at 3:35 A.M.

But this—this race—with a team of aging international stars that he would put together, well, this could do it. Push Bosco from the small time to the big time, especially if the first face across the line—a face that people, at least people who knew European racing, might recognize—was hovering over a Bosco logo, while wearing a Bosco jersey. What a chance to beat up all the national riders and leave the old timers smilin' one last time!

It was now 4:45 A.M., and he had worked out most of the details in his mind, forgotten them and worked them out again.

By six he had rolled out of bed, fed the dogs and showered, started to dress for work, but stopped, suddenly, in his dressing and slipped into his Haven team gear instead. This was a day to ride, he thought, ride into work and ponder the idea a bit more, flesh out the thin spots and just work up a good hard sweat, maybe peel off a millimeter or two of the soft pouch that was developing just above his beltline.

Ride in and use the magic to clear his mind.

Cheryl had a doctor's appointment this morning, so she'd be late to the office. He'd bring her up to speed at lunch. He wrote her a note, taped it to the coffeepot and threw his messenger bag over his shoulder, his shirt and tie and office khakis folded carefully within.

He unlocked the door of the small garage and stepped in. The cars controlled the room, but even between their heavy scents, he could smell the bikes, the sweetness of the grease, the aroma of the leather, the high-edged bite of the crankset, the smooth silkiness of the steel frame. He drank it in. He loved the smell of bicycles in the morning.

They smelled like ... he smiled ... magic.

He pulled the Colnago, stolen, without a bit of subterfuge, from the Haven cycling team two years before at the end of his professional career, and ran his fingers around the top edges of the tires.

Still inflated. No problem. No burrs. No thorns. Didn't mean a thing. He could easily flat half a block down the street. But at this moment, anyway, the bike looked and felt just right.

He picked it up under the top tube and backed out through the open door, closing and locking it behind him. He didn't want the bikes out here in the first place, but there was simply no room inside the house, no basement to speak of, and Cheryl had laid down the law. Bikes lived in the garage.

Not true.

Bikes live inside where they're safe and warm and not about to get stolen by the kids who ran the neighborhood looking at everybody's garage as their personal sports supply store.

Bikes live inside where their smells aren't forced to mix with those of automobiles.

Bikes live inside—so you can look at 'em whenever you want without having to put on your pants.

Bikes live inside.

He rolled the Colnago to the edge of the alley, clipped the helmet under his chin and slipped on his shoes, stepping up and snapping his left cleat into the pedal, pushing off and swinging the right up and over the seat. It found its home without further thought or aim.

He repositioned the messenger bag on his shoulder—he could never bear the thought of this thoroughbred having to act as a pack mule—and began to pedal slowly down the street. Six forty-five and it was still quiet here.

He could hear the distant hum of the interstate, the buzz of the city as it began to awaken, a train somewhere—light rail, heavy freight, he couldn't tell—rattling down the tracks, but here it was quiet. Morning quiet.

Birds and sprinklers and the plop of a newspaper being delivered.

You didn't get these sounds inside your commuter car, that's for sure. You just didn't get these sounds.

He drank them in, took a deep breath and made the turn down the street toward the city, the madness of traffic and his office that lived down there somewhere.

He'd meet the madness soon enough. He smiled, crouched and began to pedal harder.

The magic lay just beyond.

He dropped low over the top tube, brought his left leg up to the top of the stroke, leaned out and took the turn as smooth as baby's butt. He smiled at the thought; he reveled in the feel.

A baby's butt.

His baby's butt.

He was going to be a Dad.

The magic grew within him and he rode with a huge, stupid grin on his face through the growing traffic of downtown Denver on a mid-July morning.

※

AN HOUR LATER HE WAS SHOWERED, SHAVED, CHANGED AND WALKING INTO THE outer office of his boss's office, the office of Hootie Bosco, crazed mechanic, gonzo bike-builder, and tight-ass CEO of the number-ten bike-builder in the United States. A lot of different people, it seemed, were inside that Rastafarian-haired head.

Will glanced around the outer office. A lot of the toys that had once lined the walls had disappeared, replaced by advertising posters and giveaways and company geegaws that floated in from who knew where. Marketing had taken over. A lot of different people, inside one head, a lot of people indeed.

Will sighed and looked around. He missed the toys. He missed the man who went with them.

He heard a rustle of papers and turned toward the door to Hootie's office. Out stepped a striking blond in a white shirt covered with embroidered bicycles, her breasts accentuated by the black straps of the strapped pants she wore like rider bibs. It was quite a sight.

Will couldn't help but smile.

"Is he in?"

Nancy looked at him and shook her head. "Not any more."

Will caught a chuckle in his throat, but too late. It jumped out like a strangled burp.

"What's so funny?"

"Nothing," Will said quickly, "nothing."

He couldn't help but think of the torrid affair that Hootie and his executive secretary, Nancy, had been having since the week she got the job. Her response had caught him off guard and in a particularly dirty frame of mind.

See what bicycle commuting did to you, he thought, gets the hormones dancing.

He tried to recover. He looked at her chest.

"Nice bikes."

Without a pause, she replied, "Wanna ride?"

Will felt his face going not only beet-red, but bright beet-red.

"I'm sorry ... I didn't ... didn't mean ... "

She laughed.

"Oh, Christ, Ross, lighten up. It's a joke. It's called flirting. And you deserved it after that one-liner you walked in here with."

"Sorry."

"Oh, stop. But yes, he is in ... his office ... and he does ... at some point today ... want to talk to you."

"Now?"

"Good a time as any," she muttered, bowing her head just a touch, as if to avoid his gaze, sweeping her arm toward Hootie's inner door. "Be my guest."

Will turned, then stopped, then turned back to Nancy.

"Wait a minute. If he's in there now ... why when I said 'is he in,' did you say, 'not any ...'"

She smiled. "Let it go, Will. You'll lose."

Will opened his mouth to say something, realized that he should just shut up, because she was telling the absolute truth, he wasn't going to win any points at all here, then nodded, turned and stepped through the door into Hootie Bosco's executive office.

It wasn't much of an office.

The wooden floors were warped and scraped. The dirty, off-white walls held a few crudely tacked posters. The desk was second-hand. The computers were new, you could say that much, but that was about all that was in Hootie's office that hadn't seen much better days.

Will's eyes roamed the walls quickly. A few toys and trinkets still remained on the shelves. Prominent among them was a five-pound box wrench hanging from a peg that made an excellent weapon whenever necessary. It was intimidating, to say the least.

Hootie was staring at a little TV screen flickering in the corner of his computer screen.

"You hear about this?" he asked, never looking away from the screen.

Will shook his head.

"No. I haven't seen the papers today. What's up?"

"Hmm. Just happened, I guess. Some morning sports guy at one of the TV stations went and got himself blown up. Must have been a pipe bomb or something."

"No shit? Here?" Will said, his sense of calm from the morning ride ebbing away quickly in the reality of modern American life. "Is he hurt?"

"Dunno. Seemed to still have all his fingers when the bomb squad showed up. Can't be good, but he's not dead. Nobody is quite sure yet. What's up?"

"I can't believe this shit happens here."

Hootie turned away from the screen and looked at Will with surprise.

"Yeah, here. Christ, man. Where you been the last few years? Denver has been ground zero for just about every headline story in the country. I'm surprised Katie Couric hasn't moved here. It would make it cheaper for NBC."

"Yeah, I guess," Will shrugged. "I guess it hasn't affected me directly, so ... I haven't ... "

Hootie nodded and turned toward Will, the tiny TV screen forgotten for a moment, then circled his hand in the air as if to say, "get a move on."

Will caught on immediately, despite a pinprick of anger in the back of his mind toward Hootie or anyone that treated him like a dolt.

"What do you need, Will?"

"Yeah, I was watching the news last night, I guess before this bomb thing happened ... "

"Happened this morning."

"... yeah, but, the sports guy, Flynn, Roger Flynn, mentioned a race. Not a lot of detail. One hundred forty miles, starting in Boulder. That's at five thousand feet to begin with, then climbing immediately—in the summer, which means bad weather anytime after noon—right up and into Breckenridge with three or four hair-raising descents on dirt roads, in the rain ... "

"Yeah, I've heard of it," Hootie said.

"Well," Will replied, "I'm thinking we should be a part of this."

"Why?"

The simplicity of the question caught Will off guard. He stumbled for a moment, then caught the tempo of his argument again and jumped right in.

"Look. We're going to have a hell of a time getting into the European markets and onto European teams."

"That's what you were hired for. "

"No, that's the job that sort of got created around me. But—despite that, even with my contacts, that's not going to happen unless we get a prominent American team in Europe, because no foreign team is going to ride an American product. And we can't get an American team unless we get some publicity about the bikes here.

"Publicity that says: Bosco bikes can take it, Bosco bikes can win, Bosco bikes can win over any terrain."

Will sighed heavily, the load of his idea finally off the shoulders of his brain.

"We get into this race. Team sponsor. Something. Something big. It'll push the name and get us started. What do you think?"

"Well, I think it's a good idea," Hootie said, a small smile on his face, "and it makes sense. We haven't been able to make much of a dent in Europe. "

"Yeah, so field a team here," Will said, his enthusiasm for the idea taking control of his hands and wiggling them about madly in front of him, "and put 'em all on Boscos with Bosco jerseys and Bosco helmets and Bosco team cars."

"Bosco team cars?"

"Yeah, you can use that circus wagon Subaru you had painted last summer for that parade in Littleton. That can be your Bosco team car."

"Those are last year's colors."

Will rolled his eyes.

"So who cares? Who knows? It cuts your cost so just do it. We've got a shit-load of jerseys in the warehouse. Helmets, too, thanks to those photo shoots with that bunch of models who hadn't been on a bike since they were thirteen."

"Don't remind me."

"We've got everything we need except riders and there have got to be a couple of willing candidates floating around who would ride for the greater glory of marketing Bosco bikes."

"Anyone in mind?"

"Like ... "

"Like you?"

The two men stared at each other for a moment, then Will burst out laughing.

"Yeah, sure, why not? I'll go. Who knows ... if you're willing to front a couple of tickets from Europe, I could probably get Bourgoin and Cacciavillani here too. They'll ride 'em here in an unknown race. There's your European tie. Get them on Boscos. Get some photos. Slap 'em into *VeloNews* and *Cycle Sport* and *Bicycling*. It's a start."

Hootie turned in his chair and stared out the window toward the LoDo field that led to the backyard of Coors Field. The Rockies were out of town so there'd be parking at his favorite restaurant this evening. The idea made perfect sense. He loved the idea of old European stars stepping forward—if he could manage to keep the costs down.

Too bad Will couldn't be a part of it.

"Will," Hootie said, seriously, "I like it." His head bobbed like a drugged plaster dog in the back window of a low-rider. "I like it a lot."

"Good."

"You think Cacciavillani or Bourgoin might come out of retirement and ride again in something like this?"

"Sure. Distinct possibility. Tony for sure. He didn't want to retire anyway, even though the thought of those climbs will give him hives. As for Richard, well, you never know until you ask. We could have fun riding together again. Maybe a Haven team of old timers. Old timers at thirty-four," he laughed.

"It might be just the thing."

"Good. Good." Hootie was tapping his fingers against his chin. Will began to feel a strange chill run up his spine, some kind of prehistoric fight or flight response that had supposedly been bred out of the species by civilization, but was there nonetheless.

He moved ahead.

"I'll get on the horn to them right now."

"Naw. Naw. Don't worry about that. I've got some other people who can do that."

"It'll take five minutes. Besides, Tony's assistant will give you the run-around. I can get right through to him. Five minutes."

"No, Will. Don't worry. A good idea, but I'll have other people work on it."

"Shit, Hootie, that doesn't make any sense. This is my job, man. I can finally get something done. Let me ... "

Hootie Bosco held up his hand, catching Will in mid-sentence.

"Other people can do it, Will. Other people."

Will sighed.

"Sure. Sure, Hootie. I understand. I guess. But—it is my idea ... "

"And a good one."

"And a good one, you bet ... so why ... "

There was a long pause, as if Hootie Bosco was trying to find the words to say what had to be said, to say what had been decided long ago, but not acted on until now, the torpedo racing through the water toward a friend, a friend who simply wasn't pulling his own weight for the company and, damn, though he hated it, Hootie Bosco wasn't running a charity.

"Because, Will," Hootie said quietly, leaping into the thought feet first, "you're fired."

✦

WILL DIDN'T REMEMBER MUCH ABOUT THE NEXT NINETY MINUTES.

He listened to Hootie's explanation, something about business and market share and having the guts to go where no one wanted you anyway, and never really heard a word. Between his ears there was a panicked buzz, a jumble of sounds that he hadn't heard since the last time he had bounced down a highway at sixty miles an hour on his head, sounding much like a heavy-gauge needle that kept getting yanked across an old phonograph record by an insane kindergarten teacher.

He caught a few words, "sorry," "Lisa," "now," "Cheryl," "Nancy," "long time," but none of them made sense. He knew he was staring at Hootie and making some stupid face, eyes partially wide-open, a half-smile plastered on his face, the look of a man who has just won the lottery and lost the ticket.

Hootie then stood up and extended his hand. Will stood up and extended his. They shook.

Hootie continued talking as he came around the desk and put his arm around Will. A gesture of friendship. A gesture of sadness. And also a way to maneuver Will out of his office and toward his own that now needed to be cleaned out.

Will allowed himself to be moved.

There was some kind of raucous, rhythmic cheer pounding through his head now—babababa-Hey, babababa-HEY—that was drowning everything else out. As they walked past Nancy's desk, Will noticed she was crying.

What was she crying about? Will didn't know. Bababababa-HEY!

He felt two easy slaps on his back and nodded slowly, blindly. He stood for a minute outside Hootie's door and realized he was alone in the hall. It was as if the entire company had emptied out. He glanced around quickly, then stumbled, drunkenly, toward his own door, two down from Hootie's. He stepped in, turned the chair around, sat down and felt it.

The enormity of what had just happened hit him like a Russian sprinter on a descent. He was about to be a dad, very soon, and was suddenly out of work. This was real, basic human stuff. Major crisis time. How was he going to pay for anything? Diapers, formula, preschool, Yale? How was he going to support and pay and keep the ball rolling?

It was hard enough when he was working. Now he wasn't.

How was he going to do any of this?

There was a "clunk" at his door and Will spun the chair to meet it. Lisa Shannon, the Sammy Glick of the company, stood there, holding a cardboard box from which a tall, gangly and exceptionally ugly plant shot out the top.

"Oh, I'm sorry," she squeaked, not really sorry at all, "I thought you'd already be gone ... "

The banging suddenly stopped, in Will's head and he gave her a cold look that had absolutely no effect on her or her determination to move into his space.

"Jesus, Lisa, the body isn't even cold yet. Couldn't you wait until after lunch? I should be gone by then."

Whatever discomfort she had from walking in on him passed in a heart-beat. She walked over to the table near the window and put the box, the first, no doubt, of her office paraphernalia, down, officially occupying the space. Possession was nine-tenths of the law, she knew. But Will's ass still possessed the seat of the chair.

"Sorry, Will, that's just the way business goes, sometimes. I just thought you'd already be gone."

A small, white-hot ball of anger grew in his chest, bubbled up and raced through his system, clearing out all the shock and embarrassment and confusion of the last hour, the last day, the last few months.

He was seeing clearly now for the first time in weeks.

He hadn't really failed. Not really. He had been tripped up behind the scenes and he was looking at the tripper.

She smiled blankly and stepped quickly to the door. She stopped, turned, put up a finger as if to make a point, opened her mouth, shut it, opened it again and said, "Leave your Rolodex. That's company property."

"Get the hell out of here before I hit you so hard your kids are born dizzy."

"Hmm. Yes. Well. Leave the Rolodex."

She left, obviously to get another box and then lie in wait until the dead body in International Endorsements was carried out and hauled away to the dump.

Hauled away to the dump.

Will stared at the empty door for a few minutes, his rage boiling up to a point where his head was clear, his muscles jazzed, his path outlined perfectly in front of him. He needed a drink. One big damned drink. Maybe another. A few were good.

He stood, picked up her box, opened the window, pushed it outside, turned it over, and dumped everything, including the genetically-engineered mutant fern and the dirt it sat in, down into the dumpster that lay directly below. There was a rustle, a rattle, a crash, then silence.

Will stepped back from the chore and quickly peeled the personal stuff off his desk. A few pictures. A letter or two. The framed shots from Roubaix and Mont Ventoux, a pencil sketch of a rider on Alpe d'Huez, two pictures of Cheryl, a toy bike in Haven colors, a mini-Beast, if you will, and a radio. Not much. He looked over the rest of the desk. There wasn't much left, other than the company office supplies and the Rolodex with all his contacts in it. Rolodex. The company's Rolodex. The company's Rolodex filled with his contacts.

What to do? What to do? A small, very cynical idea filled his mind, and filled it with a happy, nasty warmth.

He shut the office door, locked it, sat down, and for the next hour, ignored the constant ringing of the phone while he carefully removed all the names of his friends and teammates and business acquaintances, and replaced them with new cards containing all new addresses and phone numbers.

The Italian ones took the longest. Those had to be creative.

He left the new and improved company Rolodex back against the wall where it lived, ready for Lisa to find it and learn, quite unhappily he was sure, that life was merely a series of screw-ups, and you survived by simply being the last person to pull one.

He picked up the box of pictures and desk junk, opened the door, fully expecting Lisa to be standing there, and found two more boxes of her pictures, geegaws, awards and plants. He smiled, put his box down, took hers, and one by one, upended them, casually tossing their contents into the dumpster from his window. It was childish, he knew, but it was fun. So very, very, very much fun.

He picked up his box again, walked the box down to Cheryl's office and dropped it on her desk with a note, "please bring this home."

He threw the Rolodex cards into his messenger bag, stood in the middle of Cheryl's office and changed back into his vaguely damp Haven racing gear.

He wondered, for a quick moment, if she knew. Had she known this was coming? No. She would have said something. Nancy wouldn't have let on, despite their friendship. Cheryl couldn't have known. So now, he didn't know how he was going to tell her. Yet another problem to deal with this afternoon.

He was going to ride home. Maybe see her there. Talk, explain, plan. But first, he was going to ride to a bar and see if liquid courage was still as effective as it used to be.

He was going to ride to a bar and have himself a drink and figure out how to tell her that he was "at liberty," "between engagements," "negotiating new possibilities," "out on his ass."

Yes, a drink would help all of that.

He remembered something he had left in his desk. He walked back, his riding shoes clicking heavily on the wooden floors. No one seemed to be anywhere in the office. It was as if he had stepped into a dead zone. His footsteps echoed throughout the building.

Will smiled.

The entire place was in hiding, as if they thought he would march through with a high-powered rifle and ventilate their skulls.

No. No way. He wouldn't do that. Well, maybe to one. Two at the outside, but not the lot of them. They were good kids. Kids. Shit.

And he was Old Man River. He just keep rollin' along.

He walked into his office, opened the right hand drawer and pulled out two rolls of quarters. Soda machine money. Close to twenty bucks worth. Didn't want to leave it for little Lisa. Let her find her own damned quarters. He walked to the door and listened again. Still silent.

Everyone was sleeping. Or hiding. Sure as shit there wasn't any work going on today. Tongues were the only body parts expending any energy today.

Nancy poked her head out of Hootie's office door.

"Cheryl's trying to get ahold of you."

"Huh, what?"

"Cheryl's been calling all morning," she said, her face drawn, her eyes red, "she wants to talk to you."

"Tell her I'll meet her at home." The most he could do was bob his head up and down.

The tears started again on Nancy's face.

"God, Will, I'm sorry."

She ran down the hall and hugged him. He patted her back slowly and wanted to pull away. Not because he didn't appreciate the gesture or the warmth of her body, but simply because if he didn't, he'd start to cry as well, and there was no way in God's green earth he was going to give Lisa Shannon the satisfaction.

"It's all right. It's all right. I've gotten sacked before and landed on my feet. Landed on my ass, too, but landed on my feet. Eventually."

He said it all without believing a word of it.

"I'm going to miss you."

"I'm going to miss you, too, Nance. You're good people."

He kissed her on the cheek, tasting her hot tears on his lips.

He nodded dumbly, his own tears now just behind his eyes. He could feel he face beginning to puff and burn.

"It's okay. It really is. Just keep an eye on Hootie and make sure he's okay, all right?"

"Yeah, sure. You're something, Ross, worrying about him after he sacks your ass." She shook her head. "Stupid bastard. If he thinks he's going to get laid tonight, he's out of his goddamned mind."

Will didn't know what to say to that, so he just let it go. His head bounced and he turned away from her.

"Call your wife," she said, quietly.

"Yeah, later. I'll meet her at home. Tell her I'm okay and I'll see her at home."

"What are you going to do?"

"Now, oh, just ride for a while, burn some of this off. Find me a thinkin' place."

"A thinkin' place?"

"Yeah," Will raised his eyebrows, "a thinkin' place. Take care, Nance."

He turned and walked heavily toward the stairs leading to the back door and his bike. Nancy watched him go, then stepped out of the way as the little shit that had undercut him zipped past with another box of office crap and quickly moved into Will's now-empty office.

Nancy smiled as she heard the cry of anguish when Lisa Shannon discovered that her four-year-old overgrown fern, La Liz, plus every other bit of personal paraphernalia had done a high-dive into the dumpster outside her window.

"Enjoy the view, you little bitch," she thought, turned and walked the few steps down to her own office. That's only the start of it, kid, she smiled. Only the start. Hell begins now. You never, ever, piss off the boss's secretary. Never. Life lesson. And you're about to learn it.

She picked up the phone on the second ring.

"Bosco Bikes, this is Nancy, may I help you?"

"He's still not answering."

"Oh, Cheryl. He said he'd see you at home."

"How is he?"

"He looked okay. Not suicidal or anything. Just said he needed some time to ride and think. He'd see you at home."

"Think?"

"Think. Said he was going to a thinkin' place."

There was silence on the line for a second, then Cheryl Crane laughed, sadly. "Not thinkin'. Drinkin'. If I know Will, he's heading to a bar."

BARS IN THE MORNING ARE NOT THE MOST ATTRACTIVE PLACES ON EARTH. THE sunlight streaming in through the windows catches the last traces of smoke and dust in the air from the night before, and odors rise up from the bar, the carpet, the tables, the seats, and the ashtrays.

Truth be told, a bar in the morning was no place to be.

But there he was, sitting at the bar on Eighteenth, 11:30 in the morning, trying to figure out how many quarters he was going to have to peel out of the first roll to get his second Jameson and water.

The first had gone down easy. The second would be even easier. The joy of good whiskey.

His feet dangled level with the last rung of the stool, the heels of his riding shoes bouncing against the wood. His helmet was pushed back on his head.

The liquor was swirling around inside his gut and bringing his blood pressure back to normal for the first time in three hours.

No sleep. No job. A couple of pops. Oooh. This was going to be some ride home this afternoon.

Late this afternoon.

"You want another?"

The bartender, who was also acting as the janitor, cleaning up the place, called down from the other end of the bar.

"Huh? Yeah. You bet. Top it off."

Will counted out sixteen quarters and pushed them across the lacquered finished of the bar.

"Don't you have any bills?"

"These spend as good as anything else. And you get a quarter tip to boot, my friend."

"Thanks, Rockefeller."

"You bet. Knock yourself out."

Will sucked the last of the Irish whiskey out of the bottom of his first glass and turned to the second. Life wasn't biting him quite as much as it had been at breakfast. At least now he might have some room to figure out what to do with the rest of it.

They weren't going to lose the house. Cheryl was working. Her pay would continue through maternity leave at least. That gave him some space to find something he really could do with his life, other than ride bikes and sit in an office calling old buddies on the phone and asking them to buy a product they didn't like, want or need.

Maybe he could get on a team as support staff or handle some company's bike team as a liaison or God knows what else. Maybe. Maybe. Maybe. Maybe he could find the answer in the bottom of the second glass. It was down there, he was sure. If not there, then at the bottom of the third glass. Maybe the fourth. The answers were there. They were always there. Somewhere.

He took another sip.

The door opened behind him. He heard the sound, but sensed it more by the shift in air pressure. Somebody was coming in.

He glanced up at the mirror over the bar, didn't see anyone right away, and went back to his drink. Looking for answers.

At the other end of the room, the bartender-cleaning crew combination stopped and glanced over at the newcomer. Will noticed that his eyes squinted just a bit as he looked.

"Yeah, mornin'. What can I get you?"

"A beer. A beer would be good," the guy called back in a sharply tense voice. "Budweiser. Tap."

"You got it." The bartender put down his rag and walked behind the bar, snagging a glass and stepping over to the tap.

Will glanced up at the mirror again and saw a young man in a long, black overcoat, a duster, walk quickly to the bar.

"I'm gonna have to see some ID," the bartender muttered.

"You bet," came the reply.

Out of the corner of his eye, Will caught a sweep of movement and saw what looked like a shiny brown stick rise up out of the coat and push itself into the bartender's face.

"Okay, asshole. This is my ID. Now, I don't want to kill you and you don't want to die. Just hand over last night's money."

Will froze with the heavy-gauge glass half way to his lips.

The bartender damned near soiled himself, by the look on his face. Will hadn't seen anything that white since his dad last wore a bathing suit.

"Fork it over, bud."

"I ... I ... I ... "

"Asshole, I don't have all day. You were packed last night. Hand it over."

"I ... I can't. The boss takes it all ... You can have what I've got ... its just change to start the day. I don't have the big stuff. He's already taken that to the bank."

A dark stain began to grow between the legs of the bartender's pants.

Will noticed that, but also noticed his own hand wasn't shaking. Whiskey, he thought. It had to be the whiskey. Food of the gods.

"You fucker ... lying to me." The sawed-off Remington twelve-gauge rose up into a firing position.

"He's not lying." Will immediately regretted opening his mouth.

"What?"

The shotgun hovered for a second, then turned toward Will. The bartender visibly deflated to the very point where he would have collapsed. In his relief, the stain on his pants grew even bigger.

"He's not lying. Jerry, who owns this joint, deposits the receipts on the way home every night. He only leaves about a hundred bucks in change to start the next day."

Will took another sip of his whiskey. He noticed that despite the fact that the gun was now pointed in his direction, his left hand wasn't shaking. His right slowly tightened its grip on the roll of quarters.

"Well, then, fuck face," the intruder cackled, moving the shotgun up next to Will's head, "I'll just be taking that hundred bucks and whatever it is that you've got."

There should have been terror, Will knew. He hated guns. Especially ones that were trying to poke a hole in his temple. He hated their feel, he hated their noise, he hated what each and every one of them he had met in the past few years had done to his friends, his life, his sense of well-being. He had seen what they could do—the gaping holes in what had once been living, breathing people, the shattered lives, the terror, the sadness, the sense that life would never begin again. He knew.

That thought was coupled with an emptiness, a lack of feeling, as if he had been disconnected from his emotions completely this morning. He should have been crying, shaking, pleading for his life. But Will felt nothing. He was almost standing outside himself.

And then he began to feel again. A feeling quite different than just about anything he had ever felt before.

At this moment, in this millisecond of time, he suddenly felt, quite unconsciously, stupidly, even, if he pondered the feeling at all, that there was no goddamned reason to allow this shit with a shotgun to push him around anymore. He was tired, broke, unemployed and just ever so slightly drunk.

The simmering white-hot pit of anger that had begun in the face of Lisa Shannon, dulled slightly a few moments ago by the drink, began to boil in his head again, now back with a vengeance. And by God, Will Ross didn't feel like being pushed around any more this morning.

Even if it meant that he wouldn't have a place to put his hat this afternoon.

"I said, asshole," the gunman yelled, "I'll take whatever it is you've ... "

He didn't get a chance to finish the sentence. As the barrel of the shotgun touched Will's ear, Will swung his left arm up, pushing the muzzle out into the room. The sudden movement forced the shooter's finger on the trigger and a deafening blast of heavyweight shot ventilated a table next to a Playboy pinball machine. With the same move, Will brought his right hand, filled with a roll of quarters, up and then sharply down across the shooter's chin, snapping the kid's head around.

The gunman went down like a sack of wet rice to the sound of Will's ears ringing sharply from the shotgun blast and his own yelps of pain.

"Oh, fuck!" Will cradled his right hand in his left, the quarters forgotten as they rained down on the floor. Will leapt over the fallen intruder and hopped around the room.

"Ow, goddamn it! Goddamn it! My hand. My son of a bitchin' hand! Jesus." He snapped it in the air as if to shake the pain out of it. "Jesus! Goddamn it."

The throbbing in his hand grew rather than faded as he tried to flex his knuckles. It blew up like an inflated surgeon's glove, red, hot and tender to the touch. His knuckles felt all sandy around the sudden inflammation. God, he thought, this never happens on TV. Bruce Willis can bash bad guys all day long and he walks away with soft, beautiful soap-commercial hands. Christ! One punch and he's dancing like a monkey on crack.

He looked up in the mirror over the bar and saw himself standing victorious over a crumbled heap of bad guy. Damn right. John Wayne.

"Damn right. Don't fuck with me, pal. I'm from Kalamazoo-zoo-zoo-zoo, oh, shit!"

His hand spoke to him again.

Damn right that hurt. Screw you, John Wayne.

This hero business hurts. He shook his hand, shaking the pain around again. God, make it go away and I'll go to church and I'll never hit anybody again. Never hit anybody again. Except maybe Bruce Willis. For lying to me all these years.

He kicked the shotgun away, the high-pitched whine of the blast still ringing in his ears. Will looked down at the kid in the duster and suddenly began to shake uncontrollably. He had a sudden urge to throw up.

His John Wayne moment had passed. He was mortal once more. He leaned on the bar, retched and stood up to shake his hand again.

Despite the fact that his eyes felt like they were bouncing around in his head like googly eyes on a Raggedy Ann, Will could focus well enough to look down the bar to see the bartender frantically trying to remember the number for 911, wet pants and all.

❉

He was the lead story on the noon news.

He was being called a hero. A savior. A man of steel. Cool in the face of buckshot. A shotgun in his ear, he stared down the bad guy, took a measure of the man and dropped him like a bad habit.

That was the bartender's story.

Will's was simpler.

"Why did you punch him?"

"He made me spill my drink."

He wasn't trying to be a smart ass. His brain had pretty much just shut down and that was all that was bouncing around in there. Have drink. Feel better. Hand hurt now. Go 'way. His sense of action had been replaced by panic, then the panic replaced by no feeling at all.

If the reporter had been fifteen minutes earlier, he would have been a babbling wreck desperately shaking his own hand. Now, he was just in a shock that made everything come out in a distantly smart-ass kind of way.

Somehow, the skinny blond reporter had figured out who he was, abandoned the bartender who smelled like a portable toilet and rushed to Will's side. The noon TV audience was getting a rundown on him to go with their Spaghetti-O's and peanut butter sandwiches.

"Will Ross, the hero of this morning's incident is no stranger to the limelight. Winner of the grueling Paris-Roubaix bicycle race (she pronounced it "Rowbakes") and a rider in the annual Tour of France race, he is now in Denver as an executive of Bosco Bikes, a new LoDo manufactu ... "

"No," Will interrupted. "No ... "

She stepped back away from the camera, her live shot still underway, her train of thought broken.

"I'm sorry?"

"I, uh, don't work at Bosco anymore. I got fired this morning. That's why I was drinkin'."

He smiled coolly for the camera.

"Oh, well. Okay." She nodded and turned back to the camera. She stood silently for a moment before turning back to him.

"So why ... " her head cocked to the side, indicating the bar.

"Oh, well. Fired. Drowning my sorrows. You know the riff. You're a reporter. You guys drink even more than I do."

"No, I'm sorry, I don't. I don't drink when I'm down."

Will laughed. "Then, sister, you are in the wrong business. I wouldn't trust any reporter who doesn't drink. At least something, sometime."

"Well, I don't."

"You must be very proud." Will waved at the camera and walked back to his bike. The reporter turned back to the camera, her train of thought now completely out of the station without her on board, and quickly wrapped up her live shot.

"Live from Downtown Denver, Terry Elliot, TV6 News."

The bike helmet had fallen so far back on his head that it looked like a packed parachute. It wasn't strapped, but held in place merely by the blood pressure expanding his scalp beyond all known medical limits. Will pushed it back to the top of his head and secured the strap under his chin. Whatever buzz he had had was now gone, thanks to time, adrenaline, three cops, two interviews and a TV reporter who liked to moralize about other people's vices. She was the kind of dame who would eventually get sick but have nothing to abstain from because she hadn't kept up with her vices.

Will looked over at one of the police officers and spread his arms.

"Do you still need me?"

"Naw, we've got your number. You can go." The cop paused for just a moment. "How's the hand?"

"I've got George Washington's mug tattooed on my palm ... "

"It'll fade. Give it a couple years. Nice punch though. Jerk's still out. Came to for a second, threatened to sue you for assault, then passed out again."

"Can he do that?"

"Sure. All he's got to find is some lawyer with an eye for the spotlight and he'll make a case. Won't win, likely, but he'll make a case."

"Swell." Some world.

Will threw his leg over the saddle, balancing precariously on the toe of his riding shoes.

"Ride safe," the cop said and slapped Will on the back. "You did good today."

"Thanks, man. This hero shit hurts, though." He shook his hand again. "Ain't like the movies."

The cop held up his hand. The fingers were bent and twisted in a variety of directions. "What is?" the officer asked with a laugh, turned, and walked back to his squad car.

Will nodded in agreement, glanced, then slid his leg down and snapped it into the right pedal. Just as he was about to push off, the blonde reporter ran up to his side.

"Excuse me, excuse me, Mr. Ross. Do you have a minute? Bill Sessions would like to talk to you."

"Who?"

"Bill Sessions? Our assistant news director?" She seemed surprised that the world was not fully in tune with her and everyone she knew and worked with.

"Why?"

"I honestly don't now," she said, growing tired of this man, "I don't. But he wants to talk to you and he's on the cell phone in my car. Can you talk to him?"

"Yeah, I guess."

Will pried his foot out of the pedal, swung his leg back over the bike frame and rolled over to the news car, using The Beast to steady a gait made all the less steady by two cleats, two drinks and a quickly falling adrenaline rush.

He took the tiny phone in his hand, raised it to his ear and then his life changed.

Three big events in one day.

Later that afternoon, a beer in his hand, the thought amazed him that a man could be struck by three thunderbolts out of the blue in the space of four hours and live to talk about it.

CHERYL WALKED INTO THE KITCHEN, THROWING HER KEYS ON THE COUNTER NEXT TO the day's mail and an open bag of bread.

"Will?" she called, hoping to finally find him and talk, but in the same moment hoping that he was out somewhere so she could put the moment off for another few minutes. It wasn't something she wanted to deal with right now, especially if he had been drinking this afternoon.

"Will?" she called again.

The TV set was on to one of the early newscasts. Cheryl crossed the kitchen into the tiny dining room and looked past the glass bookcase dividers into the living room. Will was staring at the TV set, mouthing the words of the anchorman and mimicking his hand movements.

"Will?" Cheryl said, softly, "Will, are you okay?"

"Huh?" Will shook his head, turned suddenly and smiled.

"Hey, hi, how are you doing?"

"I've been trying to get in touch with you all day."

"Really? I've been running around. I'm sorry. Did you get that stuff I left on your desk?"

"Yeah, Hootie carried the box out to the car for me. By the way, late this afternoon Lisa Shannon started screaming that you sabotaged her Rolodex. Know anything about that?"

Will grinned from ear to ear.

"Nope. Not a thing."

She looked suspiciously at him, wondering if he was drunk, manic, crazed or a little of everything.

"You all right?"

"Yep. Just fine. You got anything planned tonight?"

"No, I was just planning to help paste you back together after your morning."

"Have you seen the news lately?"

"No, why?"

"Sit down. I've got something to show you—then, we're going out. We're going to celebrate."

She squinted at him, not sure of where he was going and what was bouncing around in his head.

"Celebrate what?"

"Oh, gee, well, my day, I guess. I was fired. I beat up a bad guy. And I got a job. Wanna hear about the job?"

"I ..."

He held up his hand to silence her, then pointed at the TV screen as the story of his morning at the bar began to unfold for Denver news consumers. Cheryl felt the skin across her belly contract involuntarily and a cold hand run up her spine.

Most people don't have days like this one.

Let alone survive them.

CHAPTER THREE:

ON THE AIR

WILL STOOD ON THE SIDEWALK FOR FIVE MINUTES, TRYING TO CALM HIS heart rate. It wasn't working. For some reason, his ticker was pounding out a staccato rhythm, making him feel like a hopped-up hamster just off the wheel.

He hadn't felt anything like this since Le Tour. And then he was climbing.

This was simply walking, which he began to do, up the slight incline of the entrance, opening a heavy glass door, and stepping into an overly-air conditioned outer lobby, then standing before a slim, pleasant, smiling older woman in a glass booth. She looked at him for a second before saying, "We were wondering when you'd get here. We've been waiting for you."

Will stood, stock still for a moment, then turned to see who she was talking to in the lobby. There was no one else. He turned back with a dumb smile.

"Yep. You. We thought you were having second thoughts, the way you stood outside, but, then again, knowing this place, second thoughts aren't a bad idea. Third or fourth, even. I'm Shirley."

"Hello," Will replied dumbly.

She smiled again, very sweetly.

"It's a good idea to make friends with me. Really. I control the doors to Oz."

He stared for a second until she pushed the button and buzzed the electric lock on the doors on either side of her great glass booth. Will, suddenly understanding, nodded, then walked to the door on the right. He pulled it open, stepped through and stepped on thick carpet surrounding a huge open atrium. Shirley wheeled her chair back and leaned over the half-door leading to her sanctum.

"Impressive, isn't it? One of the greatest wastes of space in American architectural history, but a damned impressive sight."

Will chuckled at her tone.

"They're waiting for you in the newsroom. Just down there to your right."

"Here on the first floor?"

"Here on the first floor."

Will started to walk, not without a touch of fear, toward the wooden double doors leading to the newsroom.

"Watch out for the flyin' monkeys," Shirley called out behind him, "they'll get you every damned time."

Will kept walking straight ahead, but smiled to himself. He liked the image, even though he'd been dealin' with flyin' monkeys his entire professional career.

Shirley watched him walk toward the newsroom for a moment, before leaning forward and resuming her position as the first line of defense against the salesmen, fans and kooks who daily assaulted her TV station.

Kooks.

Since the bomb, everybody was a kook.

She shuddered, then plugged her headset back into the buzzing console and said with a smile, "TV6—how may I help you?"

❂

WILL STOOD IN THE DOORWAY OF THE NEWSROOM, UNNOTICED IN THE BUSTLE OF THE late morning. Was it always this noisy? How did anybody get anything done? He turned and looked down at the desk near the door. The mustachioed guy sitting at the desk didn't seem to be bothered. He was leaning back in his chair and sleeping, adding to the din with a very slight snore.

He checked his watch. 11:55. Even with chatting to ... Shirley? ... he was still five minutes early for his appointment.

A large boy trundled his way, his face flushed with urgency.

"Comin' through! Scripts! Coming through!"

Will jumped to the side, jostling the desk holding the feet of the sleeping man, who snorted, jumped up and snapped awake.

"I'm here. I'm here. What's up?"

"Oh, Jesus," Will said, apologetically, "I'm sorry. I sorta got pushed into your desk here and ..."

The man rubbed his eyes and blinked them open and closed a few times. He glanced at his watch and put on a pair of wire rimmed glasses.

"No problem, dude. Gotta get up anyway. I'm anchoring this mess today."

The man with the mustache looked across the room to a raised desk where a young woman with a frazzled look about her—frazzled hair, frazzled clothes, frazzled eyes—pounded away at a computer keyboard, screeching at anyone who came near her.

"You got scripts for me, Lynn?"

"YES. YES, I'VE GOT SCRIPTS," she shouted. She seemed to shout everything, working at a fever pitch that wound her so tight her hair curled.

"ON THE SET, EDDIE, GET ON THE GODDAMNED SET!"

Eddie moved, but slowly. He moved very slowly in comparison to the woman at the computer, who was now throwing papers and scrambling for some kind of electronic earmuffs while in mid-stomp down a short flight of steps—BOOM!—through the double doors and flop-flop-flop-flop down the hall.

"Well, if you'll excuse me," Eddie said with a faux aristocratic accent, straightening his tie, "I must go and anchor the award-winning TV6 *News at Noon* broadcast."

"Oh, sure," Will said, taken ever so slightly aback by it all.

"Eddie Slezak, by the way. I'd offer you my hand, but I have this pretty much timed out to the second."

"Credits, Eddie. *As the Stomach Turns* is in credits," someone shouted from across the newsroom.

"Gotta fly." He sauntered out the door and down the hall, in stark contrast to the frantic woman, not making a sound.

"I see you met Fast Eddie."

Will turned around to face a tall, slim man with a dark face and the heaviest eyebrows he had ever seen. They looked like two caterpillars trying to mate, blocked only by a furrowed gully that seemed carved into the man's forehead by a cold chisel.

"Bill Sessions." He extended his hand. Will shook it.

"We talked yesterday after your, uh, adventure."

"Yes, of course. Nice to see you, meet you, see you, again. Meet you." Inside

Will's head, his conscience gnome was screaming, "You idiot!" He tried to ignore the criticism.

"Whatever," Sessions said with a smile. "Barb's busy for a while, but maybe I can show you around a bit, get you acquainted with everyone. Then, in about twenty minutes, we'll sit you on the set with Fast Eddie and he can interview you about yesterday."

"Yesterday?"

"Yeah, yesterday. You were big news in the papers this morning."

Will hadn't even seen the papers. He had been on the Internet trying to get as much Tour information as he could.

"What'd they say?"

"You didn't read them? You do read the papers, don't you?"

"Yeah, I read the papers."

"Which ones?"

"*Post. Rocky. New York Times. L'Equipe* and the *International Herald Tribune*, too, when I can get them."

"Well, that's three better than anybody else around here. Add *USA Today* and you'll make Barb happy. She's got a thing about people in the newsroom knowing what's going on every day outside their own little world."

"I understand," Will nodded, wondering if he should really start reading the *New York Times* rather than just scan it looking for pieces by Sam Abt.

"We don't copy our stories out of the newspapers," Sessions said, leading Will through the long, thin, crowded and busy room, "despite what those little bastards at the papers think, but Barb's convinced that you'll get a better grasp on what makes news and how to write news if you read papers."

"Got it. Read papers."

"Watch our newscasts, too. We have debriefing sessions after each one and people are invited to criticize just about anything. Or anybody."

Will paused for a moment. That could be a problem. *The Simpsons* were on at the same time as the early evening news.

"Sounds like fun," he said with a shudder.

Sessions noticed the pause.

"It can be. It can be. Barb handles them pretty well, but they can get exciting at times. Especially when you drop Flynn and Slezak in there."

"Flynn?"

"Sports anchor. The guy you'll be working with. Don't tell me you don't know Roger Flynn?"

Will smiled. Of course he knew Roger Flynn, even though he didn't have the slightest idea who Roger Flynn was. He watched TV news, usually TV6, but sometimes Channel 4, sometimes 9, sometimes 7, but the names, the names never really seemed to matter. They simply washed over him, all sprawled out on the sofa, jumped over the back of the couch and ran out the door before he had a chance to pay the slightest bit of attention.

"Flynn. Yes, I know Flynn. Just didn't pick up on the name."

Sessions smiled and nodded. "Yeah. Just don't forget it when you're near him. His ego army will drag you out onto the helicopter pad and chop you up into itty-bitty pieces. Don't worry, though. Flynn is about the worst of it around here. Most folks are pretty sane until you get down to crunch time ..."

"Crunch time?"

"Yeah, just before a newscast. Think of it as that moment just before the end of a race. Just before a sprint."

"Gotcha," Will smiled. "Understood."

"Good," Sessions continued easily. "These are the reporters' cubicles. We keep them low so reporters can't hide from the assignment editor—this large African American gentleman right here—"

The man standing on the risers in front of the dry erase board turned and offered a huge hand.

"You must be Will Ross."

"Yeah," Will answered shaking hands and wondering for a second where his had disappeared to in this great fist.

"Jerry Tower. Nice to meet you." He shook with a force that gave Will the odd sensation that his arm was starting to unbolt from his shoulder. "That was some day you had yesterday," Tower said. "Not bad. Not many folks could make sense on TV after having a shotgun stuck in their ear."

"Did I make sense? I don't quite remember."

"Cool as ice. We can use that, Billy. Another scrawny white boy, but cool as ice. I can use that."

"Good, Jerry. Thought you'd like it. That glass booth—that's dispatch. She's shut in there with a shitload of police scanners trying to catch breaking news."

"Gotta be noisy."

"For her, but not for us. You can see we don't have a lot of room. Keeping her in there with the scanners keeps it down to a dull roar out here. This is the news conference room. And over here is the wire room. We still call it the wire room even though every reporter now has the wires on their desk computers."

"Wires?"

"Wire services. Big old wire machines, the clackety-clack guys? They used to be in here. Pulled them out years ago. CNN. Associated Press. Reuters. CBS Newspath. All the news that's fit to print. Now they're all on computers and this is a feed room. We get video from all our primary news sources in here now. All the video that's compelling enough to air."

"What makes it compelling?"

"Murder, death and destruction, mainly. We're a visual medium, Will. We're always looking for the best pictures. Even though the best pictures sometimes don't mean jack shit to the people who are watching us. Other than the fact ..."

"That they're good pictures," Will added with a smile.

"You got it. You catch on quick."

"Not really. Just like races. The important part of a race may come on a deserted mountain pass, but what people really want to see are those moments when it's nip and tuck in a fast moving pack, or when somebody has a spectacular crash."

"Compelling video." Sessions said it slowly, drawing the words out almost sarcastically.

"Yep."

They walked out the door of the newsroom and down the hall.

"Speaking of deserted mountain passes and compelling video, I pulled up some stories about you in the Tour a few years back. Pretty spectacular crash you had there ..."

The skin along Will's left side crawled involuntarily.

"Yeah. Spectacular ..." A sudden vision of Henri Bresson pedaling through the air and over a cliff made him shudder.

"Oops. Sorry. Bad thoughts. Okay. Here you go," Sessions said, quickly changing the subject. "This is editing." They stopped in front of a doorway leading to a dimly lit hall. On both sides were small rooms, each with a door for privacy, each packed with machines, two or three, sometimes four, that looked like big VCR's, all connected to some sort of computer keyboard. Most had computer screens over on one side.

Will had absolutely no idea what would make any of them work.

"Yeah, I know," Sessions whispered conspiratorially, "they look intimidating. But it will only take you five minutes to learn the buttons—then a lifetime to make your tape look good. You won't do ninety-nine percent of your own editing. But you can jump on a machine if you want to cut something small, log a tape, or just watch to see what you've got to work with."

Will gulped. It felt like he was trying to swallow an eight ball.

"No problem. Okay," he whispered, giving his voice as much confidence as he could muster.

Sessions looked at his watch.

"Gotta hustle up a bit. Give you the rest of the ten-cent tour and then get you on the set. We're going to have Reynelda and Fast Eddie interview you on air in about ten minutes."

Will's eyebrows rose dramatically. "You are?" He began to chase Sessions, who was walking down the hall, turning at odd angles into new and unknown hallways.

"Oh, yeah. I think you're going to be a solid member of the team, once you learn the ropes, but Barb wants to see you on air again and Andy, well, Andy just plain wants to see you. Period."

"Andy?"

Sessions stopped before a door and paused before opening it.

"Yeah. Andy Andropoulos. General manager. Good guy. Steer clear of his temper."

He pushed open the door.

"Bad?" Will asked to Sessions' retreating back.

"Naw," Sessions said over his back, "just try setting a four megaton A-bomb off in your underpants. About the same effect. Follow me."

Will followed. The room was dark, but filled with people. The woman who had been freaking out in the newsroom only minutes before was here, but was now much calmer than she had been before. She seemed to be in her element. The man beside her, who was staring at the bank of monitors, seemed to be in control as well, his stark blond hair almost alight in the dimly lit room. Beside him sat a black woman, both big and pretty, from what Will could see, her arms expertly moving over a control board filled with lighted buttons. Without looking down, she would take the cues from the blond-haired man, push two buttons and reach for a control arm that bore a resemblance to a tiny Hurst shifter out of the '60s.

As she pushed the control arm forward, the main monitor in the center changed.

"Hey, Gordo," Sessions called, "this is Will Ross. He's your 11:20 interview."

Gordie Branson turned, looked at Will and smiled. "Welcome to the jungle."

The woman with the frazzled hair turned and said, in a flush of words, "gethisassoutthereBill,hesupinfourminutes."

Sessions smiled.

"An eternity, Lynn. An eternity. Come on, Will, I'll introduce you to Steph and the rest of the bunch later. Let's get you on set and calm poor Lynnbo's nerves."

"Nice to meet you," Will said, following Sessions through the doors at the opposite end of the room from where they came in.

As the door closed behind them, Will could hear a raucous voice say aloud, "Nice butt. Did you see that butt? He had a nice butt. Cyclin' butt, I bet."

The laughter that followed was muted by the shutting of the door.

As they walked toward the studio doors, marked by a red and white light that flashed "ON THE AIR," Bill Sessions turned to Will.

"I dunno about them. They are always talking about my butt."

He and Will stared at each other for a moment and then laughed, loud and honestly.

For the first moment since he had stepped out of his car and into the parking lot of the station, Will Ross felt at ease.

❋

THE WOMAN LEANED ACROSS THE SPACE TOWARD HIM AND SAID WITH A SMILE, "That's a remarkable background you have in cycling, some spectacular races, but let's talk about yesterday and the robbery attempt. This is going to sound like the silliest question you've ever heard, but what were you thinking, how did you feel, when the gunman threatened you yesterday?"

The red light blinked off the middle camera, then immediately blinked red on the camera directly in front of Will. He caught the shifting lights through the corners and tops of his eyes, but never broke his concentration from the warm and friendly gaze of Reynelda Ware.

"Honestly," Will said slowly, after a short pause, leaning to meet Reynelda half way on the interview set, "I can't tell you."

He was almost whispering. It was as if the two were having an intimate chat somewhere apart from the news set.

"I was angry. I had just lost my job. I was depressed," he chuckled. "I had just lost my job, and I was not about to let some guy spill my drink. I was down to my last coupla quarters."

"Automatic pilot, then?"

"Automatic pilot is a good description for it." Will leaned back and suddenly the camera disappeared from his view. He was in the midst of a conversation with a friend, and he felt about him a new and very pleasant sense of ease.

"It's like, it's like being in a race. There are people all around. It's maddening. It's crazy, but somehow, somehow, you feel right. You're in control. Maybe it's a sprint and everybody is riding like a pack of cartoon dogs, all arms and legs and knees and elbows ..."

Reynelda laughed at the image.

"... or maybe it's a sixty-mile-an-hour descent on a tarmac road that hasn't been resurfaced since Mussolini was in power. Whatever. There comes a moment in a race, I guess there comes a moment in life, where your conscious thought, your sensible thought," he smiled, leaning back in to her to make his point, "is lost. It's gone. Completely. You don't have to be an athlete. It happens to everybody at some point. It's happened to you, hasn't it, Reynelda?"

Will was shocked by his own familiarity, but pressed ahead. She didn't seem to mind.

"It has," she said with a smile. "It has."

Will continued.

"But it certainly happens in a sports situation more often. Ask Elway. Ask Jordan. Ask Tiger Woods. You're in the zone. And you just do what needs to be done. And that's what happened yesterday. It wasn't sport but it sort of played out that way for me. I went into the zone and did what I did."

"And were very lucky."

Will sat back and thought about it for a second, making a face as the stark reality he had been pushing away for the last twenty-four hours jumped on his back like one of those flyin' monkeys Shirley had warned him about earlier.

"Yeah, Reynelda, I was. I was very lucky. Don't know if I would be again, but I was very lucky this time, that's for sure."

Reynelda nodded once or twice, showing a clear and beautiful smile, then relaxed back into her chair, turned to the center camera and said, "Will Ross, who yesterday threw a wrench into a robbery and today," she smiled broadly, "may just be joining the TV6 News team. What do you think of that, Ed?"

The third camera, which had never left Fast Eddie on the main set, blinked with its red eye. At first, Will thought he had been caught off guard, but it was a ruse, a hustle. Ed was glancing down at a TV monitor set in the main anchor desk, as if he had been riveted, absolutely riveted, on Reynelda's interview with Will.

He adjusted his glasses, looked up at the camera and then said with a winning smile that actually looked sincere, "I think that's just great Rey ... but I'll tell you ... I want him on my side in a bar fight."

Everybody chuckled, including Will, who relaxed in the chair as if he owned it. He had survived the interview, not an easy thing to do, he knew from past experience. The red light on the camera pointed at both of them blinked off. Ed, on the main news set, stentorially mumbled something about being right back, and then his camera light blinked off as well.

"Shit," Ed shouted, the volume and new timbre of his voice breaking the somber mood in the studio, "I have never seen that video before. How the hell did you ever survive that crash?"

Will wasn't quite sure what to say.

"Dumb luck, I guess."

"Bad luck for the guy who did the nose-dive."

Will winced. That was Henri Bresson. His friend, who had died in that same crash.

Reynelda saw the expression on Will's face and put her hand on his forearm. "I'm sorry," she whispered, "that's just Eddie. That's no excuse, but that's just the way he is, sometimes."

Will nodded.

"I understand. And he wouldn't know. It was just a real bad day."

She smiled and said, quietly, "I hope everything works out. It would be nice to have somebody here who hasn't had all the human emotions aside from anger and lust already squeezed out of him."

Will gave her a look that quite clearly said he didn't understand what she was talking about. Reynelda merely smiled again, her rare, enigmatic smile that warmed a room, then unplugged her earpiece from the box on the floor, unclipped the microphone from her lapel and walked back to the main set, and sat to the left of the man Will had come to know as Fast Eddie.

What the hell had he gotten himself into now?

Bill Sessions appeared at his side, a grin running ear to ear.

"Man, if that wasn't the best audition I've ever seen, that time when you turned it right back on Rey, nice and comfortable and familiar, man, you're a natural. Barb has already called down from her office. She wants to see you right away."

Fast Eddie was listening from the set, the noon show still in the middle of a commercial.

"Guard your nuts. She'll have 'em on a necklace by this afternoon if you're not careful."

"Oh, shut the hell up, Eddie," Sessions replied, a laugh in the back of his tone, "what the hell would you know about it—your first wife got your nuts in the settlement."

"Kiss my ass."

"That hairy old thing ..."

"Gentlemen, gentlemen," Reynelda said, quietly, "despite the fact that we're in a commercial break, I'd like to remind you to treat every mike like an open mike."

Sessions retreated, chastised.

"You're right, Rey, sorry about that."

"You're right, Rey, sorry about that," Eddie mocked. "Kiss my ass, Sessions."

He then leaned down to the microphone and said, in a deep, basso profundo, "This is Channel 9, KUSA-TV, Denver."

Sessions laughed.

Reynelda rolled her eyes.

"Hey," Eddie laughed, his arms outstretched, "our viewers are like ninety years old. They're literally dying off. They have no idea what channel they're watching. So—if I can get them upset at our little friends over at Channel 9, well, all the better for us."

Reynelda now had her head down, and was shaking it back and forth as if she was trying to remember when her retirement date was so she could leave this life once and for all.

"Eddie, Eddie, Eddie," she moaned, "when will you take you out of my misery?"

"Rey, Rey, Rey," he said, with a smile, "never, never, never ... once I learned I had absolutely no talent for this business, I was too successful to leave it."

Reynelda laughed. Sessions laughed. Will smiled. The camera's red light went on, and without missing a beat, Fast Eddie Slezak segued smoothly into a tease for the Four PM news, and its lead story, something about Madonna suing a hospital for a web site name.

It caught Will off guard for just a moment.

For this he had to read the papers every day?

❧

THE FIRST THING WILL NOTICED ABOUT HER WAS HER HAIR. IT WAS BLONDE. IT was not just blonde, it was strikingly blonde, the kind of blonde that women dipped their heads in tubs of exotic chemicals to achieve. But, given the rest of her coloring, it appeared to be real.

Her eyes were a piercing blue and her features sharp, but attractive. She was a tall, Nordic beauty that one wag in the newsroom had referred to as "The Ice Queen" as Will passed.

A small point of her hair, certainly her crowning glory, was at the moment being twisted with a single finger into a knot tighter than the mainspring of a cheap watch.

"Well, Will, I'll tell you, I like what I see," she said, a friendly tone in her voice that Will could hear, just barely, masking an I-don't-know-about-this question in the background. "You did a nice interview with Rey, seemed comfortable on the air. Were you?"

Will nodded. "Yeah, I'd say I'm comfortable with TV, but she was driving, so it was easy. I still might need some training wheels."

She laughed, an easy, high laugh that was sincere and open.

"At least he's honest about it, Bill. Don't get that too very often in here." She lowered her voice to make the comic point. "Can you do it? Well, can I? I've been the lead reporter for Dan Rather for ten years ... you never saw me? ... I'm shocked!"

"Shocked and surprised," Sessions added, quietly.

"Yes," Gooden said, returning to her normal tone of voice, "shocked and surprised. Forgot that one. So, you can see, Will," she leaned forward across her desk and spread her arms in a gesture of openness, "we get all kinds through here. What kind are you?"

"I'm the kind that needs a job."

She laughed again. It was a nice sound to hear. Will wondered how often he'd get to hear it once he became an employee rather than a prospect.

"Good again. Honest again. Okay. Here's the deal: you don't have any TV news experience. That's bad. And normally, we wouldn't even look at you at this level, the eighteenth largest TV market in the country. On the other hand, you've got life experience and we've got a hole in our staff."

"You shouldn't really put it that way," Sessions countered.

"Hmm," Gooden said, leaning back and twisting her hair even more tightly, "you're right. Sorry, Will. You probably heard, we lost a reporter yesterday. A bomb—right outside the station here—meant, the police think anyway, to scare more than injure, but it did his nerves no damned good. He's okay. Few burns. Few scrapes ..."

"Hair blown in a new direction ..."

"Yes," she smiled, "hair blown in a way that makes it look like he can go really, really, fast, now."

She paused. She and Sessions looked at each other and burst out laughing. Will didn't move. This was a bomb. A bomb at the TV station. You'd think that it was somewhat more serious than that. Will had heard yesterday that the employee involved had been seriously injured. My god, he thought, what do they do when they die?

"We're terrible. We're terrible." She stopped laughing, sort of coughed up one last chuckle, then looked back at Will. "He's okay. He really is. Police say he was really lucky—more a prank than anything to be worried about. Enough, though, to scratch him up and freak us out. I guess this is our way of handling it."

"Sorry, Will," Sessions added from behind.

Will merely raised his hand—cautiously. It was okay by him.

"Anyway, Andy, our general manager, has increased security and we're adding more outside lights and escorts to and from the parking lot, especially at night. Police are pretty sure we were targeted randomly. There's nothing to indicate that they were after Channel 6 or Jim in particular."

"Unless they had watched his sportscast ..." came the quiet voice behind Will. Sessions and Gooden burst out laughing again.

She stifled another chuckle and said, "You've got a three month probationary period, here, Will. If you don't make it—well, don't open any mysterious lunchboxes you find outside your door."

"Jim—not the brightest bulb in the chandelier."

They both burst out laughing yet again.

Will was appalled. He could feel his stomach begin to churn and tighten. A ball of phlegm was jammed just underneath his Adam's apple, threatening to spew out over Barbara Gooden's desk, hair, expensive tailored suit and even more expensive gold watch. What in the name of God was he doing in here, and what the hell was he doing stepping into a business that watched employees going giggle-ass-up and then laughed about it?

"Gee, he lost his hand, har har har har har ..."

The sound of his mental laughter began to retreat in his mind and Will continued to listen to Barbara Gooden with half an ear. What the hell would he want with a place like this?

What the hell was the attraction?

Why should he do it?

"... three-month probation at sixty thousand a year, then, if you do well, we'll bump you up to seventy thousand for three years, with one-year options and a six-month non-compete clause. What do you think?"

Will's eyebrows involuntarily raised, and before he knew what he was doing he had his hand out, shaking hers. Barbara Gooden smiled. There was something in that smile that said to Will, "Gotcha!" but the thought skipped by with the ease of passing a Cat. 4 rider on a Mount Evans downhill.

"Andy will want to meet you this afternoon," she said, quite businesslike, "he'll have the contracts then and will likely scare the livin' shit out of you. Before that, though, Bill, why don't you take our latest catch to the sports department, get him a desk and show him around? I'll get the paperwork upstairs so we can start on your benefits and everything."

"Benefits?"

"Yeah, benefits. We're a big ol' 21ˢᵗ century TV station. Right up with the times." She waved to Bill Sessions, who was already on his feet by the door. It was obvious to Will that the audience was over. "By the way—as you're walking him to the sports office, don't let him see the looms where we make the ten-year-olds work sixteen hours a day."

"Can't anyway, they're on their gruel break," Sessions muttered.

She laughed again. It made Will smile and feel just a touch more comfortable.

Will gave her a small, self-conscious wave and walked into the hall, right behind the assistant news director.

"Your office is on the other side of the atrium. This building is laid out like shit, but is actually better now, because Sports used to be in a hole in the wall behind the men's room. Every time somebody took a crap they knew about it. I couldn't stand Flynn gagging anymore so we moved that office over here."

They crossed behind Shirley at the front of the building and turned a corner on the side opposite the atrium from the newsroom. Bill Sessions took hold of the doorknob and opened the door.

"Beware and Fear for Your Lives All Ye Who Enter Here," he intoned.

Will smiled and noticed suddenly that the phlegm ball was now the size of a small cantaloupe. The two walked into the office. Four desks were crammed into a space about the size of a small team step van.

Three were empty. One had flowers piled on top of it that were already beginning to wilt. The desk of Lucky Jim, Will thought. Lucky break. Lucky.

The fourth desk featured a stocky young man in a Hawaiian print shirt, furiously pounding away at a computer keyboard. Will noticed he wasn't writing a story he was playing a game.

"Thought we got all those off the system," Sessions said, a bit too loud for the size of the room.

"You got the ones that weren't hidden, Sessions, now leave me the fuck alone, I'm going for Level Eight and the Mystic Dragon of Idor."

"Yeah, well, leave the nice dragon alone for a minute, Zorro, and meet your new cell mate."

Will winced at the image.

"Clyde Zoromski," he announced, "meet Will Ross. New sports reporter and sometimes anchor if things work out as planned."

"What plan is that, Bill, boy, put Zorro in a cannon and shoot him out over the Front Range?"

"No, no, no, Z—we would never give you the courtesy of a cannon. He's gonna fill in for Jim for now. Pick a desk and get comfortable, Will," Sessions said. "I've gotta hit the can then I'll take you to lunch. When we get back you can meet Andy."

"Ah, the Jabberwock hisself," the Zorro character muttered.

"Don't worry about Zorro, Will. He doesn't bite. And if he does, he's had all his shots."

Zorro bowed in gratitude. High praise, it seemed.

"Get to know each other a bit, shove him in a desk, Z, and I'll be back in fifteen."

"That's some crap you've gotta take," Zorro said to Session's departing back.

"That's some crap I've gotta put up with," said the voice already disappearing down the hall.

Clyde Zoromski turned back to Will and paused for a minute, eyeballing him, giving him the once over. Hands behind his head, he peered sharply, making Will slightly uncomfortable. He didn't know where to put his hands, whether to smile or not, or if he should just turn his back, walk out, get in his car and drive to the nearest bar.

"Will Ross," Zoromski said quietly, "Will Ross. You're the guy who got his nose picked by a twelve-gauge yesterday, aren't you?"

Will nodded. "Yeah. I am."

"Hmm," Zoromski grunted, "and, if I'm not mistaken, you won Paris-Roubaix a while back and did a couple of spectacular high dives during the Tour de France, right?"

"Yeah. That's me."

Keep it short, sweet and to the point, Will thought. Don't give this guy an opening.

"Well, you may think you're hot shit, but this is my territory and my office and my job. Don't think you're getting weekends."

"Don't want 'em."

"Good. Ol' Jimbo did. Sorry he left the way he did, but not sorry he left. Know what I mean?"

Christ, Will realized, the politics in this business, in this station, hell, in this office, were as bad, if not worse, than anything he had ever encountered on a team. You got it, I want it. Well, I got it, don't think of taking it from me.

Shit. He was right back in it again, after so long of trying to get out of it and just ride his bike.

"Naw, Jimmy boy was an ambitious little shit," Zoromski continued, unasked. "Always trying to go behind my back and get my gig. But I've had it a long time and I like it. So don't even think about it. If you want to step up, try and get Flynn's job. He's an asshole and you can have that Monday through Friday shit. He's the one who has to go to all the games. Broncos. Rockies. Avs. All that shit. Me, I can sit on my ass most of Saturday and Sunday and just introduce my friend Roger live from the stadium.

"Take it away, Roger.

"Get my drift?"

Will got his drift. He wondered again what the hell he was doing in this office. This station. This business.

Suddenly, the force of a realization body-slammed him backwards into the flowers on Lucky Jim's desk. Christ! He'd have to cover that, he thought! He'd have to go to the football games, baseball games, hockey games and every other game and figure out what the hell was going on. He'd have to do that. That was now his job.

It was as if Zoromski could read his mind.

"Yes, that's right, new buddy. You get to go out and play with Roger each and every weekend. And if you think I'm a grump, just wait until you get a load of him." The look on Clyde Zoromski's face was hard and brittle for a second, then softened.

"I guess I've hazed you enough. I'm Zorro. Don't answer to anything else except on the set. Take that desk. We'll have Jimbo's cleaned out soon if you want to have that one. He's not coming back. That firecracker that went off in his face blew the courage right out of him and back to his mama. He shoulda jumped right back on the air, no eyebrows and all. Get right back on the bicycle."

"Bicycle. Yeah, that reminds me. What kind of bicycle coverage will we be doing?"

Zorro looked at him as if he had just fallen off a turnip truck.

"Cycling. Hmm. Well. Let me put it is way: NONE!" he shouted, laughed, then turned back to his desk. "I know all about you, buster, professional cyclist and all, but around here cycling carries about as much weight as jai alai. If you get two stories a year on cycling, you've had a good year."

"Nothing?"

"Nothing."

"What about that race coming up? The point to point one day job?"

"Oh, that. Yeah. That, uh, well, that's something that some corporate buddy of Mr. Big," he motioned upstairs with a thumb, "got us roped into. But Flynn doesn't want it. I don't have time. Hey, guess, what—it's yours."

He smiled and offered two open hands to Will as if he was offering a present.

"Have fun and don't fuck it up."

He turned back to his desk. Over his shoulder he said, "By the way, I'd get your phone number up to Kris in Andy's office so that you can get cards started, business cards. You're gonna need 'em and these assholes take forever to get them to you. And—thanks to your appearance on the noon—you've already had your first call. I put it on your voicemail."

"Must be my wife."

"Not unless your wife is a man. Dial 6400 and then punch in your code. For new employees its always 6666—a mere one digit away from the mark of the Beast."

"That's cheerful."

"No doubt. For I am a cheerful guy." Zoromski returned to his computer and began to pound unmercifully on the keyboard, as if he was beating the life out of it, paying it back for each and every frustration that had come his way over the years.

Will paused for a moment and then turned to his appointed desk, glanced over at the flowers on the desk of the newly departed Jim, Lucky Jim, and picked up the phone. 6400 he dialed, waited, then punched in the code. 6666. One message. The red light on the phone continued to blink.

Not Cheryl. Maybe Hootie. He always had a set on in his office. Maybe Hootie. Hootie. Had to be.

Please come back, Will—all is forgiven.

One message. The red light continued to wink at him.

"You have one message," the machine said in its digitized female voice. To retrieve said message, press one.

Despite years of knowing where the one was on a telephone keypad, Will glanced at the phone with a look that indicated bifocals might not be too very far away and gingerly pushed one. The digital voice said "First message."

Will sat back in his new office chair and casually put his feet on the desk as if he had been there for years. New turf, home turf, his turf.

Will put the phone to his ear and listened.

The voice was quiet, distant. In the background, in the distance, Will could hear the hum of a highway. A semi horn blew somewhere in the distance.

The voice, when it spoke the single sentence, broke through the noise like a glasscutter through single-pane. Quick, clean and somehow, deadly.

Even though he had no idea what the hell the message meant, Will was suddenly disposed to listen closely and take the caller very seriously.

The voice said, softly, but with impact, "Aren't you going to thank me for your new job?"

Will listened to it twice.

"Aren't you going to thank me for your new job?"

"Aren't you going to thank me for your new job?"

He thought about listening to it one more time, but Bill Sessions suddenly stuck his head in the door.

"All set?" he asked Will.

"All emptied out?" asked Zorro.

"Yes, Zorro, I am now empty. And ready to fill myself up again. Will, come on along, there's a deli across the street that's not bad."

"Hope you haven't had your full grease intake today."

Will laughed. He wondered if or when he'd become a part of the banter.

He hung up the phone and forgot the call through lunch and a busy afternoon of paperwork and being intimidated by Andy Andropoulos, the general manager of the station. But later that day, as he was about to go home, Will stood in his office, his new office, his new office due to another man's tragedy, and stared at the message light blinking, blinking, blinking on his new office phone.

What did it mean?

"Aren't you?"

"Well, aren't you?"

"Aren't you going to thank me for your new job?"

CHAPTER FOUR:

HELL ON PAPER

"How much?"

Cheryl's eyes were wide. Her cheeks were flushed. Her smile was huge.

"Sixty to start," Will said with a smile.

"And you start ..."

"Tomorrow," he answered. "I go in for some kind of orientation kind of thing and then one of the newsroom honchos shows me how to put together a story."

"I've never heard of anyone getting to step in like this, Will."

"I just impressed them, somehow."

"Or they were desperate."

A strangled cry caught in this throat, he turned to her and smiled a nasty grin before saying, "I'd punch you, but little Gooch there might think I don't like you."

"And we wouldn't want that."

"No," Will answered, "we wouldn't want that."

"Jesus, though," Cheryl said, flopping back onto the pillows, then rustling this way and that in an attempt to get comfortable in the way-too-small bed, in the way-too-small room in the way-too-small house. "Yesterday I was about to kill you for not fighting for your job and then going out to drink it away, then, I was going to kill you for almost getting your head blown off in a bar while you were trying to be a hero."

"I wasn't trying to be a hero."

"TRYING," she emphasized, "to be a HE-ro. And then you turn around and walk into a bunch of roses like this damned TV job ..."

"Amazin', ain't it?"

"Amazin' ain't the word for it." She rolled this way then that in another futile effort to get comfortable.

"What's your benefit package like?"

"What do you mean?"

"What I mean is, what do you get in your benefit package?" She patted her stomach. "Do you get family leave? How much vacation? Do you work holidays? What's your medical like? Do we have dental? What if Gooch needs glasses? Does your insurance pay for them?"

"What about Hootie's insurance?"

"Hootie's insurance sucks royally. It pays for about half a lens on a pair of glasses and God knows what else beyond that. The co-pays are high, the choice of doctors stinks and I'm not happy about it at all."

"So, what should I look for?"

"You've already signed your name."

"Yeah, so what should I look for?"

"Oh, shit, Will. Don't tell me you didn't even look at the benefit package before you signed."

"Well, you know," he said, defensively, "I really didn't have much chance to do it. After all, I have a baby on the way and I didn't have a job, so when somebody dangled an easy sixty in front of me, I jumped. Can't help it. I just do that."

"Always look at the benefit package."

"And what am I going to do if it sucks? Negotiate? With what? Hi! I'm the new guy without a bit of TV experience. But I won't take your job unless you give me a gold plated doctor plan that pays me to get sick twice a week."

"That's not what I'm saying," she answered, suddenly defensive herself.

"Then what are you saying?"

"Jesus, I don't see why you're in such a touchy mood. Christ. Look. All I'm saying is that if you don't look at the entire package before you sign your name, too late now, I know, then you're bound to get burned somewhere down the line. Contracts are meant, in this kind of case, to protect the company. Not to protect you."

"I didn't have much I could say about it."

"Well, just get the package ..."

"It's on the dining room table. All those papers."

"Well, at least you brought them home, Will."

"Hooray for me," he snorted derisively.

"Okay, what's eating you?"

"Oh, my—I lose my job and almost get killed then out of my hat I pull a sixty thousand dollar a year job, up to seventy in a couple of months and all I'm getting is health insurance shit. Sorry. At that moment in time, it didn't seem to leap out at me and say 'Oh, wait—open me first.'"

Cheryl stared at him for a moment. Quiet. Thinking.

"No. No," she whispered, "its not that. We give each other shit constantly about all sorts of things and it never really grinds at you, but this does. Something about this does. What is it, Will? It's not the insurance. We both know we're covered, no matter what your plan is. I was just givin' you gas. But now, something else ..." She paused and looked at him, trying to find the answer deep within his eyes, his skin, the way he breathed, the way he held his head.

Trying to read him was like trying to decipher a set of hieroglyphics.

"What is it?"

"Nothing."

"Afraid you can't hack it?"

Will sighed.

"Well, yes and no. Yes, I think I can hack it, because when you look around that newsroom you'd be amazed at the wackos who can. But no, I know I'll never get it because I just don't think like they do ..."

"What do you mean?"

"They have an edge to them. A bitterness. A cynicism that's really raw. I mean one of their own guys had a bomb blow up in his face a day or so ago and they were joking about it.

"Murder, death, destruction ... yuk, yuk, yuk. Shit, I don't want to think like that. I don't want to live like that. I don't want to be like that."

Cheryl was quiet for a moment, then said, "So don't be."

"What?"

"So don't be. I read a book about soldiers once in school. How some kill and become killers. How some kill and remain soldiers."

"I don't follow."

"Some kill and grow to like it. Love it. Need it. Others joke about it, because it's the only way they can deal with the horror. And then there are still others who kill, because it is their duty, and, yet, retain their own essential humanity."

"And I should ..."

"Retain your humanity. That's what I fell in love with: the way you look at the world and keep rising up again, no matter what it has done or tries to do to you. You've seen death and murder and lost friends and still, you remain a decent human being. It's tough. I think it will be especially tough in this new business you got yourself into, but, in the end, that's what I love about you and I hope you don't lose it.

"Stay human. Keep your heart. Don't find humor in the tragedy of others."

"Or excitement," Will muttered.

"What?"

"Excitement. Excitement of the news game, you know? If it bleeds, it leads?"

"Good. Yes. Exactly," Cheryl said, wrapping her arms around his shoulders and drawing him close.

After a quiet moment, as the warmth between them grew, she whispered, "What am I going to do with you?"

"Well, there's always the thought of doing something with me in new and exciting positions."

"That's a terrible thought. Gooch will be born with a dent in his head."

"Her head."

"His.

"I want a clone of you. A girl."

"And I want a clone of you. A boy."

"No dice. I ain't gonna be no role model."

"Too late. You planted the seeds, little farmer man, now you get to raise the corn."

"I thought those were oats. As in wild oats."

"No, you're a little more basic."

He chuckled seductively. "Then let me show you something a little more basic."

"No, I don't ... ah, there ... no, okay, let me shift ... and ... ooooo."

✤

THE OFFICE PHONE RANG. WILL PAUSED FOR A MOMENT BEFORE HE PICKED IT UP. Was this the somebody wanting special thanks for giving him the job at the TV station? Will thought about it for a moment, then pushed it aside. Cheryl had said it last night when Will mentioned it while they were watching the late news. Ten o'clock. The late show.

Well, late enough. Will was getting old. He needed his beauty sleep.

"Kook. Saw you on the news and called in. Kook. TV attracts 'em. I wanna be frens' I wanna be on TV I wanna ..." she curled the words around a mocking, mentally deficient tongue, "be your pal. I got you your job."

"Kooks."

"Kooks. Definitely. But in your case, a singular kook. I'm sure in a few months you'll have a whole army of them following you around. Ask your boss, what's her name? Barbara Gooden—and is she?"

"Is she what?"

"Is she a good 'un?"

"Jesus. Your hormones are making you stupid."

"Yeah. I'm becoming more like a man everyday." She rubbed her stomach. "It's a boy, no doubt. But—point is, ask your boss if this happens to her and if you should be bothered. Ask her. She's been in the business since God created TV according to Nancy. Hey, maybe she'd know."

But that was last night. This was today, at the station, and the phone stared at him. Then rang again.

Will hadn't had a chance to ask Barbara yet, but maybe he would this afternoon. Until then, he simply couldn't be afraid of picking up the phone because maybe some loony would be on the other end dithering at him for some unknown reason.

"Hello? Wait. Uh. Ross. Sports, can I help you?"

"Don't worry, dear, practice your lines and someday you'll be good enough to get a phone of your own."

"What did I do to deserve you?"

"Something really good, I'll wager," Cheryl laughed in the phone, "but knowing you, I suspect it was something good in a previous life."

"Thank you so very, very much," Will answered sarcastically. "What's up? How's Gooch?"

"Gooch is fine. I'm fine. I just wanted to give you a heads up. Nancy just gave me a call and Hootie and your ol' pal Lisa Shannon are on their way over to the station. Your very own station to talk about getting involved as sponsors in this bike race deal."

"You know that's my idea."

"Yes, I know. You told me."

"But it was," he whined.

"I don't doubt it a bit, Will. Lisa's taking credit for it, though. Not to my face, mind you, but Nancy says she's crowing that it's quite a coup and it will look good on her resume."

"Her resume? Jesus. The bitch just got the job forty-eight hours ago."

"True. But most of the folks around here miss you already and are offering to help her polish up her *curricula vitae* for future job opportunities. We're goin' to Peter Principle the bitch right on out of here."

"Sounds fun."

"Well, the fun's in your court now. They left about ten minutes ago, so they should be there anytime. You might want to find a good place to hide."

"There's a makeup room in the back of the station. I'll go there and take a nap."

"On your first day?"

"Sure. Is it really fair to make them wait until the end of probation before they see just what they've hired?"

"Just watch your ass. Cute ass, I might add. But, one thing, Will," Cheryl said, her tone suddenly serious, "watch out for Shannon. She's really steamed about that whole business with the Rolodex. She was shouting that she wanted to sue your ass."

"What'd Hootie say about it?"

"He only found the humor in it when Nancy said he'd never see heaven again unless he laughed ..."

"Theirs is a strange but wonderful relationship."

"And aren't you lucky it is. Head down, I'll talk to you later. Let me know what happens."

"I will, sweetheart," Will said, a smile growing on his face. Somehow, more than any other person on the planet, this woman could do this to him. "Keep an eye on Gooch for me ..."

"Got to. That's all I can see when I look for my feet ..."

"I love you."

"Love you, Will. Be careful"

They hung up. Will sat silently for a second, then checked his watch. It would be half an hour before Steve, one of the weekend producers, was back to give him his next computer news writing lesson. Maybe it would be a good idea, thought Will, to sneak out back, miss Hootie and Lisa completely, and just zone out for a few in the mid-summer Colorado sunshine.

He didn't even make it to the door.

"Hey, Bill ..."

"Hey, Will. This rhyming shit is going to be good for us. Uh, Barb wants you to sit in on a meeting about this bicycle race we've got going in a few weeks."

Will's heart sank. Shit. Thirty seconds more and he would have disappeared out back.

"She thinks you'll be able to bring some hard realities to the table here, even though you don't have a lot of TV experience. Like how many cameras we'll need, where we need reporters, what to do and how to do it."

Trapped. Only one door open.

"Sure," Will said, forcing a smile that Sessions immediately knew was fake. "What's the problem?"

Will sighed. Might as well just jump right into it, he thought. "You know the folks who fired me earlier this week? They'll be at this meeting today."

"Really? Good. Rub their fucking noses in it. You work for us, now."

"I don't know about that."

"I do. If you don't, Barbara will. She doesn't let anybody give any of her reporters shit. She's like a mother hen. She'll tear anybody a new asshole who even looks at you cross-eyed."

"Really?"

"Really. No shit. It's something to see, too. Just wait. Come on."

And Will went.

Walking down the hall, in the distance behind him, Will heard the ring of a phone. His, he could tell from the tone.

He let the machine get it. He followed Bill Sessions around the atrium toward the news conference room. Strangely enough, he felt an odd sense of excitement.

❖

"I SEE YOU HAVE A NEW FRIEND," BARBARA GOODEN WHISPERED IN WILL'S EAR. He nodded and looked across at Lisa Shannon. If looks could kill, Will would not just be dead, he'd be dangling from a large oak tree, with vultures, crows and finches picking bits and pieces of flesh from very uncomfortable places.

It wasn't just anger, her anger at finding the Rolodex, the company Rolodex, her Rolodex by inheritance, so completely and totally useless, but jealousy. She had won, but the person she had beaten had stepped up to something better immediately and doubled his salary in the process.

He had doubled what was now *her* salary.

It wasn't fair. She didn't even have time to revel in her victory and he was already rubbing her nose in it.

Her eyes said it all. And Will found it entertaining to keep her gaze, a small smile forming on his lips.

Even jumping up, clutching himself and shouting, "Rolodex this, bitch!" wouldn't have had nearly the impact of just that simple smile.

She glared. He smiled. Life was suddenly good.

Barbara rose to open the meeting.

"We're glad to have the reps from Bosco Bikes with us today. It's a pleasure to have another sponsor in with us, especially a money sponsor."

Everyone chuckled. Will didn't break his gaze. Neither did Lisa Shannon. They both chuckled blandly.

"Ken, could you just take a second to bring everybody up to speed on what the race is and what it's going to entail?"

"Sure, Barbara," said the thin man at the end of the conference table, his standing up from the table breaking Will's gaze and drawing it down to him.

"It's nice to have the support we've got here in this room, and really nice to have Will Ross, who had a great final season two years back with Haven in Europe, joining us for this very first Zephyr Classic. For those of you who don't know," he pulled a packet of stapled sheets out of his briefcase and pushed it down toward Will, "the race is one hundred forty miles over seven mountain passes. A one-day point-to-point race. Not quite as endless and colorful as the old Coors Classic, but in one day, given weather and road conditions, probably one of the most difficult races in the world."

Will glanced at the map then, and the numbers on it began to catch his eye. Ken Whoever-He-Was continued to mumble in the background while Will added them up. It was a rough estimate, but it staggered him.

"Excuse me," he interrupted. Ken stopped.

"Yes, Will?"

"Do you realize here that you've got fourteen thousand feet of climbing in one day?"

"Yes."

"With the first climbs within four miles of the start?"

"Uh-huh."

"If you had read some of your mail you'd already know ..." Lisa Shannon snorted.

Will ignored her.

"This is one of those things like the first Tour de France. Unpaved roads. No guardrails. How many riders do you figure will start?"

"We've got one hundred twenty so far. Room for fifteen more."

"How many you think will finish?"

"Not sure."

"Try fifteen to twenty."

"That makes for good TV," Barbara said.

"Yeah, unless you're picking them dead out of the treetops."

"Little chance of that ..."

"Really? Look at this map. Descend 'Oh My God' Road. You know why they call it 'Oh My God'? Ever driven it? Try riding it on a bicycle without the speed getting away from you. There isn't a guardrail within two miles of that thing. And—it's all gravel. One wrong move and you're picking gravel out of your teeth on the way to heaven."

"We've ..."

"Guanella Pass. That's dirt at the top. The temperature change alone in mid-summer will kill you. That's twelve thousand, isn't it? It's damned close. What about Hoosier Pass at the end of the day in late July? You gonna give each rider a lightning rod? Nobody's gonna be riding into Breckenridge but a bunch of crispy critters if you get a good storm up there."

"I take it you don't like the race, Will," Hootie said. "And after you suggested it to me, too."

Lisa Shannon blushed a dark red with anger and resentment.

"Didn't say that," Will answered Hootie, his voice never wavering, his gaze never faltering. "I'm just saying that logistically you had better have all your little ducks in a row on this and have three things—a shitload of backup plans; one damned big broom wagon and an ambulance handy. Oh, yeah, and at the very least, rolling medical aid, well-equipped rolling medical aid inside that enclosure."

"Enclosure?" Barbara asked.

"Yeah. I assume, correct me if I'm wrong, Ken, that you're figuring on a rolling enclosure for this, right? Colorado State Patrol closes it down a mile ahead of the leaders and a mile behind the pack? Something like that?"

"We've got it timed out pretty much. Any rider fifteen minutes behind the pack for whatever reason gets pulled. But, yeah, you've got it. We'll close the roads as we go. The CSP is being pretty cool about it."

"What times are you figuring for the race to pass any particular point?"

"Late in the race, anywhere from twenty to forty-five minutes. That's the outside."

"Okay," Will nodded, then lapsed into silence, staring at the route map and the climb profile.

After a few moments of uncomfortable silence, Barbara spoke up. "You have a problem with any of this, Will?"

"Hmm? No. No. It's going to be tough, that's for damned sure. It's certainly more than I figured it was from the stories I've seen on it so far, but it can be done. Has a chance of becoming America's Paris-Roubaix, doesn't it, Ken?"

"You should know. I can only hope."

"So can we," Hootie said, quietly.

"No doubt, Hootie. This is a hell of a race for proving a bicycle. You put one in the top five and you'll have something to crow about. It's not Europe, but it'll make noise."

"Somebody told me that once."

"Probably Lisa," Will said flatly, flicking his finger her way.

She turned red again. Will smiled inwardly.

"What about TV coverage. How difficult would it be to do?"

"Live would be next to impossible in the mountains, unless you're willing to break the bank for relays all over the place."

"We don't have that budget."

"The French government doesn't even have that budget," Will muttered. "What were you planning on?"

"A few live locations during the day. Satellite trucks. Microwaves. A special show that night."

"Have you ever done anything like this?"

"Not since the Coors Classic. Even then, it was hit and miss."

"What about this? Have a camera on a motorcycle in the pack. Another with the leaders. Just shooting, uh, videotape." He remembered to say video-tape rather than film. He was proud of himself. "A helicopter, you've got one, right?" Barbara nodded. "The helicopter shoots pack and leader pictures on the flats and in the mountains. Wherever it can go in the mountains. Along the way, they've got landing zones where they meet a TV6 runner and maybe a fuel truck. They drop the tape, fuel up and miss maybe ten minutes, during each, what—hour? I dunno."

One of the producers, who Will didn't recognize, was shaking his head.

"Won't work. Where do you cut tape? How do you know what you have?"

"No, it will work. It's just leapfrogging. I've seen it done in Europe. They do live shit as well, but we blow that out and just leapfrog tape all along the way. You have somebody, a producer, I guess, in charge of the whole mess back here. All the pictures come here except the last stuff. That goes into Brecken-ridge for the finish. Ken, when do you figure the race will be done?"

"Anywhere from four to a little after five."

"Okay. We have the race finale live ... no, better ... we hold the finale, take the hour to cut everything together and put it in the hour show as if we don't know what the outcome is ..."

"That's staging ..." Sessions said, in a singsong voice, full of warning.

"No," Barbara said, quietly, "we're not creating anything, we're simply holding. Building suspense until a more convenient time." She gave Will a sly smile.

"It's showbiz."

Will allowed himself a proud smile.

She looked at the operations manager of the station, another sudden coworker that Will had yet to meet.

"Could it work?"

He nodded, slowly, thoughtfully. "Yeah, it could. Hell of an idea. Out of the mouths of babes. Simple. Clear. Takes a lot of the hassle out of what we were trying to do."

Sessions looked at Will with pride. "See—I knew it. Just watching him the other day. Thoughtful, on the mark, no bullshit."

And, Will thought, able to pull roses out of his ass at a moment's notice. He had been speaking and drawing little squiggly-eyed marks on the race map and profile that those looking on might take as detailed notes, but he knew to be nothing but mindless doodles. He had, in fact, been bullshitting. Throwing out ideas he had ripped off from watching the TV crews in Europe with the ragged hope that one of them might actually stick on the wall. To his shock and surprise, all of them did.

That, he knew, was prime bullshit.

He wouldn't be able to do that again in a million years. Every shot hit. Every one of theirs missed. Even those nasty-assed glares from little Miss Lisa.

Will let his eyes drift casually over to her and noticed she was looking down at the race map. She clutched her pen so tightly her fingers were turning white.

She raised her head, looked at Will and started to speak.

"On the other hand, I think ..."

She never got any farther. The door of the conference room burst open with a 'bang!' and there, in the doorway, stood Roger Flynn. He was bronzed, sweating and wearing the most obnoxious golf pants Will had ever seen, a bizarre combination of colors that Mother Nature would never put in the same county.

"Sorry I'm late. What have we got here on our little bicycle race?"

"Glad you can call it little, Roger," Barbara grumbled. "Glad, in fact, that you could bother to show up."

"Late, but here. Better than never. How you doin'?" Roger reached for Hootie's hand, "Roger Flynn, nice to meet 'choo ..."

"Nice to meet ..." Hootie replied, then stopped when he realized that Roger wasn't listening, but was already on to Lisa Shannon.

"Enchanté, my dear," Roger smarmed, picking up her hand and kissing it full on the back.

"I'd wash them lips if I were you, " Will muttered under his breath.

"And you ... you are ..." Flynn had turned toward Will, "you are the new guy, the fresh meat, aren't you? Roger Flynn, your boss."

Oh, Jesus, Will thought, not this shit again.

"Will Ross," he answered quickly, "your serf."

Bill Sessions choked back a laugh and had to grab at a handkerchief in order to keep his snot within its nasal boundaries.

"Good to have you here, Ross," Flynn said, quietly, sizing up Will as he did. "We'll go through the rules of the sports department a little later. As for this race, what are we looking at in terms of stories? Because, frankly, I've got Broncos camp coming up pretty quickly and I don't really want to be saddled with this shit."

Barbara Gooden blanched at the word. Everything had been going so well, up until now. Flynn did have a point. There was a lot going on in other sports, but Sessions' inspiration to give Will a tryout might have been a real saving grace, having him doing this race coverage until such time that he could move off that and onto coverage of the real sports that people cared about: football, baseball, basketball, hockey and soccer—as if anyone over the age of sixteen really cared about soccer in this country.

Her answer was there. Sitting right in front of her right now. And he had signed his name to a little piece of paper that said, "duties as assigned."

Roger Flynn was still going on about the Broncos and the bike race, something, he felt, no one in their right mind would ever watch, so why were we wasting the time and manpower and ...

Barbara held up her hand. "Enough, Roger. That's enough. Ken, your eyes are bulging. Don't stroke on me. We are committed to this race. We are committed to the coverage. Roger, you will not have to be a part of it at all, except for some promos ahead of time. The person who will anchor the coverage and make it work is sitting right there."

She pointed at Will. Immediately, he felt his sphincter close up like a spring-loaded mousetrap.

"Huh?" was all he could say.

"Will can handle the majority of our coverage. It's a good way for him to get his feet wet in our business while giving us insight into his business. His *past* business. Just off the top of your head, Will, what would your first story be about the race?"

He paused. He had no idea what to say. The bullshit wagon was now empty and he was in big damned trouble.

"Well, I guess some background on how it got started, but then, you could give me a camera guy and let me ride the course."

"I can't really give you a couple of days on this," Sessions said.

Will looked at the race profile again and swallowed hard.

"I can do it in one, no worries."

Everyone nodded except Lisa Shannon, who looked at Will with an undisguised hatred in her eyes, and Roger Flynn, who matched that look and went one better, mouthing, "See you in the office" to Will before he turned and hurried off.

Swell, thought Will, my list of office enemies is growing and I've barely begun to work here.

❈

"BOTTOM LINE IS, BOY," ROGER FLYNN SNAPPED, STRUTTING AROUND THE SMALL office like a lion in his den, "I rule the roost here. I'm not about to take any kind of shit from the new kid. You can dazzle them all you want with your style and whatever it is you have, but don't you fucking well dare get in my way, because I'll chop you to pieces. Pieces. Small pieces. Easily digested.

"Is that clear to you, boy?"

"Crystal," Will said, debating his next sentence. Should he be politically correct or fight back? With a new job, the idea was to be careful. Smooth the angry outburst over, but, then again, he was an adult now, probably as much as he would ever be. There was no way anybody was going to call him a 'boy' anymore. Not even if it meant that this department, this new job, turned into a living hell.

"I understand, Roger, and I apologize if I made you feel uncomfortable. That wasn't my intention."

"Bullshit," muttered Zorro, intent on his computer screen, but obviously just as intent on listening to what was going on less than forty-five inches away from his head.

Will turned and addressed Zorro directly, "Don't be so paranoid, guys," he emphasized the "guys." "I'm not trying to make anybody look bad and I'm not trying to take anyone's job. There's no way I can. I've never done this before and I don't even know what the jobs are or what I might possibly be good at."

"You'll find out," Zorro grumbled. "They all do."

"But," Will continued, ignoring the last interruption, "I will tell you this: I don't put up with crap and backstabbing from anybody. Not you, Zorro, not you Flynn. You want me out of here, go to Barbara or Mr. Andy and get me tossed out. But otherwise, get off my ass."

It was said in such a fiercely controlled tone that both Zoromski and Flynn stared at Will without reaction. Then, there was a flicker in Flynn's eyes and Roger opened his mouth to speak.

Will shot a finger into the air.

"Eh! Don't even think about it, Roger. You've already called me 'boy,' at least twice. I'm asking you not to diminish me again."

"OOOooh," Flynn sang, "diminish me. Oooooo."

"Don't challenge me, bud."

Flynn held up his hands in mock horror and backed down, buying himself enough time to come up with a new argument.

"Tell me, *sir*, is that with enough respect, Mister Ross? Tell me, this is big market TV ... "

Zorro hiccupped a laugh.

"Sorry."

"This is big market TV," Flynn continued, "so what are you, a guy who knows jack about any of the local teams or local sports, doing here as a sports reporter?"

"As Dante said as he entered the fifth ring of hell, 'just lucky, I guess.' "

"Oh, shit," Zorro whined, "we've got Dennis Miller in the office."

"Sorry. Last classical reference. Lost on younger viewers, huh?"

"Lost on me for damned sure."

"But I don't get it," Flynn bellowed, "WHY? Why you? You're not even an amateur. At this level, they're supposed to be hiring professionals. Why? I just don't get it. I'm a pro and you're shit. And now, I've got to help haul you up in the ratings or, shit, I'm gonna get blamed for it."

"How's that?" Will asked.

"Great. Now I get to teach TV 101, right? Ratings, shit for brains. Ratings. They go down because the audience doesn't like what it sees, then who gets blamed? The newbie, Barbara's Butt Buddy? Or me—the flagship. The guy at the front. The keystone."

"The big cheese, top dog, head man," Zorro followed.

Will stifled a laugh and tried to focus on Roger Flynn.

"Exactly," Flynn continued, completely missing the *Airplane!* reference. Will smiled.

"And, frankly, I'm not going to get blamed because you can't do the job."

"We don't know that yet, do we?" Will asked quietly.

"I do. I know that you don't have it and won't. You don't have shit, pal. You don't have shit, as far as I'm concerned."

Will was quiet for a second, taking the measure of the man. It didn't take much of a tape measure.

"Yes, I do, Flynn. I do have something. I have a life. And I have a rep and I have a past and I have a future. I have a life. To me, this is only a job. That's it. Don't know what it is, don't know where it is going. But by God, it's okay for now as far as I'm concerned. You don't want to help me, fine. I'll muddle through on my own and try not to muddy your shoes. But I will promise you this, pally, pally pal: if you get in my way—if you trip me up—if you try to fuck me in any of a million different ways, by God I will pull off your ears and use them for beer coasters."

"I'd like to see you try."

Zorro interrupted by harshly clearing his throat.

"Uh, Roger, I'd uh, just like to interject here, um, I've been doing some reading on our friend here and at least according to the web, there are, like, fifteen people who knew this guy and aren't around to celebrate birthdays this year."

"Hard ass, huh?" Flynn moved in tight, his chest pressing against Will. What the hell was going on, Will thought. He hadn't had to deal with anything like this since the sixth grade playground.

Flynn was charged. His blood pressure was up and he was breathing hot and hard into Will's face. It wasn't a pleasant sensation. There was nowhere to move and Flynn kept pressing in on him. Finally, Will did the one thing he could instinctively do and did it without thinking. He raised his left leg, put his instep just below Roger Flynn's right knee and pushed down—hard.

Flynn screeched and jumped back clutching his leg, the fabric of his Italian trousers torn from the friction and the skin of the leg scored from the sole of Will's shoe.

"Oh, damn! You son of a bitch! These were brand new pants! Oh, goddamn you! You fu ... ow, damn it." He struggled upright and lurched toward the door.

"You have already blown it. You have blown your job, your bike race, your future. Nice life you're gonna have after I get done with Andy. Shit, you little creep. You are dead. You are fucking dead."

Roger Flynn turned and limped over to the elevator, just outside the Sports Department office, rang for the second floor and stepped in, ready to lower the boom on the little son of a bitch who was taking up both oxygen and space inside his office.

Will watched him go and turned to Zorro. Zoromski quickly held up a hand and listened. There was a "bang!" as Flynn, at least Will assumed it was Flynn, slammed close the door to Andy's office, just above.

"Shit."

Zorro shook his head and kept his hand up. Then, breaking the silence of the atrium, there was a page: "Barbara Gooden, Barbara Gooden, please come to Andy's office. Barbara Gooden to Andy's office."

Within seconds, Barbara was quick-stepping across the atrium toward the stairs. She stepped in the doorway below and almost immediately opened the door at the top of the stairs, as if she had taken them two or three at a time.

Andy's inner office door opened more quietly, then closed with a snap that reverberated around the lobby as loudly as Flynn's slam of a few moments before.

Zorro lowered his hand, smiled, stood, walked to Will and hugged him tightly.

"Oh, thank you, thank you." He turned and looked toward the ceiling. "Thank you, God. You have sent me an ally. Thank you, God."

Will shook his head.

"Okay, Zorro, I'm going to be leaving now," he said, gently.

"NO!" Zoromski shouted, "you can't leave me now. You have proven yourself. Little Jim Bob was a suck-up who was trying to get Flynn to toss my ass and put him in my place. I had to make sure you weren't, too, man. I had to be sure."

"And now?" Will asked suspiciously.

"Now, you're in. You're part of the inner circle. Zorro's Phantom Legion. The Masked Riders. Our goal: to bring down the evil Emperor Flynn. Right on his righteous fat ass. What do you think of that?"

Will had no idea what to think of that, but, hell, you take your friends where you can find them.

"I think that's just dandy. Just plain, HA, dandy."

"Good word, dandy. I should use it myself instead of bitchin'. Or fuckin' bitchin. Or ..."

The paging system interrupted his thought, small as it might have been.

"Will Ross. Will Ross. Please report to Andy's office. Please report to Andy's office."

"Yikes," Zorro squeaked, "just when I find a new friend, somebody goes out and kills him."

"Thanks for the thought," Will muttered.

"Don't keep the Grand High Executioner waiting, Ross. He's a fidgety type. When he starts yelling at you in Greek, duck."

Will nodded and stepped out the door toward the elevator. He pushed the button and waited. No wait. The car was already there. He stepped in. The doors shut as quickly as those on "Star Trek" and the elevator shot up toward the second floor. Was moving this fast this safe?

He barely had time to ponder how he was going to explain it all to Cheryl.

Hi, Sweetie. Remember the new job? Yep, I sure do, too.

And he still wasn't sure about the benefits.

The doors slid open soundlessly and Will walked forward. He stepped in the hallway and Andy's executive secretary looked up. Without saying a word, she simply pointed at the door. Will nodded, stepped over and grasped the handle.

Well, he thought, TV has been nice. Two days. Ten hours total. A good run. He opened the door.

Andy Andropoulos stood behind his desk. Both hands were pressed firmly on the top piece of wood. If he was pressing with any of the force that his face suggested, the desk would soon be a part of the sports department directly below.

"Ross, I want an answer, goddamn it, and I want it now."

His voice wasn't raised, but the force behind the words made his spine rattle like it was on cheap hinges.

"Yes, sir," Will said, as loud as he could muster.

Andropoulos stepped from behind the desk, a man of medium height, but great stature. His personality commanded the room. He was a force of nature, and not a simple man.

He was a force of nature who was presently bearing down on Will.

"DID YOU—did you—do that," he pointed, "to our lead sports anchor? "

Will looked over. Flynn was displaying his leg and torn trousers like a badge of honor.

"Yes, sir, you bet I did," Will said, turning back and looking Andy in the eye.

Andy nodded. "Okay, Roger. You can go. We'll handle it from here."

"Thanks, Andy," Flynn said with a simper, "I really appreciate it."

He smiled smugly at Will and left the room.

As the door closed behind Flynn, the general manager turned his attention back to Will.

"Why'd you do it, son?"

Will looked in his eyes. Their gazes never wavered.

"He was being a bully. He physically backed me in a corner, and, frankly, sir, I didn't like the smell of what he had for lunch."

Andy stared at Will for a second, then burst out laughing.

"Good! Good for you, Ross. By God, good for you! Shit, Barbara, it's about time you got somebody in here with balls big enough to stand up to some of the prima donnas ... you're not a prima donna are you, son?"

"No sir. If I'm a donna, I'm at least third or fourth down the list."

"Good! A humble, modest smart ass. Just the kind of guy I like. Nice call, Barbara. He's going to work out just fine. Heard you had some good ideas about the bike race, right?"

"Yes, sir."

"Gonna save me some money?"

"Oh, you bet."

"I like him. I like him. Be in at nine A.M. tomorrow, Ross. Right after the manager's meeting I want to sit down with you, Barbara and Sessions and figure out how we're going to do this damned thing without losing our shirts. You were a big deal in Europe, weren't you? European biking?"

"No, sir. Won some races, but David Hasselhoff's a big deal. I was just a teeny deal."

"HA! Yes. Like him. Take Flynn out back and shoot him, Barbara, I'm tired of his bitching. And don't let him replace those pants with my money. You, Ross. I'll see you tomorrow at nine. You too, Barbara."

He sat down behind his desk.

"You've got it, Andy," Barbara said, quickly rising from the chair and pulling Will off the chair he had been frozen to and toward the door. They stepped out into the outer lobby and closed the door behind them.

"Now, that wasn't so bad, was it?" Barbara asked.

"Ask me again when my knees stop shaking," Will answered.

The executive secretary never looked up. Never broke a smile. Never reacted at all.

Will and Barbara walked into the hall and stepped through the doorway into the stairwell leading to the first floor.

"Don't let Flynn bully you," she said, "but don't mess up his suits, either, if you know what I mean. He's got a litigious temper."

Will nodded. "I know the type. He just pushed me ..."

"He will. You just can't let him."

"Understood. Hey, with this Andy meeting, I've got computer training and some sort of story shoot tomorrow at 9:30. Will we be done by then?"

"I'll move them. Don't worry. Andy likes to jaw, especially if he likes you. So far, he likes you." She patted him on the shoulder. "Don't screw it up."

They parted at the base of the stairs and Will walked back to the sports office, carefully looking in to make sure Flynn wasn't there. The room was empty.

Will gathered up his things and prepared to go home for the day, but first noticed, that the red message light was flashing on his phone. Cheryl. More gossip. Wonder what old Lisa had to say once she got back to the office.

Couldn't have been good, Will thought with a smile.

He punched in the number. He punched in the code.

He listened. His spine stiffened.

"You still haven't thanked me," the voice said quietly, almost in a whisper, "you still haven't thanked me for your job.

"And that—disappoints me.

"Very much."

CHAPTER FIVE:

BAD DREAMS

WILL LAY AWAKE FOR A LONG TIME THAT NIGHT. TIRED AS HE WAS, HIS mind was alight with ideas and thoughts and memories of the day. The station, the job, the run-in with Flynn, Zorro's change of attitude, the money, the contract, Lisa Shannon and the race.

Christ, the race.

This was no race. This was hell on wheels. He had been expecting something out of the old Coors Classic: tough, challenging, long, lots of climbing, but doable, a ride through the Colorado mountains that made everybody sit up and say *howdy*. Not something that made everybody stand up and scream *Murderers!* at the promoters. This race profile was a stage from the Tour that no team would accept. One hundred forty miles, starting at five thousand feet. Most Tour climbs didn't go over five thousand feet. The starting altitude was enough to suck the last bits of oxygen out of everyone's lungs. Even his, while sitting in some media car. Then fourteen thousand feet of climbing on top of that. How many passes? Seven? Eight? Too goddamned many.

And he had offered to ride the course in one day as a story.

Couldn't he make it two days? Three days? Nice little cycling vacation? Couldn't he do it on a motorcycle? Big ol' Harley?

He'd still be scared shitless riding down Oh My God on a Harley, but at least, that way, the climbs wouldn't kill him. He wouldn't be found days later at the top of some pass gasping for air like a bluegill tossed on the dock by a retriever.

On something motorized, at least he wouldn't be found in a mangled heap at the bottom of a ledge off Oh My God Road. He flopped over in bed, harder than he expected.

Cheryl stirred beside him.

"What-is-up-with-you?" she grumbled.

"I dunno. Just lots of thoughts. Go to sleep."

"That's easy for you to say. First, you don't have Skippy the Bush Kangaroo jumping around on top of your intestines. And you aren't trying to sleep next to an out-of-balance Maytag on a hard spin cycle."

Will stopped thrashing a moment to ponder both images.

"You need a happy thought," she mumbled, repositioning herself to look at him. It took her some time.

"Like what? Raindrops on roses? Whispers on kittens?"

"It's whiskers. Whiskers on kittens."

"I could use a happy thought," Will whispered, though he didn't know why he talked so low. Will and Cheryl were the only ones in the house except for Rex and Shoe the Wonder Dogs, who were busy snoring and farting under the bed.

"Happy thought. Happy thought," she said. "How's this? I gave you this at dinner, but somehow, you've obviously forgotten: Lisa Shannon came back to the office today looking like she was sunburned from an unprotected week in Honolulu. Any idea who did that to her? You did that to her."

"I didn't do anything to her. I just looked at her." He paused. "With undisguised hatred and the hope that a Kansas farm house would drop out of the sky and land on her, and then her feet would curl up and I could get her ruby slippers."

"Now you're not making any sense. You are tired. According to Nancy, who got it from Hootie, who had to ride back with her ..."

"What is that, about eighth hand?"

"Whatever, its good shit. All the way back she was grumbling about you. How could they listen to you? How could that station give you a job? How could they think you were some kind of expert when it's obvious you don't know jack shit?"

"Is it that obvious?"

"Only when you're drinking. But she walked in there with a whole plan for this race. Coverage. Cameras. Sponsorship. She was going to put Bosco Bikes front and center ..."

"Kind of tough to do when you don't run the cameras ..."

"I know. But—she had a plan. She was going to take over the race and tell TV how to do it. It was a plan she never got to unload because you stole the show."

"I was babbling. It just came out right."

"Then it wasn't babbling. Look, Will, everybody knows you paid more attention to the media in Europe than anybody else on the circuit. You watched
them. You listened. You paid attention to what they were doing. That's why
they loved you two years ago. You didn't push them off. You cared about them
getting their stories."

"I didn't care all that much."

"You cared enough. It was more than the rest of us. And, obviously, you
gathered up enough information that you were able to make some kind of sensible pitch."

"Maybe I've got a talent for organization, then?"

"Not according to your sock drawer ..."

He leaned over and pinched her on the arm. "Hey, I'm your friend here.
Remember that. And don't wake up Gooch. Little bastard has finally stopped
bouncing around tonight. My diaphragm's back in place for the first time all day."

"That's what got you in trouble in the first place, wasn't it?"

Now it was her turn to pinch him.

"Tit for tat."

He yelped, then opened his mouth.

"Don't say it," she warned. "I'm not in the mood for any tit jokes. I feel like
Elsie the Cow."

Will sank back onto his pillow, rubbing his arm as he lay there.

"So she was pissed, huh?"

"Lisa? Royally. I didn't see it. She gives me a wide berth, but yeah, Nancy said
she was just screamin'."

"But why? I mean, she won—right? She got the job."

"Yeah, but you didn't die. Remember," Cheryl said, turning back to her left
side and trying to get comfortable, "it's not enough that she succeed, everybody else has got to fail. It's sort of the Daffy Duck vision of life."

"But Daffy always loses."

"Exactly. Now go to sleep."

Within moments, she was gently snoring. Will smiled. Visions of
Daffy Duck danced in his head. Ducks's face, however, looked vaguely

like a waterfowl version of Lisa Shannon.

His mind fell into a drifting remembrance of some long ago Looney Toon, something about trouble with pronouns. He couldn't have it right. Bugs and Daffy were arguing while Elmer stood at the side with a loaded shotgun and a stupid look on his face.

Too much fun. He needed to get more cable channels so he could see all those again.

He needed. He needed. He needed ...

Within moments, he was snoring, too.

OUTSIDE THE SMALL BUNGALOW SAT A SMALL, NONDESCRIPT CAR, ONE YOU MIGHT see each and every day on your commute without ever noticing the style, the color or the occupant.

Which, was, of course, part of the problem, he thought.

He had never been noticed. Not from day one. And now this: He had been forced to ask for thanks. That's all he wanted. A bit of thanks for a job very well done.

A smoker. A test of a firing system.

It had worked beautifully. Beyond beautifully, really.

It had gone off just as planned, blackened the face of the target, although not the target originally hoped for, but a target nonetheless, set off one hell of a bang, and landed lots of off-the-mark press coverage on TV and in the papers, including a nice picture of the device on the front page of the *Post* that showed off the inner workings in great detail.

But while Denver bomb experts puzzled over those same innards, only he knew that the real device had been burned away by the magnesium flare, leaving a bunch of intricate, highly intriguing, much–to–ponder junk behind along with a disconnected nine-volt battery.

Weaving that together, and making it look realistic rather than ridiculous, had taken longer than building and setting the device itself. Now it was in the hands of the Colorado Bureau of Investigation or the Denver bomb squad and they were picking it apart and trying to decide what they had. How long would it take them to decide what they had was a maze with no center?

Not too long. Just long enough to make it fun.

They'd ponder the lunchbox, too. What was the significance of Gomer on a bicycle? Andy of Mayberry? Nothing, really. He just had it handy and it fit his mood of the moment.

He also wondered how long before it disappeared from the police evidence room. How long before someone discovered the collectibility of the thing and pinched it? Even with a magnesium scorch on the bottom, the box had seemed to deliver itself well.

A little cleaning, a little wash and off we go to one of those collector's conventions that always seem to be taking up space downtown. It should go back there. After all, that's where he found it. Just complete the circle.

He paused in his own thoughts and listened. The neighborhood was silent. It had been so for some time now, but he paused before he made his move. He sensed some stirring. He took the time to let it settle.

Let the neighborhood dogs get used to his scent.

Let the car sleep. Let it become a natural part of the neighborhood's creaks and groans and overnight sounds.

There had been no traffic. He hadn't had to drop over on the seats even once in the time he had been there.

He reached over to the plastic bag on the passenger seat, and pulled out the single sheet of paper with his gloved hand. He quietly opened the door and let it drop closed without latching.

No extraneous noise. Only the noise of the sleeping neighborhood and the distant sounds of a city in the last few moments of the witching hours, the last few moments before the false dawn.

He stepped quickly across the street and paused on the sidewalk. Listening. He heard nothing at all, outside of the natural rhythm of the neighborhood, itself asleep.

Casually, he walked the few steps to the walkway, turned and glided silently up to the wooden screen door. Without touching anything, he slid the single sheet of paper, folded twice, into the gap between the door and the frame.

It rested tightly within.

Without a pause, he turned, and moved quickly, but comfortably, back to the sidewalk, across the street to the car, slid behind the steering wheel and started the engine. Quickly, but without haste, he pulled into the street and drove down the street, only pushing open and slamming closed the stubborn driver's side door when he was around the corner.

He had done it all in such a way that he was merely another sound of the city in the morning, the first neighbor who had to get up early for work that morning, unusual, but certainly possible, the first neighbor to break the overnight silence. The first neighbor to start a new day.

Just me, he smiled. Just a neighbor.

With a little reminder for a friend.

A friend he suddenly wanted to meet now.

A new friend.

The car turned the corner and sped up to catch the green light at Colorado. He turned north, drove quickly toward the museum, then turned back west toward town, toward home, toward sleep.

He smiled to himself.

That note was finally going to get him noticed.

That note was finally going to make him a star.

That note was going to bind him to his new friend.

That note was going to light the fuse on a spectacular career.

"Light the fuse," he snorted. He laughed out loud.

The sound carried out of the car and into the night at Eighteenth and York. He caught the light at the corner of City Park and hurried off toward home.

❀

THE MORNING BREEZE, WHAT THERE WAS OF IT, CAUGHT THE SINGLE SHEET OF PAPER and made it gently wave from its perch in the gap of the wooden screen door. It moved side to side, but never loosened, staying in place for three-and-a-half hours until Will Ross, in a pair of moose-and-pine-tree motif boxer shorts stumbled out the door to retrieve the *Rocky* and the *Post*. He missed the note as he opened the door, the single sheet of paper suddenly released, dropping to the second step and out of his immediate line of sight.

He picked up the papers and walked back inside, noticing the letter only when it stuck to the bottom of his foot. He peeled it off, in his stupor figuring that it was some part of the newspaper, and stomped back into the house, causing the most noise the neighborhood had heard in some seven hours.

He walked into the kitchen and poured himself a cup of coffee, sat down and began to read the *Rocky*.

He finished the paper with his coffee and refilled the cup. As he sat back down to begin working on the *Post*, he noticed the sheet of paper.

Blindly, he picked it up and flipped it open with one hand, taking another gulp of coffee with the other. As he began to read, the coffee suddenly congealed in his throat, forcing him to turn and do an Uncle Tonoose spit take onto the kitchen floor.

Rex and Shoe were on it in a heartbeat to see what was causing all the interesting sounds.

Will stared at the letter, feeling his hands growing cold, and the very breath sucked out of him.

He put the letter down and slowly slid away from the table, as if any movement, any jostling, would ignite this single sheet of paper.

Turning first to the bedroom, as if to get Cheryl, he paused, thought, rubbed his head in an attempt to clear it, then walked quickly to the front window to see if, for some stupid reason, he was being watched.

The street was quiet.

He rubbed his eyes, then his forehead and hair, walked back to the kitchen, picked up the phone and dialed 911.

After replacing the phone, he only had time to read the note twenty more times, pacing around the living room between each read, before the first squad arrived.

He didn't get to the *Denver Post* that morning.

He barely got to work by noon.

The letter had done its job.

My dear Mr. Ross,

Congratulations on your new position with TV6 News.

I would suppose it is quite a coup for a man with no experience to win such an important position in a major TV marketplace.

On the other hand, such a position cannot be won without a job becoming available. Like yours became available.

Suddenly.

You should always thank those responsible for creating your good fortune. It is the only polite thing to do. And it makes me angry when matters of courtesy such as this are so blindly ignored.

I will not be ignored Mr. Ross. You owe me your thanks. Just as the town of Crooked Lake owes me their thanks for what has got to be the most spectacular Fourth of July celebration they've ever had.

Think about that, Mr. Ross.

Think about that.

CHAPTER SIX:

NOTHING TO IT

B Y TEN O'CLOCK, THE POLICE WERE GONE, ALONG WITH THE LETTER AND the hundreds of fingerprints they had found on the aluminum screen door of Will's house. All his, Will figured. Cheryl rarely, if ever, used the front door.

The coffee was gone as well, but Will had helped with that.

What irked Will, more than anything, what clawed at his insides like somebody who had cut him off in a sprint and picked up the inside lane, was that no one had taken him seriously when he first called in, until he mentioned the connection to Crooked Lake found in the note. Then, and only then, did it get serious with lots of people running around and shouting.

People shouting loudly and banging through his house as if they owned it. He didn't even own it. Some bank in Dallas did. He kept wishing one of its tellers were here to protect their investment. The police kept him sitting at the kitchen table, drinking his own coffee, not even letting him wander off to Ishmael's for a fresh latte.

"Did you hear anything?"

"No."

"Where were you?"

"Sleeping. After a fashion."

"What?"

"I didn't sleep well last night."

"Did you hear anything?"

"No."

"What do you know about Crooked Lake?"

"Only what I read in the papers."

"And what's that?"

"Fourth of July fireworks display all went up at once? Operator killed? Every piece of glass in town shattered from the concussion? Lots of people hurt from the blast wave and flying glass? Three or four heart attacks? Lots of people with hearing problems? It's what I learned in the papers."

Detective Raymond Whiteside let himself into the house and whispered something to an officer who was looking for evidence of last night's snack in the tiny front room.

"You know, I don't think he came in the house," Will called out to them.

Whiteside turned, smiled and walked into the kitchen, offering a hand, then silently motioning the question, "Can I have a seat?" Will nodded.

"Good morning, Mr. Ross. I'm sorry we have to dig around like this, but this is a serious investigation. We've got to see if this is in any way related to the Crooked Lake blast ..."

"I thought that was an accident," Will interrupted.

"Yes, well, that's what we thought, too, but it may not have been."

"What does that mean?"

"It means that it may have been a plan, a plot—a bomb. We don't know. Until this morning, Mr. Ross, we didn't know anything, frankly. We just had our suspicions. We had eyewitness testimony from up at the lake that made us question the first reports of what had happened.

"You see, I never believed the report to begin with, simply because gunpowder, the gunpowder in fireworks, doesn't act like that. Specialty military explosives do, but gunpowder and fireworks explosives, even personal concoctions, don't. They don't have the power, the oomph, the zing."

"The what?"

"The power. Let's just leave it at that," Whiteside said. "Have you had any other contact with the person who left this note?"

"Not that I know of, well, not a note, but I've had a couple of strange calls at work ..."

"Which is where?"

"TV6. I got hired at the sports department two days ago. I've had calls both days."

"TV6?"

"Yeah."

"Sports?"

"Yeah. Anyway, I got two calls. One each day and both of them said, pretty much, what this note said: 'you oughta thank me.' Like I wouldn't have my job without his help."

Whiteside paused in his note taking and tapped the pencil on the notepad.

"Did anyone help you get the job?"

"Not that I know of."

"What did he sound like?"

"What? Some kook, that's what he sounded like."

"Are the messages still on your machine at work?"

Will thought for a second. He shook his head.

"The second one maybe. I dunno if I erased that one. The first one I did erase, though, when I was learning how to use all the features of the phone system. Sorry about that."

"Mind if we access your phone at work and check your messages?"

"Feel free. I've already called in to the station and explained the situation. Said I'd be late. They said they'd take care of everything when your men ..."— Will noticed the female officer standing in the kitchen turn to him—"... your officers, your people get there."

He stumbled over the last words and turned red with embarrassment. The female officer merely smiled and turned back to taking notes.

"We know most of the people at Six," Whiteside said, "from our investigation out there earlier this week."

"Do you really think they're related? All this stuff?"

"It's a little too neat for my blood, but could be. Crooked Lake may have been the big show. Crooked Lake may have been an accident. We're still not sure what happened there. Most of the evidence is scattered over and under the lake. The smoker at the TV station may be a hook, just to get us interested. Could be a copycat, too—which is how I'm leaning at the moment. We just don't know at this point. All we've really got is one note and maybe a phone message from somebody badly in need of appreciation, if you saved it ..."

"It might be there, I can't ..."

Cheryl walked into the room. She had been in the midst of this early on, but had been allowed to step upstairs to shower and get ready for work.

"Have you figured out what's going on yet, officer?" she asked Whiteside directly.

"No, ma'am," he answered, standing as she entered the room, "not quite yet, no."

"Do you need me, anymore?"

"As long as we have your statement ..."

"We have it, Ray," the female officer said.

"Then, Mrs. Ross, you are free to go. Officer Phillips here will walk you out to your car, if that's alright."

"That's fine."

"The garage has been checked, hasn't it, Phillips?"

"Yes. And both cars."

"Then, you're free to go, Mrs. Ross, but," he paused to pull out a business card, "please get in touch with me or my office if you notice anything unusual."

"You mean more unusual than this morning?"

"Anything. Anytime."

Will stood and gave Cheryl a long, deep hug. It was for both her and Gooch, still packed away in the Sta-Fresh Pouch. He whispered in her ear, "Be careful. I don't know what I would do without you."

She pulled back and looked at him. For the first time in a long time, the mask of natural confidence she wore was shaken. Her eyes were red-rimmed under the makeup. She was just as frightened as he, maybe more so, with even more to lose.

"Whoever this is seems to be after you. I'll keep my eyes open, but you, Will, you have to be truly alert. To everything around you. Be careful, please. We, and I do mean *we*, need you. Badly."

He nodded. She pulled away and walked to the door with Officer Phillips. She took one last look at Will, smiled, waved and stepped out into the mid-morning sunshine.

"I'll be careful," he said to her departing scent, not really knowing, in his heart, what any of that meant. He had said it all his life, but had wandered through minefields it seemed, each and every day, surviving more by the luck of the draw and his own number not rolling to the top of life's Wheel of Fortune.

He had been shot at, bombed, slashed with knives, poisoned, punched, and cursed with evil, foul deaths. And that was just the bike stuff. The rest of his life was a series of misadventures that made him look like an ad for an insurance company.

"Don't let this happen to you ..."

"What? Don't let what?"

"Nothing. Random thoughts. Too little sleep, not enough coffee."

"Well, if any of those random thoughts have anything to do with this case, I hope you'll bring them up to me."

"I will," Will replied. "Promise."

"Hmm. Alright," Whiteside mumbled. "Would you mind, Mr. Ross, if a few officers retrieved that message? Maybe kept an eye on you today?"

"No, not at all. They'll be bored spitless, but they're welcome to come along. I'm not doing much yet at work. At least, anything that's interesting."

"They're not there to be interested in your job. They've got their own work to do."

"Fine. Happy to have the company."

"You've already got company, it seems, Mr. Ross," Whiteside said ominously. Will smiled, an incredibly fakey smile that couldn't hide what he felt inside.

"Swell," he mumbled, shook the detective's hand, and showed him and Officer Phillips to the door.

He stopped Whiteside at the door with a hand on his elbow. "Look, Officer ..."

"Detective ..."

"Detective, I've really got to know: Am I going to open a car door today or sneeze or take a piss and blow sky high?"

The detective sighed, not wanting to give away what he was thinking, but then again, not wanting to leave this guy hanging all day long when it was obvious that there was nothing really to concern him.

"Look, Ross," Whiteside whispered, putting his hand on Will's shoulder and bending his head toward his, "what I figure we've got here is a stalker. A copycat, maybe, who was thrilled with what happened at Crooked Lake, but in the end doesn't have the expertise to match it."

"Swell. I'm his practice range ..."

"No, not really. He just wants to be noticed. By a TV star ..."

"I haven't even been on TV yet."

"Don't worry about him. We'll keep an eye on your house and the station for a day or two. You should be a little more vigilant. But beyond that, there's not a whole lot we can do."

"Until he hurts somebody."

"Well, yes. But I don't think he will. This just doesn't read right to me. He wants attention. He wants you to thank him."

"So what should I do?"

"Thank him," Whiteside simply said, then smiled, turned and walked down the front steps.

"We'll continue our investigation outside, Mr. Ross," Officer Phillips said. "When you're ready to go to work, just let us know and two officers will be sent along with you to the station to take a look around and retrieve that message."

"Can I still get a ticket if they're with me?"

"They'll probably be the ones who give it to you."

"Thanks," Will said, waved at Whiteside, who was already halfway down the walk, then shut the door. The house, which had been alive with activity for the past four hours, was suddenly silent.

Despite the police officers surrounding the bungalow, Will had never felt quite so alone.

But then a realization made him shudder. He wasn't alone at all, was he? They might not think it was all that big of a deal, but it sent an icy hand down his spine.

What a way to wake up.

❖

BARBARA GOODEN PACED BACK AND FORTH ACROSS HER OFFICE, TWISTING A CURL in the back of her hairspray-frozen hairdo until it was about the size of a spring in a cheap ballpoint pen.

She pulled the finger out of the hair and, amazingly, the strand immediately went perfectly back into place with the rest of her hairstyle.

"Well, the question now is: what do we do?"

Bill Sessions shook his head.

"There's more than one question here, Chief," he said with a dark seriousness underlying his tone, "we've got to wonder if Will is a target, or the station, or our people, or if we're just being used to get this little asshole all the free TV time his ego could ever use. That's the way it breaks down to me."

"You're right, of course, there's a lot to deal with, simply in terms of the station ..."

"And me," Will added quietly, "... and me."

"Yes, of course, Will," Bill Sessions agreed. "We know you're the primary contact."

"At the moment, Will," Barbara mused, "I'm thinking this guy likes you. I don't know if you're a target at all. Psychologically, somehow he thinks that you are his personal media contact. Almost his press agent, if he works things right."

Will smiled.

"Well, that's all well and good, but I don't want to be his press agent and I don't want him following me around waiting to shove a pipe bomb up my ass if I upset him. And—excuse me for asking, but where did you get your psychology degree?"

"Denver police seem pretty convinced this guy is a low-level stalker in need of attention. You just happened to be in the right place at the right time," she said, ignoring his sarcasm, "and so are we. He wants to be on TV. He'll take credit for Crooked Lake and shooting Lincoln if it will help."

"Help make him a TV star? Get his manifesto to the 'pipples'?"

"Something like that."

"Great." Will slumped down in the chair, somehow hoping that the expanse of leather would soak him up and he could disappear, easily, happily and forever. Why in God's name did every maniac and oddball on two continents seem to be drawn to him? What did he ever do to them? All he did was ride a bike, marry wrong the first time out and then be in the wrong place at the wrong time. What the hell. This was getting ridiculous.

"Denver police also think," Bill began to add, as he drummed his fingers on his chin and stared blankly into the glaring sunshine of Denver's early afternoon, "that you've drawn him to you, just because of the reputation you've got. You're a name in Europe, as a rider, you've been involved in a lot of, well, media coverage ..."

"Murder, death and destruction, you mean," Will grumbled.

"Well, yeah," Bill continued. "And it's just one of those things that a guy like this would be drawn to ..."

"Ah, great. Freud and Jung, TV Shrinks. I'm in the right place, you betcha."

"Get a grip, Will," Barbara said sharply. "We're as concerned about this as you are. We're just trying to find our way through the maze this guy set up, just like you are and we're just as worried about your ass as we are about our own."

Will sighed and waved her off.

"Sorry. It's just been a long night. Long morning. Long everything."

Barbara nodded her head in agreement. "It has been for everyone. I do agree with the police, we should be on our toes, but we can't let this change our lives ..."

"Unless I get blown up."

"That would be a change," Sessions said with a laugh. Will gave him a tired smile.

"Stalkers are a part of this business, Will. I had my share while I was on the air. You keep an eye on them, you watch out, you keep going, simple as that. The nut who calls, you take note, but you mostly ignore them. We've got to stay alert, but otherwise our big concern right now is that we've got to get you on the air. We've got to make you a part of this station and get you up and running before this race coverage begins. You've got to know TV and TV construction before this race. You've got to know how to handle yourself on the air, write a story, go live and anchor a segment if I need you to."

"Nothin' to it." Will paused for a moment, a thought rattling around in his head. It took a few moments to form to where he could actually get a handle on it. "Am I going to have to anchor, actually carry this thing?"

"Could be," Bill said. "Flynn is still giving us a hard time about the race. He says nobody gives a rat's ass about cycling—especially American cycling. Even the guys in Spandex tights around here are more interested in European cycling. They say we've got no history in it."

"They're wrong. He's wrong. One hundred years ago, America was the cycling center of the world. The champions came from here. Everybody came here to ride. Newark. Salt Lake. New York City. Every town had a velodrome. We just let it all get away. We turned the bicycle into a toy. Cars took over."

Barbara smiled. "See? That's the kind of comeback I want from you. That's why we hired you for this race. You know the real story, not just the bullshit sports reporter stuff that Flynn tosses out. You get into it with Flynn, and I want a camera there."

"Want me to punch him?"

"Only if he asks for it. Beyond that, just get in his face and let him know the history."

Will shook his head. God, how did he keep getting himself into situations like this? Why couldn't he just have a nice little job where he fit running shoes into little cardboard boxes for twenty cents an hour? Work the line, get bored, go crazy, and leave at five P.M. for home?

Where were these jobs?

Mexico. Damn that NAFTA thing!

"Okay, so after I beat the crap out of Roger Flynn, what do you want me to do?"

"Well," Sessions laughed, "that should get you to 1:15 ..."

Will looked at the clock. It was 1:12.

"Why don't we just throw you into the deep end, Will?" Barbara said, thoughtfully. "Why don't we just get you out ... starting, well, tomorrow? What do you say, Bill?"

"Got something in mind?"

"What if he had our former professional cyclist here ride the course tomorrow? We'll send him out with Dale Dwyer and they can ride from Boulder to Breckenridge? We'll send a live truck along the way and cover it for noon and four, then see him come into Breckenridge live during the Five. How about that?"

"Sounds good." Sessions stood up. "I'll talk to Engineering and make sure we've got a satellite truck up and running this week and somebody to run it." He walked toward the door.

"There's only one problem," Will called after him.

"What's that?" Barbara asked, surprised that someone would question the soundness of her plan.

"Well, you see, I've got to ride the damned thing. One hundred and forty miles. A boatload of mountain passes. Fourteen thousand feet of climbing. And— do it without any training, and stopping every few miles to puke on camera?"

Both Barbara and Bill stared at him as if he was not making a lick of sense.

"Best of all—I have to make it as far as Breckenridge by five, all fresh and ready to go? Is that the plan?"

"Well," Gooden said, slowly, "yeah. That's the plan. Dwyer will shoot. You will ride. Simple"

"Simple," repeated Sessions. "Besides, it gets you out of town and away from your adoring fan."

"Singular," Gooden laughed.

"Singular," Sessions repeated.

"I'm glad everyone takes this so goddamned seriously," Will muttered, feeling his stomach fall somewhere down into the lower reaches of his shoes.

The plans were already well underway. Sessions had left to call Engineering and set up the satellite truck. Barbara was under a full head of steam tromping toward the assignment desk to set up Dale Dwyer, a seasoned photographer, for the shoot.

Will's work wouldn't really begin until tonight, when he started getting the gear ready for the ride, while, at the same time trying to shutter over his fear about it.

To say he was dreading the day ahead would be an understatement.

Suddenly, all thoughts of the mysterious stranger with a seemingly desperate need to be thanked left his mind, replaced by the challenge and stomach-cranking fear of the road tomorrow.

He stood up, walked out and went to find a bike.

He needed to stretch.

He needed to think.

He needed to ride.

✻

WILL STARED AT THE CEILING, LOOKED AT THE CLOCK. TWO A.M. HE LOOKED AT THE ceiling, flopped over once, stared at the wall. Listened to Rex snore and Shoe fart.

He flopped over again, back to his original position.

Cheryl sighed in exasperation.

"Trouble sleeping?"

"Yeah," he answered. "You, too?"

"Not necessarily, but its tough to sleep with a field-goal kicker in your gut and twelve miles of bad road in bed next to you."

"Sorry."

"That's okay," she muttered. "I wasn't sleeping all that well anyway. Your son or daughter, take your pick, has been busy as hell, and, despite the concern of the Denver P.D., I'm not all that comfortable knowing that somebody out there likes you."

"Yeah. That's there. That's there."

"There's something else about it, though, isn't there?"

"Yeah," Will admitted, sheepishly. "Yeah, there is." He paused, thinking of what to say and how to say it.

"I'm really afraid of that guy, whoever he is. That's he's watching us. That he's found us. That he's—out there. The cops don't take him all that seriously. The station doesn't, either, but I do. I don't know why, but I do. Then, on top of that, I'm afraid of this job. I've never done this shit before. I mean, Flynn is right. They're hiring assholes off the street. I have no idea what to do. And then, I'm afraid of tomorrow. I've gotta be in the station at seven and catch a ride to Boulder and then ride a hundred and forty miles through the mountains."

"You've done that."

"In the past, dearie, in the past," he said, patting her arm. "After I've been in training for months. And not like this. I don't know if I've ever seen a ride like this."

"You can make it. When do they need you at the finish?"

"Sometime inside the five o'clock show. Live."

"You can do it," she said, sleepily, moving in closer to him and wrapping her arms around him. She put her forehead on his shoulder and was instantly asleep.

She had won the battle. No matter how much he wanted to move now, he couldn't. She held him in a vice-like grip and was comfortably notched in beside him. There was no place to go and no room to move. He couldn't flop. He couldn't stir he couldn't reach out into the night in search of some kind of help, relief or salvation.

The shadows crawled across the walls of the room. One car. Two cars. He slept. He woke. Another car, and another. He slept again. And woke. He watched the leaves move on the tree outside the window and slept again. He woke again, still in darkness, and heard the birds begin to wake. He drifted and dozed, seeing people wander through his room: Tomas, Kim, Bresson, Bergalis, and the entire damned Bergalis family from Stephano to Martin to

Henri. He was in the strange half-sleep between awake and asleep, between life and death, like the empty space between the walls of a house, in the netherworld between the walls of a life. Who knew if he really was between those walls and could see those ghosts, or if he was just dreaming? They were there, talking, at the foot of his bed, pointing, laughing, discussing the situation in which he found himself, but none with the least bit of inspiration or advice.

They drifted away and he drifted beyond.

And it was morning.

Suddenly, it was not just another day to face. It was a day to simply survive.

CHAPTER SEVEN:

MR. TOAD'S WILD RIDE

THE FIRST FEW MILES WERE NOTHING BUT STOP–AND–GO AND STOP–AND–WAIT and stop-and-go and wait some more. Stoplights, traffic, then more stoplights kept bringing him to a halt. The racers wouldn't have to worry about this, but a lone idiotic rider led by a single news SUV did, even though the intern behind the wheel took the first few seconds of a red light as a signal to simply "go really fast."

Will was wired for sound, the black wire running up and under the Louis Garneau Haven jersey, the transmitter pack clipped to a pair of older, off-brand riding shorts with crummy elastic As a result, he felt quite sure that he was dropping trou and giving the city of Boulder a quick glimpse of his butt-crack pencil-holder on a regular basis as he hunched over the top tube.

Luckily, Dale Dwyer, the photographer—or photojournalist, as he kept telling Will on the ride up to Boulder earlier that morning—was ahead on the course, shooting out the back window of the station's Cherokee after enlisting a station intern to drive the Jeep through the mountains.

He didn't know how legal that was, but at least it would give them some rolling video they otherwise wouldn't have.

Will was taking his time. There was no one else to set the pace for him and so there was no great need to push himself. However, he knew it was going to take him forever to finish at this pace. He'd have to goose himself somehow and get some speed up, otherwise he'd still be on the course when the race actually took place in two weeks.

But Breckenridge by five o'clock? Who the hell did Barbara think he was—Moser? Merckx? Bourgoin? Speedy Alka-Seltzer? Maybe he could cadge a ride with Dwyer over the rough spots and they could fake it. He would have ridden the course—ridden it in the back of a Jeep Cherokee, but he would have ridden the course.

He could smear some dirt on his face and make it look like he had been through hell. It would look right, but it just wouldn't be quite honest.

Naw. He could hear Gooden now: staging. Dwyer said that was her big thing: you can't stage the news. You can't say you did something without having done it, saw something without having seen it, or shot something without having it naturally happen right in front of you. There was no hard-and-fast rule about how much of this he was going to have to ride until last night on the ten o'clock news when Roger Flynn said that Will Ross, the new TV6 reporter, a former professional cyclist, would ride the entire course—start to finish—on his bicycle and be in Breckenridge by five to file live reports on the difficulty of the race course.

Thanks a lot, asshole, Will thought. Until you opened your mouth and made this participatory journalism, Will was planning on just riding sections of the course. Nobody had really said otherwise. Now, the whole world knew he was supposed to be riding the entire course.

The light finally changed.

Will pushed off again, The Beast slowly coming up to speed, the ancient Colnago stolen two seasons ago from the Haven Pharmaceutical Cycling Team in Europe just as reluctant to make the ride as Will. Bikes knew. This one certainly did, anyway.

His legs knew it, too, and this was just the start, the slow rise on Highway 93 as he headed south out of Boulder. He made the next light. Thank God. At least he could keep up his hard-won pace for a while, at least until he hit the mountains, that were just a few miles, one right turn and a few foothills ahead.

His pushed his pace, listening closely to the sounds of the bike, which were beginning to fuse themselves with the sounds of his body into one rolling metronome of rhythm. Click-click-click-click-scrun-click-click-click-click-scrun ... His right knee was beginning to give him trouble again. The tear down the back of his calf suffered on Mt. Ventoux some summers before had affected just about everything on his lower right side. His ankle would roll without warning, his knee would grumble with a raspy, filled-with-sand kind of "scrun" sound that bothered him no end. Meanwhile, his back was impersonating a pan of Jiffy Pop on high heat, as it snap, crackled and grimped so often that he only recognized the sounds and the little shots of feeling dimly in the dark recesses of his brain.

He was falling apart, no doubt, but he was falling in such slow motion that he might be in his late seventies before he could finally admit that he couldn't do certain things anymore.

The turn onto Highway 72 caught him off guard and he drifted wide for a moment. He almost gave the newsroom a piece of spot news by taking on a small Japanese sedan driven by a teenage girl whose eyes widened to the size of Thanksgiving platters as Will maneuvered around her.

He cut back across the road, convinced he had created another driver who hated cyclists and picked up the pace to put as much distance from her as possible. He looked up ahead and caught Dwyer in the back of the Jeep, his camera down, his face pale, his mouth perfectly round and open in a silent scream.

Then he laughed.

Hmm, Will thought. Maybe I was closer to playing a harp than I figured ...

A mile down the road and then the climbing seriously began up Coal Creek Canyon toward the peak at Wondervu.

Will could feel his legs begin to question what they were doing. They had spent so much time over the past few months merely being stretched, certainly not being asked to perform at any sort of world-class level, or in this case, asked to perform an honest-to-God miracle. Will realized the one thing he had going in his favor was that despite the lack of conditioning he felt, there was a certain muscle memory he could rely on. He had done hard climbs before, he could do them again, especially if he paced himself and didn't try to overextend. No matter what Roger had said the night before in his subtle on-air challenge to the new guy, Will knew he could make the ride.

He wouldn't be able walk for a few days, wouldn't be able to sit down, but he could do it. He just had to get his mind right.

Get his mind right.

Get his mind right.

Find the magic. Find the magic.

It was out there, somewhere, out there stepping just out of reach whenever he came close, now at the top of the climb, now at the bottom, now just around the corner after that short, lush meadow just ahead. It was always just ahead.

Will rode toward the magic, and lost track of the car, lost track of the trees, lost track of the world around him. He had no sense of when he passed the peak at Wondervu, or the exhilaration he knew he felt on the descent, or feeling as if the bike was made out of old coffee cans as it crossed the railroad tracks at the bottom of the hill

He realized he was just outside of the gambling town of Blackhawk on a quick descent, thanks to the fact that Dwyer was yelling at him from the window of the Jeep, now driving alongside him on the wrong side of the road.

"We're going to jump ahead and set up in town. You'll see the Jeep, then I'll be about fifty feet beyond that. Start sprinting at the Jeep."

"Why?" Will could see no point in sprinting. He had barely started the day. He glanced at his watch. 11:45. He had already been on the road for more than two hours.

"Yeah. Okay. Okay."

"Don't forget. See the Jeep, make the sprint. There's a prize in Blackhawk for the best sprinter, so I need the video."

"Sure, no problem," Will shouted back as the SUV sped ahead. Will just hoped that he didn't sprint himself right into a fat, drunken gambler out for a pleasant noontime stroll. That would bring the whole day to an end real fast.

Wait a minute. Do you think ... no such luck. Fat, drunken gamblers are certainly quicker than he suddenly felt. They could easily beat him to the curb. He'd have to finish the ride.

The Cherokee disappeared into the gambling town, while Will sat up on the bike and coasted toward the turn, far below and beyond where Dwyer and the intern had turned off the road.

Will finished a bottle of water and absentmindedly tossed it to the side of the road for the fans. The fans, he then realized, that didn't exist. He had littered, and worse, he had tossed away one of only two water bottles he carried for the day, the other buried somewhere in the back seat of the Jeep. There was no support crew, no feed station, no water relief along the way except that he brought himself. He had just mindlessly tossed away half of it. That was going to prove to be an expensive move right about the top of Guanella Pass.

Will made the first turn into Blackhawk and cruised through some back portions of the eastern side of town. He thought for a moment he had made a wrong turn, but then remembered that the course was a bit confusing just before they hit the casino sprint. He came up toward town again, turned around at the back of a large industrial-looking casino, turned back onto a main street and saw, just ahead, the TV6 News Jeep, dressed out like a circus wagon. The Jeep was a rolling billboard, full of logos and colors and promotional information, and, Will thought in a sudden, ugly moment, a perfect, colorful target as well.

He rose up out of the seat, pushed himself into a bigger gear and began to sprint. He was no sprinter. In fact, he wasn't quite sure at the moment what he was as a rider, but a sprinter he wasn't. Still, he had watched Tony Cacciavillani enough during his time with Haven to know how a sprinter moved, how a sprinter looked, how a sprinter held himself to make the sprint look fast and deadly on TV.

Before he knew it, he had swept past Dwyer and up to the next turn, a left that would take him up through Central City, the poor sister of the gambling towns, and then onto Oh My God Road. Of everything he had to do today, that was the stretch he dreaded the most, at least until he passed it. Then he would dread Guanella and then Kenosha and then Hoosier, but now, it was Oh My God. He had driven on it in a car once and knew how it got its name—he came around that first turn, looked over the valley, saw the steep dirt road without out guardrails and invariably said, "Oh, my God." Happened every time.

Will rose out of the saddle and began the climb to the top of Central City. The road conditions were not good at all, narrow and spotted with open potholes and potholes that had been filled both above and below the level of the street.

He heard a quick beep and moved to the side. The news car raced past him, Dwyer pointing ahead as if he was going to shoot Will at some point above. Will nodded. Go ahead, shoot me, jerk off, but do it before I begin the descent.

It wasn't to be. Will corkscrewed his way through the top of town, past the Central City Opera House, then back and forth through a series of short switchbacks, to the top of the hill overlooking Oh My God and Idaho Springs, somewhere ... out there. The road suddenly turned to gravel. Will's insides suddenly turned to jelly.

He was in it now. And he was already heading down.

The first turn wasn't bad, a long sweeping left that carried him out and down, the unprotected cliff only four feet away. Will's right eye drifted to the side for a glance that might reveal how far he would fall before he crashed into the pointy rocks, the pointy trees, the pointy road down below.

The Beast fought him, trying to find its own line through the hard-pack and gravel. Will came over a short rise and plowed straight into a pile of loose sand and pea gravel dumped in the middle of the road waiting to be spread. It was like throwing out an anchor. His pace pulled back, his nose shoved right. He headed toward the drop-off.

It was lousy bike handling, but rather than lean straight out of the drift and back to the middle of the road, Will pushed the fork to the left and leaned internally, shifting the weight in his butt to the left, as if trying to think the bike back into a center line.

What the hell was he doing? This was Riding 101 and he was riding like a goddamned amateur. He hadn't ridden like this since ...

"YEAH! YEAH!" Dwyer was screaming and pumping his fist in the air as Will rolled past. "That's it! Man! I thought you were going over! Great video!"

Will noticed the intern standing next to the driver's side door. Her face was ashen white. It was obvious that she thought Will was going over as well and that she would have been held responsible.

It hadn't been all that close, Will thought. Then again, maybe it had.

A shudder ran up through the bike and the rider.

Too close. Amateur night. Too damned close.

As he began to sweep through an easy turn, he felt the pace begin to rise from the road once more. The Jeep again shot past him , blanketing him in a cloud of dust and very small rocks. He'd have to talk to Dwyer about that at some point. This was hard enough without having to dig gravel out of his pores. As the dust began to settle, Will looked ahead in panic. A tight hairpin turn without a guardrail loomed ahead. He grabbed the brakes and squeezed hard, unconsciously shifting his weight to the inside, something he had neglected to do at the top of the road. As he popped his foot from the right pedal for support, the rear of the bike swung out easily on the gravel and he slid around the turn, a little wide, but safe enough, the move more a matter of physics than athletics.

Jesus Christ. He had almost reached the bottom of the hill first and fastest.

Old tricks. Old dogs. Good one more time.

Will picked up the next turn and went into the long, straight descent. He could see the Jeep continuing on down below, kicking up a cloud of dust as Dwyer and his driver tried to get into position for the entry to Idaho Springs. Will tucked and picked up speed, trying to gauge it carefully so that it didn't get out of control on the gravel descent.

Ahead and to his right, was a car, a gray, nondescript car pointed in the wrong direction. He wasn't sure what kind, a shitbox on wheels as his brother would say, obviously broken down or the ride of some nature lover who had pulled over to the side to examine the flora and the fauna and to take a leak among them.

A man began to step out of the rocks and weeds beside the car and into the road. At that moment, Will noticed what had bothered him about the car from the moment he first saw it: it had no license plate.

Colorado law demanded two—front and back. This had none on the front. Didn't see that very often. He raised his gaze to the man, standing now beside the rear right corner of the car. He was waving his hands over his head, as if in distress, or warning or wishing Will to stop. As Will braked, he realized something else: the man's face wasn't real.

❁

THE VOICE WAS SLIGHTLY MUFFLED. THE VOICE WAS SLIGHTLY HOLLOW. THE VOICE was threatening, in a smooth and silky way. Will stared with disbelief at the mask, a frosted plastic thing that you could see through, but so distorted the features that there was no way to make out anything distinct.

He tried. Eyebrows were impossible. Hair, maybe dark brown, but Will couldn't tell with the light and angle of the hat. As he moved closer, the man stepped back and held up one hand.

"I said ... that's close enough. You don't listen well, do you?"

"Sorry."

Will glanced to the left and pulled his right foot up to the top of his pedal stroke. He could push off and be past this guy in seconds, flying down Oh My God Road before he even had a chance to react.

As if he read Will's mind, the man with the mask said, "That's not particularly wise. You'd be panicked and panicked people make mistakes. That's a treacherous hairpin at the bottom. If you are panicked, you might not make it."

Will eased off on the pressure on the right pedal.

"Better. Better. I'm not about to hurt you. I'm just here to remind you. You can have a million cops around you, but I can still get to you. Every day. Any day. Any hour. You aren't safe, Mr. Ross. I control your fate. Your future. So, pay attention: You are now my voice. I will speak through you when I speak in the future to the world. You will pass on everything I have to say, not only to the police, who I'm sure will be right there with you, but also to the television public, just so they know that I am here and I am real. Not today. Not tomorrow. Maybe not for weeks to come, but you will. You will be my voice, do you understand? Understand?"

"Uh, yeah," Will said, stumbling over the words, "but, I, uh, don't know how ..."

"You'll figure it out. After all, we all have a lot to lose here, don't we?"

As if someone had pushed a button, Will felt a pulse of anger spring up in his chest.

"What the hell ... what the hell is that supposed to mean?"

"It means nothing. It means everything."

He turned away and looked across the valley.

"They'll be coming soon. Coming back to find out what's holding you up."

"The police will catch you."

"The police couldn't catch their own shit with both hands. But even if they get lucky, it won't be today. Not before the word is out."

"What word?"

"I want credit."

"For what?"

"For everything, Mr. Ross. Figure it out."

"I won't ..."

"You will. You will, indeed. You, in particular, owe me, Mr. Ross."

He paused, was if waiting for Will to say or do whatever it was Will was supposed to say or do.

Will shook his head and offered up both hands.

"What?"

The man in the mask sighed, then shook his head back and forth sadly.

"Mr. Ross, you are as dense as the police. As the media. You'll fit in well there."

Will thought, for a second, that he could see a sardonic smile behind the frosted plastic mask.

"Think about it all, Mr. Ross. Think about it all. We'll talk again. But not for a while. By then, I would hope that you will have suddenly developed some brains, some common sense, some insight into dealing with the people who control the world around you."

It seemed as if he smiled again behind the mask. Then, the man nodded his head, walked slowly around the back of the car, opened the driver's door, got in, started the engine and pulled away without another word.

Will, stunned, watched him go up the hill, around the hairpin, then up the switchback toward Central City. He could swear the guy waved to him through the cloud of dust on the way up the cliff.

Shit. Shit. Will hadn't taken the time to figure out what kind of car it was, any identifying marks or logos. The dust and the distance made that impossible.

Will turned and scanned the valley below, looking in vain for Dwyer or the intern, the Jeep, anything or anyone who might be able to help him. His heart pounded. His throat felt dry.

He took a jacket out of his jersey pocket and put it under a rock beside the road, marking the place the car had been. Tire tracks. They can trace tire tracks.

He scanned the road to the horizon again in search of the news car. He realized he was wearing a wireless microphone. He didn't know the range, but it was contact, in some way, nonetheless.

"Dale! Dale, goddamn it, Dale! Do you hear me? Come back. Come back to Oh My God Road ..." He continued to babble with an urgency that surprised even him. He was scared, as scared as he had ever been, but it was also true that he was out of range. Dwyer and the intern were in Idaho Springs, or, worse, they were in Georgetown, setting up for the ride over Guanella Pass.

There was only one thing to do.

With the spot marked, Will threw his right leg over the top tube of The Beast, clicked into his right pedal and pushed off. Keeping his hands off the brakes and his chain in the big ring, he powered down the side of the mountain, hit the heavily graveled hairpin at the bottom and dropped into a high bank turn. He was somehow sure that he was going to lose it and they'd find his body pressed into the red rock that lined the descent, like some kind of modern fossil in stretch fabric. But luckily an invisible hand held him in place and he came around the curve, gravel flying, his yell echoing off the stone walls.

Don't lose this momentum, he thought, and shot forward toward Idaho Springs, suddenly back on pavement and sprinting like Cippolini was right behind him, the prime straight ahead.

Don't lose it. Don't lose it.

Dwyer was somewhere ahead. But, more importantly, a phone was somewhere ahead. And with that phone was the ability to call the station and Cheryl and the cops and warn everyone he could that as far as he was concerned, his life and that of his wife, and, therefore, child, had been threatened, and by God he wasn't going to put up with it.

As he made the turn into the first Idaho Springs neighborhood, he glanced ahead, saw Dwyer, and rode, straight as an arrow, toward the camera, slamming the binders at the last minute and sending the photographer scurrying for safety.

"GIMME THE PHONE," WILL SHOUTED, SHOVING HIS HAND TOWARD THE PHOTOGRAPHER like a battle lance. "Gimme the phone!"

"What?"

"Give me the phone!"

"I can't—these are station phones for station ..."

"Gimme the goddamned phone, Dale!"

Dale handed over the phone, his eyes wide and frightened.

Will punched in the number for the station and waited for the ring. The assignment desk picked it up on the eighth one.

"I've got to talk to Barbara."

"Who is this?"

"This is Will Ross. I've got to talk to Barbara Gooden, please."

"I'm sorry, who?"

"Barbara Gooden."

"No, who are you?"

"Will Ross. I work at the station?"

"You do?"

"Just put her on, goddammit, this is important."

He was put on hold, which lasted an eternity. Not one of those eternities where time passes quickly but seems forever, but one of those real life eternities where the person on the other end hopes you'll go away.

"Who were you holding for?"

"Barbara. This is Will Ross."

"Well, I'm sorry. She's in a meeting."

Will felt his blood pressure push his heart up into the back of his skull.

"Look. Get her. I don't care if she's meeting with God and all the elect right now—get her. This is a matter of life and death ..."

The woman who had answered the phone sighed with an air of resignation. "Aren't they all?"

The Muzak started again.

Finally, after four numbers and an overture, the phone clicked.

"Barbara Gooden."

"Barbara, this is Ross," Will fumbled, his words spilling out in the hopes of getting the story out before the battery on the phone went dead. "He was here. He was on the road. Oh My God Road."

"Who?"

"The stalker. The guy who left the note at my house. He stopped me on the road."

"How do you know it was him?"

"He said so, shit, how many people are going to make something like that up?"

"Where was Dale? Did we get a shot of the guy?"

"No, we didn't get a shot of him. Dale had moved ahead with the camera. The guy," Will whispered with a growing exasperation, "he threatened me. He threatened my family."

"Did he threaten the station?"

"Not that I can recall, no."

"Okay. This is what we'll do. You keep riding and get your story done ..."

"Bullshit ... I'm coming home."

"No, there's nothing you can do here and we need you to get that story done."

"Hey, Barbara, if it didn't sink in for some reason, there's a guy heading back to Denver right now who threatened my wife and child. There's no way ..."

"Don't worry about them. I'll call the police and get somebody over there right now." She broke up for a second. "... talk to her. We'll make sure she and your house are being watched. Are safe. Just finish the story and come on back. Everything"—she broke up again—"fine."

"Not good enough, Barbara, not good enough by half ..."

"Will, are you there? Will? Just finish the ride, Will. Get the story done. Everything will be just fine here."

"Barbara, goddammit ... Barbara ..." The phone went dead.

The endless wait in Phone Purgatory had worn the battery down to nothing. Will's temper popped. He slammed the phone down on the pavement and stomped over to a gas station, Dale Dwyer squeaking behind him, "That's company property signed out to me! You're paying for that one, pal!"

Will didn't care. Maybe he'd buy them a phone with a battery that lasted more than twenty seconds.

Just outside the door of the gas station was a bank of phones. Will picked up the handset of the second, least scummy looking one, dialed in his AT&T code, then the number for Bosco Bikes. Jenny, at the desk, put him right through to Cheryl, in a manager's meeting.

See, he thought, wasn't this the way it was supposed to be?

"Cheryl Ross."

"Hi, there. Look. Be careful this afternoon. That guy who left a note at the house, the one who has been calling us, met me on the road today ..."

"What did he look like?"

"Don't know. He was wearing a mask. No plates on his car that I could see."

"Great."

"I've called the station but they don't seem all that cranked about it. I am. Unless I steal a car, it looks like there's no way I'm getting back until about seven tonight."

"Don't worry. Finish the ride. Don't worry about us. We'll be fine."

"What the hell is this? Nobody's worried but me?"

"Look, I'm not happy about it, Will ..."

At the sound of his name, Lisa Shannon shouted from the other side of the conference table, "I want my Rolodex, you asshole!"

Cheryl picked up and passed the phone on to Lisa, mystically just as Will shot the bird. She fell into a silent funk.

Will felt like everybody was going mad. He was being threatened, along with his family, the station, shit, who knew, and nobody was taking it seriously. Go ride your bike, Will. Do our story, Will. Get yourself blown up, Will, by some guy in a frosted plastic mask who looked like your sister after she covered her face with that nighttime goo to remove all the little hairs.

He was going mad. His blood pressure rose, then dropped suddenly, and he felt all the fight go out of him. It was like somebody had opened a high-pressure valve on the top of his head.

All he wanted to do was lie down.

"Okay. Okay. But, do me this favor, go home with somebody. I'll pick you up and we can go home together. Please."

"Alright. I'll go home with Nancy. How's that? I'll go home with Nancy and then we'll meet you someplace and go home together. How about that?"

"Fine. Okay. Good."

"Just go ride your bike, Will. If you come running back to town, he wins. He wins."

"Okay. Just ... just watch yourself, okay? Please. There's just too much at stake here."

"I'm not afraid of nuts, Will."

"He says he did that Crooked Lake thing ..."

"You heard the cops this morning. They still say that was an accident, Will. That's like some fifteen-year-old kid taking credit for putting the iceberg in the Titanic's way."

"Really?"

She sighed. "Go ride your bike, Will. We'll be fine."

He sighed. "Okay. Okay. Alright. I'll finish and be home as quickly as I can."

"Don't kill yourself."

The words sent a cold hand down his back. That two-bit piece of shit on the road wasn't kidding, Will thought. He wasn't making this up. Something in his tone wanted recognition, appreciation for a job well done.

And only Will took him seriously.

"I love you."

"I love you. See you tonight. Be careful."

"You too, love. Gooch and I will be just fine."

The line went dead.

Will quietly hung up the phone and turned to see the gas station drive filled with a casino bus packed with seniors on their way to the gambling dens in Blackhawk and Central City. The bus was very nearly overflowing.

One short, dark haired woman with a wild look in her eye caught Will's attention. She shook a bag of coins at him through the partially opened window.

"Spending my kid's inheritance!" she shouted.

Will smiled and nodded, then hustled himself back to his bike. Dale was kneeling down in the street beside the camera trying to piece the phone back together.

"You're paying for this, buddy."

"Happy to. Let's get going."

Dwyer shoveled the last of the pieces into a plastic bag, as if somehow, some technician, somewhere, could magically restore the equipment he had signed out for. He knew that Andy, upstairs in the great glass office, didn't look kindly on people who broke equipment. He remembered, far too well, the tripod leg that had given way, dropping his camera into the middle of a stairway in the middle of a basketball game in the middle of the Pepsi Center.

This was Ross's fault, and by God, Ross was the one who was going to get his ass chewed into a thousand pieces.

Dwyer gathered up the last of it, picked up the camera and tripod and walked back to the station Jeep, where the cute intern with the amazing chest and little tongue stud sat waiting for him.

Dale Dwyer smiled and hoped that the college senior behind the wheel couldn't see the wrinkles that had developed around his eyes or the thinning that had taken over the top of his head.

He heard the shout behind him.

"Let's go!"

He turned to see Ross pedaling hard down the streets of Idaho Springs toward Georgetown. God, just what the station needed again, another high-strung, high-maintenance sports asshole like Roger Flynn.

He broke his gear down quickly and threw the tripod in the back of the Jeep. The hatch clicked as he pulled it down and he said over his shoulder: "Let's go—magic awaits us just up the road." He climbed into the back seat and set himself in position to shoot Ross as he rode over Guanella Pass.

The intern laughed, which make Dwyer smile. Who knew? Maybe so, maybe this time, maybe so.

The SUV pulled into the street, crossed over Interstate 70, then picked up speed on the frontage road in the hopes of catching up with its target, a lone cyclist who suddenly wasn't feeling the effects of age, training or lack of same and was powering down the flats trying desperately to find the magic of the road before the demons of Guanella came out to rip them from him.

The Jeep continued to speed up.

The intern clacked the tongue stud against the back of her teeth.

Nobody could ride this far this fast, she thought. Not on a silly-ass bicycle.

She came around a long turn and saw him. Far ahead, and losing them.

She sped up again to catch him, but the little shit continually seemed to pull away.

❧

GEORGETOWN WAS A ROUGH RIDE. THE CITY FATHERS HAD INITIALLY APPROVED THE race running through town itself, but had lately changed the course from main streets to back streets, many of which weren't in great condition.

Will tried to find a line, but it slowed him down. If he flatted here, or damaged a tire, he'd pay for it with a shattered pace on Guanella.

Don't lose the pace, he thought, don't lose the pace. Gotta get this done. Get this ride over and get home. Get home and convince Cheryl and everybody else involved that this guy wasn't just some two-bit stalker.

But why? Why did he think that? All he had to go on was some damned bell ringing in the back of his head. That's it. Nobody else seemed to be all that concerned. Not Whiteside, not Officer Babe, not Barbara, not Sessions, not Cheryl.

His pace began to slow down. Only him.

Only he thought it was worth worrying about. Ignore your instincts at your peril, he thought. At his peril.

Will rose up out of the seat and began to ride.

He set the metronome in his head and let it click away. Building. Building. Click click click click click click click. He knew this course, though he had never ridden it before, and took the turns he knew the pack would take, click click click click, and zipped through the quiet town without a pause, click click click click, onto the run up to Guanella, a steep climb up to some nine thousand feet click click click click get into your climbing rhythm click click click click click click click. He was up out of the seat now, shifting without thought, finding the proper feel, watching the road, close, far, mid, close, far, mid, click click click click. That turn came up faster than he expected, click click click while an approaching pick-up truck went wide on the turn into his lane, click click click click throwing him off his line, goddammit, goddammit, click click click, find the rhythm, find the pace, click click click click, find them. Somewhere outside himself, there was a honking sound and he unconsciously moved to the side of the road, still pedaling, still trying, still climbing. The station Jeep shot past him, Dwyer shooting Will out of the back window. Will's attention was caught, for just a moment, by what seemed to be a single, middle finger propped up against the side of the camera. It shook his concentration, but Will pushed it away and dropped back in.

Fine, be like that, he thought. Who gave a rat's ass about your damned phone anyway? Don't lose it, don't lose it, find the line, find the center, find the escalator to the top of the climb. It's in you. It's in you. Click click click click. He caught himself skidding too far right into the scud on the edge of the road, full of pea gravel and road shit and tree bark and burrs that would rip a road tire to shreds without a second thought. Find the line, find the line. A diesel pickup passed him and shifted just beyond, belching a cloud of black smoke into his face.

He gagged and retched, then held his breath for a second, blew out, and found a clear patch ahead of him. Find the line. Find the line. Ignore the truck. Ignore the traffic. Find the line.

It was hard to breathe. The altitude was beginning to claw at his lungs, along with the diesel fumes, and they burned, they burned like he had inhaled a spray of lighter fluid then touched it off. He reached for the water bottle.

The one he hadn't replaced. Shit. He needed a feed station someplace soon. Food and drink. Somewhere, ahead.

"Dale—meet me at the top of Guanella. Christ, I hope you can hear me this time. I need you to hand me that blue and white bag in the back of the car when I ride past. Meet me up there, man or this ride ain't going much farther at all."

Who knew who he was talking to? Maybe Dale. Maybe thin air. Maybe some trucker down on I-70 who just happened to be on the same frequency.

Maybe Mars. Who knew?

Just be there, man, just be there.

The climb continued, steep, less steep, more steep, never flat. Never really flat. Find the line. Find the line. Click click click click. Don't wander. Don't let the bike wander. Don't let your mind wander. Stay on the line. Stay on the line.

Click click click click.

There was a turn, then another, then another, and Will looked into mid then far range to realize he was at or near the crest. Dale Dwyer and the intern were ahead, Dwyer standing with the musette bag at his side.

Will sat up on the bike, breaking his concentration for the moment and put his arm out straight, telling Dwyer to reach out with the bag. Dwyer did and within seconds Will had snatched it and was gone, the musette over his shoulder, the contents already finding new homes into cages and pockets and his mouth.

He stuffed the empty bag into the back of his jersey.

Tossing the water bottle earlier had made him paranoid about throwing anything away.

As soon as he drank, he felt the power begin to rise inside him again. The watered-down Gatorade was just what he needed. Yet, despite the large bottles, he knew he wasn't going to have enough liquid.

The van shot past him again and this time Dale was shooting out the back with a thumbs-up symbol beside the camera.

Will couldn't hear him but he could see him mouthing: "Very cool. Very cool."

Then he pointed at the camera. Will shook his head. Dwyer turned to the intern and shouted something. The news car immediately began to slow down. As they drew closer, Will could hear Dale shouting, "That was so COOL, so damned COOL. I want to catch that ahead. Get a shot of that ahead. Do we do that again?"

"Yeah, at about Fairplay," Will shouted back, coming up even to the back edge of the car. "After we go over Kenosha, you can drive ahead to Fairplay. Get in position and buy me more Gatorade and water. Stuff the bottles in my next musette and pass 'em over. I'm dehydrating like crazy up here."

"Got it. Got it. This is so cool. All the mountains and trees and riding and shit, I've got an Emmy here for sure."

He continued to babble on, but Will returned his concentration to the road. Something ahead was making his spine tingle and he wasn't sure why. He backed away from the SUV as Dale continued his monologue, then hit the brakes as he saw the front of the Jeep drop off the pavement, hard, onto the gravel road leading down the backside of Guanella. Dwyer and his camera bounced in the back of the SUV and he shouted something Will couldn't make out to the intern.

Despite the dust and gravel thrown up by the Jeep as the intern tried to get it under control, Will found a line over at the edge of the pavement onto a somewhat smoother part of the hard pack.

It still rattled his back fillings, but it was something that he could handle.

The Jeep he wasn't so sure about, it was scrabbling down the mountainside, now this way, now that, the wheels trying to find purchase, the intern, who obviously hadn't been paying attention to what was ahead of her, trying to regain control.

Dwyer, Will could see, was bouncing around in the back seat like a pea in a dried gourd. He was trying to protect the camera, but it was going this way and that, despite being cushioned by a 160-pound photographer.

Will could hear Dale Dwyer screech at the intern to slow the hell down.

He would have laughed, but he had his own problems. The road was a mess of potholes and oddly shaped stones, some pointed, some round, some shaped like God's first attempts at a map of Idaho. He couldn't slacken his pace too much, but he still had to find a line through the worst of it. The Jeep ahead had regained control and was heading away quickly to set up for another shot somewhere down the road. Will, on the other hand, was wondering if he'd ever make it that far on this set of tires and rims and buttocks. What he wouldn't give for a mountain bike right about now, something with fat tires and a full suspension. Somebody else riding it, even, while he just watched from the back of the Jeep.

As he rode, picked his line and prayed not to flat, Will considered Dale for a second. It was a strange duck, Will thought, who got all hot about a feed station, the most basic aspect of the race; sit up, pedal, grab, eat, and the guy went nuts. There were other things more dangerous, more thrilling, more exciting, but, for some reason, the power and majesty of catching a ratty old musette bag, like some Milwaukee Road express grabbing the mail bag, had Dale in a tizzy of award possibilities.

Will knew he would never understand the TV business or the people in it for the life of him.

His thoughts came back to the road. This was a hairy descent. Because of the grade and the surface of the road, it was like hurtling down a glass wall on marbles. It was hard to control your speed, it was impossible to find a line that saved your tires and it took God's own bike handling skills to make the turns. They were coming up too fast. Too fast.

Will felt himself sliding too wide on one, and pictured himself going over the edge, no one to see him, no one to hear him for days or weeks or months, while the vultures picked out his eyes and had fun with the soft spot around his gut.

He slid back the other way, his thought being that it was easier to deal with road rash than death, but caught himself with his left foot at the last second, popping it out of the pedal by instinct and getting it down to the road.

He very nearly lost it, again, in putting his foot down directly in front of an eight-inch rock that had materialized out of nowhere. It caught him on the point of his left ankle and the pain made him sit bolt upright on the bike, his mouth in a tight "Little Rascals" circle of surprise, the road, the ride, the threats, the whole damned thing forgotten for a second as Will dragged his foot behind him, the pain a needle at the hinge of it.

Slowly, he started moving it around. It felt like mush, but it didn't feel broken. Man. That was going to leave a mark.

He came around the next turn and shot past Dwyer, who had set up for a descent shot. Rather than capturing the drama of riding, all he got was Will sitting up on the bike and wiggling his left foot.

"Do something!" he screamed from the side, but Will just kept rolling his ankle.

This was going to make a better shot than you can imagine, Chumley, Will thought. The dangers of the course. What every rider faced. It was going to be something to break up the ride ride ride ride ride ride ride ride ride.

The endless ride from hell.

Will looked down. His left ankle was soaked in blood. The rock had torn the sock and his top layer of skin. Not bad, but compelling video. If dipshit got a shot of it, then that would be a story tonight on the air.

The TV6 Race—full of danger, excitement, bloodied riders, idiots in Spandex! The thought brought him back to the descent. Flynn. He began to look ahead and dream of pavement. Flynn. Flynn hated this race. Hated Will. Hated everything about it.

The riders. The sport. The equipment. The course. The demands.

Was it the American sports reporters' natural dislike of anything that didn't serve him a buffet lunch or happen directly in front of him? A case of stadium ass, stadium eyeballs, stadium mindset?

Or, was it the fact that Americans hadn't, with a few spectacular exceptions, done much in the sport since the turn of the century? The last century, when cycling was king and cars were slower than riders?

Or was it Will himself? Will had done it. Will had been on the playing field. Then had the gall to intrude on Flynn's life, his rice bowl, his territory, his fiefdom. Flynn, he gathered, had been one of those kids who sat in the stands and dreamed of athletic glory. AV club.

"Hello, my name is Roger and I'm here with the projector for the movie today, 'Wheat—the Glory that is Kansas.'"

Will snorted. Snot ran down his lip. He picked it up with the tip of his finger and flipped it into the pines lining the descent.

Watch the line, watch the line. His concentration was skittering like a puppy on a freshly waxed floor.

He was feeling the first stirrings of dehydration bonk, but he didn't want to take his hands off the bike until he hit pavement. Man, he needed a stop and another feed station.

Breaking his stare from the road ahead, Will shot a look down at the water bottle he was still carrying. Covered with dust, almost mud at the tip, it was about half full. If he got to it soon, it should carry him. Should.

Christ, he needed a support team that was focused on him. Ha! Focused. That was the problem. Dwyer was focused on him. Watch the road. Watch the line.

Bring it right. The center of the road was piled with gravel pushed there by the cars. The cars. Who the hell would drive this goddamned road? It can't be open in the winter. Can't be. Bring it back. Keep it here. Will swept around one turn, then another, then a third, long sweeping turns that gave him the sense that the mountain itself was flattening out. He avoided one pothole in a panic, and instinctively lifted as much weight off the front wheel as he could, to take the lip of the returning pavement.

It was jarring anyway.

The Jeep was behind him on the gravel, going fairly slowly, Will noticed, with a glance over his arm. As soon as it hit the tarmac, it picked up its pace and shot past him, dropping in just in front of him as they came off Guanella and stepped almost immediately onto Kenosha Pass. Nothing like Guanella, that's for sure, but still another climb before Grant.

Will snatched up his water bottle, flipped open the cap and greedily drank down the last of the performance drink, the last of the Haven stuff he had stolen from the team two years before. Now the tie was officially and forever severed. He felt his body hungrily grab at whatever it could find to use in the scientific concoction, while his mind felt a sadness bordering on maudlin grief over what was past.

Look ahead. Look ahead. You've got a future and it's all ahead.

He almost tossed the bottle again, but leaned in and put it back in the cage. He called out to Dwyer with the wireless microphone and the photographer jerked his head back from the eyepiece of the camera in the car ahead.

"Dale, get a shot of my left foot. It's covered with dust and mud now, but it's bloody. They'll want to know this ride is dangerous ..."

Dwyer gave him a thumbs-up.

"Kenosha isn't much, at least I don't think so. Forget Fairplay. Run ahead to Grant and get me set up for the feed station. I might actually get off the bike there, for a few minutes. But run up there and get ready for me. Get me some fluids. Gatorade, All Sport, whatever you can find."

"Budweiser?" the photographer shouted from the back of the car.

Will saw him say the word more than heard it. He nodded, then replied, "You're buying in Breckenridge."

Dwyer shook his head and threw a thumb back toward the intern driving. Will laughed and nodded, then waved him off. Dwyer returned the salute, said something over his shoulder and the Jeep was gone.

The Haven sports drink was doing its job. Will felt energy return to his left side and he stretched himself out over the top tube, trying to release the knot that had formed on his right side as he squeezed the handlebars for all they were worth on the gravel descent.

There were going to be a million flats on that section. Nothing short of a million. Why he had made it through today? Who knew? Maybe God looks after idiots and professional cyclists with bum legs and no job prospects. Wait a minute, he had job prospects. He had this. If he buckled down and made good, he could make it in TV sports.

He could beat the guy from the AV club.

He'd have to do a lot of sports he didn't care about all that much, football, baseball, basketball—college hoops were fun—hockey, hockey he liked, no soccer, no cycling, nothing the least bit out of the ordinary until the race came up again down the road. Could he do that? Could he stick with it through all the other stuff, ignoring cycling eleven months out of the year, getting geared up only for this race and a few seconds each night on the Tour de France?

The Tour. It wasn't even Le Tour anymore. Christ.

He was home.

He crouched, dug deep and found some speed left in legs that were ready for nothing more difficult than a steam, a soak and a beer.

He shot forward toward Grant.

❋

GRANT WAS LITTLE MORE THAN A FEW BUILDINGS AND AN INTERSECTION, BUT DWYER had been good to his word. Along with the musette bag, he held out a plastic bag from a local market, weighed down with something. The intern was across the street staring into the camera. Dwyer must have set the shot up earlier and put himself in position to be a part of the story. Alfred Hitchcock lives.

Will decided to make this one look slick, so he straightened himself up on the bike and picked up a little speed. Sticking out his hand like a hook, good TV style.

He snagged the bags and immediately ruined the take.

"Shit."

It was like he was picking up groceries for a week. The plastic bag, especially, yanked him over to the edge of the road and he had to fight to pull himself back toward the middle of the tarmac to set up for the turn into South Park.

Clearly out of control, he leaned forward, touched the brakes, came to a slow, if wiggly stop, then, almost as if in a slow motion silent film, fell over onto the side of the road, barely keeping his head out of thistle growing there.

"What the hell? What the hell?"

Dwyer came running up, far more frightened than he was concerned. The equipment he carried in his Batman-like utility belt jingled and shook with each step.

"I fell down."

"Yeah, no shit, I can see that. I thought you weren't supposed to fall down when you were a pro."

Will snorted and thought, for a second, of all the far more spectacular falls he had endured on the road over his career. This was nothing. This was just another way of getting off the bike.

"What the hell did you put in that bag? Christ, it was like trying to catch a brick on the fly."

"I got you some Gatorade," Dwyer said, sheepishly.

"Thanks. Swell. Did you have to buy"—he looked in the bag—"a half-gallon of the stuff?"

"I thought you'd be thirsty."

Will slowly pulled himself out from around The Beast, standing up as best he could and pulling out the bottle of sports drink.

Even alone, without the bag or the surprise, it weighed a ton.

"Besides, it was the only size they had."

"That's fine. That's fine." Will dropped the musette beside the bike, cracked open the bottle and began to guzzle the stuff full strength. He usually liked to cut it fifty-fifty with water, just so he didn't get that sort of sugary/salty heartburn and aftertaste down the road, but there was no water in sight and what the hell, he could use the fluid. He guzzled a third of it before he looked back to Dwyer.

"Where's your phone?" Will asked, putting out his hand, "I want to call home."

Dale Dwyer looked at him as if he had completely lost his mind.

"It's in pieces. If you recall. Back in the middle of Idaho Springs."

"Oh ... yeah. Idaho Springs. Yeah." Will recalled the frustration. "Sorry." He also recalled the reason for the frustration, which the ride, the climb, and the descent had pretty much knocked out him.

He thought about the course and the rest of the ride ahead. He looked at his watch. It was easier to go forward and hope for the best, than panic and go chasing back to Denver. The finish was closer than the start by now. It was going to be quicker to go ahead than go back and fight with them for missing a live shot. It would be midnight before he got to Cheryl that way.

Midnight and no job prospects, that's for sure.

He guzzled another third of the bottle of Gatorade as if he was filling a gas tank, the scientific refreshment formula filling him up and churning away as if it was actually building an apartment building in his guts.

"You know, I'm not pissed about the phone anymore," Dale said, quietly. "It was a piece of shit and the station is buying us new ones in about a week—dual mode. That was an analog thing that couldn't keep a battery charge more than ten minutes."

"Still, I'm sorry. It was a pretty shitty thing to do. I'll rat on me to Barbara, okay?"

"Mrs. Freeze? Shit, man. That's walkin' into the lion's den. You wasted money. She'll have your nuts and wear them as a necklace."

"Really? I haven't seen that."

"You will, my friend, you will. She's always nice to the pukes until she knows whether you're on her side or not."

Without thinking about it, Will finished the bottle of Gatorade. He was now sloggy, the stuff sloshing around in his poofy guts like water in a fishtank.

"I gotta ride. Gotta get back on the bike or I'm going to stiffen up and never ride again."

"We'll meet you on the flats a couple of times then catch you in Fairplay on the run up to Hoosier Pass."

"Cool," he nodded, handed Dwyer the empty Gatorade bottle, then stepped back to The Beast. It didn't want to get up and he didn't want to get on, but the course was two thirds finished, only one bad climb left to go and he had a live shot to do.

He slung the musette bag over his shoulder, not even bothering to unpack. The churning, fermenting Gatorade took the edge off any hunger he had. He stepped over the bike, snapped his right foot into the pedal and pushed off. He could feel it. Even a few minutes off. Off the bike, off the pace, and everything had begun to stiffen up. Nothing wanted to work, to climb, to sprint, to pedal.

Everything just wanted to sit in a chair and drink a beer with him.

Watch TV. Didn't matter what was on. Even that relationship dame with the crummy life who gave advice to everybody else in a loud and angry way. Infomercials at two A.M. Australian Rules Football at three.

He pushed off, every muscle screaming. His desire to ride had been left somewhere behind him on Guanella. Ahead was only effort. And home.

Cheryl. The thought of what was threatened and whispered. It hurt. His right knee hurt, a sharp, bothersome little pain running along his right leg, likely a result of all the tears and pulls and damaged muscles that were trying to remind him that he couldn't play this way anymore.

Couldn't ride with the big boys. Couldn't ride like this at all.

He rose up out of the saddle and began to build up some speed for the flats ahead. Slowly, ever so slowly, the screaming began to subside and the warmth began to flow and the ride began to move again, slowly at first, then faster, a climb toward the magic that lay ahead in the road.

Flats, climb, descent, Breckenridge.

Live shot. Home.

Cheryl.

In that order. Let's take 'em, he thought to himself.

He rose up out of the seat and began to build his pace again.

Click click click ...

❋

HELL, WILL DECIDED, WAS LOCATED IN THE MOUNTAINS OF COLORADO AND WENT under the name of Hoosier Pass.

It wasn't as steep as Guanella, but it was long, just plain long, with endless climbs that rose up out of South Park and just kept rising and rising and rising to the bottom of God's shoe.

For a trained cyclist, someone who was actually in shape, this would be the point of the day to lose anybody that was still hanging on with him. For Will, this was just yet another moment to survive.

The pines on either side were swaying gently, he thought at first, in praise of him for just plain making it this far. What he failed to recognize was that after a long, hot and very dry summer, a front was coming through and the monsoon, which usually arrived in June, was about to make an appearance on the top of his head, in his face, on his legs and through his shirt.

That suddenly made him remember his jacket. His jacket that lay back at the side of the road just outside of Blackhawk and Central City, marking a meeting spot that no one but Will seemed to care about. Given that fact, he thought, it would be a pleasure to have his jacket back again. Maybe he should go back and get it. At least the first part would be downhill.

Short descent. He sat back on the seat and tried to catch his breath. He couldn't. His pace was up ahead or far behind, he wasn't sure which. He just knew that it wasn't with him.

The temperature dropped, the mist disappeared and the raindrops began to pelt him, lashing him through his jerse. Already super saturated with sweat, the jersey now took on the feel of a cold, wet washcloth.

The wind chilled him. Ice cube time.

Dear God, get me through this one and I'll never be bad again, he thought. "I know I've promised that in the past, but this time, this time, I really, really mean it. You betcha, God. I'm not lying anymore. Really."

"WHAT?" Dale Dwyer was shooting from the back of the Jeep, a mere twenty feet ahead. "What are you talking about?"

"Nothing, nothing," Will answered, waving him off. He had to remember the live microphone. The SUV was now kicking up a spray that threw fallen rain and road grit into his face. He waved them ahead and Dwyer waved back.

He stood on the pedals and moved a little closer before whispering in the mike, "Look, Dale—you're killing me here with these boulders the tires are throwing up. You've got plenty of climb, why don't you catch some descent on a long shot then head into Breckenridge to catch the finish and set up the story we have to do at five?"

He said it calmly and quietly, and nicely, he thought. Still, Dale Dwyer sat up in the back of the SUV as if someone had touched him with a 220-volt line. Dwyer stared for a second, nodded, yelled something over his shoulder and the intern popped the gas. Away they went with a little puff of blue exhaust in the freshly scrubbed mountain air and then up and up and up and eventually over a ridge, out of Will's sight.

As soon as they were gone, Will missed them. He hated the stuff in his face, but appreciated the company, as well as the windbreak the Jeep had been giving him that he hadn't really noticed until now.

Now he noticed. He had been wet and muddy. Now he was wet and muddy and cold and being pushed back by a head wind, one foot for every three he went forward.

It was like a gigantic hand was not so steadily pressing on the Haven logo in the middle of his chest. Oh, it would be so easy, so very, very easy, to turn around and let the hand push him right back to Fairplay.

Come get me, Dale. The ride is done and this is where I am.

But no, Dale was ahead, Breckenridge was ahead, and so was his very first live shot. He shifted gears and crouched low, trying to pick up the pace and reduce his profile. His very first live shot. On TV6 *News at Five*. The big show. What Zorro called the barge, though he wasn't quite sure what that meant yet. The barge. What would that mean?

The barge. A full hour of news. A news barge.

He didn't know. He kept low and kept pedaling. This wasn't the posture, that's for sure. He was crimping his diaphragm and cutting off his own air. He shifted again and stood up on the pedals. As if in response, the wind picked up and a gust slammed into him, actually pushing him back on the bike seat.

If he hadn't been hanging onto the handlebars, Mother Nature would have used his head to erase the center line as he dangled off the back of the bike, attached only by his butt crack and his cleats. He readjusted again and slogged on. This wasn't a race, never really had been, but it wasn't even a ride anymore. It was a slog, an honest-to-God slog through the mountains of Colorado.

He looked to his left. Out there somewhere was a beautiful mountain meadow, a countryside that would take your breath away. All he saw was a gray wall of water that hung like an ugly shower curtain over the scene. At least it could have been a diversion, something to look at. God wasn't giving any diversions today. The slog continued.

Up, up, always up, always heading toward another false summit just ahead. The metronome was gone. The damned thing was broken by the side of the road for all he knew. No rhythm. No pace. Just slog. Once and around and around and again. He realized that his ankling was off and that now, thanks to a torn calf, the right side, his weak side, was letting the left set the pace. One strong turn, one weak, one strong, one weak, all leading up the grade to another false summit. A honk behind him and a pickup truck passed him close on the left, the rear view mirror damned near brushing the back of his helmet. The driver was shouting something he couldn't make out. Something pleasant, he could only assume.

Well, the guy had his reasons, Will thought. He had his reasons. Will was all over the road. First, far right, then centerline, then right, then left, then center again. He was riding as if he was in the Colorado State Patrol rolling enclosure and he was in nothing of the sort. He was just plain lucky that mid-week he hadn't met much traffic on this ride. Especially the way his mind was floating across the climb and taking the bike with it.

Enough. Enough. Enough of this wandering, enough of this climb, enough of this ride, enough of this day. This slog. Once again and around and again and around and again. He was riding as poorly as he ever had in his life. He did better as a seven-year-old on that cast iron bike on a Michigan country road.

Zip zip zip it went then, and faster than he had ever gone before. Faster than he could run. And he could run fast. Faster than he thought was possible to go, except maybe in his Grandpa's car, driven ninety miles an hour down Michigan Highway 43 with Grandpa's two fingers lightly on the top of the steering wheel and a Camel hanging limply out of his mouth. Faster and faster than he had ever gone before and now, now ...

THERE WAS A TURN! THERE WAS A TURN!

Will clamped on the brakes and fishtailed toward the guardrail, the road suddenly heading down instead of up. He had crested at some point and hadn't even realized it. Now all he realized was that he was going to die a horrible, cold death, all alone, while Dale and the TV6 audience waited patiently, endlessly, in Breckenridge for his pearls of wisdom.

A wiggle, a catch of the tires, a lean and he regained control, bringing the bike back into the center of the right lane. He sat up for a second to catch his breath, took a quick look over his shoulder to see the summit that he had completely slept through. With renewed vigor, easy to find since the gale was now somewhere above him, above the massive pines that were affording him a break, he shifted, dug in, paid attention to the road and began a fast descent on the wet road.

He was finally on the descent, he thought, so let's just get this sonofabitch over with. He pedaled hard, leaned through another turn, felt a bit of a slip and eased off, caught the road again and dug back in.

"Let's take this thing home," he said, to no one in particular.

❧

THE RAIN WAS STEADY IN BRECKENRIDGE, BUT THANKFULLY THERE WAS NO WIND TO push it around and bring it under the back hatch of the station Jeep. Dwyer had put up the hatch and was using it as a shelter to keep the camera dry as he waited for Will to arrive.

As he waited and smelled the heavy scent of the intern from the front seat (why did they always wear so much perfume, he wondered?), he thought about how this one was going to react.

Each reacted differently to the news. Flynn, now Flynn would have a freakin' heart attack. He'd rage and stomp and call everybody a goddamned bastard then stomp off someplace and kick a dog and stomp back and yell at Dale then curse Barbara Gooden and every one of her body parts, hair to toe nails in language as colorful as a hardware store paint chart.

Zorro, on the other hand, would smile and laugh and pump his fist in the air and shout "yeah" a couple of hundred times because it meant he didn't have to work all that hard. You bet. Do what you like. You're the brain trust of news and I, I am but a humble jester here only to amuse. Do what you will, my lady.

Dwyer laughed. He liked working with Zorro.

This guy, though, this guy was an unknown. The phone thing made Dale suspect that he had another Flynn on his hands. He was a former pro athlete, too, and despite their apple pie and America image in the papers and on TV, they were usually royal pains in the ass. Everybody had treated them as something special all their lives and by God, you should too.

What did he have here? Who was this Ross guy? The phone thing he could let slide because the guy was cranked. Somebody was threatening his wife, Dwyer figured. The phone was a piece of shit anyway. He had thought of "dropping" it himself any number of times. It was even better that this Ross guy had spiked it. Made it a lot easier for Dwyer to get a new one without being hauled on the carpet in front of Sessions and Gooden and the big boss with the bad temper whose name he could never pronounce.

The big A. As in asshole, he laughed. He himself had never been on the receiving end of a blast from the general manager. Frank Makarios had been, though, any number of times, for never using his tripod. Frankie Boy always hand held his video and it always looked like he had shot it from the deck of the Titanic. Kids were always riding their bikes uphill and the Mayor was always falling over to his left.

He laughed and looked up the road. He had seen a figure on the mountainside some time ago, but he couldn't be sure. He could only hope that it was Ross finally bringing this day to a close. He needed a can, a drink and something to eat. Then, the heater turned up full-blast as they drove back toward Denver.

Come on, man, he thought, come on. Get here and start the rest of my life.

Will popped around a corner in the distance before Dale Dwyer could complete the thought. He fumbled at his camera, getting it up and running, finding Will in the view finder, then focusing, then refocusing because the distance kept shifting, then adjusting the iris to deal with the fading light, then refocusing again and hitting the record button to catch Will just as he snapped past the car, arms in the air in triumph.

Dwyer clambered out of the van, released the camera from the tripod, adjusted the weather hood and hustled down the street, as best he could, to catch Will for some quick sound right at the end of the ride.

Will was about fifty feet beyond him. Still on the bike, balanced on his toes, hunched over the handlebars, trying to catch his breath.

"Nice job, man, nice job," Dale wheezed, the altitude getting to him more than he wanted to admit. "Nice ride."

"Thanks, thanks," Will wheezed right back, just damned glad that he didn't have to pedal anymore. The last three miles had been an icebox of a ride. There was no wind, really, except what he himself had been generating, but it was cold and wet and whatever bodily defenses he had earlier in the day against the weather were now gone. He was beginning to shiver. Uncontrollably. Oh, for that damned jacket. Why the hell couldn't he have used a rock or something? A stick to mark the spot? Never, never give away your clothing.

Lesson learned.

He looked at his watch. 5:01. He had done it. He had completed the ride with plenty of time left to set up for the live shot. Let him just gather his thoughts in the car, get warm, get a jacket and something to eat, an umbrella, one of those things to put in his ear so he could hear the anchors back at the station and he'd be good to go.

Set. Ready for my closeup, Mr. DeMille.

"Crank up the heat in the car, Dale. I am ready to get warm."

"Good. Good. Uh, Will ..."

"I figure you sent back film already ..."

"Video, we use videotape."

"Video, I'm sorry. Getting my terms bassackwards." He smiled. Dwyer hoped that was a good sign.

"Let me just get myself together and we'll set up for the live report."

"The live shot. Live shot."

"Thanks, Dale. Thanks for the help. Really sorry about the phone today, man."

"Don't worry about the phone. But I do have something to tell you."

"What?" Will didn't like the look on Dwyer's face, a mix of fear and intense interest, as if he was judging Will on a fine point of etiquette.

"The live shot has been dumped. This is really the first rain we've had in a couple of weeks. The fire danger is really high right now. So, they got a weather woody back at the station and changed their whole newscast plan to cover the rain."

Will stared at him. Stumped. Just plain stumped. He didn't have the slightest idea how to respond.

"You're telling me, Dale, that I just rode 140 miles, climbed my ass off to get here, just to be told that because it's sprinkling that my story doesn't count anymore?"

"Well, not until tomorrow, anyway. They've rescheduled you for tomorrow. A package and a live shot from the starting line in Boulder."

"What if we get rain tomorrow? Or snow?"

"Well, if it's rain, then since it's the second day of rain, it won't make all that much difference. They'll just handle it from 'TV6 Storm Central,'" he intoned, half comically, "but, if for some reason it is snow, well, then all bets are off because any snow, anywhere in the state and the newsroom goes into a full court hard-on. Flakes make compelling video. Weather sells big in this town."

"Jesus, why?"

"God, I dunno. People watch. We get three heavy snows a year in Denver and everybody drives a four-wheeler. Don't ask me why. The whole town is one, big SUV. Don't ask me why."

"So, after all this, no live?"

"No live. I sent back thirty seconds of you riding in the rain on Hoosier Pass. That's all they could use. Sorry, man."

"Well, that's the way it goes, I guess. Well, I tell you, if I had known this I would have either given up in Fairplay or ridden one hell of a lot slower today."

He laughed darkly and Dwyer smiled at him.

Dale still couldn't read Ross. He wasn't going ballistic, but he wasn't happy about it either. Dwyer figured he should just be happy that Ross wasn't banging his bike into the hood of the news car.

"You wanna, you wanna," Dwyer fished for words, "wanna get something to eat, warm up a bit and head back down?"

The whole day came back to Will. The ride, the climbs, the pain, the threat, the calls, the brush off.

Exhausted, he looked at Dwyer. The day had just plain done him in.

"Yeah, let's make it fast, though, can we? I've got to get back to town."

"No prob, no prob," Dwyer answered with a smile. He turned and hustled back to the Jeep, waving his hand at the intern to indicate that he wanted her out of his seat. He was driving home and speed limits were no object. As he slid the camera into the back hatch, he thought, "That went okay. He handled that well. Different, but well. Quiet resignation. He'd better get used to that. It's a way of life in the newsroom."

Will rolled the bike to the side of the Jeep, and with some difficulty, since his muscles were stiffening like some ancient Twinkie, wrestled The Beast onto the roof rack. He tightened the clamps and shakily added two straps for added support. It was a good ride. He didn't want to lose this one. He rattled the bike once to make sure it was secure. Dwyer passed him and slid into the front seat behind the steering wheel.

"Fast food okay?"

"Fast food's fine. Just crank the heat."

"Easy to do, easy to do," he answered.

Dwyer shut the driver's door and for a second, Will was alone on the streets of Breckenridge. The rain fell in heavy, harsh, cold drops as he stood beside the car. He could smell the pine in the air for the first time since Wondervu. He could feel the day creeping up on him. He would be sore tomorrow.

He had to get home to Cheryl and Gooch and make sure all was well.

The smallest part of his day, the most insignificant, when you really thought about it, had been the live shot. The live story from Breckenridge at the end of the ride.

It was nothing. Two minutes of empty TV chat. There was no reason to bemoan its passing.

And yet, he did. He had set the goal, he had reached the goal, and the final punctuation had been snatched away from him.

He raised his face to the cold rain and let it beat on his eyelids, his cheeks, his lips, his neck. He spit once to the side, looked back at the road that led up to Hoosier and before that Kenosha and before that Guanella, whispered "shit" under his breath and opened the back door, climbing into the warmth that was already growing in the Jeep.

CHAPTER EIGHT:

THE CRIMSON KING

H_{E BROKE FROM HIS WORK AND SLAPPED THE TABLE HARD, AND AGAIN, IN} frustration.

What was he expecting? A band? Confetti? A parade?

He didn't get it. He didn't get any of it. He got nothing. All his offers of friendship. All the chances he offered for gratitude and he got nothing.

Ross was even too stupid to give him a thank you. Just a proper in your face, shake your hand, and from the heart thank you.

That wasn't right.

He had gotten Will Ross his job in TV. Made him famous, for Christ's sake. And the guy clearly didn't deserve it. It was obvious to see that. He didn't deserve it. How many ex-jocks ever get to step right into major market TV without an ounce of experience? None. None at all. None that he knew of, anyway. Not beyond network football.

He shook his head.

Since he was the man who opened the door for Mr. Will Ross, he was the man who deserved thanks. A handshake. A thank you. A bit of bow-ing and scrap-ing ... bow-ing and scrap-ing. My efforts, he thought, my efforts gave you a life, he thought. He slammed his fist down on the workbench in rhythm with the words.

He was shaking now. He had to stop. The workbench was shaking. Everything on the workbench was shaking. That was not a good thing.

You can't work properly when you're shaking.

The RDX goes everywhere, the powder flying in the air and attaching itself to anything and everything. The C-4 goes outside the lines. The nitroglycerin blows up in your face. The Semtex didn't care. You could be shaking like your fat old aunt Hannah and the Semtex didn't care.

But the Semtex was not what he was working with at the moment. It was the nitro. And he had to calm himself down. Nitro didn't like to be shaken or stirred or aggravated in any way, shape or form.

He watched the bottle. The clear liquid bounced and splashed within, rolling from side to side.

He held his breath. It calmed. And he calmed. He carefully picked the bottle up and moved it back into the cupboard with the elaborate locking system.

Take your time, he thought, take your time and do it right. One device at a time. And while he was anxious to work on the device featuring the nitroglycerin in a starring role, he was content to work on the others first. The more difficult. The more creative. The more central to his drama.

His anger and resentment began to flow again. It wasn't right.

No, it wasn't right. It never had been. But now came his chance to make it right. To make it right with Ross and TV and sports and the state of Colorado and the City and County of Denver and everybody who had refused to thank him all his life for the moments in which he made their lives better.

All the little people who had inspired him along the way.

"Thank you, thank you so much," he whispered, with a smug smile, bowing to the unseen crowd filling the room behind him, "thank you for my destiny. Aren't you going to thank me for yours? What? No thanks? No ears to hear, no mouth to say ... thank you?"

Aunt Hannah. Lovely old Aunt Hannah. And Ron Warner in high school. Oh, yes, you deserve my thanks, too, Ron. And I deserve thanks from you, for I gave you the gift of flight.

He laughed sardonically. Oh, yes, Ron, you wanted to fly. You flew, thanks to me.

Aren't you going to thank me, Ron? Thank me for turning your car into an airplane?

His fists were tight. His eyes stared straight ahead to a point of nothing on the workbench. His set his jaw in a hard, macabre smile and felt the pressure in his head grow and expand.

Just a little thank you. Was that too much to ask?

Is it ever too much to ask? Let me make it right. Let me make it right.

Now, it was his chance to make it right.

At least for him. They had it right all their lives. Now, it was his chance to make it right for him.

He slammed his fist down on the top of the workbench again. The chemicals around him jumped, beside the tools and the burners and the soldering guns and the timers.

"Relax," he said aloud, "relax."

He gripped the table to control his anger.

Revenge, they say, is a dish best served cold. Wait. Wait until your moment. Despite the fact he liked his food hot, he would wait this time. And bide his time, and plan his time, and make sure that nothing, absolutely nothing, got in the way of his second act.

More thank you's. Thank you for the face in the toilet. Thank you for the face in the wall. Thank you for the slap. Thank you for the giggles. Thank you for the look of disgust. Thank you. Thank you. Thank you, ever so.

They had tried so hard to diminish him, to make sure he knew his place in their world. But they had overlooked a few simple facts—he was better than they were. He was smarter than they were. He was greater than they were.

And they paid for their ignorance, they paid for their rudeness—with the full-face fury of his greeted destiny.

And now, more would pay.

Crooked Lake was the first. The race would be the second. And they would know him. They would know him.

And they would come to fear the third act.

Oh, they would fear the third act.

Just like they were supposed to.

He smiled.

They'd finally know him.

And they'd forever remember him. They'd know, finally, that Crooked Lake and the race were merely a reflection of his gifts, his ingenuity and his talent. They would then fear the third. They would so fear the third act of his first drama.

And so to the race. The second act.

Concentrate now. Let all the anger and resentment subside. Anger and resentment got in the way. They spoiled the effect. They made him shake. There would be no act, second or third, if he shook something into ignition. If what was on this bench decided to ignite beyond his control.

He hummed.

And the nitro's connected to the RDX, and the RDX is connected to the C-4, and the C-4 is connected to the Semtex and they'd all go up—kaboom. He chuckled.

If that happened, none of this neighborhood would exist anymore. He'd be atoms. There'd be a pit about thirty feet deep. And Mrs. Rand, who lived next door, well, they'd find her in the next county, hanging from a cottonwood in her perpetual housecoat.

He would return to the matter of the universe and they'd never find enough of him to put in a thimble.

And so to concentrate. And so to work. He pulled down the magnifying glasses and soldered a tiny wire.

Planning. Molding.

Wiring.

Small and careful.

No big blasts this time.

Just small.

And targeted. Each with a tiny plan. Each with a tiny job. Just enough to get their attention and show his range.

Show his range. The range of his talents. The range of his creativity.

They'll realize that they've been wrong all along on Crooked Lake. It wasn't an accident at all. Never was. It was part of a great, pyrotechnic drama. And it was merely Act One.

They'd always remember this race. Act Two.

And they'd write in the history books about Act Three.

His eyes caught the pink oversized tennis ball he had found in a pet store. It was a sideline, really, a secondary. Very simple. So very, very simple.

But creative. Oh, he liked this part of the game. So very much.

Catch me if you can, you dolts.

He smiled and bent back to the table. Back to his work. The soldering gun smoked. The solder melted. The connection was made.

Once again, he was creating life.
And he, himself, felt alive for it.
Thank you, Peter, he could hear it say.
Thank you ever so.
And he smiled.

CHAPTER NINE:

DON'T TOUCH
THAT DIAL!

"WHAT DO YOU HAVE GOING ON TODAY?" CHERYL ASKED, BRUSHING an errant eyelash off her cheek and smoothing a bit of makeup left crooked in its wake.

"I figure I'll spend the day standing up, the way my ass feels. Remind me— we used to do rides like that for a living, right?"

"Right."

"Jesus, we were stupid."

He stretched up his right leg onto the back of the footboard of the bed and tried to stretch out the muscles that had congealed over the thirty-six hours since his ride over the mountain tops. Everything from his toes to his butt to the middle of his back screamed bloody murder, but at least, today, he could move without looking like a maniacal marionette.

"So, what *are* you doing today?"

"I guess I'm editing my first piece. The ride piece. It'll be three minutes long and air in tonight's Five. Dwyer logged all the tapes yesterday and he's ready to rock. I wrote a script that Gooden rewrote and that I rewrote and that Gooden rewrote. So, I figure I'll stick with her rewrite now."

"Was it tough?"

"Not all that tough. I was just telling what happened. No, it was, you're right, it was in a way, because everything has to be so goddamned short in TV. Read a book or even a newspaper article and they can go on forever about all kinds of stuff. Do a TV news story and it's squeeze it, squeeze it, squeeze it."

"Squeeze it?"

"Squeeze it. Every time I saw Barbara yesterday, all she ever said to me was

DEADROLL • GREG MOODY

'Squeeze the water out of it.' "

"The water ..."

"Yeah, like, uh, the extra words. The points you don't need. The repetition. Fast, punchy, ratatattat. In and out, like a thief in the night."

"So," Cheryl said, her eyes wide in mock sarcasm, "by the time you've done all this water squeezing and everything else, is there anything left?"

"Any what?"

"Any news? Any story?"

"I dunno. I'm too busy squeezin' water to notice. Ask me again after we cut the thing today."

"I will. Sounds kinda thin to me. But I'll watch."

"That's very good of you," he muttered.

"Hey, aside from that, how are you feeling?"

"Fine, why?"

"No, I mean, how are you feeling?"

For a moment, Will couldn't figure out what she was asking. He then realized both the point of her question and the reason for the secrecy. They had decided to keep talk of *him* out of the house. But there still were those moments it had to be asked.

"Oh, yeah, well," he thought for a second, "okay, really. I mean, I haven't heard anything. No calls, no oddball appearances, and, as I think about it, it's getting harder and harder to remember what he said on the road during the ride, you know, so I don't know. I guess we are just dealing with kook-ville."

"You're sure?" she asked, with quiet concern.

"Yeah. At least I think so. We'll see if he keeps bothering me. Otherwise, Barbara is pretty sure it's nothing. The cops were surprised that we met face to face, but they don't seem to be taking it all that seriously. And so and so and so ... as you can see, it didn't affect my sleep last night."

"Or your appetite, chunk boy," Cheryl said, poking at his gut with the end of the hairbrush.

"Thank you ever so much for bringing it up. I'm still trying to rebuild myself after that ride."

"That was one day. You're eating like you're in Le Tour."

"All part of my recovery plan."

"Well, don't 'recovery plan' yourself right into the plugged arteries ward. I'm going to need you around for a while."

"How long?"

"Long enough to drive me to the hospital on the appointed day. Then, you can crap out and I'll live off your huge insurance settlement."

"Nice to know you care. Oh, just so you know. I changed my will. It all goes to one of those overnight cable-TV evangelists now."

She hit him with the hairbrush.

❧

THE EDITING SEEMED TO TAKE FOREVER. EVEN KNOWING WHERE EVERYTHING WAS on the tapes, it still seemed to take forever. How anything ever made it onto a daily newscast was way beyond him. Find the sound. Check the sound. Cue the sound. Time the sound. Enter the "in" points on one machine, then the other, enter the "outs" if you need them, preview the sound to make sure everything works, readjust your in-cue and out-cue to fit the mental rhythm of the person actually doing the editing. Check, check and recheck until you're sure, then, hit the red button that says auto-edit and make the thing permanent.

Unless you have to change it again.

Then, set it up to do it again. Sound, pictures, narration, all in a carefully constructed package that takes forever to build. If Will was working the buttons and making the choices, maybe, then the time would move quickly and the day would be more fun. The piece would look like a pile of Tinkertoys after an earthquake, but it would be done. But even with watching every edit, he couldn't figure out the progression of buttons that brought Dale to the point where he was ready to "lay one in," the point where he could hit the red button with confidence and put an edit together for posterity. Will tried, but Dwyer liked to carefully set everything up, then, at the last second maniacally slap a bunch of buttons before making the edit.

That completely lost Will.

The day moved along slowly, the story building until they were two minutes in, putting in another map built by graphics with a little cartoon Will huffing and puffing up and over Guanella. Bill Sessions stuck his head in the door of the editing room.

"What color shirt are you wearing?"

"A delicate orange and blue Bronco shirt, as you can see, Billy boy," Dwyer chortled, never looking away from the editing screens.

"Not you."

"Blue and white stripes," Will said.

"Do you have a tie to go with it? A jacket?"

"No. I didn't think I'd be on air today."

"Always dress like you're going to be on air."

"Okay. Why?"

"Because you're going to be on air today. Dale, you're going to have to finish this up alone. Will, come with me."

Dwyer looked up with huge eyes at Will and nodded.

"Good luck. Into the frying pan, pal. Don't worry about this, I've got it."

Will said thanks and followed Sessions out of the editing suite and down the hall, cutting across one corner of the atrium. Will could see an ambulance at the front door. It sent a chill up his back, while his mind flooded with memories of the man on the road.

"Come on, we don't have a whole lot of time."

Will followed Sessions into the newsroom. The staff was bunched in three small groups around the room, earnestly discussing something. Will didn't know what, but he instinctively knew that it was going to somehow affect him.

Sessions looked at Will, eyeballed his shirt, looked around at the staff and said to one reporter, "Elliott, give me your tie."

The entertainment reporter, a short round man with a mustache, red glasses and surprisingly bland taste in his clothing beyond his tie, pointed at his sharply red neckwear, sighed, untied it and began to hand it to Sessions.

"I want it back."

"You'll get it back at six."

He refused to release his end of the tie.

"I don't want any coffee stains on it, that's my Mark Twain tie."

"Oh, Jesus, Elliott, just give me the tie." Sessions snatched it from him without a lick of patience and tossed it to Will.

"Put that on," he said, harshly.

Will started adjusting his collar while Elliott mouthed, "No coffee stains." Will nodded.

They walked into Barbara's office just as Will was turning his collar back down. Sessions turned to him and, like a mother hen preparing her children for Sunday services, tightened and centered the knot.

Gooden hung up the phone and looked at Will.

"Nice tie. One of Elliott's?"

"Yeah," Sessions answered.

"Don't get any coffee on it," she said to Will.

Will nodded, still wondering what was going on today.

"We've got a problem, here, Will. Roger Flynn is off in San Diego with the Bronco's for Sunday's game. As for Zorro ..."

"As for Zorro," Bill said, rubbing his eyes.

"Yes, as for Zorro," Barbara continued, "he just stuck a pencil in his eye."

"He what?" Will asked, incredulously.

"He just stuck a pencil in his eye. He was sitting at the assignment desk, with a pencil in his hand, point up on the table. Somebody said something to him, at which point he said, 'Oh, shit,' and slammed his head down on the desk. He is now on his way to the hospital with a pencil sticking out of his head."

"Jesus, is he okay?"

"As okay as you can be with a pencil sticking out of your head."

"Holy, shit."

"Well, yes, holy shit indeed. You ready?"

"Ready for what?"

Barbara stood up, glided around the end of her desk, put one hand on Will's shoulder and looked deeply into his face.

"You ready to go into the barrel? Because we're down two and you are number three."

"For what?"

"Since we can't extend Roger Flynn's satellite window, he can't anchor the sports report from San Diego—live. And since he can't anchor, you're anchoring sports tonight. Five and Ten."

"Oh, shit."

"Oh, shit is right. Just about everything is written, right Bill?"

"Yeah, Zorro finished a lot of it before he did the pencil trick. I've got John finishing up now. He used to be a sports producer in Minneapolis."

"Okay. So, you got a jacket with you? No?" she said in a rush. "Then we'll find you a jacket. Bill, check with Elliott. He's always got a jacket hanging on the back of his chair. His little round person clothes will fit just about everybody. And while we're finding you a jacket, we've got to get you a little rehearsal. Where, Bill? They're starting the Four now. Is the *Call 6* set still up in the small studio? Good. Light it up and we'll put him there. I'll be there in about five minutes to watch. Get him set up and we'll start givin' him grief."

She turned and walked out, a woman on a mission. Bill didn't waste any time. He took Will by the elbow, which Will realized was just about the driest part of his body at the moment and began to drag him toward the other end of the newsroom.

As they walked, Bill glanced back and forth at everybody's desk, as if searching for something. He finally found it.

"Elliott. I need your jacket."

"Oh, Jesus, Bill. Can't anybody around here actually dress before they come in?" he whined.

"Put a sock in it, pal. This is an emergency."

He tossed the jacket to Sessions who handed it to Will.

Elliott opened his mouth to say something, but Bill beat him to it.

"No coffee stains. Gotcha, Elliott."

With that, Sessions was off again, Will in his wake, waving a thank you to Elliott Green fuming and nearly naked in his cubicle. Sessions' pace was affecting Will's sense of calm, either that or the pace of the newsroom was beginning to grow in anticipation of the Five, or Will was just starting to fully realize what lay in ambush for him just around the next turn of the clock.

He was going to anchor. Anchor a major sportscast. In a major TV market. Without a bit of experience in doing such a thing. What kind of business handed over such a major job to an inexperienced newcomer?

"Hey—good news—we've got a double fatal," the skinny kid on the desk shouted as Sessions and Will passed. The kid paused and listened to the scanner as Will followed Sessions out the door into the hall. As the door closed, Will could hear the kid behind him shout, "Even better! It's a triple fatal!"

What kind of business? That kind of business, Will thought. That kind of business put an inexperienced noodge at the plate for no better reason than the improper placement of one sharp Dixon #2.

As they turned the corner leading to the small studio, Will wondered if the company was now going to have to put warning labels on their pencils, "Do not place sharpened pencil in eye! Injury may result!"

He shook his head. He was merely trying to postpone considering the inevitable. He was now on the downward slide of a roller coaster, and ahead in the dark, he wasn't sure if the track continued around the corner or collided with a brick wall in the depths of a tunnel.

Whatever the case, he was in the car now, it was rolling ahead, and he was in for the ride of his life.

Sessions moved some buttons on a control panel and lights came up on a small news set, almost a miniature version of the main set in the main news studio. He pointed at a chair.

"Sit down and let's get started. We've got just under an hour to make you great."

All Will could hear was Cheryl's voice in his head answering Sessions with a cheery, and heavily sarcastic "good luck."

❧

WILL TRIED DESPERATELY TO REMEMBER ANYTHING THAT SESSIONS HAD TOLD HIM during the crash course, or whatever is was that Barbara had told him, something like her list of "The 100 Things to Remember When Anchoring," as they walked into the main studio for the start of the show.

"Flynn and Zorro both like to ad-lib a lot of stuff—highlights and such. We didn't think you'd want to do that, not on your first night. So, everything is in the prompter."

"The what?" Will asked, from the numb, shock-like state he was currently residing in.

"The TelePrompTer. It's that piece of glass in front of the camera lens. You can see your script, but you can't see the lens. The audience can see you, but they can't see the script. Cool, huh? Just read. Whenever it's your turn, just read. All there is to it."

"Yeah. Uh huh. Yeah." If someone wasn't leading Will he'd be running into things. Walls. Posts. Doors leading to the outdoors and freedom.

Then all chance of that was lost. They were in the studio, the show was starting and Sessions had him by the hand. Someone was smearing makeup on Will's forehead, cheeks and chin. He walked Will around behind the robotic cameras and waited on the sports side of the desk, screen left, set right, until Tom Blakely introduced the first news package.

After the package started, the set was quiet. Nobody spoke to one another. Tom Blakely didn't say a word to Martine. Martine didn't speak to Tom. Will wasn't sure if there was no love lost between the two or this was a matter of professionalism. The people on the floor crew didn't speak to the people on the set. The people on the set didn't speak to the people on the floor crew.

Will didn't speak. He was too nervous. He'd jabber. He knew he'd jabber.

He looked down and kept reading the scripts over and over and over again to become familiar with them, to get a sense of their words and rhythms and the directions of the stories, the emotions that he had to bring to each tale, "The 100 Things to Remember When Anchoring," and the book he was going to write in about forty-five minutes, "The 100 Ways to Puke on Live TV Without Making It Appear that You're Throwing Up Something You Ate When You were in Kindergarten."

In the silence of the set, broken only by an occasional introduction to a story or something that was read on the air, Will watched the clock speed toward the magic hour of 05:12:34 P.M., when the studio door swung open. Fred March, the weather man, casually strolled in, turned on his wireless microphone, sat down on the opposite side of the set from Will and the Round Robin SuperTease, "Stay with us for the rest of the hour because you wouldn't believe the stories we've got for you" promotion began. First Blakely, then Martine, then Fred. Each smooth and short and right to the point. With the exception of Fred, who had been doing this for nearly thirty years, they were all smooth and short and right to the point because it was all written out smooth and short and right to the point in the camera lens.

And then—the camera shifted toward Will. The red light came on. The floor director made an exaggerated move and pointed toward the camera. Will stared into it and sought the words he was supposed to say.

They weren't there.

The computerized prompter had crashed.

Will opened his mouth to say the first and said nothing. He just sat there, his mouth open, a bluegill on a hook hanging off the side of the boat, his brain as blank as the screen in front of him. For what seemed like an eternity, they sat there, man and camera, both hoping the other would make the first move.

Neither did.

And after eternity came to an end, and another began, the camera faded to black, the red light went off, and some guy selling couches covered with tigers came up on the screen. Commercials.

It was over. Man, was it over. And he was delivered. Soggy, but delivered into the safe zone of the commercial break.

No one on the set said anything for a moment, before Tom Blakely turned to Will and whispered, "Red light come on—you talk."

Will nodded. "I know. I know. Sorry. I was just expecting words to be there and when they weren't, my brain went blank. Sorry."

"Ain't much room for sorry at this level, son," Blakely said, smoothly.

Martine looked over at Will with a sympathetic smile. He got the feeling that she had been in the same situation from time to time and that Blakely had given her the same advice, such as it was.

Fred March was smiling. Will was pretty well convinced that this tape was going to be saved and wind up on a Dick Clark Blooper Show.

The studio door opened and Sessions strode in. Will wondered if he was going to be yanked from the set and thrown out the door. Sessions gave him a wave. Will disconnected the microphone and stood up, realizing for the first time that his jacket was soaked and his hands had left two water marks on the faux walnut desk top.

This was worse than climbing Ventoux.

Sessions walked over and put his hand on Will's shoulder.

"That was ... that was interesting. You'll be happy to know that you didn't go blind. We just forgot to script in a tease for you. We'll take the blame for this one. But right now, I want you to sit on over here on the interview set and just relax. Watch Tom and Martine. Watch how they do it. Watch how they interact. Watch how they read. And just relax."

"I don't know if I can, man. I just played fish on the beach there on live TV."

"It happens to all of us. Fred March over there, so cool and easygoing? Got so wound up one night on air that instead of saying Rabbit Ears Pass, said Rabbit Ass Pierce. Martine, calm and professional, was doing a story about dog training and how the dog had to respect you. When someone asked her why, she said, 'Well, would you come if you didn't respect me?' " He paused. "Whole set went up for grabs on that one."

Will bit his lip to keep from laughing.

"Yeah, you see," Sessions said with a nod, "everybody's done it. Everybody has done it. Barbara had some doozies as an anchor. It's live TV and anything can happen. Even Mr. Blakely. Ask him about Anna Nicole Smith one day. That was a good one. Let's just figure you got your first doozy out of the way the very first thing. From here on, just relax and do the job. Okay?"

Will nodded. "Okay."

"Just sit over here in one of the easy chairs on the interview set and watch and relax and try to watch what they do," he pointed back toward Blakely and Martine. "They can both be a pain in the ass at times, real divas, but they know what they're doing. And you can't learn from anyone better."

Will nodded. He walked over to the interview set, peeled off the wet sports coat and draped it over the edge of the chair. He sat down to watch and to bring his breathing back to normal.

The show began again and Tom and Martine slid gracefully back into "news chat" and the second block. It all went smoothly. They just talked to each other. They just talked. To the reporters in the field or on set, They knew what they were going to say and they simply said it. Real, I'm in your living room kind of stuff.

Will read over his scripts again. And again. And again.

Get to know them. What was it Barbara had said? One of her 100 things? Ownership. Own the story. Own the segment. This is you and your work. Own them. Let the audience know that you care enough about what you're saying to take the time to write it, and cut it and put it on the air for them.

Own it. Own it.

The show was moving on. Another break started. What was it? Fourth? Or fifth? Whatever. The floor director looked at Will with a smile and waved him over to the chair. He stood, slipped on the sodden jacket, walked over, sat down, clipped on his microphone, and arranged the scripts before him. If the prompter went down, this time, he knew where he was going to go, even if that meant that Denver would be watching the top of his head for the majority of the sports cast.

The floor director called out, "Ten seconds!"

Tom Blakely leaned over.

"If you pull a stunt like that tease again, I'll make damned sure you never work in this business again."

"Stand By!"

Will sat silently for a second, stunned by the threat.

He turned to Blakely.

"Thanks. I appreciate it."

The red light came on. Will turned to the camera and opened his mouth. This time, words actually came out.

❀

THE ROCKIES HAD THE DAY OFF, BUT THE REST OF BASEBALL WAS BUSY. WILL rambled through the scores, bobbling only one, Seattle/New York, but he picked it up and moved on. A little video of a great catch broke up the scores as he shifted from the American League over to the National. He had to keep referring to the TelePrompTer to make sure he knew who was making the catch. No matter how many times he had read the name, he couldn't remember it, and made himself so nervous over it that he mangled the pronunciation anyway.

Hockey and the Av's trade. The Nuggets once again promising a top-flight season that would likely never materialize. The circus is just out of The Pepsi Center, leaving an interesting aroma for the sports fans to follow. And then, on to the live shot from San Diego with Roger Flynn.

Will read the introduction, turned to a second camera, where his head was stuck in a box next to that of Flynn's in Southern California, and said hello. Flynn either couldn't hear him or wasn't listening, for he was off on a rant and didn't slow down at all to do his report on the Broncos and their pre-game preparations.

"... I couldn't believe it, either. Can you believe this shit, putting that FNG in the anchor chair? They'd be better off having Blakely or the babe do it."

"Roger ..." Will said sharply. He glanced over at Martine and saw her turn a deep shade of red.

"Nothing like working for a two-bit operation. Not a bit of professional ..."

Blakely moved in as if to say something. Will quickly put up his hand to stop him.

"Roger!" he shouted. Flynn reacted with a start and turned to the camera.

"What?" he asked in a low and patronizing tone, obviously thinking that he was talking to somebody in the control room.

"Roger, hey, buddy. Will Ross here LIVE in the studio with you LIVE in San Diego. Live TV. Ain't LIVE grand? Being LIVE, I mean?" Flynn had caught the point. He looked at the ground, he looked to his side, he looked at the camera and smiled. He had found his calm. Will went ahead as if nothing had happened and nothing had been said. "How are the Broncos doing this week and are they really up for this game? They've reached a point where this is a must win for them, isn't it?"

Will didn't have the slightest idea if it was or it wasn't. He didn't follow the Broncos all that much, even though he was paying for their new stadium as a Denver resident. But he wasn't. It wasn't really his sport. Baseball, maybe, on a sunny day with a beer and a hot dog between him and the field. Hockey, that was a game. Hockey he loved. Madness on ice. Cartoon dogs racing back and forth, beating each other senseless with sticks.

Now, that was sport.

Flynn was rattling on about injuries and schedules and records and must win situations and something about a "red zone," which left Will completely in the dark, then went to a package. While that was on air, Will could see and hear Flynn fly into a towering rage on the preview monitor.

"What the fuck kind of operation is this? I need CUES, people, CUES. Did anybody back at that dump ever think of that? CUES! We're about to go on, here, folks. Let me know, I've got to know so I don't look like an asshole."

"Too late," Martine muttered.

Tom Blakely laughed and patted her hand.

Flynn ranted until cued to the end of his package. He stopped, turned back to the camera, ran a hand through his mop of hair, smiled and picked up on his cue like the true professional he was convinced he was, finished the live report and tossed it back to Will in the studio.

"Back to you, Will, nice to have you on board."

"Nice to be here, Roger. Thanks for the warm welcome."

Tom Blakely snorted beside him.

"See you tomorrow before the game, Roger." The cameras shifted to a new shot that replaced the boxes holding Roger and Will's heads with a wide view of the three people on set: Will, Tom and Martine.

"Well, that was fun," Will said with a smile. "Should be a good game."

"Indeed," Blakely said with his serious, sonorous tones. How he got his voice that deep and profound with only two testicles was beyond Will's comprehension.

Will turned to the camera.

"Make sure you watch us tomorrow. I'm sure Roger will have more insights." He paused. "About the game."

Martine turned away. Blakely froze a smile and marched on.

"Speaking of insights, Will, you've got quite a history and reputation in professional cycling, don't you?"

"I spent some time riding in Europe."

"Did quite well, too, if I remember correctly."

Will was fairly sure that Tom didn't remember much of anything before noon today but he nodded his head politely.

"Yeah. I rode in the Tour de France a few times. Paris-Roubaix. A few other races, a lot of other teams. It was quite a life."

He turned to the camera again.

"But nothing like trying to do this," he turned back to Blakely and Martine, "each and every day. How you two do it, how this staff does it, is just beyond me."

He turned back to the camera again.

"It's tougher than it looks, friends. It is tougher than it looks."

"Well," Martine said, "so is riding a bike, at least through the Colorado mountains and on the course that has been created for the Zephyr Classic in ten days. Will, you rode the course this week. What did you think?"

"Think? Thinking really had nothing to do with it."

Before he could say anything else, the package began and everyone in the studio turned to the monitors to watch. One of the floor directors stepped over to the wall and turned up the audio monitor so everyone could hear as well.

Will knew that the package was coming, but it still surprised him. He had-n't gotten a chance to read the introduction as they had planned, a little set up that went from three shot to single shot to package, clearly a smooth transi-tion since no one was screaming at him.

He turned his attention to the screen and watched as he struggled up toward Wondervu, then bounced over the railroad tracks at the bottom, then sprinted through Blackhawk and powered down Oh My God Road. Martine made a face and looked away for a moment, convinced that Will was going to miss the turn, sail off into the ether and die a painful death on the sharp and pointy rocks below. He had made the ride, but he turned away as well, convinced of the very same thing.

Music was running through the background. Dynamic music of struggle backed the charge up Guanella, flying down the gravel on the other side, and zipping up and over Kenosha, then some John Tesh rhythmic stuff across the flats of South Park, and then dark and throbbing music for the slog over Hoosier. The video focus was as much on the crappy weather and a close up of Will's nose, running like a fire hydrant , as the ride itself.

Martine looked away again.

Will crossing the imaginary line in Breckenridge, flashing down Main Street in the driving rain, Dwyer with the camera running up to him as he coasted to a stop and leaned over the handlebars.

Will peered at the image.

He didn't remember this part.

"How was the ride? How was the ride," you could hear Dwyer call from behind the camera.

The shot showed Will's tired face, dripping with both sweat and rain, turn-ing to the camera, and pausing for a moment before whispering, "never again, never again."

The camera held on his exhausted, dirty, wet, face for a long moment, then faded to black. Within a second the camera faded back up to the three on the set, all still intently staring at the monitors built into the desk.

Tom Blakely looked up, shook his head in some rough approximation of amazement and said, quietly, "We'll be right back."

Within moments, the guy with the couches and the tigers was back and the station was in commercial.

Will leaned back, the sudden relaxation, the sudden release of pressure, giving him the sense that the best thing he could possibly do right now was puke his guts up for the next thirty days.

Martine winked at him. Tom Blakely turned and said, quite seriously, "Rough start. Nice job. Good story. You'll get there. You'll get there."

Will nodded his thanks and rose up out of the seat to go back into the newsroom.

His back was soaked, the jacket so wet it was a different hue, his hands were clammy and his legs didn't want to move. He shuffled, more than walked toward the studio door.

He loosened the tie, but the knot was wet from the sweat and makeup running down his neck, and untying it took some doing as well. He continued to shuffle alone, back toward the newsroom and the post mortem he knew lay just beyond. He stood before the door, took a deep breath, pushed it open and walked in to the sound of long and sustained applause.

Everywhere he looked, people were smiling. Barbara. Bill. Dale. Jim. Terry. Frank Makarios. Shirley the Receptionist. Even Andy Andropoulos, the grand high muckety-muck of the station.

Andy was nodding his head up and down.

Only one person in the newsroom wasn't applauding. That was Elliott the Entertainment Reporter. He recoiled from Will with undisguised distress.

"My jacket! My goddamned jacket! What the hell did you do in it? Go swimming!?!"

CHAPTER TEN:

THE MARK OF ZORRO

ZORRO HAD LUCKED OUT. HE HAD DROPPED HIS HEAD STRAIGHT DOWN onto the point of a pencil, but rather than piercing the eye, the point had slid between the eyeball and the right corner of the socket, merely scratching one side of the eye. He was an extremely lucky bastard.

Now he sat in the sports office, staring at the computer with his one good peeper, the other covered with a huge patch of gauze, goo, guard and tape.

When he had come back that morning, every pencil in the building had been fitted with a one-by-one-inch chunk of Styrofoam on the tip. He hadn't laughed.

Everybody else did, but he didn't. Something else was on his mind.

"You think you're set now, don't you," he muttered to Will after a half hour stretch of silence in the sports office.

"What do you mean?"

"I mean, you think you're set now. I'm injured. You're anchoring. Got it made."

Will nodded. He had wondered when this hydra head of TV land was going to be raising its ugly head. Jesus. Where in the world did you find so many big egos more fragile than spun glass Christmas balls?

He looked over at Zorro slumped in his chair, staring straight ahead at his computer screen, one eye staring at one eye, his lower lip jutting out in an angry little pout.

"Enough," whispered Will. "Look, Zorro. I like you. I really do. And that doesn't matter one damned bit if I'm also out to get your job. I just had a job taken away from me. Stolen. Just like you think I'm doing to you. It was stolen by somebody who spent a lot of time dancing around in the background, trying to get it. I'm not dancing and I'm not trying and I don't want it.

"Sitting out there with Tom and Martine is one of the most boring experiences of my life. Having to work weekends is against my religion. Always has been."

Even though I've done it for years, he thought.

"There is no way in God's green earth I want your job. I don't know mine. I sweat like a pig every time I'm out there. I'm bored to tears. And I just want to get back into the editing booth and finish whatever it is I'm working on."

"Really?"

"Really, man. I don't want it. No fun at all."

"You're not shittin' me?"

"No, I'm not shittin' you. I don't know enough about this business to take it. I'm too rough on the air to take it. I don't want it enough to take it. And besides, it's yours. You're too good."

He paused.

"And I don't steal things from friends."

Zorro stared at the computer screen for a moment, then turned, and with one glistening eye, offered Will his hand.

"Thanks. Thanks for thinking that way. Thanks for saying that."

"No problem. It's your job. You're stuck with it."

He laughed. "Newsroom says you did a good job."

"No. What the newsroom is really saying is I dodged the bullet. Except for the one dead bluegill incident in a tease, I got through it without throwing up. That's a cause for celebration. There are a lot of definitions in this world today of what makes up a 'good job.'"

"Maybe, but you've set little Barbara's heart all atwitter. You're the second coming of Steve Montoya."

"Who?"

"Reporter dropped in here a few years back. Small market guy. Good style. Good look. Okay, you know, but with a lot of confidence and a good voice. Huge voice, a real three-nut job. Worked here for two years and the network hired him away bang. And he popped up on one of their newsmagazine shows. He's a big anchor in Atlanta now."

"Not bad."

"Yeah. Well, Barbara is convinced that she created him, rather than just giving him a launching pad. And since that moment, the moment of *his* success, she's been trying to make lightning strike twice."

"How's that?"

"Just short of jamming lightning rods into our heads. So, you can see why I got the feeling that you were doing the same leapfrogging and such."

"Don't be so paranoid, bud."

He chuckled darkly.

"It's the nature of the business, Will. It'll suck you in as well. You never learn anything. No one tells you anything. You get a sense. Some feeling that the rhythm of the job is off. Each day doesn't quite play out the way you expect it to—the managers fight you on story ideas, they leave you out of conversations, you ask to see them and they're never available. You start hearing rumors and seeing new faces around, and even your pals in the newsroom don't quite seem right to you, and then, pop, you're slung out onto the sidewalk behind the studio. Quick, painless. Get gone. And all the people who were your friends watch you leave through the great glass windows of the newsroom waving sadly while thinking 'Thank God, thank God, better you than me, pal, better you than me.'"

Will knew the feeling. That same intense cold hand of that same reality had squeezed his heart any number of times in the past.

"So, whether you like it or not, Will Ross, that's the business you have chosen. Or, in your case, has chosen you. When the bomb falls on you, I promise you this: I will watch you go in sadness.

"But I will also be thinking to myself, 'better you than me, pal, better you than me.' And I hope you do the same when the hair breaks and the sword falls on me."

Will sat silently for a moment, then put out his hand.

"You've got it Zorro. You've got it."

They shook. And the atmosphere of the room immediately brightened.

Will turned back to his computer screen and stared at the day's rundown for the five o'clock Saturday show, another hour-long news barge, another endless ride down the river of life, with nothing to speed up the progress of time, and little sandbars of commercials slowing the progression even more.

It was Saturday. Nothing happened on Saturday.

Then he smiled. Until next week.

Next week was the race.

That would be something happening. That would get him out of the station and off the set and back into the real world.

As real as any cycling world could possibly be.

He glanced at the red message light on his phone. It was dark. No calls from the mysterious stranger, not for days. No contact at all. It had reached the point where Will went whole stretches of time without thinking about it.

But he was there, something deep in a more primitive portion of his brain told Will. He was still out there somewhere. Still out there. And he was clearly someone to still take seriously, as hard as Will might try to forget that notion.

❦

THREE CREATURES OF LIGHT.

Three creatures of sound.

Three creatures of death.

Three announcements into the world.

The soldering iron glowed too hot and broke the connection.

He cursed.

The primary was finished and ready to place.

The special added attraction was ready, waiting only to be handled.

The secondary, though, the secondary was giving him fits. Maybe he had just grown tired and clumsy today. Maybe he was trying too much. Maybe when you try this much, the quality suffers over all. Maybe. Maybe it was just too small. Maybe. It was going to be tough to plant anyway. Too many people. Too many. Whatever. He sat back and raised the loupe to the top of his forehead. Too much. Step away from it. It's too much for right now.

You've still got a week, he thought. Still got a week.

He carefully covered the RDX, he didn't want that floating around the room. He put away the Semtex and the remaining C-4. He'd have to get more of that at some point. Problem was, his last contact had been arrested and was cooling his heels for the next fifteen to twenty somewhere in the middle of Kansas.

He'd have to find a new source. Shouldn't be tough. It was out there if you knew which rock to look under. It was out there.

He covered everything and then turned his attention to the nitroglycerin.

This went somewhere special. He slowly and carefully slid it back into the padded box, each small glass-stoppered bottle held firmly in place by a cloth frame. No movement. No heat. No cold. No disturbance.

Not until this time next week, when he would call upon it to unleash its terrible, glorious, beautiful power.

He had never really used nitro in the past. Too unstable. Too inelegant, he thought. Never allowed for a lot of creativity.

Ah, but the creativity was in the soul of the creator, now, wasn't it? The creator. And he was the creator. He could give life and he could bring it to an end. He could do it with love, he could do it with pain.

Just like Daddy.

The door opened in his mind and he could see the concrete steps leading down to the basement. He could hear the screams rising up as his father threatened his mother and his sister. As he hit, and hit, and hit once more.

"Goddamn you—don't be forgetting again! I work my ass off and I expect some appreciation around here for what I do! Everyday I work at that goddamned mill and I expect appreciation for what I do. I don't get it from those candy-ass college boys in their goddamned glass offices, but I do expect it from you!"

"Daddy! No, please!"

"Carl! Stop!"

"I can—I can and I will kill you if I damned well feel like it! I brought you into this world and I can take you out of it. I"—*swat*—"expect"—*swat*—"some"—*swat*—"thanks, goddamn you!"

And he proved that. He proved that with Bobbi and Momma whenever she tried to protect her daughter.

And, so, it fell to him to protect them, to release them.

And he did. And he did. All three. Bobbi from her pain. Momma from her shame. Daddy from his evil.

I forgot something, he said, some homework, and he jumped out of the car and had just made it inside and across the kitchen when Daddy turned the key to start the car and back the huge Oldsmobile into the driveway.

The car lifted into the air and Daddy began his long, slow drive to hell.

The creator had died, thanks to three wires, two blasting caps and four sticks of ancient dynamite stolen from the dairy farm over the hill.

The creator was dead. Long live the creator. And yet, there had to be someone to take his place.

There always had to be a creator.

And that someone, that someone, was him.

And this time, this time the creator had found the perfect place and the perfect container and the perfect target.

Perfect.

So you won't thank me, Will Ross? You won't take the time to thank me properly for all my hard work? You ignore my messages? You don't take my calls?

You reroute me to the police station or put me on an immediate trace?

Bad form. Bad form.

So, you won't thank me.

Then, you will damn me.

You will damn me for the rest of your days.

And will never know how you brought it all upon yourself.

He turned out the light and walked up the stairs toward the sounds of a TV blasting out a rerun of *The Simpsons*.

CHAPTER ELEVEN:

IN THE GATE

THE QUIET AT THE STATION WAS NARCOTIC IN ITS EFFECT. THE EXCITEMENT of the last few days had settled, the summer days stayed long and hot and lazy, while the pace of news—spot, live, long form or otherwise—seemed to draw to a long and languid stop.

The race rose up ahead—five days, then four, then three—with Will quietly putting together stories along the way. But he was in no rush, occasionally dropping everything to anchor for Flynn or Zorro, now returning on Friday from his brush with a pencil point, then stepping easily back into his stories again: the race, the climbs, the primes, the history of racing in Colorado, features on Davis Phinney and Connie Carpenter Phinney and the bikes themselves. One news manager desperately tried to get a story about doping included. Will didn't see the point, and, thankfully, neither did Barbara. Sessions had raised an eyebrow, but had let it go, bless his pointed little head.

Finding pictures and props was proving to be a challenge, unless Will wanted to go back out on the course, which he most assuredly did not want to do. How are you going to illustrate this or that, or this moment, or that climb? Some of the ride from last week was usable, but the video already had an old feel to it, seven days after the fact.

The key words had become something new, something different, something compelling. Will didn't know what was compelling in a story about climbing your guts out. Maybe pictures of the guts actually exiting, he thought. Eh, maybe not. Despite its age, Will used The Beast for one story, then gave up the fight and went for a tricked-out little number that one of the photographers paid the price of a small home for just because the same kind of bike had been used in The Tour.

"This one has actually been in The Tour," Will whined, holding up The Beast by the top tube, "it's not based on a design. It is a design."

"Yeah, a design from the first Tour," the kid replied, then insisted on his Postal Service Trek.

What the hell, Will thought, and put it on the air. It was after all, a sweet bike and the kid was into it, he figured justifiably, given the price tag. Will shuddered. He had never paid retail for a bike in his life. That was changing. He was going to have to learn. Big price tags awaited him for everything from his personal rides to the kiddie bikes that Gooch would demand. Hundreds of kiddie bikes. One for each new inch of growth.

He shuddered again and did the story.

Oddly enough, the more stories he did, the less he thought about them as he did them, the better the stories seemed to turn out.

He stood around, interviewed somebody, looked at what pictures he had, typed a little bit of narration, squeezed the water out all along the way, recorded the narration, handed it to the photographer or editor and stepped back, hoping that once again they could turn chicken shit into chicken salad. More often than not they did. Will mentally picked out the names and faces that he knew he could rely on to make him look better than he ever really was on air.

There was a bit of magic in that as well as in riding, in doing just about anything worth doing in the world. Will figured you do it, you do it right and somehow, just somehow, there had to be magic in it for those who loved to pick up its daily challenge.

He watched the story unfold on the air, saw Barbara nod at the screen in her office, then Sessions pop his head out the door, give a quick look around, catch Will's eye and offer him a thumbs up. Ah, instant gratification, approval, line two, no waiting.

Will nodded at Sessions, checked with the news desk to make sure he was no longer needed, then picked up his bag, walked into the men's room and changed into his riding gear.

The station was still close enough to downtown to do this, lost in the Golden Triangle of Denver, just south of Downtown. An area littered with six different television stations, four network affiliates, an independent and a PBS, all within about eight blocks of each other. Enough microwaves floated around the neighborhood that a cheese sandwich thrown from the top of an apartment building would hit the ground toasted.

Will figured it couldn't be healthy, but was just another danger of modern life.

If the microwaves didn't get you the bullets would. If the diesel fumes didn't get you the high-fat diet would. If the traffic didn't squash you, a runaway light rail train would use you as a hood ornament.

Welcome to the 21st Century.

As he waved to no one in particular and carried his bike to the front door, Will honestly thought that he'd rather take his chances with radiation and heart disease. At the turn of the last century, a cold could kill you. Now all you got was a runny nose and a prescription you didn't need.

He knocked on Shirley's window and waved at her.

"Night, Will," she called out behind him as he stepped through the main doors of the building.

He strapped on his helmet, threw his leg over the seat and gingerly lowered his butt onto it. He had put the soft leather European seat back on the bike, but realized as soon as he slid onto it and pushed off that "soft leather" was a misnomer. It was no such thing anymore.

His ass had grown old and soggy and demanding of comfort. Much more comfort than this, that was for sure. There were also still a few tweaks from the week before still remaining. Seven or eight days before when he had ridden the course, it had damned near killed him. Knees, ankles, back and butt. Now only the *derriere* continued to complain. Loudly.

He stretched, certainly not as much as he needed to, then pushed off, using the down slope in the driveway of the station to get him rolling and down into the turn of the parking lot.

He shifted gears, cut across the main streets, heavy with late afternoon traffic, and cut into the neighborhoods. It wasn't much of a ride from work to home, not much at all, fifteen to twenty minutes max, if he didn't push it.

But tonight, he felt like pushing it.

The job was going well. He was feeling happy. Life had turned on a dime for him and everything past the new starting line seemed bright and pregnant with hope and opportunity. He was succeeding, succeeding as he never had before in his life.

Job. Money. Notoriety. He was respected, on a somewhat small and limited basis, but it was a start. In one week, he had gone from Flynn's FNG to a member of the TV6 sports staff, despite the fact that Flynn still seemed to hate his guts and Zorro slid back and forth between "you're my best friend," and "you're after my goddamned job, you bum."

Left turn home. Right turn gone.

He turned right. This was a night to extend it just a bit, stretch the muscles, find the center, release the magic and chase it down the road. As the sun dropped lower in the sky, as the shadows grew longer, Will could feel the breeze cool, taking the edge off the piercing Colorado heat of a late-summer day. There was really no place like this, he thought, no place in the world.

He slammed on the brakes as a car missed a stop sign and blew through the intersection, missing Will by inches, the driver flipping him off as he raced past.

Well, even magic apples contained the occasional worm, he thought. He pedaled on, using the adrenaline caused by very nearly seeing the word Ford imprinted on his left cheek to pick up the pace, drop him down to the Cherry Creek Bike path and then back up along Speer to University.

Where shall I travel today? He wondered, Where should I go? There was more of the Cherry Creek path, the Highline was ahead, that could take him so far east of town that he could spit his way into Kansas. He could run south into the suburbs, then bring himself back up on the Platte River Greenway. Any number of choices, distances, backgrounds, rides.

Where was it?

Where was it hiding today?

He glanced over his right shoulder and took a quick look at the sun. Ninety minutes to two hours left, he figured, before he was using a white cane to find his way home. Maybe Cheryl would send Rex and Shoe out to look for him.

Which way?

Which way?

This way. He turned south on University and dropped off the bike path into a narrow, pebble-strewn bike lane that ran alongside the traffic. No one seemed to notice him, but brushed close in the race home from work, and within a few blocks he didn't notice them either. After a time, he knew, you sensed changes in traffic. You sensed danger coming up on your right or left, ahead or behind, but beyond that instinct, you simply rode. It was the only way to get anywhere.

Through the University of Denver campus and across Evans, down to Hampden, Belleview, Orchard, Dry Creek and County Line. Across on County Line to the west and up Santa Fe, a street where everyone drove as if they were in bumper cars and they had paid their fifty cents and, by God, were going to get their money's worth. A jog to the Platte and the bike path, heading north and out of the traffic, while the sun slowly set to the west, losing itself first in the mountains and then the foothills and then the developments at the foot of the Rockies. He pedaled on, digging in more and more, no longer sitting back and simply riding, but now chasing, looking for the power of the road, seeking out the magic. He was feeling somewhere deep within him, once again, the burning need to go farther, faster, longer, the need to win and win and win and ride and find it, chase it, hold it once again.

Find the magic.

The southern suburbs gave way to the southern city and the southern city led back and forth across the Platte River to Confluence Park, where the path reconnected to Cherry Creek. He turned east, surprised by the lack of traffic on the path, but then again not surprised at all, since it never seemed to be crowded at all in August. May, June and parts of July, you couldn't move on this path, with the cyclists and walkers and Roller Bladers here, there and everywhere. Now, in mid-August, with the summer drawing to a close and everyone sick of exercising until next May, he had it pretty much all to himself.

Himself and the homeless.

He kept an eye out for them. You never knew when one person or two would block the path, inadvertently or on purpose, and he was never sure how to react to them: like his dad and scream "get a job"; or like his mom and give them everything in the house.

He didn't have anything on him tonight, so the question was already answered for him, but that didn't stop the question from crossing his mind, as it did every night, every day, every time he rode, drove, or walked through downtown.

And after all of his thought, the path was empty this evening. The question was moot.

Life rolled ahead, with the wind at his back, the sun creating long, frail shadows, dark, thin arrows pointing the way toward home, final goodbyes until tomorrow morning before him.

He left the path near Channel 7, cut down Seventh to Pennsylvania, then worked his way back and forth, to Colorado, across the street that was little more than a moving parking lot sixteen hours a day, and cut behind University Hospital.

Home was just ahead.

And as he slowed down to make the final turns, now sitting up on the bike, he once again smiled, in full possession of the magic.

❧

"ARE YOU GOING TO TELL HIM?"

"Am I going to tell him what?"

"Are you going to tell him what the police said?"

"What the police said about what?"

"What the police said about his stalker? That maybe, just maybe, there is something to be afraid of? The whole Crooked Lake business?"

Barbara watched as the sunlight faded and lights began to come on in the downtown Denver office buildings, six blocks away. She teased her hair, pulling one piece, then another free, and twisting them, slowly, sensuously, as if the answer to her problem was somewhere in the follicles.

Bill Sessions shook his head.

"A pilot has got to know what he's flying into, Barbara. That is one of your first rules."

"I know. I know," she said, twisting her hair harder, her eyes focused outside the building on a point and an issue that was farther away than she thought.

She released her hair and turned back to Sessions, leaning down and forward on the desk, fixing him with a hard stare.

This, he thought, was the Barbara Gooden he knew and loved, the one who would find a decision, know it was right, infuse it with the bright light of journalistic morality and then hold to it through the maelstrom that would most assuredly come.

"They're just dealing with suspicions? No one knows anything for sure? Right?"

Sessions didn't answer.

"Right?" she repeated.

"Right," he whispered with resignation.

"Fine. They're not sure about anything. These are just suspicions. Suppositions on their part. Anything they say, they're just guessing at. Let's keep our eyes open, watch Will this weekend, get through this race and hope for the best. I'm still thinking we've just got a goon out there who likes TV people. Wants to be on TV. I don't know that we've got the mad bomber loose in Denver."

"Okay," Sessions said quietly.

"Bill, you don't sound like you agree. Well, I'm sorry. Will is a concern and I am concerned for his safety. We'll keep him on a tight leash all this weekend and then on Monday, after the race, we'll let him know what the police are thinking and saying."

"Making it sound like we just heard it, right?"

"Bill, the police told me not to say anything. I'm not even supposed to know any of this—I've got contacts inside the department. I can't jeopardize them on suspicions. And truth be told, the station has got a lot invested in this race. Will is part of that investment. We can't just hand it off to Roger or Zorro because we're afraid some obsessed fan is going to try to hurt Will. And, frankly," she said, waving her hand, "I don't think Will would go much for that, either. Do you?"

"Probably not."

"What is it? Something about this is bothering you."

"It's nothing."

"Spill it."

Bill Sessions stared at her hard, for a moment, trying to fathom the thought process that was going on somewhere behind those icy blue eyes. He had never been able to do it before, so why he thought he could now was anybody's guess.

But he did. He hoped, he looked, he tried but he could not find it. He turned, walked to the window and stared out at the mountains, the peaks now shuttered in shadow, backlit with what he liked to call "God Light," all golden rays and pronounced cloud formations.

It was a beautiful view from here. Looking back from there it wasn't pretty at all.

"What? Come on, Bill."

"Frankly, Barbara," he said sharply, with a sudden turn, "this sucks. And, I hate you when you're like this. I truly do. It isn't very often, but when its there, it's just the ugliest goddamned thing I know. You get this manager's mentality and you start thinking of the bottom line and getting the programming on, no matter what it takes or whom it hurts. It doesn't happen often. Your feelings for that group of people out there," he swung his hand toward the door leading to the newsroom, "are greater than anyone I've ever known in this business, but sometimes, sometimes, goddamn it, you make me nuts."

"I do, huh?"

"Yeah, you do, huh. I don't know what sets it off—Andy or some call from corporate, but you get all white shirt, red tie, dark suit on us. That's not what news is, kid, and you know it. You—YOU—taught that to me. News is a living breathing thing that demands—demands—that it be free from the bottom line."

"Within reason."

"Screw reason. You want reason, go work for the *National Enquirer.* They make a shitload of money doing a shitload of shit news. Here, you gotta be fair, you've gotta be mean, you've gotta have guts. And—you've got to let your people know what's up, even if it means that person says, 'screw you, I ain't doing your goddamned bicycle race.' "

He had spent himself in the effort. He slumped down in a chair in front of her desk.

She silently watched him for a moment, then leaned back in her chair, took another strand of hair, and began to wind it again.

"You're goddamned lucky I hate violence. I should throw you through that window for that little speech."

Sessions sighed. "Sorry, but I'm right. And you know it."

She stared at him for what seemed like a very long time, her eyes dancing as the argument raged inside her head. She knew it. She knew what had to be done, in terms of the station, programming and the company, but none of it, none of it at all, seemed to really matter. Where was the answer? Where did it lie?

But she knew all along. Barbara nodded. The dam burst and she felt the old argument slipping away in the rush of ethics. She knew. She knew what had to be done. Not for the corporate reason, but for the right one.

"Thank you, Bill," she said, quietly.

He didn't move.

"You're right. He deserves better. They," she pointed at the newsroom, "deserve better. Thanks for keeping me on track."

Bill Sessions relaxed. He nodded.

"Thank you, Barbara."

"No, thank you."

"Let's not get into that—just know, Barbara, that I thank you for being the boss you are and being the journalist you are and being the manager you are—but—more than anything, I thank you for being the person, the human being that you are."

They were silent for another long moment.

"Thank you for that. I appreciate it. Sorry I let it get away from time to time."

"That's nothing to be ashamed of, especially in your case, because you walk a fine line between corporate and human needs, and keep coming down on the right side—whatever that side may be, whatever is right for that situation. It's a delicate balancing act. You do it well."

"But I look like shit in tights."

"Brad and the boys don't think so—and they're the only ones who matter, aren't they?"

She smiled at the thought of her family. She turned to the picture of the tall, slightly balding man and the two blond-headed boys that held a position of honor on her desk. She nodded.

"I suppose you're right."

"Think if it was you. Think if it was them."

Tears welled up in her eyes. She waved her hand as if to silence him, and began to nod.

"I will. I will talk to him first thing tomorrow." She ran a finger under her nose. "Damn you. And I'm out of Kleenex."

"First rule of photo-journalism: don't let them wipe. It makes for better pictures."

"You're full of first rules tonight, aren't you?"

"You bet. Here's another one. Sessions' first rule of the newsroom: When your mission's finished, go home."

He stood and extended his hand. She stood, took it and they shook.

"Thanks," he said.

"Thank you."

"See you tomorrow."

"First thing, Bill. First thing."

He smiled and walked out. She watched him go, gather his things, turn out the light in his office and close the door behind him. He gave her one last wave as he walked toward the newsroom door.

Barbara sat down again and turned to stare at the mountains, now darkly framed in the gathering dusk. She'd have to tell Ross tomorrow.

That was the right thing to do.

She would have to tell him that maybe this was more than just another station stalker, another loser who has fallen in love with an anchor, thinks a TV show is real, or thinks that celebrity is something that rubs off just by being close.

She would have to tell him that maybe, just maybe, this threat was real. She would have to tell Will that something found in the bottom of Crooked Lake made the police think they were dealing with something other than an accident, with something other than a copycat or a wanna-be.

She'd have to tell him that maybe, just maybe, his life was on the line this Saturday, that the bike race was a target and that Will Ross of TV6 Sports was in the crosshairs.

Maybe.

She'd have to tell him all of that.

Maybe.

Tomorrow.

Maybe.

CHAPTER TWELVE:

THE FLAG IS UP

FRIDAY WAS SPENT GATHERING.

Gathering gear. Gathering clothes. Gathering last-minute bits and pieces for Saturday's race. Will was in the station and out of the station, checking with engineers about where the live truck would be tonight, and then tomorrow along the route, checking with producers as to where and when they wanted their live shots both today and then first thing tomorrow, checking with the assignment desk about who would give him a ride up to Boulder and how the hell he'd ever get back from Breckenridge.

"We got you a room."

"Right, in Boulder, for tonight."

"Yeah, but we got you a room in Breckenridge for Saturday night, too."

"No. I'm comin' home on Saturday night. Find out who's coming back after the live show and put me in their car. There ain't no way I'm staying up there when I could come home and sleep in my own little bed."

"Free night out ... eh?"

"No thanks. Just get me home."

"Company's payin'."

"No, just get me the hell home." God, what was it with these people? Save the money, get me home. Simple concept. There was no reason to stay and party with people he didn't really know all that well after he had spent the day cooped up in a news car traveling the 140-mile bicycle course.

"Home. Think about it. Do it. Simple."

The assignment editor looked at the dry-erase board and checked the afternoon assignments.

"Home. Got it, Will. Tony C. will take you up to Boulder this afternoon and be the photog on your live shots from the starting line."

"Who?" Will said, so surprised to the point that he stood back a step from the desk and shook his head.

"Tony C. Tony Carver. Dwyer's out with Flynn. You got a problem with Tony?"

"No, no. God no. I was just ... just thinking about somebody else."

"What time to you want to leave?"

"When do you suggest?"

"Boulder live at four. Traffic ... I'd say no later than 2:30."

"Okay, just have Tony," Will he paused, remembering another, "C. touch base with me in the sports office. We'll go from there."

"You got it, Will."

Live shots. Live shots. He had to remember what each one was about and to take the earpiece along with him for the IFB, the little single channel radio receiver that played back station audio from the live truck. Then he could hear his cues, along with the producer breaking to tell him what to do and when the hell to get off. Little things. He had to remember tons of little things.

This business was nothing but little things. Turn this way then. Turn that. Eyebrow up for emphasis, let it down. Squeeze the water. Talk to the camera. Be personable, but credible. Don't be a goof. Remember your hair, your earpiece, your makeup. No sunglasses on the air, even if the sun is making your face look like a two-year-old prune. Emphasize the vowels only for emotion. Emphasize consonants to make a point of logic.

Oh, yeah, and remember your story. Don't forget to do your story. Don't forget your roll cue so they know when to start the video. Otherwise, while you're babbling out on location, they're laughing their asses off back in the control room, taking pity on you only when they run out of time and need to move on to something else in the show. Then, and only then, they'll start your package. Laughing their asses off all the way.

He walked over to the sports office to go through his bag once again, to check and recheck all the little things he had to make sure he remembered. Once he started toward Boulder this afternoon, there would be no going back to pick up something he had left behind.

Shit. This was worse than packing for The Tour.

As he walked across the atrium, he spotted Barbara Gooden heading the other way, along the carpeted outer track, deeply involved with some piece of paper.

"Hey, Chief," he called out with a wave.

"Hello, Will," she said, glancing up quickly and then returning to her paper.

He continued walking. She continued walking. They both walked into their respective offices on the opposite sides of the atrium.

And for that moment, the atrium was silent, except for the sound of the visitor's TV monitor, quietly playing back the sights and sounds of another day on TV6.

CARVER WEAVED IN AND OUT OF TRAFFIC ON HIGHWAY 36, ALMOST CHALLENGING the law enforcement of three communities to pull him over. He drove like Will's grandfather had, sprawled out, fingers barely touching the steering wheel, going ninety miles-an-hour. Will tightened his seat belt and gritted his teeth for the impending collision with something—car, animal, concrete piling—that was sure to come.

"So, you were a pro rider, once, huh?" Carver said.

"Yeah, about twelve years or so."

"Rode all over Europe, Dwyer said."

"Yeah."

"Win anything?"

"A few races. Mostly, I was cannon fodder for the big guys."

"What's that mean?"

Will had been getting better at explaining this over the past few days to people who had little or no concept of what cycling was all about.

"It's like I was hired to hit nothing but sacrifice flies so that the big stars of the team could make all the runs."

"Jesus, that sucks."

"It does indeed," Will chuckled, darkly. He gripped the console tightly as they missed the back end of a slower car by a mere quarter of an inch. "How about you, Tony? You do a lot of sports coverage?"

"Naw. Not much. I'm divorced and I've got my boys. They live with me. So I don't have much chance to go out of town for games anymore. Do some stuff in town on occasion. Don't travel much, though. This is my one connection to the race. Do the live shots, then go home and be Super Dad."

"That's gotta be tough."

"It's not easy. But they're good boys."

Both men nodded, then lapsed into silence. Will pondered the challenge this guy had to have: working full time, being a dad, doing the single parent thing with a half-gainer and a twist. He couldn't help but wonder what happened.

And he couldn't help but wonder what would happen to him. Could he be a dad? Could he do this? It was too late to be askin' this sort of thing, but the question was there, nonetheless. Could he be a dad at all? The responsibilities, at times, seemed overwhelming, but there was no turning back now. He was going to be a dad. He'd have to learn. Just like Tony had, and his own dad had and every other dad had who ever lived and cared. You just decided to do it. And you did it.

'Nuff said.

"What?" Tony turned away from the video race game he was playing on Highway 36 and stared at Will. "What'd you say?"

"Nothing. Nothing at all." Will changed the subject. "You like being a dad?"

"Best thing in the world. Nothing like it. Nothing better."

"If I can ask, and you can tell me to stuff it, how'd you lose your wife?"

He snorted.

"You make it sound like I misplaced her. Left her at the mall."

"Sorry."

"Naw. No. It's okay. No problem. She left me. Suddenly decided she didn't want to be married anymore."

"Why'd she leave the kids with you? I thought they usually went with the mom."

"Well, she loves 'em, but she didn't much want to be a mom anymore, either. And when I dug in my heels and said, 'they stay,' she said, 'ok,' and made herself scarce."

"Shit, that's cold."

"That's why they call the wind Mariah. Especially in February."

Will chuckled.

"You're going to be a dad, right? Somebody at the station told me."

"Yeah. Not much longer, now, really, four, five weeks."

"Good stuff, man. Good stuff. You're gonna love it. Believe me, no matter what else I ever accomplish in my life, I've accomplished something with them. Together with Mar or alone, doesn't matter. They are the good stuff. They are the good stuff of my life."

"That's good to know."

"You don't need to know it. Just happens, man. It just happens. Boy, girl, doesn't matter. You're gonna love it."

Will smiled. That part, he knew already.

❊

THE BOULDERADO IS A ONE-HUNDRED-YEAR-OLD HOTEL IN DOWNTOWN, JUST NORTH of the center of the Pearl Street Mall, the rallying point for just about anything that ever happens in the People's Republic of Boulder. With the possible exception of the CU stadium, it's close to everything, with enough style and atmosphere to make it a destination hotel.

Will liked it from the moment he stepped in the door.

He checked in and dropped his gear in his room, sadly a room in the new part of the hotel. It was a great room, but he had wanted one of the classics, one of the rooms that Teddy Roosevelt had stayed in or something. Then Will wandered back to the main lobby where the race organizers were having a press conference. It was open to all the media in town, but only TV6, the sponsor, was there to shoot it. It was as if the race existed only on one channel of reality.

It was likely to stay that way.

The race teams weren't forthcoming at all about strategies or comments on the course. The riders, the few that had come forward or been sent by the teams in sponsor colors, were loathe to let fly with any inside information, or personality, for that matter.

Will sat depressed in the second row, tossing out questions to each of the five riders who were lined up in front, hoping, with dying hope, that one of them, some of them, would suddenly drop the facade and become a character. No such luck. The youngest rider, the amateur, was a possibility. He was excited to be in the company of the pros and be a part of the press conference. He was bouncing off the walls, but it was all too much for him. Whenever a camera turned his way or a question was asked, he rattled off a three or four word answer, Tasmanian-Devil style, then turned to the experienced riders at the table to let them carry the ball.

All Will could think was, Come on, guys, I've gotta sell this thing to an audience who cares more about that video where the dog squats in the middle of Mile High Stadium than this race. You've gotta be excited to get them excited. Be blasé and they'll ignore you, waiting for the baseball scores and the dog poop. You had to break through and none of these guys was doing it.

"How are you going to pace yourselves?"

"What are the killer portions of the race?"

"How does this compare with every other one-day course in the country?"

The rider from Holland realized after a few questions what Will was up to and rose to the bait. He admitted he was a sprinter and not a climber and that this wasn't his kind of course, but that the challenge of riding something like this—for the prize money they were offering—made it something that he just couldn't turn down.

"After all," he said with a smile, "who hasn't wanted to spend one day riding through hell itself?"

Will smiled and nodded. He had his sound bite. Tie that to the race director's comment, repeated endlessly, that this was the American equivalent of Paris-Roubaix, 140 miles of bad roads, heavy traffic—and, in this case, hard climbs—and Will knew he had his story.

He hadn't created anything, hadn't twisted, too much anyway, the facts as he had found them, but he had gone looking for the spice of the story, the excitement he knew existed in this race that no one at the station, or in this event, seemed to understand. It was there. All you had to do was unleash it so people could see it. No, it wasn't as simple and easy to watch and understand as a bunch of guys tossing a ball back and forth in an enclosed stadium. Four plays, take a break, four plays, take a break. Stadium games were built for TV and making money.

But this, this was for those who asked for something more, who asked for their challenges to be grueling, who asked for the drama to be spread out over hours.

Aged over a day, like wine. It wasn't simple, but the drama that was there, Will knew first hand. And, somehow, he was going to convey that to the television audience of Denver, an audience that had known cycling once, in the days of the Red Zinger and the Coors Classic, and had seemingly let it go forever.

It was back, and by God, Will was going to make it interesting. There was no way in hell he could stick with a job in the sports department if all he ever got to cover was baseball, football, basketball and hockey.

There was more to the sporting life.

The news conference ended. Will marked his sound bites, took the tape from Carver and walked down to where the engineer was waiting in the live truck.

"Do we have a shot in to the station yet?"

"Oh, yeah. Easy from here. Point the dish at Bow Mountain, hit low power and you're boomin' and zoomin'."

"Thanks, Bill." Will crawled into the truck and sat down in front of the digital editing system, inserted the tape and began rewinding it to the sound he was going to need. Ken, the race director, with his opening remarks, then Kurnitz, the Dutch sprinter, riding to hell and back. He wrote down the times and tore off the sheet, leaving it on the editing console for Carver, who at that moment appeared at the side of the microwave truck loaded down with his gear.

"Did you find your bites?"

"Got 'em. All logged and ready to cut."

"What are you going to use for extra video? In and out stuff? There wasn't much to shoot in there. Never is at a news conference."

"They've got Coors Classic stuff back at the station as well as the video that Dwyer and I shot on the course. Editing is cutting that up."

"Okay. Let me in there and watch the magic begin."

They switched places and Carver began swatting at the briefcase editing station, slapping buttons and switching tapes. It was fun to watch this personal ritual, but Jesus, it couldn't be good for the equipment.

Carver slapped at the machine for five minutes, twisting the shuttles this way and that before slapping again, popped the recorded tape and smiled.

"Magic. What did I tell you. Two bites. Tied tight. We'll let the kids back home worry about the A roll and video out. Billy, I need to feed this back."

Bill Royal took the tape and nodded, gently sliding it back into the editing deck, easily pushing some buttons on the truck panel and quietly dialing in a number on a cell phone.

"This is EJ-3. Ross in Boulder. We're ready to feed, Cathy." He paused for a few moments while Cathy, the engineer back in the feed room, got a tape up and rolling in a machine. "Here you go," Royal said and delicately touched the button, as if he was merely stroking it.

The leader started, the video clips were sent and that, as they say, was that.

"See, Tony," Royal said, with just a hint of sarcasm, "you don't have to beat the machines into submission. Often, they'll do your bidding even if you're easy on them."

"Yeah, yeah," Tony muttered, opening his tripod to set up the live shot.

"No, you see, I've finally got this truck the way I want it. After nearly five years of working on it, it is now—officially—perfect. And I want to keep it that way. And I can't keep it that way if you're going to bash on everything with those goddamned hams you call hands. Okay?"

"Yeah, yeah," Carver muttered, leveling the tripod head.

Will got the idea that this was a regular ritual between the two, that every live shot included had the banging on the machine and the lecture that went with it.

"Will, grab my camera, would you?" Carver said.

"You got it." Will carried the digital Panasonic, lighter than he imagined, over to Tony and set it next to the tripod.

"You're not supposed to do that, but I'm just too goddamned lazy to care."

"That's for sure," Royal called out from the truck.

"Union rules," Carver whispered. "We don't have much of a union, but what we got says that talent ..."

"Such as it is," Royal called out from the truck.

"... isn't allowed to handle the gear. Other markets, bigger markets, with stronger unions, and you would have been grieved for that—or even just carrying the tripod."

"No shit?"

"No shit," Carver answered. "They take this stuff seriously. Not here so much, unless we're pissed at management. Then we grieve everybody. But otherwise, we're happy for the help."

"Okay, I'll keep that in mind," Will answered.

He started gearing up for the first live shot, a quick pop in the four o'clock "News Lite," as it was called around the station. This was Elliott's show for entertainment reports and his chance to rip-off David Spade's "Hollywood Minute" from *Saturday Night Live*.

This was the show with the doctor and the home repair guy and the news you can use—the station's in-your-face, solve-your-problems consumer guy—"Media with an attitude," he'd crow—before he'd leap in to save a life or destroy one on air. The show also had lots of weather reports and traffic, as if the people sitting in it on the Boulder turnpike were somehow watching from the comfort of the driver's seat. Will's shot was strictly promotional: promote the race, promote the five P.M. report, promote the promotions that he'd be promoting in his next stories.

Push the audience on, always push them on to the next story, Gooden told him.

He shoved the little plastic earpiece into his right ear, looped the clear hollow plastic over the top of his ear and clipped the end to the back of his collar. He snapped the tiny receiver to the end of the earpiece, then ran the line down the middle of his back to the wireless IFB receiver. He flipped it on and could hear Fast Eddie Slezak reading a news story about an attempted carjacking that left the carjacker squashed in the middle of Colorado Boulevard. Fast Eddie had stayed late today.

Will took the wireless microphone from Tony and clipped the transmitter onto the leading edge of his back pocket, clipped the microphone on his shirt-front, and ran the microphone cable into his shirt, then around the top of his waistband. Reaching behind, he turned it on, then uncomfortably craned his head over to make sure he could see the little red light on the transmitter. Forgetting a microphone, in any way, shape or form, was a cardinal sin in Barbara Gooden's Big Book of Television.

Will could hear the show music start and Eddie go into his "Coming up Next" vocal routine. Sylvia Merrill, the regular anchor of the show, picked up her cues. This was the SuperTease, the end of the first segment and they were up next. Will couldn't hear the commercials, but somebody in the control room had left a switch open and Will could hear the conversations floating around, as if in a dream, all off-mike, all without their knowledge. It was eavesdropping from thirty miles away.

"Tell Elliott to stop whining and get on his little box," Amanda, the director, called out to someone. "No, tell him I don't really give a shit," she said, a tone of comic harshness in her voice. "I don't care if he's in the light or not. If he can't stand in the same place each day, then I'll just take the shot and let America see his right half. What the hell do I care?"

Will could hear chuckles and agreement in the background.

"Tell Ross two minutes," Amanda said.

"Will, two ..." Carver said.

Will nodded and held up his hand.

In the background, even more distant than the rest, Will could hear Elliott complaining that the live shot was cutting into his time and nobody, not nobody, ran before HIM on HIS show or cut into HIS Hollywood segment.

"Someone please tell Elliott to please go fuck himself," Amanda said. The room chuckled around her. Will could hear it all.

"One minute to Ross."

"One minute, Will."

Will nodded and gave the camera a thumbs up.

"Got it."

"Can this guy actually do this shit?" Amanda asked.

"He's doin' okay," Will heard the technical director say.

"He's another Barbara special though, isn't he? Come on in and I'll make you a star? That sort of thing? Thirty seconds."

"Thirty seconds, Will."

Will nodded.

"I mean—can he really do this? This is big time, professional TV. We hire pros ... is he a pro?"

"No, Amanda," Will answered with a laugh, "but Zorro says I'm a gifted amateur."

The control room burst into laughter and over it, and Will could hear Amanda scrambling, laughing at the same time, "Okay, okay, what son of a bitch left a key open ... let's just find it and ..."

The control room sound went dead in his ear and he could hear the end of the commercial break. The restart music began and the show continued.

"We'll have Elliott's *Hollywood Beat* in just a second," Sylvia said, brightly, "but first, let's head up to Boulder, where Will Ross is on the starting line of tomorrow's inaugural Zephyr Classic. Will, how much is this like the old Coors?"

Will knew this question was coming. It was scripted out early on just to get the audience from Eddie and Sylvia on the set to Will on the streets of Boulder. There was very little that was left to chance, up to and including catching a reporter off-guard in a live shot with a question he or she didn't know was coming or had no idea how to answer.

"Well, Eddie, the deal is this—where the Coors was a multi-day race, this is one day—point to point—over some of the most treacherous terrain that Colorado has to offer."

The sound shifted in his ear as the package began, a two-minute cut-down version of Will's ride over the course.

"Tape," Tony said, and relaxed.

Will slumped and listened, everyone standing around and waiting for the end to come. "One minute," Will heard in his ear.

Halfway through.

He continued to relax and listen and look around until he heard "fifteen out" in his ear, at which point he straightened up and looked into the camera, ready for his cue. Tony Carver adjusted the shot. Will heard his final sound, then a slight shift in tone in his ear. Without a cue from the studio he went ahead with his story.

"... and we'll have more, including reactions from the riders and the hopes of the promoters, at five. Eddie? Sylvia?"

"Will, you rode this course," Fast Eddie asked, "is it really as tough as everybody is making it out to be?"

Now, here was a question that Will hadn't been ready for. He thought for a second, trying to think of a direction for the answer, then, just suddenly thought screw it and jumped ahead.

"Look, there are rides in Europe that I would say are longer. There are rides in Europe with worse roads. There are rides in Europe where the climbs are just as tough and long and brutal. But there are no rides in Europe that jam all of these things together into one package like this ride does. This is hell on wheels. No doubt. You add altitude into that and this is the biggest one-day racing challenge in the world."

"Really?"

"Really." It was hyperbole, he knew. But, what the heck. If it got them to tune in ... hey, he was starting to think like Gooden.

"So what is the toughest part? The one toughest part of this whole thing?"
For this question, he didn't have to pause. He didn't have to think.

"Eddie, it's just getting yourself to do it. And be competitive. Halfway through this, there are going to be 120 guys all saying to themselves, 'I shoulda had a V-8.' And they've just got to keep going."

"There you have it, from a guy who rode it. Will Ross, live in Boulder at the starting line of tomorrow's first annual Zephyr Classic. See you at five, Will."

"See you then," Will answered and stood smiling until Tony nodded and said, "clear."

Will relaxed.

The control room popped in his ear.

"Nice job, Will," Amanda said.

"Thank you, Amanda," he answered with a smile. He gave the camera a thumbs up and walked out of frame.

He turned and made sure his microphone was off before he said a single word.

❋

THE REST OF THE NEWSCASTS WENT EASILY. TWO SHOTS IN THE FIVE, THEN ONE IN the ten, both answering Roger Flynn's questions about the course. Will hoped that Flynn had watched the stories and read the information he had left him about the race. He didn't want to wind up carrying Saturday's hour-long show on his own. He had never done this before. He had never tried it. No, just relax. Flynn was a pro. He was a pro. He knew, more than anything else, how to make himself look good on the air—with style and knowledge and attitude. That's what sold on TV, and Will realized that all he had to do was relax, talk to the video and answer Flynn's questions.

It was going to go just fine.

Just fine.

By 10:40, he was in his room at the Boulderado, laying out Saturday's clothes, packing up the extra gear, hoping to just make it all as simple as possible when he sat down in the press car. He changed and stretched out in bed.

He had a live shot in the Saturday morning news, but luckily, it wasn't until 7:10. And it was the same thing he did at ten. Repetition is good for the soul. No one expected anything more.

He picked up the phone and called Cheryl.

"How'd that one look?"

"We liked it. Me and Gooch. I've got to say, Will, you are getting better."

"Thanks."

"You're better than that Flynn guy. You oughta be the main anchor."

"Oh, don't you start. Zorro hears you said that and he'll go into another funk."

"Sorry, but it's true. You've got a sort of natural way about this ... Flynn reminds me of that guy in Michigan on TV when I was a kid, who always shouted everything at the camera and wore bright checked sports coats that made the TV wiggle."

"Hey, it's a style. Besides, the sports networks love that sort of thing—anything you can do to break through to the 'pipples.'"

"Ah, yes, the pipples."

"Now, don't get all outraged about the viewers. I hear that at the station all day. 'The viewers don't get it. The viewers are stupid. The viewers don't appreciate the good stuff ...' Jesus, you and Zorro ought to get together. Or Elliott, the entertainment guy. You can listen to him complain about how nobody appreciates his sarcastic sense of humor."

"Well, they are stupid, sometimes."

"No, they're not stupid. They're just not listening. Nobody pays full attention to anything on TV. We all just let it wash over us. News and cartoons, it's all the same coming out of the box. Look. Think about how we watch the late news. What we watching for?"

"Weather, usually."

"Right. Think about how many times we sit through an entire weather report and then turn to each other and ask, 'what did he say?'"

"I just did that," Cheryl said, sheepishly. "I had to ask Gooch what the guy said, but he was sleeping, too."

"Yeah, so no wonder people yell and wear weird coats and say outrageous things and show the most shocking pictures they can get away with ... They're all screaming 'notice me, notice me, notice me, notice me,' to a bunch of people who aren't paying all that much attention."

"Hmmm. You going to be careful tomorrow?"

"Yeah. All I've got to do is sit in the back of the press car and listen to Race Radio all day. Make notes and do the show at six. You gonna watch?"

"No. Those travel and entertainment shows I like are on Channel 4."

"Thank you."

"Why couldn't you get a job there? I like the people there."

"Thank you. I guess they just didn't see the instinctive television stardom in me like Barbara did over at good ol' TV6."

"And some said his ego grew three sizes that day ..."

"Thank you again. Jeeze, you're just full of 'em tonight, aren't you?"

"I am." She was quiet for a long moment.

"You going to miss it tomorrow?" she asked.

"Hmm. Tough question," Will said, slowly. "I don't know. I've actually been scared that I would, and somehow, even more scared that I wouldn't. That I'd be happy to be out of it. When I'm off the bike, sometimes, I'm just damned glad that I am, but there are other times, when I see somebody ride, and dig deep, that it hurts like hell to be away from it. You wanna go forever. But you can't. You just can't."

"I know. All too well." She yawned.

"Get yourself to bed," he said, "you and Gooch get some rest."

"You, too, love," Cheryl sighed. "What time are you going to be home tomorrow night?"

"About 8:30. Show's done at seven and I'm gone. One of the field producers is coming back to town and she'll drop me."

"Okay. See you then?"

"See you then. Sleep well."

"Doubt it. Your child has been playing soccer with my kidneys the last few nights. But you get a good sleep. You'll need it for tomorrow."

"Well, it's not like I'm really working, but thanks. I love you, Cher."

"I love you, Will. More than you'll ever know."

"Thanks."

"For what?"

"For loving me."

"Most times, it's easy. 'Night."

They were both silent for a moment, then hung up the phones.

Will rolled over, stretched, turned out the light, and laid on his back, staring at the ceiling. Sleep was going to be as difficult to find tonight as the magic of the road was starting to be.

❖

AT THE SAME TIME, AT HER HOME IN AURORA, BARBARA GOODEN HUNG UP THE phone for the third time.

Still busy. Another message left. Call Barbara at home.

The day had gotten away from her. She had started it with such resolve, a resolve to call Will and tell him, despite what her contact at the police department had begged her not to do, but life had intervened. There were the weekly management meetings and then a news meeting and a meeting with the lawyers because one of the younger reporters might have accused someone of murder based on what a family member said on air. The reporter didn't say it, but she let the sister say it, which in the end, meant that the station said it based solely on somebody's emotions. It was a legal minefield if anybody wanted to sue.

Then, Andy got a bug up his ass about something. Andy had come out of sales and he wanted to make sure the client was served and Barbara had to keep reminding Andy that this is a news organization and we can't kowtow to the clients. If we lose a big contract over a story, then so be it, but nobody will ever listen to us if they think we're kissing a sponsor's ass. He grumbled, but he understood. At least he seemed to, and he generally left Barbara alone to deal with the newsroom.

He was a good boss. Sometimes dealing with him was like handling dynamite, but he stood by his people and let them drive their own departments.

Will. Every time she tried to call him it had just gotten away from her. He was on the air. The control room didn't pass on the message. Producers didn't remember to call him.

For a communications business, she thought, they were pretty damned lousy at communicating with each other.

She looked at the clock. 11:15. Chances are he was already asleep.

She'd set her alarm early and make sure that she got in touch with him at the truck right before or after tomorrow morning's live shot.

Sessions had been right, at least at first, she had been avoiding telling Will, but now, she convinced herself, it was just life and circumstances getting in the way.

She held her forehead with her hand.

No, you just can't say that. You just can't. She knew that somewhere, deep down, she had been afraid to tell him. Not just for how he might react, but for what could conceivably happen on that course tomorrow. The course of a race that her station was sponsoring. That her newsroom was committed to covering.

It was too late, now. Too late to back out. Too late to call Will. Too late to start putting up red flags.

Just too damned late. She walked up to bed, knowing that she wouldn't sleep, knowing that the first job in the morning, no matter what life threw at her, was to get in touch with Will Ross.

That she would do.

Despite how the possibilities for the rest of that day frightened the living hell right out of her, that, she would do.

❋

However, another person had no trouble sleeping that night.

He was in a deep sleep and had been since eight.

He had an early morning.

And he always slept well the night before a show.

CHAPTER THIRTEEN:

NEUTRAL START

THE SKY BLAZED COLORADO BLUE.

It forced Will's eyes into a raggedy squint, his nose crumpled up on his face, the moment he stepped out of the hotel. He stood on the steps of the Boulderado and dug for his sunglasses somewhere in the depths of his shoulder bag.

Christ, but he should have known. A sky so blue that it actually hurt was a three hundred day-a-year phenomenon here. Why this morning should be any different was beyond him. Still, it caught him by surprise, stepping out of the dark wood of the lobby into the bold blue of the morning. He had scorched his retinas beyond repair.

And he hadn't even been drinking.

Finding the sunglasses deep in the bag, cradled between a cut down reporter's notebook and a half roll of Tums, he slid them on and pushed his face back into a rough approximation of relaxed. Damn. That hurt.

He scanned the street, looking for his contact, a photog or an engineer, a truck or some kind of signage that would give him direction to where he should be and whom he should talk to this morning.

The live shot came late in the six A.M. show. He checked his watch. He'd better get a move on, or the weekend producer would be screaming.

He slowly scanned the crowd again and then noticed what he had missed before. He spotted a camera, and beside it a diminutive photographer with tight pin curls. Will decided to start there. Right station or wrong station, the small photographer would likely know where the others were.

"Good morning," Will said.

"Morning. You're Will Ross, right?"

"Yeah," he answered, somewhat surprised that this person, this woman, this photographer, knew him.

"Hiya, I'm Sarah. Your photog this morning."

"Hi," he reached out and shook her hand. "I'm sorry, I didn't recognize you."

"No reason why you should. We've never met, I work a shit schedule and you just got here. Three reasons. Good enough?"

"Yeah, I suppose."

"Okay, then. I'm Sarah, hello." She put out her hand. Will shook it.

"I'm Will. It's a pleasure."

"As for me. You'll hear about me at the station. They call me Smurf."

"Smurf?"

"Smurf. I'm five-foot nothing, have a high-pitched voice and am annoying as hell when people get in my face. Smurf."

"Okay. Mind if I call you Sarah, instead?"

She visibly relaxed, her shoulders dropping as she pulled herself upright.

"Uh ... I'd appreciate that."

They shook hands for a third time.

"Thanks, Ross."

"Will."

"Will. I'm sorry if I came out with my guard up. Working as a woman in a very male portion of TV gets me a tad defensive at times."

"Strange. Working in TV at all for two weeks has made me very defensive."

She laughed. "Touché." She glanced at her watch. "Where do you want to do this? We're getting close."

"Hey, you call it. You're in charge of the visuals."

Sarah smiled.

She checked the sun, then shaded her eyes to examine the various backgrounds. She shifted the camera—attached to a black cable that ran down the street and around the corner—about six feet to her right.

"There, that ought to light your face pretty well and give us the starting line as a background. You like that?"

"Works for me."

"We better get you wired up."

Will looked at his watch. He still had fifteen minutes before his live.

"Don't even think it," Sarah said, "you're dealing with Cassie, Mistress of the Morning. She comes in at one o'clock in the morning, has her show ready by 2:30 and won't put up with anybody screwing it up—not you or Yasser Arafat—until it's over. No breaking news, no late lives, no nothing. She started screaming for you to get in place five minutes after the show started."

"Sorry I couldn't oblige."

"Well, talk to her. I know she'd love to hear from you."

Will plugged his earpiece into the wireless IFB, then clipped the microphone to the zipper of his TV6 windbreaker. "Yo, Cassie, are you there?"

In his ear, he heard the ops engineer back at the station respond, "She's not. I am. Give me a level, would you, Will?"

"1-2-3-4-5 ..."

"Say something real."

"Welcome, sports fans to the inaugural running of the twenty-first annual Zephyr cockroach parade, here in sunny, downtown Pamplona."

"Got it, thank you. Cassie's next."

There was a click in his ear and Will heard a scratch, a pop, and a screech. The screech belonged to Cassie.

"You there? About damned time."

"Yes, ma'am. Here and ready to go."

"Well, you're ten minutes away."

"Got it."

"What are you planning on here? When do you want me to take the video?"

"What video?"

"The video that goes with your story?"

"I dunno. When we get talking about the race, I suppose, just hit a button."

"I don't like to work like that."

"I get that feeling. It'll be fine. This is just a talk back with Steve, right?"

"Well ... yeah."

"Then relax. When we get talking race, just push the button. It's all just video wallpaper at this point."

"I hate doing that."

"And I am just promoting a race, kid. Let's just do it."

So early in the morning and his mood disappeared. Damn.

Will stood in his spot and watched the race begin to gather around him. There were no riders yet, not even the eager beaver new kids, just race organizers setting the start barriers. The media coordinator, a former race director himself, rushed about to make sure he touched base with everyone about everything in his manic, pushy, funny, sincere sort of way. The first spectators, those who had been around for the end of the old Coors twelve years before, were on the line already to be sure to catch the rebirth of racing in Colorado.

They wore ancient wool jerseys that Eddie Merckx would have refused, old uni's embroidered with logos from companies that no longer sponsored cycling, if they still existed at all. Or they sported old Coors Classic merchandise that looked like it had spent the past decade crumpled in the bottom of a box in the corner of a basement next to the furnace.

"Two minutes," Smurf said.

"Got it," Will answered.

He could hear a car commercial in his ear. Dealin' Doug. The guy was everywhere.

He took another quick look around the scene to grab what he could in the way of color and background, turned to the camera, heard his introduction, smiled, and started yakking away.

TV. He had come to realize that there were times when he was telling stories and there were times when he was just filling air. At this moment, he was just filling air. Everything that he could think to say about this race he had already said.

And now, he was just trying to get through previewing it one last time so they could actually throw the flag and get the damned thing started.

Blather. That's all it was, blather.

Not always. But he knew it when he heard it. And he heard it now.

He said goodbye to Steve. Steve said goodbye to him. He heard the magical "Clear" in his ear as Steve rattled off all the promotional information. The race goes all day. The race ends tonight in Breckenridge. TV6 will have a special tonight on the race. TV6 will have another special next week. TV6 is your Sports Leader in Colorado.

Will smiled. That would come as quite a shock to Green at 7 and Zarrella at 9 and Soicher at 4 and Conrad at 2 and Treadwell at 31. If Flynn led any of these guys in anything it was simply in the Ego Parade.

"We're done," Sarah said. "Nice job."

"Eh, for what it was," Will replied.

"Look, I've seen it all, man. Some can do it. Some can't. There wasn't much here, but you made it a comfy conversation with some video and a few facts. You might have thought it's bullshit because you've been doing nothing but this story for the past three weeks, but I'll tell you, it's real to the folks who are watching. You moved the story ahead. You got them closer to the start. You did the job. What more do you want?"

"I want to be Edward R. Murrow."

"Who is, at this moment, food for worms. Be Will Ross."

She folded up her tripod.

"Be Will Ross. And give me my microphone."

Will disconnected himself from the IFB and handed that to her, then worked the microphone cable and transmitter box out of his jacket. He wound the wire carefully and handed it back to her.

"Hope I did it right."

"Close enough." She clipped the wire onto the transmitter. "You're one of the few who even does that. Most of them leave it all in a pile wherever they were standing."

He helped her break down the shot and wind cable. The engineer came around the corner and tugged on the black cable running to the live truck to make sure it was free. He disappeared and seconds later, the cable and all its connectors, a hydra head of plugs, snaked its way down the street and out of sight.

"Thanks for the help. I'm shooting the start and then I'm out of here. So where should I be?"

"I'd say catch the riders while they're getting ready, then put yourself down on that corner," Will pointed about half a block away, "and catch the roll out."

"That's it?"

"That's it. Get as much of the pre-race stuff as you can. Who knows, if this shit doesn't work it could be all we have to work with today."

"Got it." She looked over to the side. "You've either got a fan or somebody who really has to go to the bathroom over there."

Will turned and saw the media coordinator bouncing toward him.

"That guy is wound way way way too tight."

"Race personnel usually are. Thanks for everything, Sarah."

"Thank you, Will. I appreciate it. It was fun."

She gathered up her gear and walked off toward the team trucks. Her spot in the universe was almost immediately filled by Mark Sistrom, media coordinator.

"Hey, Will Ross, how you doin'?"

"Doin' fine, Mark, what's up?"

"I've got your media pass here and a race packet. I've also got you a spot in the Press Car. You can go with a TV6 car, but they'll be behind the race and this will be right in the thick of it."

"I'll do the right-in-the-thick-of-it."

"We could put you on a moto."

"Naw. My ass can't take it."

"I understand. Mine can't either anymore. Okay. It's the red Lincoln Navigator over there. And—just so you can stay in touch on the course, I got you clearance on a satellite phone. Ever use one?"

"No."

"Easy. You'll love the thing." Mark handed him what appeared to be a large walkie-talkie featuring a black plastic dowel on a side pivot.

"This is great. What's the catch?"

"No catch. You're a sponsor. It's important you stay in touch. Just mention MerdTech a few times in your stories and they'll be happy."

"That's a catch."

He wiggled his head back and forth.

"Yeah, maybe, but not a big one. Use it today. Let me know what you think about it. Product testing. You'll be in the mountains all day. Your cell phone will be useless."

"Yeah, I suppose." Will wondered if he should call and clear this with Barbara before he agreed to anything or slapped a logo on the air.

"Okay. Great. Just push the buttons and point it straight up. Satellite picks it up, routs it through San Francisco, then connects you to the land lines. Great. Talk to you later." And he disappeared into the growing crowd.

Will checked his watch. 7:20. A few riders, bouncing up and down beside their bikes, were already wandering around the starting area. Will smiled. New guys. Flynn's favorite FNG's.

He remembered. He lived that. He knew it. The memory warmed him.

He walked back to the hotel and went in search of breakfast at the outdoor cafe. While he sat at the table, picking at his Denver omelet, slurping coffee and hoping he wouldn't have to pee every twenty minutes all day long, a clipboard was shoved in his face.

"Will Ross? You got your satellite phone yet? Nobody wrote it down."

Will peered up, but only make out a silhouette, thanks to the position of the morning sun directly behind his questioner's head.

"Yeah. I got it right here."

Will nodded, then bent down and began to dig in his bag for the phone. He glanced at the guy's shoes, worn work boots edged with white dust, covered at the tops with khaki's. It surprised him. Everybody else was in sneaks and shorts today.

Will dug and found the phone, then stopped.

"I thought Mark wrote down the number."

"Well, I don't have it. What's he got for you?"

Will read off the number, then peered up at the man with the clipboard again. He still couldn't see his face, but he could tell his hair was a light brown. Maybe. He blinked twice and looked back at his breakfast to clear his eyes of the little blue and yellow dots.

"Wrong one. Goddamn it. Mark gave you the wrong one. You've got the one signed out to the race director, Len ..."

"Ken."

"Ken. Yeah. I'm gonna need yours back. You going to be here for a few minutes?"

Will looked at his watch. 7:45.

"Yeah, until at least 8:15."

"Good. I'll be back with your phone in just a second."

He left. For a split second, Will wondered if he should have done that, just handed a multi-thousand dollar portable satellite phone to a guy he didn't know, but it was too late now. He disappeared into the crowd.

Nothing much to do, except wait and hope, Will thought. He turned his attention back to his eggs and sourdough toast, and nodded yes when the waiter asked if he wanted more coffee.

He'd pee, but at least he'd be awake to do it.

He read the headlines of the *Denver Post*, then skipped over to the *Rocky*

Mountain News for the comics. At 7:55, the young man returned, stepped up to Will's table and put the satellite phone next to Will's plate of congealed eggs and bread crusts.

"You're set. I guess that they knew what they were doing. Here's your sat phone back."

Will sat back, relieved. It had all worked out after all.

He looked up at the young man, who oddly enough, had moved himself into a position in a direct line with the sun again. The shadows cast by his face didn't help, nor did Will's sunglasses. He couldn't make out much of any sort of facial features with the morning sun and a startling blue sky directly behind the guy's head.

"Thanks. I appreciate you bringing it back," Will said.

"You got it. You're all registered and everything."

"Should I give it back to you at the end of the day?"

"Me or the guy who gave it to you to begin with ..."

"Mark?"

"Mark is fine. We'll all be around to watch the excitement at the end. So, I guess, give it to any of us."

"You got it."

"Have fun." The young man turned sharply and walked away. Will noticed the long-sleeved blue work shirt, the khaki pants and the work boots again. Not the sort of thing most wore for a summer day in the mountains, unless, of course, you had been up since three A.M. setting up platforms and scaffolding and barriers.

"Thanks ... uh, what's your name?" Will called.

"Peter," he said over his shoulder, never turning back, "just ask for Peter."

"Thanks, man," he answered.

"Oh, you bet. You bet." Once more, the growing crowd quickly swallowed him up.

※

THE RACE BEGAN WITH A NEUTRAL START—ESSENTIALLY—A PACK OF CARTOON dogs in Spandex, pedaling, laughing, jostling for position for the first few miles It was a parade lap of Boulder, in a way, until reaching the mark on Highway 93 when the race official flipped the donut sign from red to green and the Zephyr truly began.

With the other reporters in the car, Will knelt on his seat, facing backward, to catch the moment.

As it happened, a small electric thrill chased up his spine, and a memory flashed, a memory of a hundred moments like this, when the donut flipped and the race began and all the joking and jostling fell to the wayside as the racers got serious about their jobs.

Within seconds of the start, one rider jumped away, pedaling furiously in a breakaway. A great idea, only about eight hours too early. Seconds later, a second member of the same team jumped out.

"There's your winner. We might as well just head back to the bar," a mountain town radio reporter on the other side of the car said.

Race radio crackled.

"Breakaway—Big T Texas Volkswagen Team."

There was a pause, then the radio crackled again.

"Dumb shits."

Will smiled while the others in the car laughed. Sure it was dumb. These guys had no more chance of winning than Gary Coleman had of ever seeing five-foot-eight. But this was their one moment to shine; this was their one moment to leap ahead, to sparkle, to ride, to lead. They'd die in a matter of miles, likely on Guanella, but they'd always be able to say, "I led once."

He knew the feeling. He knew what drove it.

He smiled. The others laughed.

And they had no idea what they were laughing about.

He scribbled some notes on the early action, then glanced back to see the pack slowly catching the two riders, already burning themselves out with their efforts. Guanella? Hell, they'd be lucky to make Wondervu now, he thought.

The station helicopter swooped past, the rotors cutting the air with their distinctive thup-thup-thup. The 'copter looped ahead, then turned back toward the race itself. The spectators along the road were more interested in the chopper than the bikes.

There was the problem, Will whispered to himself.

The more noise a machine created, the more interest it held. Maybe if everybody in the race clipped the Jack of Hearts in their spokes with a clothespin. He shook his head and dug down into his bag. He found the cell phone first and turned it on. They weren't in the mountains yet and he saw no need to irradiate his brains with the satellite phone until absolutely necessary. He dialed the number for the assignment desk and was put through to Billy Caton, the sports editor who was set to cut the day's events into some coherent form.

"Hey there, it's Will. Before we wander into the mountains I thought I'd let you know, race got off on time. Neutral start out of Boulder. As soon as the flag went up, at," he checked his notes and rattled off a time, "we had a breakaway. Riders 145 and 146 on the Texas team. Turning toward Wondervu now and they look like they're about ready to die."

"Got it. Got it," Caton answered. "Hey, drop off any notes you've got with Gene. He'll be shooting the race as it crosses Wondervu, then he's coming back here, okay?"

"Yep, no problem."

The phone hissed and popped.

"... ey, did Barbara get in touch with you?"

"Gooden? No, what's up?"

"She's been trying to talk to you since yesterday. Now, she's in the station and all pissy because you never returned any of her messages."

"I don't know where she left them, but I didn't get them"

The phone cracked, then dropped out and came back.

"... she ... say ... "

"I'm losing you man, we're going up into the foothills."

"Just call her ... Just call ..."

The phone popped, squeaked and died. Will pushed the power button and dropped it into the bag. That was that, until probably Idaho Springs and Georgetown for twenty minutes, then South Park two hours later, then Breckenridge an hour after that. He looked at the satellite phone, picked it up, and turned the antenna to the sky.

He pushed the power button, watched the LCD glow, then register, then beep, then ask for a number. Will tapped a second button and the phone dropped into standby mode. He placed it on his lap, thought better of it, and put it back into the top of the bag, with the pole antenna pointing toward the open window.

Who knows, he thought, I could need my nuts again someday.

He turned back and watched the race, a new rider beginning to make a move on the climb toward Wondervu. This, Will knew, wasn't a simple shot at momentary glory. This was someone who was thinking ahead, through the climb and descent and into Blackhawk, where the first sprint would hand someone a check for five thousand dollars at the end of the day.

Not bad for an hour's worth of busting your ass. As long as you didn't bust it so wide that you couldn't finish. No finish, no money, no shit.

The kid looked strong. He climbed with confidence.

Will smiled. He did that. Once.

In the meantime, he had forgotten completely about calling Barbara.

❁

THE BREAKAWAY KID MADE GOOD ON HIS PROMISE, CHARGING THROUGH BLACKHAWK for the sprint prime before fading quickly back into the pack. There was no way he could or would win the day, he was a sprinter after all, a very specialized art in a sport that was filled with specialized arts, but all he had to do now was finish to win his prize.

The press car picked its way through the pack on the narrow streets of Blackhawk and Central City, passed the leaders and sped through the switchbacks leading out of town over the top of Oh My God Road.

"I'm gonna run ahead to the hairpin—anybody care?" the driver asked.

"Naw, go ahead," Will said and the rest of the reporters muttered in agreement. It was already getting stuffy in the car and it was already time to get out and stretch their legs.

Will made more notes, then snatched the sat phone out of his bag. He was going to need this to call in the times and prime winner to Caton. Oh yeah, and call Barbara, he remembered.

What had he done now?

What was she going to yell about?

Why was he worried? He was fifty miles away. All he had to do was turn off the phone and he was free. At least until Monday.

As the car pulled to the side of the road near the switch-back, Will scrambled out, very nearly losing his balance and tumbling over a ledge. He caught himself, dialed the satellite code then the station number and waited for Caton to answer.

When he did, Will was thrilled. This sounded better than that pay phone in Idaho Springs.

"Hey, there, I've got a prime winner for you and the race order going over Oh My God."

"That's okay. I've got the sprint winner thanks to Rob in Blackhawk and the 'copter is feeding back live microwave right now, so I've got race order. Did you ever talk to Barbara?"

"Naw, I forgot."

"Well thanks, man, she's been chewing my ass for the past half hour wondering where the hell you are. I'm going to transfer you. Hang on."

"The phone clicked and snapped, on the station's end, rather than his. This satellite phone business, Will thought, was cool shit. Maybe he should buy some stock.

The phone jangled in his ear, as if someone had answered in the middle of a ring, or it had been snatched up so quickly that it had rung the bells that hung inside Will's brain pan.

"Will?"

"Barbara? Hi." There was a pause. "What did I do wrong?"

"God, you're impossible to get a hold of."

"If I was God, I would be. What's up?"

"Will," her voice dropped into a very serious tone, "we've got to talk. Do you have a minute?"

He looked up the road. The leaders were strung out like a strand of pearls down the incline of the descent, while the pack remained close behind. Everyone was taking their time on Oh My God.

"Well, not really. The race is coming. We're gonna fly pretty quickly."

"Okay," she sighed, "then, I guess, I'll make this short and sweet. Colorado Bureau of Investigations and the Feds found a switch at the bottom of Crooked Lake. A launcher and a switch. Both were covered with residue of PETN. Do you know what that is?"

"No idea."

"It's a high explosive. A military explosive. An explosive that shouldn't have been in any kind of fireworks display."

Will looked up the road. The race was coming. The driver was back in the press car and the other riders were moving back to the car in anticipation of following the race again. Will stumbled toward the car, a cold hand beginning to make its presence known along his spine.

"Okay," he gulped. "What does this mean?"

"It means that Crooked Lake wasn't an accident."

"Okay."

"It means that maybe your guy was being serious. It means that maybe your guy was—your guy on the phone—was telling the truth. It means that the police aren't sure what they've got. Maybe. It means that your little friend, the one from Oh My God Road may be ... may be ..."

"Real?"

"Real. Yes, he may be real."

"Jesus." Will ran his hand through his hair. "After all you guys went through to convince me otherwise, he's more than a kook. More than a celebrity wanna-be?"

She took a long time before she answered.

"Maybe, Will. Just maybe. This was too detailed, too professional for the kind of guy who stakes out TV reporters. But Will, they just don't know. It's just a possibility. One of many. They don't know what it means."

The race was on them. The pack hurtled past in a sea of dust, clanking bikes and muttered oaths. How anyone made that gravel-strewn hairpin turn at the bottom of the drop was amazing. The driver looked at Will and honked.

"Okay, so what do I do?"

"At this point," Barbara reasoned, "just continue on with it. The police aren't sure what they've got—and the race is just too big to stop. But they're investigating. They're taking precautions. They do want to talk with you on Monday again. Everything should be fine and they'll deal with it."

"Should be."

"Should be."

"Cheryl." The word popped out of his mouth. "What about Cheryl, what about my family?"

"Don't worry. I'll get in touch with Cheryl. The police said they're not expecting any move toward her. They're not expecting a move toward you or the race.

They just have a connection. A possible connection, that's it. So keep a close eye on yourself. Keep a close eye on what's going on around you. Watch for this guy."

"I don't know what he looks like," Will barked. "Screw this, I'm coming home."

The driver honked again.

"No. No. How Will? You're out in the middle of nowhere. Keep with the race. The police are on this. I wasn't even supposed to tell you. The cops get wind of this and my contact inside will freeze right up. I'll call Cheryl. I'll make sure she knows to be careful. Just be aware. That's all this is ... be aware."

The driver honked and gestured angrily.

"That's all this is. We'll see you in Breckenridge and we'll get you right home."

She hung up the phone. Will stared at the dial for a moment, then pressed the END button and walked toward the car.

The race was ahead of him now.

And Will didn't care.

❀

BARBARA SAT AT HER DESK AND STARED AT THE MOUNTAINS. SHE HAD CONVINCED herself that, any second, Mount Evans or Guanella or something along the I-70 corridor would erupt, showering downtown Denver with debris.

The police still weren't sure what they were dealing with, that much was true. They gathered up nothing more than a collection of maybes.

But one thing remained true.

The trigger, covered with PETN, found at the bottom of the lake was a duplicate of the one partially burned by a magnesium charge, found in a lunch-box outside the TV6 door.

Coincidence or continuation?

She didn't know. They didn't know.

The police, some officer named Whiteside, said not to panic, they still weren't sure what they were dealing with but they were on the case. The station was being watched. Will Ross should report any further contact.

There had been none. No one knew the next step.

All they could do was wait for one. One next step.

Barbara stared at the mountains, flinching at any loud noise on the street.

CHAPTER FOURTEEN:

REACH OUT AND TOUCH SOMEONE

T HE DRIVER WAS PISSED TO BEAT ALL HELL.

He missed his chance to drop in between the leaders and the pack because Will held him back with a phone call. Now he was chasing the broom wagon down Oh My God Road toward Idaho Springs, on a short blast of flats, then into Georgetown with its run up to Guanella Pass.

The driver juggled possibilities in his head, saw an opening and decided to take it, no matter what the crowd in the back of his car wanted.

Driving through the tight streets of Idaho Springs, he turned down an unbarricaded side road, cut through a neighborhood of old, boxy homes, popped out on a main street and picked up the business route to the Interstate.

The race would stay on the frontage road, while he hopscotched to Georgetown. He drove up the entrance ramp and put his foot on the accelerator. The Navigator sucked the gas, leapt ahead and was doing eighty-five by the time it merged.

Will looked across the other lane and saw a lone rider on the frontage road, pounding hard and glancing over his shoulder to see who was chasing him. That had to be the leader, he thought. He was acting like a leader.

A leader or a rider determined to stay just ahead of the broom wagon.

He looked back down the frontage road. There was no one following, yet. This was the leader.

He wouldn't be leading over Guanella, but if he was lucky, he'd be reeled back in by the leaders and would be able to use them to stay up front. It wasn't a particularly good strategy, but it was a strategy, better than that of the guys who had leapt off the front just outside of downtown Boulder.

It would be interesting to see if he could hold on. Or how long.

Will turned his attention back into the car. Everyone was making notes, taking a glance out the window, then scribbling in their reporter's notebooks. With an athlete's disdain for the press, Will wondered if they had the slightest idea what they were looking at. A lone rider with two and a half minutes on the pack, flying down a back road with two major climbs still before him. What were they seeing?

Why did he care?

He cared because this was his new pack now. He rode in a new peloton. The game was to get the better insight first, to get to the public first, to put your stamp on the story first. He cared because he had to make this one work. He had already frittered away one career in the bicycle business and had stepped out of the shit and into a rose bed. If he could only avoid the thorns.

The thorns.

Despite the words, he could hear a tension in Barbara Gooden's tone.

There was something else there. Screw it, he was calling home.

He reached for the satellite phone, thought better of it, then grabbed his personal cell phone. In the Idaho Springs/Georgetown corridor, he'd have service. He was sure of it. He didn't know who was billing out the sat phone time, but he did know they'd be a lot happier if they didn't see personal numbers on the final invoice.

Besides, this made the call seem his, gave him possession of it, made it a personal stand away from the station, the race and the infinitely long reach of Barbara Gooden. He punched in the numbers and leaned toward the window. There was a hiss and a pop. He pulled it down and looked at the screen. It was searching for a cell. The signal indicator dropped to one, then jumped to five, dropped to three, then jumped back up.

He listened. It rang. And she answered.

"Hi, this is me. How are you?"

"I'm fine. The question is, how are you?"

"Why?"

"I just got off the phone with your boss," Cheryl said, "she's a piece of work."

"Is that good or bad?"

"That's management. She's a manager who wants to be your friend at the same time. Don't know if that can happen."

"What did she tell you?"

"She said she talked to you. Some kind of evidence at the bottom of a lake—like the smudge pot outside the station."

"What's your take on it?" he asked.

"I'm not sure. She didn't seem too creeped out by it. But I don't know if that's because she's convinced herself that nothing can happen, or if she's convinced herself that the police are wrong, or if she's worried to frighten the little woman. I dunno, Will. I just don't."

"What should I do?"

"Well, I've been thinking about that and I can't really come up with anything. We're fine, if that's what you're asking. Gooch and I are just fine. But—you … I mean, look, Will … you can't change your life and hide away because some asshole jumped out and said 'boogie, boogie, boogie' to you. You've got to keep moving ahead. Just ..."

The signal broke up and returned.

"... and watch yourself. I worry about you. Gooch does too. He kicks every time he hears your voice."

Will smiled and felt his heart grow.

"I like that."

"I thought you might. Get this finished and come home to us. We'll figure out where to go from there."

"Okay. Okay. I need a day. Maybe we can take Monday off and go somewhere."

"Sounds good, Will. I love you."

"Oh, God, Cheryl, I love you too. More than you'll ever know."

"That's nice," she said, "that's nice."

"Be careful."

"You too. I'm not going anyplace and you're wandering through the mountains all day. You be careful."

"I'll try. Love you."

"Love you, Will." She hung up the phone.

Will pushed the end button and stared at the display for a long moment, his home number still flashing at him. He'd give just about anything to be out of this car and away from this race and at that number right now.

But he was in it. He was of it. And he was heading toward the finish, whether he liked it or not.

He pushed the power button and tossed the phone into his bag. It would be pretty much useless until Fairplay. He heard it "clack" against the satellite phone. He reached in and picked it up, dialing into the station. He talked to Caton again and gave him the latest notes he could decipher from the notepad of the guy sitting next to him in the car—rider's numbers, position, lead times. It was difficult.

The guy kept moving his pad around and Will couldn't always read it while looking like he was doing something else.

Have to pay attention and take my own damned notes, he thought. Have to do the job.

He closed his eyes and scratched his head, telling Caton to wait for a moment as he visualized the race. He laid it out as best as he could, telling the editor that he'd call him back from the top of Guanella, as it was there and on the descent that the race would truly begin to form. This was a sprint for position, while Guanella would break up the race and reform it into its final configurations.

Guanella. Guanella was the key.

His mind began to slip toward the stalker.

Do the job. Pass the time. Finish the mission. Do the story. Go home. Deal with it then. Deal with it then. Deal with this now. Deal with this now.

Deal with it.

The car pulled off Interstate 70 at Georgetown, negotiated the narrow city streets, and popped up onto the footsteps of Guanella Pass. The crowds were impressive all along the way. People were actually making a day of following the race. There were moments he could have mistaken the scene for Europe.

The driver pulled into a parking spot on a switchback about a quarter of the way up the pass.

"We'll stretch here and wait. But as soon the leaders come by, I want everybody in the car. Everybody," he said, sharply, eyeballing Will. "Then, we'll pack in right behind the leaders and follow along."

Will climbed out of the car and stood leaning against it. Meant for me, he thought, 100 percent meant for me.

He turned his face up toward the sun. Screw you, pal. You don't have a fan demanding gratitude in your face while lighting matches near a garage full of dynamite. He rubbed his face again, moving his fingers underneath the sunglasses to work his eyes.

What a pisser. What a goddamned pisser.

The satellite phone rang in his hand.

The surprise caught him off guard and he nearly dropped it. He turned the phone up to him, looked at the display, which merely said "Incoming" and then searched the pad for a button that would allow him to answer. He saw a small green one, took the chance, pushed it, and lifted the phone to his right ear.

"Hello?"

"Your magic number is four today."

"What?"

"Listen to me, Mr. Ross," the voice hissed, "your magic number is four. There are four devices that you've got to deal with today. You've got to find them, you've got to disarm them, you've got to deal with them."

"Who ...?"

"Don't patronize me, Will, you know exactly who. Nobody is taking me seriously, Will, not you, not the promoters, not the police, not your station, not nobody. And, so, I've got to change all that. The magic number is four. It should be six, in honor of your station, but I really didn't have time. But you'll think these all devilishly clever ... the magic number is four, Will, four."

If Will was breathing, he didn't know it. It was as if his entire body had been dropped into a deep freeze, with his brain removed and put in the coldest corner of the locker.

"Where? When?" was all he could say.

"I'll give you a hint, Will, I'll give you a hint. What if a tree fell in the forest and there was only a race to hear it? Would it really make a sound?"

"I don't understand."

"You will. I'll be in touch."

"Wait."

"You should have said thank you, Will. You should have said thank you."

"WHY?" Will shouted, "WHY? TELL ME WHY!"

The sat phone clicked dead, but Will was frozen. He held it to his ear and didn't move for a long second. Then he turned, looked up and down the road, and began to march uphill, toward a motorcycle cop twenty yards up the Pass.

He arrived winded, shocked that such a short walk had left him so out of breath. Walking the Pass was almost harder than riding it thanks to the grade.

"Hi, how ya doin?" Will wheezed.

"Fine," the cop replied, "what can I do for you?"

"My name is Will Ross. I'm with TV6 News. Call in to, what, your central base. Get in touch with Denver Police. Some guy named Whiteside. Tell them I've been in touch with his suspect. You got that?" Will hacked and spat. "He called me on this," he held up the sat phone, "I don't know how he got the number."

"Well, if you've got a phone, why don't you call this Whiteside?"

"Look. If this guy's plugged into this number, I don't know what else he's plugged into. Just call in. Call Whiteside. Tell him to get in touch with me."

"How?"

"I dunno. I dunno."

"What's that phone number?" He pointed at the sat phone. Without thinking, Will gave him the number, then stopped. "Wait. Not that one. Use my cell phone number." He rattled it off. "Tell him to call on that. He's calling me on this. I dunno. I want to keep this open. LISTEN TO ME! He says there are four devices on the course. Tell that to Whiteside. FOUR. Four I-don't-know-whats. He gave me some clue, something about a tree in the forest ..."

The motorcycle cop held up his hand.

"I'll call in and have the station call this Whiteside. Explain it all to him. Okay?"

There was cheering and honking behind Will. He turned to see the first rider coming up and around a crest on a curve. The driver of the press car was the one who was honking and waving Will back down the mountainside. Will waved him up and turned back to the motorcycle cop.

"Call in. Call Whiteside at Denver PD. Please. Tell him he's got to get in touch with Will Ross. There are four devices, remember that, please, four."

"Got it. I'll call it in right now." He picked up his microphone and waved it at Will. "Got it. Right now."

The press car pulled up beside Will and he ran around the back to his side. He looked back over the roof. "Call him. Call it in."

"I will. I will. Trust me."

The press car pulled onto the road behind a group of eight chasers and began its march toward Breckenridge again.

At his motorcycle, the officer replaced the mike on its hook and went back to watching the race.

The assholes he got in the mountains. The assholes he got.

He watched the peloton crowd toward him on the narrow mountain road. Pretty impressive, he thought, but better done on a Harley.

He was thinking to himself how he could blast through these skinny bicycle guys on his machine, when—WHOM!—he was startled by what sounded like a double barreled twelve-gauge firing off both barrels at once. He jumped, then turned himself quickly to see a thirty-foot lodgepole pine fall toward the road, then hit another tree beside it, crack, turn, and fall directly toward him.

He at least had the presence of mind to scramble out of its path. It fell, hard, on top of his tricked-out police Kawasaki and flattened the bike.

After a moment's hesitation, brought on both by the sharpness of the blast and the falling of the tree, the peloton passed the tip of the lodgepole in a steady wave, while Motorcycle Officer Ted Burns simply stared at his motorcycle and wondered how the hell he was going to explain this to his boss.

❄

WILL RELAXED A BIT AS THEY CROSSED THE PEAK ON GUANELLA AND HIT THE DIRT roads on the back side. The knot in his stomach began to ease and he turned his attention back to the race. The leaders, just ahead, were now eight strong, including three from the Chartwell Team, a pickup team of strong riders from both Europe and America, plus Team Hermes, a powerful American team sponsored by an auto maker.

He made some notes, his heart not really in it, then picked up the sat phone. He stared at it for some time, convinced that it had, somehow, become dirty, and finally talked himself into dialing the number. Will didn't know how his stalker might be tied into this phone: number, certainly; read back, maybe; eavesdropping, who knew. Given modern technology, all were real possibilities, but he had already called in to the TV6 Sports office earlier in the day on the thing, so another call wasn't going to make that much difference. Once in the station's system, Will figured, he could be transferred to any other number within that system without registering on the sat phone.

He dialed Caton's number. The sports editor answered on the second ring.

"Caton. Editing."

"Hi, this is Will."

"Holy Shit! Where you been, man?"

"Listen to me, I've got some race leaders ..."

"Hell with that. Did you see the tree?"

"What tree?"

"Some tree on Guanella snapped off in the wind or something and was falling right toward the road, woulda made a hell of a marmalade if it had fallen when the riders were there."

"What happened?" Will asked, the question coming out in a way that made him frightened of both it and the answer.

"Man, oh, man, we got some great video of it on the ground. Not falling though, shit-beat-all-hell, but we got some great video of it. It was falling toward the road, then hit another tree and twisted weird and fell on some cop's motorcycle. Squashed it flat."

"What about the cop?" Will whispered.

"What? The cop. Shit, he's okay. Surprised, sure as shit, that's for sure." Caton laughed. "Man, I wish the hell I coulda seen his face."

"How ... how ... did it happen?" It was taking an effort to say the words, like the altitude was affecting him.

"What? God, I dunno. Some people said they heard something like a big firecracker, others said it was just a dead tree and a gust of wind. Hell of a coincidence if it was just the wind, but they're not sure. The race passed, the crowds are gone, the motorcycle's flat and I'm not sure how close they're looking at it."

"Give me to Barbara."

"I need the leaders from you."

"Give me to Barbara."

"I need ..."

"FUCK THE LEADERS! GIVE ME TO BARBARA!"

There was silence both on the other end of the line and in the car next to Will.

"Give me to Barbara. Please."

"Okay. I'm gonna need those ..."

"I'll leave them with her. Give me to Barbara."

"Yeah, she's here. I'll transfer you in ..."

The phone clicked, snapped and then rang twice. Barbara answered on the start of the third ring.

"TV6 News. Barbara G ..."

"Barbara, this is Will. He called. He called."

"Who? Will?" She paused as the words soaked in. "Oh, my God."

"Listen carefully. I don't know if he's plugged into this line or not. I'm starting to freak here."

"Take it easy, Will. What did he say?"

"He said there were four devices. Four bombs, I've got to figure. Somewhere on the course. He gave me a hint on the first one ... what if a tree fell in the forest ... you know, that old line ... well, Caton just told me that a tree fell on the course and landed on a cop's motorcycle. A cop, I'm thinking, that I had just been talking to ... so, he was not only there, he was watching me and setting it up for my benefit."

"Okay, Will, tell me exactly what happened. And what he said. First—how did he get in touch with you?"

"He called me on the satellite phone that the race gave me."

"How did he get that number?"

"I don't know. I don't know."

"Think. Think about it. Denver PD is going to want to know. Any possibility. Alright. When did he call you? And exactly—what did he say?"

Will closed his eyes to the theater of memory and repeated everything he could remember. Where they were on the course, what time the call had come in, he just had to guess at that, and what was said. He struggled to hear the voice in his head again, the hiss, the warning, the danger. The stupidity of it all. Christ, why hadn't he just said "thank you"? Why didn't he just kiss the guy's ass a little? Why didn't he build a goddamned shrine to him when he had the chance?

"Will, you there? What was the thing about the tree again?"

He cleared his mind and told the tale, as carefully as he could, to Barbara Gooden.

"That's it."

"Okay. Look. You keep your satellite phone clear as much as possible. I'm not so worried about that guy listening in as I am that when he wants to call you he can't get through. I'm still wondering how he got that number ..."

"Believe me, I'm fried about it, too."

"... but I'm going to call Denver Police about this, that officer, what was his name ..."

"Whiteside was the one I talked to ..."

"Whiteside, that's it. From now on, talk to me by cell phone. You'll be in Grant soon. You can hit a cell there. Let me know if he calls again and I'll let you know what the police say."

"Okay. I'll keep the satellite phone open."

"Good."

"What about the race?" Will asked.

"Screw it." Barbara replied. "We'll make it up once we get to Breckenridge if we have to. You're in the eye of the hurricane right now, Will. Your job is to make sure you pass along everything you hear from this guy in the hopes that nobody gets hurt."

He never expected to hear this from the mouth of Barbara Gooden, TV News Director, Vice President of News and Community Affairs, Corporate Officer, way down the list, and all around symbol of sweetness and light and goodness in the City and County of Denver.

"Got it. Got it."

"Don't worry about the race, Will."

"No. Just worry about everything else."

"Exactly."

"I'll be in touch."

"I'm calling Denver PD now."

She hung up. Will pushed the red phone button and the line cleared.

He leaned back in the seat, the satellite phone falling into his lap, the stick antenna still pointed toward the window.

Will leaned his head back and closed his eyes, trying to force the growing crest of the headache back to a manageable place behind his eyes. He turned and looked at the other reporters riding with him, all of whom were listening to his calls, but acting like they weren't paying the least bit of attention. Just as well. They turned back and were focused on race radio, the play-by-play coming over the driver's walkie-talkie.

Just as well, he thought, dropping his head back and slipping into an uneasy meditation. Just as well. His thoughts ranged uncomfortably over the day. The call. The tree. What if a tree fell in the forest and he wasn't there to hear it, was it still connected to him? He had to be there. Whoever this guy was, he had to be there, close to Will. Close enough to watch him talk to the motorcycle cop. Close enough to pick a tree and set a charge. Was this one of the four, or a special surprise guest? And the number? Where did he ... where did he get that satellite ... son of a bitch.

Will sat up in the seat, his eyes wide open and staring at the back of the driver's head, a head he did not see.

"Son of a bitch!"

"What?"

The driver was looking at him in the rear view mirror, a look of concern on his face. Will shook his head.

"Nothing. Nothing." He settled back again into the seat, glancing out the window into the Colorado afternoon, along the back gravel roads of the state, on the descent of a major pass over the Continental Divide.

The clouds were closing in, both on the day and Will.

He realized. He knew.

He had seen him.

He had looked into his face and seen him. Sunshine and all.

Khaki pants. Work shoes. Out of place. Dust. White powder streaks on his pant legs.

He had seen him.

How had he gotten the satellite phone number?

Will had given it to him.

Hell, he had given him the whole goddamned phone.

"Shit."

It was the only reaction that seemed the least bit appropriate.

❀

ONE OF THE LEADING RIDERS HAD SWITCHED BIKES AT THE TOP OF GUANELLA, going from a road to mountain bike. Will dully wondered how far outside the rules that might be, but since none of the officials were squawking, he put it out of his mind. Besides, this was the one rider who didn't flat on the gravel- and pothole-laden descent.

He jotted down some notes in his reporter's notebook, but his heart wasn't in it. Next to the words "Hermes/Mt Bike/Switch" he had written the word WHY and traced over it, time and time again. The race was behind him now, Grant was ahead. And all he could do was wait.

He had become nothing more than a pawn, with a faceless man in khakis on one side, Denver PD and Barbara Gooden on the other. Both sides feeling they could move him—not white, not black, but some strange shade of gray—across the chess board hurly-burly at will.

He had suddenly become the everyman pawn, showing no control over his own destiny. It made him nuts, but there was nothing he could do about it, at least until Grant. At least, until the next call. At least, at least, shit. He couldn't do a goddamned thing.

Pawn.

Moved at will.

To any mark on the board.

He leaned his head back and closed his eyes, letting his mind drift aimlessly through a forest of firing synapses. A face, a word, a ringing of the phone, Barbara, him, silhouetted by the sunlight, Cheryl, a ringing of the phone, a voice, low and deadly, a ringing of the phone.

He shook his head violently and sat up straight. The ringing came from his carry bag. The satellite phone had fallen off his lap and into the bag. He dug, madly, found it, straightened the antenna, leaned toward the window and pushed the green button.

"Yes?"

"You're a difficult man to get a hold of," the voice whispered.

"Sorry. I couldn't get to the phone."

"Oh, that's fine. What surprised me was that I called a while ago and tried, oh, I don't know how many times, and just couldn't get through. Talking to the police?"

"No. The station."

"Oh, I thought maybe the police. Or your wife."

"What about my wife?"

"Nothing. I just figure you call her a lot. I guess I just expect you to."

"Leave her out of this."

"Oh, no doubt. No doubt. My trouble is with you, Will. Ungrateful bastard that you are ..."

"Hey!" Will said, sharply. "Hey. All right. Jesus. I am sorry. I am sorry for whatever I did to you. Or—for whatever I DID NOT SAY. OKAY? But, man, don't do this ... somebody is going to get hurt."

"Oh, no doubt. No doubt. Did you hear about my first device? Didn't quite work out the way I planned. I should have taken more time to figure out what direction the tree would fall in ... but, I was in a hurry. You were on the move."

"Me? So you *were* there ..."

"God, you're a dope. Yes, Mr. Ross, I was there. And if a tree falls in the woods ... Are you always this dense?"

"What's next? What's next? Aren't you going to give me some kind of clue? Isn't that your game?"

"Not a game. Not a game, my friend. Deadly seriously. I have arrived. Today, I have arrived. As of today, Denver, hell, all of Colorado—if not the country— is going to take me seriously. Crooked Lake was only the first act in a long and magnificent career."

Will's anger grew.

"Cut the shit. What's next? Don't you want to threaten? Play with your mouse? Come on. What's next?"

"Patience, patience, Mr. Ross. As if you'll even have the ears to hear it. You've got some time. Within the hour, all with be in place, with the eye of a Holly-wood art director. And then, then, maybe I will tell you. We'll have to see about that—if you have the eyes to see and the ears to hear."

The line went dead. Will snatched the phone away from his head and stared at the readout. He still had power. The voice on the other end of the line had simply hung up.

Next? Next. Next was Grant. And Grant was a key for whatever Barbara had in mind.

Will carefully rested the satellite phone in the crook of his arm, aiming the antenna up and out the partially open window. There were few times in his life when he had felt this useless, this helpless. He looked around the car and realized he was trapped, both physically and in a situation so completely out of his control.

He shut his eyes and let the day play out against the back of his eyelids. He focused on the young man at breakfast, so carefully positioning himself in relation to the sun. It was impossible to see the face in his mind's eye. But what else, what else?

The way the sunlight filtered through his hair. Easy. No shading. No light blonde. Light brown to blonde. How far did he rise above the table? Will remembered the angle of his head. Five ... five ... eight. About five eight. Skinny. His clothes hung on him. The shirt. Loose fitting. Button down work shirt. Blue denim. Not the stylin' polos that the race staff were wearing, but denim. Pressed. Pants. Khaki. Dirty. No, clean. A bit wrinkled. Clean except for that streak of white powder above the cuff. Powder. No. Not like flour. Grains. Like corn meal, only white. White corn meal. Grainy. But not too much.

Shoes. Shoes. Work boots? No. No. Work shoes. Like those steel-toed low-slung jobs his father had given him the summer he worked on tile floors. Work shoes. Not work boots. That funky brownish red. What do they call that? Cord ... cord ... cordovan. Cordovan? Yeah.

He could feel the car starting to slow down again. They had been busting their asses down the mountain, then back up, then down, the driver slamming his foot back and forth, brake, gas, brake, gas, gas, gas, brake, brake, until Will had passed the point of seasickness and just came to expect an irregular rhythm from the ride.

This time, however, the car was slowing to a stop.

Will opened his eyes, sat up, and saw a Colorado State Patrol officer in his Smokey the Bear hat, looking in the driver's side window at the various journalists in various states of alertness in various places in the car.

"Which one of you is Will Ross?"

❋

THE PATROL CAR SHOT ALONG HIGHWAY 285 THROUGH SOUTH PARK TOWARD Fairplay, the fields and farms passing in a blur, not only because of the speed, but thanks to Will's skittering focus. He was here, he was there, he was everywhere, he was absolutely no where at all.

"Yeah, I've got him," the officer said, then passed the cell phone to Will.

"Will? Raymond Whiteside, Denver Police. We met at your house?"

"Sure. Yeah. I remember."

"Look, Will. I'm sorry about the way this has all turned out, but if we're lucky, and you're game, we might be able to nail this son of a bitch today."

"Yeah, okay. What do you need me to do?" Will asked without any level of enthusiasm.

"Has he called you since Guanella Pass?"

"He called me on Kenosha, just outside of Grant."

"Got a time?"

"No."

"From now on, write them down. What did he say, exactly?"

Will took a deep breath and told Whiteside as much as he could remember. He referred to his notes once, but really didn't have to. He could remember, quite clearly, the references to Cheryl, his ears and a Hollywood art director.

"A what?"

"Hollywood art director. That's what he said."

"He's fucking with us."

"Yes and doing a mighty fine job of it."

"Don't lose faith. Not yet. The game has barely started."

"Not according to him. He's already in the second act."

"Crooked Lake was a fluke. He won't try that again."

"You're probably right. He'll probably try something bigger."

"Don't lose hope ... I'll be in touch. I'm on my way to Breckenridge now. I'll meet you there. Let me know if he calls again. Use a cell phone or a land line. Leave that sat phone open for him to call you."

"Alright. Hey, Whiteside, sir, could you do me a favor?"

"What do you need?"

"Have somebody check on my wife. Please? If you would?"

Whiteside paused for a second, before saying, "Sure, no problem. I'll send somebody over to take a look and give her a high sign. But I really don't think he's aiming at her. It seems to be the race."

"And me."

"I think it's the race. You can't do him that much good. Screwing up the race, then he gets a ton of publicity. Maybe even the cover of *Time*."

"Just check on her."

"I will. See you in Breckenridge."

The line went dead. The car shot forward. The scenery blurred. Despite the company, Will felt incredibly alone.

❁

THE RACE WAS ON THE FLATS OF SOUTH PARK NOW, WITH FOUR RIDERS TRADING PULLS at the head of the pace line. Team Hermes had its lead rider in the mix, while the Chartwell pickup team had two in the lead. Class will tell. Hanging on, and showing more staying power than anyone had given him credit for in Georgetown, was the kid from a mountain bike team who had made his jump before Guanella. He could have been leading alone at this point, if he hadn't flatted twice on the descent of Guanella, but chances were he wcould have been swallowed up by the roadies anyway. Who knew? The kid showed power. The pro's showed experience.

A few more races, this kid would be impossible to beat.

Will rubbed his eyes, almost obsessively, as he listened to race radio in the police car. He couldn't make his budding headache disappear, not in this day, reeking of phone calls and threatening voices, not in this car, smelling vaguely of gasoline, sweat and the occasional cigarette.

He cracked the window, listening to the whistle of the wind charging through, carrying a random raindrop along that hit Will in the right side of the forehead. He opened his eyes and slowly focused on the scenery; the pine trees were no longer shimmering in the sunlight. The trees were now hunkering down against the clouds and growing cold at altitude as the rain crept in.

Looking north, Will could see the clouds growing in color and height. They were moving this way, backing up against the Divide. Hoosier Pass was going to be a mess. Cold, windy, and rainy.

He didn't envy anyone on the course right now.

Then, again, he didn't very much envy himself.

Truth be told, rain and all, he'd rather be riding.

He returned to rubbing his eyes with the determination of Captain Queeg with his ball bearings.

AT THE TOP OF HOOSIER, THE SATELLITE PHONE RANG DULLY IN HIS BAG. WILL dug to find it, following the stick antenna down to the body of the phone, wrapped now in a jacket that had been crawling around the bag of its own volition. He pulled it out, searched the pad quickly and found the green button.

"Yes."

"I couldn't reach you," the voice said coldly.

"We were going over Hoosier Pass."

"The race isn't there yet. Who are you with?"

Will felt a cold sweat pop out of his forehead. Damn. He had to think. He always had to think.

"I'm in a station car. We have to go ahead because of the show. The weather is holding the race back."

There was silence.

"Hmm. Maybe. Actually, I was just checking on you. Wanted to find out how you were holding up, Mr. Ross. And how are you holding up?"

"Fine. Just fine.

"Good. Good to know. There are three left, Mr. Ross, three. The tree, well, the tree was just a little too clever, even for me. Too many things left to chance. The next three, though," his voice brightened, "while clever, I won't deny that, are far more sensible. Tough to find and very sensible. The tree got your attention, though, didn't it?"

"I wasn't there. I just heard about it later."

"Yes, so much the pity. You'll be around for the next three. I've made sure of that."

"Thanks," Will said, quietly, "ever so."

"Yes. Tah."

The line went dead. And Will Ross hung his head on his chest. It felt like it weighed a ton.

Or as Martine back at the station would say, "Is it two thousand pounds or a ton? People! Let's make up our minds!"

✿

As the police car pulled into Breckenridge after a hairy, wet descent of Hoosier Pass, the rear end of the police car fishtailing frantically on the switch-backs, Will heard race radio call the run through Fairplay, the small town on the other end of the pass. The four riders were still together. One from Hermes, two from Chartwell and the mountain bike kid, hanging on like grim death.

Will smiled. Good for him. Good for him.

Raymond Whiteside of the Denver Police Department was waiting for Will at the finish line, wrapping a too-light jacket around himself, while taking a drag on a cigarette.

As Will stepped out of the patrol cruiser and looked up at Whiteside, he could see the people around him eyeballing the cigarette with disgust. Will slung his bag over his shoulder and carried the satellite phone in his hand, the wand pointing toward the sky.

No more chances, no more chances.

Whiteside saw Will and walked across the announcer's platform, the cloud of smoke trailing behind him, followed by looks that could kill. Most times, these same people would speak out loudly against anything and everything, but somehow, Whiteside spoke just as loudly back, without saying a word.

Cop.

He could smoke anywhere he damn well pleased.

"Mr. Ross ..."

"Will."

"Will. Good to see you. Glad to see you made it. We're watching the race carefully. Keeping everybody tight. Pulling riders who fall too far behind. Keeping in the center of the road. No problems so ..."

"I don't think he's going after the race."

"What do you mean?"

"I just had another call from him. At the top of Hoosier Pass. He said that I'd be on hand for the next three. I'm nowhere near the race ..."

"He doesn't know that."

"Maybe not, but—change your theory here for a minute—what if the race isn't the target at all? It's always been me not saying 'thank you.' The race is show, a backdrop. I'm the target, because I'm not grateful. Think about it."

"Well, that would mean ..."

"That would mean, he's here. Somewhere in Breckenridge. He's here. Three more devices are here. Somewhere. Near me. Wherever I go and whatever I do ... they'll be somewhere close to me."

"That could be anywhere."

Will snorted.

"No shit. That announcer's stand. I'm supposed to call the end of the race from there. A men's room near the set for the TV show. The set itself. The car driving me home."

"We'll check them all."

"Just be aware," Will said, "he was pretty clear that these would be tough to find. What did he say?" Will looked away and squinted his eyes, as if, somehow, the answer was written on the back of his eyelids.

"Sensible. That's what he said. He said the tree was too clever. Too much was left to chance."

"What tree?"

"The tree at the top of Guanella that got the motorcycle."

"Nobody told me that."

"He was there. He had to be there. Close to me," Will said quietly as he worked it through. "He watched me. Watched me walk up to the cop and planted the device on the side of a pine tree while I was there. The leaders caught up to us before he could fire it off. The media car picked me up. We went up the hill. Out of range. The leaders passed. He fired it. The tree broke, but he was off. It didn't hit the road or the pack. It hit another tree and rolled off into the cop's motorcycle." Will stopped and looked at Whiteside as if coming out of a dream.

"That's why he said it was too clever. Too much left to chance. Timing. Angle. Everything had to be just right. Not for the next three. They'd be simple. Simple and direct. Sensible. They'd be sensible."

Whiteside nodded.

"And I may have seen him."

"What? I saw him, I think, in Boulder. At the starting line. He wanted the number for the satellite phone. That's how he's been getting in touch with me all day."

"What? What did he look like?"

"I don't have a face, he kept standing in the sun. I could never get a clear look at his face, but he was young. Early twenties, maybe. And the hair, the hair was sandy. Sort of a dark, sandy brown, from what I could see when he walked away."

"What was he wearing?"

"Boots. Worn work boots. Light brown from wear. Khaki trousers. Wrinkled. Not bad, though. They had white streaks on them. Kind of grainy white. Like coffee grounds, only white. And—and—a blue work shirt. One of those light blue denim work shirts—long sleeve."

Will paused for a moment, thinking, then shook his head.

"That's it. That's all I can remember."

Whiteside turned away from Will and snatched his radio from a holster on his belt. The new Western Lawman.

"This is Whiteside. We've got three. We're looking for three devices. I want you to check everything connected with the TV set-up. Cameras. Chairs. Microphones. Everything. I need somebody over here at the finish line. Go over the booth with a fine-toothed comb. And people—talk to folks—find out if they've seen anything and I mean anything unusual. Anyone or anything that didn't belong. We're looking for a young male, white, in his early twenties. Sandy brown hair. Khaki pants, possibly, blue work shirt, worn work boots. Keep an eye out and keep in touch."

He turned to Will.

"You okay?"

"No. Frankly, I don't mind telling you that I'm not okay. I've got a headache the size of Cleveland. I'm being pushed around and I don't like to be pushed around, I've got to take a piss and I haven't gotten to see ten minutes of the entire goddamned race that I'm supposed to talk about for an hour in—what— ninety minutes."

"You're going on with the show?"

"I guess," Will said. "I don't know what else we could do. They've been promoting it all week. Unless they've got an hour long infomercial up on the rack, they're stuck with us."

"Could prove to be exciting," Whiteside said.

"You bet. You'll stick around to scrape me up off the camera, won't you?"

"Don't talk like that," Whiteside said.

"Easy for you—you're not the staked-out goat."

Will turned and walked across the street toward the TV set-up, frantically being covered because of the growing rain.

It would be some show, he thought, with everyone's final image being a flash, a bang, a puff of smoke, and Will's belly button smacking into the middle of the camera lens.

Here's looking at you, kid.

He stumbled on the curb and stomped, head down against the wind, over to the set.

❧

OUT OF ONE HUNDRED AND TWENTY RIDERS, ONLY TWENTY HAD ACTUALLY FINISHED the ride. The sprinter from Blackhawk brought up the rear, but at least he finished, making his prime check negotiable.

Of the four leaders at the Fairplay side of Hoosier, the mountain bike kid had held on until the first attack, then fallen off the pace. The two Chartwell riders had faded on attacks numbers two and four, leaving the Team Hermes leader to crank it up, pop over the peak, and drop down in a manic, wet run to Breckenridge.

One loop of the park and the race was his.

Will glanced at his watch. The race was forty minutes behind schedule finishing, leaving them only forty-five or fifty minutes until air. There were going to be a number of editors cursing under their breath and crash-cutting video to make the show happen.

But the show would happen, no doubt about that—according to those who had left the station this afternoon, the producer was already losing his handle on reality at about two in the afternoon. That was a good sign. The sooner Boswell lost it, the better the shows usually turned out.

The rain picked up, driving down, then sideways and down again, the wind whipping it into an icy cold shower.

Will couldn't feel his feet.

He watched as the police looked under each chair, examined the microphones, the connections, the cameras, the lights, the risers, both above and below, then wrapped the set in yellow Police Line Do Not Cross tape. Two officers were stationed on opposite corners to detain anyone unauthorized from approaching the "hot set."

He glanced back across to the finish line, where he had not announced jack shit. "Not prudent," Whiteside had said.

Another group of officers were digging around underneath that as well.

Other police were breaking up the crowd and moving everyone along and out of the center of town. It was an easy job, as not one wanted to hang out in the cold mountain rain.

The racers had departed. The leaders were interviewed and gone. All that remained were the cops, the kids who set up and tore down the announce booth and a bunch of TV people, shivering in the rain to do a TV show that would be ready to go only through the benevolent grace of God.

Will called Cheryl on his cell phone and explained the situation. She was worried.

"Can't you just leave?"

"No. I wish I could," Will said, "but they want me here. Do the show. Draw him out. Be the bait."

"I don't like you being the bait."

"I don't like me being the bait. Did the police stop by? Check on you?"

A police officer stopped by to chat, to look around, she said, but hadn't stayed long and hadn't told her anything. After that, her day had merely crept along.

"I'm scared. About you."

Will smiled. "Thanks. I appreciate that. I'll be fine, I think." He chuckled. "But you watch out for yourself. I don't like how this guy keeps bringing up your name."

"He's just trying to spook you. Have them check that set again, will you? Please?"

"I will," he said, even though he knew the police would tell him to go piss up a rope.

"I love you."

"I love you too, Cher. Pat Gooch on the head for me."

"I will."

"I love you."

There was a long pause. "I love you, too, Will. Be careful. Please."

He pushed the end button on his cell phone and stared at it for a long moment.

Let me be blown to smithereens, he thought, but let me see Gooch before I go.

He hacked and spit into a gutter. His stomach was a knot, too tight to undo by any conventional non-alcoholic means. Damn, he wished this was over.

Will turned his face toward the sky and let the rain cool his forehead, his eyes, his lips.

Dear God, just let it be over.

The satellite phone, now a fixture in his hand, rang. He jumped.

Will took a deep breath, raised the phone to his ear and pushed the green button with his thumb.

"Yeah?"

"It's *show time*," was all that was said. The line went dead.

Will took a deep breath and looked at his watch.

Indeed it was.

○

WILL COULDN'T FIND WHITESIDE UNTIL HE WAS ALREADY SITTING ON THE SET WITH Flynn and Morgan Farrenty, the race analyst. Their microphones ran up inside their shirts, essentially tying them down to their chairs. Trapped. Trapped like beavers, right in the bull's-eye.

He saw the police officer march quickly from the announce booth to the TV set, covering his head along the way with an errant sheet of soggy newspaper.

"Whiteside," Will called out.

"Twenty seconds," the floor director said.

Whiteside hurried over to the set.

"Fifteen seconds."

"I just got another call," Will said.

"What this time?" Whiteside asked.

"All he said was 'showtime.' Very theatrical."

"Ten seconds, stand by."

"That's it?"

"That's it."

"Nothing else, no hint?"

"No, just 'showtime.' That's it."

"We're close then. We're close and we're losing the race."

"Oh, that's comforting."

"Stand by for the open!"

Whiteside hurriedly turned away from Will and jogged over to two officers. Will wanted to watch them, but he heard the opening music in his ears and turned to face the camera.

A fern blocked the lower left edge of his view. He leaned forward to move it to the side, but his microphone cable held him back. He could only reach the bottom of the vase with the tips of his fingers. It was heavy. He didn't have enough leverage to get it to move.

He smiled and sat back. They were on the air. The only word in his brain at that particular moment, was the word "shit."

❁

You had to hand it to Roger Flynn. He was a notorious prick and general screwup, but when that red light came on, he was as smooth as fresh paint on glass. He knew what to say, he knew how to say it and he moved a show along well.

He introduced Will and Morgan, then dove right into race day. The decision had been made to keep the winners a secret until the end of the show to build suspense. Some suspense. If anyone was paying any attention they had given it all away in the first five minutes.

But, then again, Will wasn't paying all that much attention.

Morgan Farrenty had a history of doing race coverage, so Flynn, in his inimitable style, was passing everything his way, Flynn's back continually turned toward Will. He was effectively shut out of the show. The body language said it all.

Will leaned into the shot, removing the fern from his line of sight, and tried to make himself a part of the conversation. It was impossible to do. Every time Will opened his mouth to add something to what Morgan Farrenty had pointed out about the race, Flynn stepped in, broke the rhythm, and pushed Farrenty in a new direction.

They were on a tight shot of Farrenty. Will sat back, then leaned forward to the limit of his microphone cord, stretched out his hands and broke off the top of the fern, tossing the branch to the side of the stage.

The viewers would be amazed, he thought. The plant had lost nearly ten inches before the first commercial break.

At that moment, Flynn turned to Will.

"Will, what did you think about that?"

Will hadn't been paying attention for the last twenty seconds. And Flynn knew it.

"What did I think about what?"

"About what Morgan said—was this stage of the race key to the win?"

For what seemed an eternity, the two men stared at each other, Will's mind racing to come up with an answer.

He opened his mouth and one barreled out, completely and totally spontaneous, completely and totally bullshit.

"Well, Roger, every portion of a race is key to the win. Holding back at the right time. Attacking at the right time. Allowing yourself to be reeled in at the right time ..."

It was tough to concentrate. It was tough to bullshit. In his ear, the producer, back at the station, was screaming over the IFB while Will was in middle of his rambling reply.

"... everything you do means something at the end of the race ..."

"WHAT'S THAT GODDAMNED TREE DOING ON MY SET? I DIDN'T ASK FOR ANY GODDAMNED TREE—IT LOOKS LIKE A MOOSE HAS BEEN GNAWING AT IT ... GET THAT GODDAMNED THING OFF MY SET!"

"... the key is putting all the things you do together at the right time to put yourself in a position to win."

"Morgan said it wasn't as important as it looked."

Flynn smiled. The producer screamed in Will's ear. The world waited. A thought was trying to force its way past Will's on air panic and into the front of his head.

"Morgan is wrong," was all Will said. Flynn sat back in his seat with a laugh and turned to Morgan Farrenty. The three were on a wide shot, Flynn smiling, Will distracted, Morgan Farrenty ready to defend his honor and insight.

"GET THAT TREE OFF MY SET!" the disembodied voice screamed.

Morgan began to say something, egged along by Flynn's frantic nodding in agreement. Will stared at them, then the floor, then the camera, then the fern.

"DO I NEED A GODDAMNED LUMBERJACK TO GET THAT TREE OFF MY SET?"

The tree, Will thought, the tree. The fern. The too-tall fern in the black glass vase. The black glass vase that was too heavy to move with your fingers.

His breath went into short, noisy gasps. Everything about Will collapsed into one, tight, brightly-lit view of the vase in front of him. His skin crawled. His hands shook.

He was staring at his own death, not more than two-and-a-half feet away.

Will caught himself and turned away. Don't look at it. He's watching. He knows. Don't look at it. Is it a timer? Can he trigger it? From a distance? Who knows? Don't look. Don't give it away. Don't let him know that you know.

Although he already had. His look at the fern was about as subtle as hitting the asshole directly on the head with a two-by-four.

In the middle of Flynn's seemingly private conversation with Morgan, Will leaned into the two shot.

"Time for a commercial, wouldn't you say, Roger, time for a quick break? We'll be right back."

Flynn looked thunderstruck. Thunderstruck and annoyed.

Will could hear the producer screaming a litany of profanity into his ear, but couldn't make out any of the specific curses. His brain was on autopilot. His mind had shut down.

"TAKE THE BREAK, TAKE THE BREAK, TAKE THE BREAK!" the producer screamed. The scene mercifully faded to black and the guy with the tigers popped up selling furniture.

Flynn spun on Will and grabbed him by the collar.

"You son of a bitch—what the hell are you doing ..."

Will brought his arm under then over and again under Flynn's, pinning Roger's wrist with his armpit and putting pressure up against the elbow.

"Yeeeeaagh!" Flynn mewled.

"Whiteside! Whiteside! The vase. It's the goddamned vase!"

Whiteside ran over from the door of the production truck where he had been watching the broadcast.

"What? What vase?"

"This one—" Will nodded. "This one right here."

Without thinking, he released Flynn, who pushed him away and off balance. Will grabbed at the arm of the light wood director's chair but it simply fell along with him. Suddenly, they were all tied up together in the microphone cable.

Will cracked his shin against the coffee table, which set the vase to rocking. Will grabbed at it, blindly, but got his wrist caught up in the cable. He slapped at the vase rather than grabbing it and could only watch in horror as it wheeled and rolled and finally toppled off the table to the floor of the set and then, with a bounce, to the concrete of the ground below.

He heard a shatter of glass and waited for the explosion that would be followed quickly either by heavenly choirs or hellish polka bands.

"What the hell are you doing, Ross?!" Flynn screamed.

Will simply stared at the mess on the ground: a shattered vase, scattered dirt, a broken fern and a mass of wax and rock and gray powders, mixed together to form some kind of weight and drainage at the bottom of the vase.

"Well, at least we've got the TREE OFF MY GODDAMNED SET!" Will heard in his ear.

"Jesus, Ross, you've thrown everything off—the show is going to be a mess now."

Will looked quickly over at Flynn and Farrenty with apology, then back at the shattered remains of the vase. Whiteside ran up to the edge of the set, glanced carefully around, then walked carefully up to the ball of waxen filler that now carried the imprint of the broken vase.

He crouched down beside it, squinted, took it gingerly and rolled it up toward Will.

Vases, potting soil, ferns and drainage—all the things that normally go into a vase, never came complete with digital timers.

Digital timers that now read 5:30 and :29 and :28 and :27 ...

Will felt God reach down and squeeze the air out of his lungs.

Flynn continued to babble behind him.

"Get everybody off the set," Whiteside said, quietly. "Take cover."

He picked up the wax ball carefully, cradling it like a child, and walked quickly behind the stage toward a creek that ran through an open space in the village. He yelled orders to the other officers, who began to quickly clear people away from the scene, including the production crew, lookie-loos, Flynn, Morgan, and Will. As Will clambered down the slick, wet stairs of the set, he watched Dale Dwyer run, camera in hand, in the opposite direction to catch a shot of the breaking news.

Will stopped to yell a warning in Dale's direction, then turned back, ran up the stairs, and grabbed his bag. He then ran back down, slipped, twisted his ankle sharply and hobbled away toward the police officers. They were waving everyone across the square, behind the announce booth and back behind a building.

"Down, down! Cover your heads! Cover your heads!"

"What the hell is going on?" Flynn was whining, loudly, behind the next building, "What is going on?"

In the gathering dusk, Will could see a police officer grab Flynn by the collar, push him down to the ground and whisper something to the back of his head.

For the split second, Will would have given anything to have heard it.

✿

THE SCREAMS QUIETED.

The shuffling and yelling ceased.

Will could only hear the wind, the rain, an occasional cry, and the beating of his heart. Too fast to be used as a clock. Way too fast. He tried to estimate the time. He looked at his watch.

What time was it, what time was it when they ran off the set, when the digital display read 28-27-26? What time? How long? How long?

He bent his head down and began to cover his ears when he heard it.

A sharp report, like a handful of M-80's going off too close for comfort. The sound pierced his ears.

"Jesus!" he screamed and dug his head into his hands.

His ears rang from the shock of the sound.

He slowly opened his eyes and looked around.

He was still here. Still alive.

The walls were still here. He looked down the alley.

The town was still here.

He rose up into a crouch, then stood.

"Get down!" the officer next to Flynn yelled.

Will waited. And listened as best he could. Then, ignoring the orders of the police officer, he turned the corner of the building, walked to the rear of the announcer's trailer, peeked underneath it, crawled out and stood on the main street of Breckenridge.

The town, wreathed in a cloud of smoke that smelled like that from a thousand Black Cats, was silent.

Will crossed the empty street and headed for the creek.

❀

RAYMOND WHITESIDE SAT BESIDE THE CREEK, HIS RIGHT HAND HOLDING A FANCY folding knife, both covered with a gray, waxy substance.

With this left hand, he casually smoked a Marlboro.

"Is it clear?" Will asked quietly, walking up behind him.

Whiteside glanced over his shoulder.

"For now, it's as clear as it's going to be."

Looking down at the mangled ball of wax in the shape of a vase, now with a digital clock cut from its heart, Will said, "Sorry about knocking it off the table like that."

"It's not something you normally do with a bomb, man," Whiteside took a long drag off the cigarette, held the smoke in his lungs, then blew it out through his nose. "That's for sure. But you probably saved this town and everybody in it. If this thing had gone off as planned, there would have been nothing left but a hole where Breckenridge stood. You gave me the time to dig the detonators out of the charge and throw them in the creek."

"Aren't you supposed to defuse these things?"

"Sometimes, Mr. Ross, you forget your training and go by primitive instinct. Separate bomb from detonator, throw in water. Watch go boom."

The bomb squad members were surrounding them now, carefully gathering up the wax ball and wiping material off Whiteside's right hand.

He worked the cigarette around them and took another drag.

"What was it?" Will asked. "It looked like candle wax."

"What do you think, Chuck?"

One man in blast gear stood back and looked at the ball of wax as it disappeared toward the bomb truck.

"Hmm. I'm thinking RDX and aluminum powder. Wax binder. Easy to work with. Relatively safe until detonated. Good range on both primary and collateral damage."

"Check the wax," Whiteside said, quietly, "it may be D-2."

"Calcium chloride?"

"Maybe. Handle it with care."

"You should talk," the armored officer said, "you're the one smoking around it."

The officer pointed at Will. "Get this civilian out of here," he said, then pulled down his visor and walked back toward the truck.

Another helmeted officer moved toward Will but Whiteside waved him off. "He's involved in the investigation. Let him stay." He looked at Will.

He took another drag off the cigarette, held the smoke and slowly blew it out.

"You know, after a moment like this, I should be listening to the stream and the babbling brook and getting in touch with life, that sort of thing. And all I can think to do is chain-smoke coffin nails."

"If I didn't think I'd throw up," Will said, "I'd join you."

He sat down on the hill beside Whiteside. The grass was wet and cold, and seeped right through his pants.

He didn't care.

"That's two," Whiteside said. "Two out of ... how many did he say?"

"Four. Four devices. Two clues."

"Only two. Why not more?"

"He said I didn't have the ears to hear them."

"What's he got against your ears?"

"I dunno. I've always liked them, pretty much. They keep my hat on and my brains in."

"Sounds like he wants your brains out."

"According to my wife that would be like breaking open one of those puff ball plants. All powder, no insides."

Whiteside chuckled and took another drag.

"I know we should be looking for a third, but, hmph, somehow, I can't get my legs to move." He sucked again on the cigarette.

For the first time, Will noticed that Whiteside's hand was shaking. And that the shaking was getting worse.

Will stood and turned to one of the bomb squad officers walking the scene, looking for pieces of the detonator.

"Officer—could you get him some help?" he nodded toward Raymond Whiteside.

"The medical officer was here immediately following ..."

"Yeah, well, I think you had better find him again."

Will looked over and saw Whiteside now guiding the cigarette and his left hand to his mouth with his right.

The officer nodded and whistled sharply, waving his hand toward the bomb squad truck. An officer nodded and quickly began to run toward Whiteside carrying a medical bag.

Will hoped there was something magical inside.

He could use some of it himself.

Will turned and walked back toward the deserted set, the lights smoking in the cold, wet air, the chairs fallen at odd angles in the rush to get away, the cables snaking away to a dead end in the truck. He looked at the monitor. The station was showing a repeat of one of Elliott's entertainment shows. He was interviewing the stars, his best friends.

Will stepped over to the edge of the stage and watched the monitor for a moment longer, before dropping his head to his hands.

Christ. He had never been so exhausted. Not on Ventoux, not on Alpe d'Huez, not nowhere, not no how. He just wanted to crawl into a warm, dry, safe place and just die.

He thought for a second.

No, not die. Sleep. Always a chance you'll come back from sleep.

His mind drifted. He could hear the medical officer trying to get Whiteside to stand, asking for help as he did so. The bomb hadn't gone off as planned, Will thought, but how many lives had been forever affected by the fact that it very nearly did?

The bag at his side tingled. Will felt the vibration but didn't react to it for a moment. Then, he stood up straight, a shot of adrenaline coursing through his brain, like lightning in a bottle.

He looked over at the medical officer, now standing beside Whiteside and supporting Whiteside's left arm.

"Call! I've got a call coming in!"

Will dug in his bag, the satellite phone, its antenna extended, catching on the notes and cords and cables and bullshit that he had carried through the day.

"It's him! It's him! He's calling!"

Whiteside jerked up and away from Chuck and the medical officer, the call energizing him as much as it had Will. He ran to Will's side yelling, "Wait— wait ... NOW ... take it now!"

He leaned in close to Will's ear as if to listen.

Will hit the green button.

"Yes?"

"Oh, well, Will," the voice cooed. "How nice to hear your voice. Let's see, what could this mean? Well, that little look I saw on your face just before that last commercial break made me wonder if you might have realized that I consider myself quite a florist."

"Go on."

"Oh, you don't want to play? Too bad. You know, Will, if I had known that they were going to replace your show with that entertainment reporter of yours asking John Travolta horrible questions about shitty movies, maybe I should have sent him a present, eh?"

"Whatever," Will said sharply. "What's next?"

"Oh, my. We are impatient, now, aren't we Will?"

The anger and frustration rose in Will's throat, hot bile that demanded to be spewed toward an enemy who was only a voice on a phone, a pair of work shoes and khaki pants under a table, a silhouette in the sunshine of a bright Colorado day that had turned dark and gray and empty.

He wanted to rage, he wanted a miracle, he wanted to reach through the phone and throttle the man responsible.

Tired, afraid, frustrated, and filled with a mounting fury that had to target, Will forced his voice into control and merely said, "What's ... next?"

The voice popped on the other end of the line. There was a hiss of static and audio wave, as if a station was being dialed in on an old A.M. radio, followed by another pop and the voice returned.

"... your emotions, Will. All in good time, my friend. All in good time. By the way, Will, did I ever mention to you how much I like—children?"

The question clawed instantly at Will's throat.

"What?"

"Children. I love children Will. Love to make them laugh. Love to give them presents and watch them laugh."

"You ... you son of a bitch! You son of a bitch!" Will screamed into the phone.

"Yeah, I'm back in Denver right now, Will. Was watching TV at that bar just down the street from your little bungalow. Now, I'm watching your front door, Will. Now I'm watching your front door."

"Oh, God, please no ..."

"What, Will, what?" Will had turned the phone away from Whiteside. "What's he saying, Will?"

"He's going after my family. He's at my house now."

Without another word, Whiteside ran off toward the police cars near the bomb squad truck.

"Look, please. Don't do this. Don't do this."

"Aw, too late, Will. Done. Done. Unless of course, you luck out again and can stop her from coming to the door. You should have said 'thank you,' Will. Should have said it."

"Thank you. Oh, God, THANK YOU! PLEASE! I BEG YOU—PLEASE! OH, MY LORD, PLEASE DON'T. PLEASE. THANK YOU. THANK YOU."

"Aw, that's nice, Will. Begging and crying and everything. And I do believe you mean it. But. I've rung the doorbell, Will. I've rung the doorbell."

"Oh, God, NO!"

"Try and stop her, Will. Try and stop her."

Will froze. His ear to the phone. His mouth open in a silent scream. His temples pounding. His eyes forcing back tears of terror.

What? What? What? What to do? What to do?

He pulled the phone away from his ear and punched frantically at random buttons, hitting, finally hitting the red "disconnect."

"Don't do that," one of the officers cried out, "stay in contact with him!"

Will ignored him.

"Fuck you, Chuck," he barked, and then began pounding at numbers. Call her. Call her. Call her. Get her on the line. Get her away from the front door. Call her. Call her. The numbers wouldn't work. He couldn't make his fingers hit the right buttons. The numbers wouldn't work. Wrong area code. Wrong satellite code. Wrong numbers. Wrong Numbers. Wrong FUCKING NUMBERSSSSSSSSSSSSSS!

He slammed the phone to the pavement in front of him, the case shattering into at least four pieces—battery, handset, antenna and ... and ... putty.

A gray, mass of putty stuck to the ground. A large computer chip of some kind poked from its top, with two wires leading into the guts of the phone.

Ears to hear. Would you even have the ears to hear?

Everyone crowding around him looked at the broken satellite phone on the ground before them. Officer Chuck spoke first.

"Shit. Clear the area. CLEAR THE AREA!"

A bomb squad officer in full blast gear grabbed Will by the shoulders and pulled him while running towards the trucks and squad cars. Will ran, then remembered, and broke away. He pawed, madly, at his carry bag.

Cell phone. Find the cell phone. Cell phone.

It was down there. It was down there somewhere. Somewhere deep. He hadn't used it since Grant? Was that it? Grant? A thousand years away.

The officer grabbed him from behind.

"Come on!"

"GET THE HELL AWAY FROM ME!" Will screamed. "GET THE HELL ..." He found the phone, threw the bag to the ground and ran away from the officer, in the opposite direction, down to the creek and around a building.

"Come on, come on, come on, power up you son of a bitch, power up!" The phone beeped and the lights flashed and the display read "Ready."

"Take your time. Take your time." He carefully pushed in 1—the area code—the prefix—the suffix—take your time—take your time—he looked at the numbers—right. They were right. He pushed send.

"Please. Please please please. Hit a cell. Hit a cell. The line hissed. Click. And took. A second later, he could hear and recognize the ring of his own phone.

"Pick up. Pick up, pick up. Pick up, Cheryl ... PICK UP THE GODDAMNED PHONE!"

❀

CHERYL WAS NEARLY AT THE DOOR WHEN THE PHONE RANG. SHE WANTED TO TURN and answer it, maybe it was Will. She had been worried ever since the show had gone to break and never returned. No word from the station. No word from him. No word from the police. She turned back to the phone and hesitated. The doorbell rang again, insistently.

She was there—she'd get that first.

She opened the door to no one.

She was about to step back into the house when something colorful caught her eye: a large, bright tennis ball, two or three times the normal size, sitting on her front step. A bow decorated the top. A card dangled from the base of the bow. It read, in large letters, "For You, Little One."

She bent down to pick it up. The colors, the size, the texture all amused her. It would amuse Gooch as well.

"Hey, look, pal ..." She shook it over her belly.

The phone continued to ring. She hadn't set the machine. She should get that now.

She turned to step back into the house, then stopped.

Something about the ball bothered her.

It was filled. It was filled with water. She held it close to her ear and shook it easily.

It was full of something, like a dog's tennis ball left out in the yard during a heavy rain.

She pulled it away from her face and lowered it to her side.

The phone continued to ring.

She thought for a second, then turned back to face the yard.

"We'll leave this one for Daddy," she whispered, tossed the ball lightly toward the grass, bow and all, then turned back in to answer the phone.

She was picked up bodily by the blast wave and hurled back through her own living room toward the dining room and the kitchen, where she hit the wall and fell in a crumbled heap on the floor.

She raised her hands to her side to protect her womb from the shower of glass and splinters that followed her to the floor.

She let out one cry each.
One for herself.
One for her child.
The phone had stopped ringing.

CHAPTER FIFTEEN:

REAPER

"CAN'T THIS THING GO ANY FASTER?" WILL BEGGED, TRYING TO KEEP his voice quiet, his tone, his tone calm, his emotions under control. The Colorado State Patrol officer looked at him quickly and turned back to the road.

"Not on this road. Not on this night. We're doing close to a hundred on the straights, but this road is like a snake. It's raining, and with traffic the way it is—you still want to get there alive, don't you?"

Will didn't answer. Maybe he did, maybe he didn't.

Five minutes after Will's cell phone broke the connection with the house, one of Whiteside's officers had arrived there and called Breckenridge about the situation or what was left of it. What was left of Will's life.

Will had gone mad. He had raged, he had pleaded, he had cried, he had fumed, he had begged. God, Allah, Jehovah, anyone, please, please, someone, help me, drive me, give me a car. He had tried to steal a police motorcycle. They had physically stopped him, the doctor shooting something into Will's hip that warmed his leg but did nothing for his soul.

He wouldn't have made two miles before killing himself.

He wanted to kill himself, put himself out of his own misery.

But who would cared? It was certain that he himself didn't. Cheryl couldn't. The others wouldn't.

He just had to get to Denver. Simple as that. He had to get home. He had to get to Cheryl and Gooch.

He had to get to the woman who had saved him. He had to get to the child who would make him whole. He had to get to his family.

Bending his head down, Will clasped his fingers behind his head and pulled. The police car sped on through the gathering darkness, with the man in the passenger's seat pulling his head down to his chest, stretching his spine, and repeating obsessive movements in some vague hope of making the time pass more quickly.

He pulled his head down, feeling the painful stretch in his back. And he pulled harder.

Will couldn't think. He couldn't feel. Not externally, anyway. His heart grew to bursting, his face flushed, he rocked back and forth, trying to release some of the pressure. He wanted to hit something. He wanted to shoot something. He wanted to act.

He wanted to rage. He wanted. He wanted.

He wanted to die.

Without them, he wanted to die.

After forever, the police cruiser pulled up to the trauma entrance at Denver Health Medical Center. CU Health Sciences had been closer for Cheryl and the baby, but Denver Medical had one of the top trauma centers in the country, Whiteside had said. Will remembered the remark vaguely. Trauma. They would need a trauma center. Not just that, but one of the best in the country. Will flushed as the cataract of thoughts crashed through his mind, uncontrolled. All ugly. All fearful. All shrouded with death.

Will threw open the door and jumped out into a thunderstorm as the car rolled to a stop. The sky rolled and cracked in the distance, the rain a steady, heavy downpour. He slipped, stumbled, caught his balance, grabbed a pole to stop himself, twisted around it and ran through the sliding door of Emergency. He skated across the polished floor to the nurses' station.

"Cheryl Crane. Ross. Cheryl Ross. Any word?"

"Who are you?"

"I'm her husband. Any word?"

The nurse's face changed from suspicious to sympathetic in a heartbeat.

"I'm sorry Mr. Ross. We ... we don't know about her, yet. There is a waiting room—right over there. I'll let the doctors know you're here. They'll come out and talk to you as soon as they know anything."

"It's been an hour. An hour and a half. Don't they know anything yet?"

He looked at his watch. 9:15. He didn't know how long anything had been. It had been forever.

The nurse looked at him, but refused to meet his gaze.

She knew. She knew something.

"Please ..." Will begged, reaching across the desk top and touching her left shoulder. "Please ..."

She jumped back as if shocked.

"No, Mr. Ross, I'm sorry. But the doctor is going to have to talk to you. The doctor is going to have to see you. As soon ... as soon as he knows anything. Please. Take a seat in the waiting room. Your friends are there."

"Friends? Friends. Yes. Thanks." He wanted to scream, to lose his temper and spread it over the walls of the trauma center, but there was nothing left to lose, nothing there emotionally. His feelings were scattered across a courtyard in Breckenridge and in the passenger seat of a police cruiser that had broken every speed limit known to man down the Interstate 70 corridor while seemingly moving at a snail's pace.

As if someone or something had just turned a valve in his head, Will felt empty, alone, and exhausted.

"Yes, alright, the waiting room," he nodded, turned and shuffled to the doors leading out of the main traffic patterns and into the warmer, calmer, and quieter atmosphere of the waiting room.

He stood at the door, as if he had just walked through the curtains of a Broadway stage. All eyes in the room turned to him. One family—father, mother and sister—looked at him with a bright moment of expectation, then turned away, their wait continuing. A young man, his hand wrapped in red gauze, waited to be called. At the end of the room sat Hootie Bosco. Beside him was Nancy, her arms wrapped around him. Beside her, and talking quietly into a cell phone, was Barbara Gooden. Bill Sessions was standing in the corner, leaning his head against the wall.

They all looked toward him as he stepped into the center of the room.

Barbara was up first, across the room, and smothering him in a tight hug.

"Oh, Will. Oh, Will. I am so sorry. So very sorry about all of this ..." She began to weep, quietly.

As if in a drunken dream, Will slowly reached up and patted her absent mindedly on the back.

"That's ... okay. Barbara. That's alright. Please." As gently as he could, he broke the hug and pushed her away. It wasn't her. It was him. He didn't want to be hugged. He didn't want to be smothered. He was already being smothered by the atmosphere of this hospital, of the world around him and by the pressure inside his own chest.

He wanted to scream. The rage, which had so completely left him seconds ago at the nurses's station, had returned in full force to make itself known in the back of his head. A squall line, not unlike the storm outside, rose, rained and passed quickly through his mind.

Nancy could see it behind his eyes. She squeezed his arm, leaned forward and kissed him lightly on the cheek.

"We're here, Will. No matter what. Come. Sit down. Sit down with us."

He nodded his thanks.

Hootie stepped up and shook his hand.

Bill Sessions smiled from the corner.

"Has anyone heard anything?" Will asked. "Has the doctor been out to say anything?"

"Not yet," Barbara Gooden said. "They brought her right over ninety min-utes ago. I've been here for an hour. I guess the longest. They haven't been out. The station has been calling, but they're not giving out any information on her condition."

"Or the baby?"

"Or the baby, Will. I'm sorry."

He nodded. He mindlessly patted her shoulder, as if he was walking through a fog. A fog in a dream. He wasn't sure about anything anymore. Where he was, how he was walking, what he was doing or saying or looking at. The wave of anger had passed again, leaving him exhausted. All he wanted to do was collapse in a heap.

He stepped over and sat down next to Hootie.

"You want some coffee or something?"

"No. No, that's okay." He paused. "Thank you."

He rubbed his face, hard, then leaned his head back and closed his eyes.

So, he thought, his mind wandering aimlessly through his own life, this is what it felt like. This is what all those other people, and their families and their friends, had felt like during that long, distant summer when he had been at the eye of the hurricane.

When people had been hurt and injured and killed around him—how many people, how many—it had never touched him at all. He had seen death, face to face, but it wasn't his death. It didn't affect him personally. Beyond Thomas, it wasn't anyone he knew or cared about, and he had been the man standing at that funeral making the jokes, telling the jokes. The life of the party.

He had seen them die. It had kept him up at night. One night, maybe. Two at the most. But it hadn't changed his outlook. It hadn't touched his soul.

Hey ... sorry about that. Too damned bad. Where's the buffet?

Now, it was his day in the barrel.

The reality of it all was upon him.

It weighed him down and squeezed his lungs and fried the connections in his brain in such a way that he felt he must go mad.

And it gnawed at his soul.

Will felt helpless, adrift, alone and frustrated. There was no way to do anything. He was out of the loop. God and the doctors had to handle it all.

Helpless. Just so goddamned helpless.

And alone. Hootie lightly put his arm on Will's shoulder.

He didn't even feel it.

And the night wore on.

❁

LATER—FIVE MINUTES, FIVE HOURS, WILL DIDN'T KNOW, WILL DIDN'T CARE—there was some mumbling outside the entrance to the waiting room. A doctor, in blue surgical scrubs dashed with blood, looked in, pulled his head out, checked a medical chart he had on the clipboard in his hand, pushed his head back in again and said, "Mr. Ross?"

Will stood as if electrified.

Barbara, Hootie, Nancy and Bill all stood as well and stared at the doctor.

"Mr. Ross, could I see you?"

Will nodded, slowly, and started to walk toward the doctor. His feet were encased in lead shoes, those old diving shoes the hard-hat guys used to wear. He wanted to walk. He wanted to know. But, he never wanted to reach the doctor, he didn't want to hear the possibility of bad news. Only the possibility of good. He only wanted to hear good news. Good news, please.

The doctor's face didn't register an emotion.

As Will finally stepped around the corner of the waiting room, an eternity later, he could see the news trucks and the lights outside. Blindly, Will looked at his watch. 10:10. Late news live shots. He was news. Cheryl and Gooch were news.

TV6 was there. He could see the logo on the truck. Nine. Four. Seven. Two and Thirty-one had to be somewhere nearby.

He saw a reporter he didn't know point through the windows at him, the camera turning suddenly in his direction, the photographer frantically focusing to get the shot. The moment of truth.

The moment the husband learned. The father learned. The man learned the fate of his family.

News? No. But compelling, that's for damned sure.

Will pulled his gaze away and looked at the doctor.

He took a deep breath. It came out in a rattle. He wanted to ask what he couldn't, but something deep within him still found the power to speak, to speak words outside himself.

"Please, sir, tell me. What ... how are they? How is she?"

The words came out in a gush, in a clumsy, frightened pile.

"Mr. Ross, I'm sorry. I am so very, very sorry."

Will was trying to say "What?", but there was no air, no power behind the word. His lungs were squeezed shut, his heart was pounding, his mind blank with the horror of the news more frightening than anything he had ever heard.

"I'm sorry."

"Your wife, Mr. Ross, I'm sorry."

He placed a hand on Will's shoulder. Will could hear Nancy burst into tears behind him. Barbara Gooden cried out. Hootie, or Bill, or someone, shouted "Oh, God!"

But Will, Will wasn't even there. He wasn't even there.

The pressure grew in his face.

The tears began to flow.

And, yet, he wasn't even there.

His mouth moved, disconnected to the rest of him, his lips moved unrelated to the world.

"H ... ho ... how?"

"The blast. The blast wave. There was a lot of trauma, Mr. Ross. We tried. But ... she, well, instinctively, turned herself so that she took the majority of the blast. And, I can only tell you that she willed herself to stay alive until the baby was born."

"The baby?"

"The baby. She's four weeks premature, Mr. Ross. She's in Pediatric ICU now."

"She? She."

"A girl, Mr. Ross. You're the father of a baby girl."

Will shook his head. No, not that. He didn't want to know about that. Not yet. Not now.

"Cheryl? What about Cheryl?" He began to scream as if he hadn't heard.

"I'm sorry, Mr. Ross. The strain of the blast and a c-section ... there was just too much ... she just didn't make it."

"Noooo! No!" he wailed, clutching at the shoulders of the doctor to hold himself erect. "Make it different! Make it come out different! Goddamn you! Make it turn out different! Please, please, please."

The outburst drained him again, bringing a calm into the center of his head. The storm ended. He could hear himself think, even if just for a moment, as if a calming hand had touched his heart.

"Did ... did she see the baby? Did Cheryl get a chance to see her baby?"

The doctor sighed. What should he do? Tell the truth or the comforting lie? He decided on the truth. This man deserved the truth, even if he might not be able to handle it. "I honestly don't know, Mr. Ross. I'm sorry. If she did, it was only for a moment."

Will nodded, dumbly.

The wave of serenity passed as quickly as it had come. His emotions were out of control again. She was gone. He was a father. She was here. The baby was here. She would need him. But she was gone. Cheryl was gone.

There was suddenly nothing but jelly in his legs, his arms, his chest, his head.

There was nothing he could think.

There was nothing he could feel.

Slowly, Will collapsed to the floor of the trauma center, as if deflating, and wished that he could seep through the pores of the floor and into the earth and disappear and just be dead. Just be dead.

And be together.

And be together with Cheryl.

With his face pressed against the cold, hard surface of the polished marble floor, through his tears he could see sunbeams in the night, reflections in the wet glass of the rounded wings of angels. Oddly, the sight brought him comfort, comfort in the thought that she was not alone. She would never be alone.

The angels. The angels of light would be with her. To take her. To take her to heaven.

He closed his eyes. He wanted to sleep. He wanted to die. He wanted to disappear forever.

And the cameras, all six of them, focused their cyclopean eyes through the window and onto Will, collapsed on the floor, so burdened by the news he had just heard that no power on earth could keep him standing. The wall of portable lights on the cameras created circular pools of light in the rain, like golden angels' wings descending through the horror.

The videographers drew their breath and the pictures shot through the cameras, the cables, the microwave trucks, through the air and to the station. There people watched, nodded and shook their heads over the tragedy of it all, as they sent it out again, the image winging its way across the city and into the warm and lighted living rooms of the audiences around the city and watching on cable and satellite dishes around the state.

All packaged, dispensed and already placed in an easy to digest emotional context for the information and entertainment of the viewers.

It became live. Compelling. Award-winning coverage, destined to be a part of every Emmy-nominated story at next year's contest for photography, spot news, use of violins and triple-lap dissolves, glorious emotional writing and hard-hitting reporting.

And beyond Denver, the image became wide-ranging human-interest news, that was soon to be a part, a highly promotable part, of every newscast in the country.

"Tragedy in Denver. See what happens when a man learns the fate of his family ... right after this ..."

Commercial.

And in newsrooms across the city, producers, reporters, writers and production assistants watched, in guilty fascination, as reality fell into their hands and once more played itself out before their very eyes.

And they knew they had a hit on their hands.

EPILOGUE

SHOE AND REX COWERED AT HIS FEET IN A FITFUL SLEEP. THEY HAD BEEN outside when the blast took place, but they had heard the noise, smelled the blood and knew the terror.

They searched for comfort at Will's shoes and found none.

Will sat at the kitchen table and finished his second beer.

He stared at the wall where Cheryl and Gooch had come to rest.

He put his head down and cried again.

✿

HE HAD SPENT THE NIGHT AT THE WINDOW OF PEDIATRIC ICU. THE BABY HAD been stabilized, checked and upgraded. She was finally moved to Denver Children's Hospital across town.

Hootie and Nancy drove him there and waited with him. They reassured him that they would see to whatever arrangements needed to be made. Will nodded dumbly. His mind simply wouldn't accept the thought of what had to be done.

There was still hope, he thought. There was still a chance to wake up and know that this was only a dream—a terrible, terrible dream.

At Children's Hospital, he finally got to touch his daughter for the first time through the glass of the incubator, feel her tiny fingers in his hand. She clutched. And she slept.

If this was a dream, it was a dream without waking. This was no dream. This was no dream.

There was nothing else he could do, other than watch the baby sleep. Finally, a doctor took a look at Will and nodded, gave him a shot and sent him home.

"She'll be fine. We've got her. Come back later today when you're rested."

Will nodded.

Hootie and Nancy drove him home, at first arguing for him to come with them, but no, he wanted his own house. His own things. His own wife.

The light grew through the kitchen window. First came the false dawn, followed by the smoky gray of the real one, then the orange, yellow and pink light that would soon lead to the blue of the day.

In the living room it was all darkness. The front of the house was covered with sheets of thick plywood, replacing broken doors and windows and blocking the light.

Blocking the light.

The blood was still here. The glass. The wood shards. He had to step around it all. The police weren't a cleaning crew, he had been told. It was up to him to wash his wife's blood out of the carpets and off the walls.

Maybe he knew someone? No, he didn't know anyone.

No one.

It was up to him.

He'd scrub the moment away later.

He looked at the clock. It was 5:15. The day was starting to brighten. Sunday. Sunday morning.

He picked up the phone and called the hospital.

The same phone that she hadn't answered.

The call that could have killed him.

The call that might have saved her.

And Gooch. Together.

"ICU."

"Hi. This is Will Ross. Is there any change?"

"No, sir, Mr. Ross. She's resting comfortably. She's resting."

"Okay. Thank you. When can I see her?"

"Anytime, Mr. Ross. Anytime."

"Is ten okay?" he couldn't control the catch in his throat.

"Anytime, Mr. Ross. There are no visiting hours as far as you are concerned."

"Thank you."

He hung up the phone and stared out the window. It was going to be another glorious Colorado day. Glorious. Just like yesterday. Glorious.

Glorious.

The dogs were quiet until the moment he rose from the kitchen chair. They were up beside him in a second. Silent. Staring. He nodded down to them and picked his way through the debris field to the stairs. He walked up them, the dogs following close behind. He'd have to get that glass cleaned up quickly, he thought. Protect their paw pads.

Random thoughts. Everything was random.

So this was shock, he thought. This was shock.

He stepped into his bedroom, his and Cheryl's room, and peeled off his clothes from the day before. They were dirty, damp and ancient history.

He opened the drawer and pulled out a fresh change of clothes. Riding clothes. Pants. Jersey. Socks.

Slowly, he dressed in his room while in a fog, in a daze.

Zipping up the jersey, he let his hands keep moving upward to smooth back his hair. Pieces were in it. Pieces of … stuff. The day. The show. The night.

Pieces. All in pieces.

He flicked them onto the floor, turned and walked downstairs, picking his way through the glass again, the dogs close behind, until he reached the back door. The dogs balked. They didn't want to leave the house again. They hadn't protected. They didn't want to leave. They didn't want to fail again.

He stepped out and closed the door behind him.

Let them stay. For now. Let them stay.

Will crossed to the garage and unlocked the back door, opened it, stepped in, and took a deep breath. He could smell the bike among all the other smells, he could smell the bike in here. Somewhere.

He picked his shoes up off the work bench and slid them on, same order as every day of his life, right foot, left foot, tighten right, tighten left.

He picked up his helmet and gloves, the Haven logo staring at him, reminding him of the past, of the first day he saw her. Of the first day he fell in love.

He smelled his way to the bike, sliding on the gloves, resting the helmet on the top of his head. He lifted the bike off the wall pegs and touched the tires. Close enough. Close enough for government work.

He didn't have the heart to pump tires. He was flying on automatic pilot.

He rolled the bike to the edge of the garage and pushed the button, the door lifting like the curtain of a cheap theater.

Will rolled the bike out and pushed the button again. The door came down. Slowly. With effort. It closed inches behind the rear wheel.

He looked out onto the street, expecting to see newsmen and photographers still staring at him, watching for another prize-winning reaction. He was alone. Then he realized it was Sunday morning. Only skeleton crews worked on Sunday morning in the newsrooms. Whoever was on duty had other things to cover. He would be focused on later in the day, with the blistered and broken house in the background of the evening's live shots.

Compelling video. Right in your very own neighborhood, folks.

Will sighed. Let it go, he thought, just let it go.

Throwing his right leg over the seat, he leaned the frame near him and snapped his right foot into the pedal.

He felt it begin. Deep within him it lay, dormant and forgotten for so many years.

Not the magic. He could ride forever and never find the magic again. He pushed off into the street, his mind a blank, his soul empty, his heart … his heart cold at the edges, with just a spark … that single spark, still alive at the core.

As he rode, the spark grew into a desire, a need, a hunger to take control of his own life, to make his mark upon those around him who had so easily taken advantage of him—those he had allowed to take advantage of him. Kim. Carl. Barbara. Bergalis. Haven. He had spent so many years being pushed and pulled and used by so many in his life. Now he felt a need to make that change, for both himself and for Gooch. And for Cheryl. He had to make that change for Cheryl.

And as that spark grew, something else grew within him, something he hadn't felt for years, if truly ever before.

What grew within contained a raw, unfettered bitterness. An icy anger. A cold and brutal fury.

It grew from the small coal in his chest into a consuming rage that engulfed his very soul. The rage exploded, battering all feeling within him, until that moment when he felt he could no longer sustain it, no longer survive it ….

Will sprinted, sprinted in the biggest gears he could find.

His legs screamed. His lungs dug for air. His chest burned. His eyes burst red with hot angry tears.

He began to dig frantically for a human emotion, a basic, primeval emotion, that his heart had planted in his head—buried, somewhere deep below his mother's lessons, the rules of the church and the laws of civilized society.

He dug for it as he climbed a hill through a quiet tree-lined neighborhood.

He clawed for it as he sprinted across Broadway and into Cherry Creek. He searched for it as he rode through the city for hours, finding it, holding it and knowing it.

He found it, knowing that it was within him all the time, there below the heart, the morality and the desire to be good, there below the lessons and the ethics and the admonitions, there below the laws and the rules and the wagging fingers of teachers, priests, rulers and those forever in charge.

It was what drove men to madness, drove men to throw themselves in front of an unreachable, unbeatable foe for nothing more than an idea, a dream, a closely-held concept. It simply wasn't done in a modern, civilized, well-ordered society. It was put aside. It was buried deep. It was hidden under blind ambition and the frantic rush for possessions, human or material.

But it was here, now. It was here within him as he rode. And it grew within him as he rode until he could no longer hold it close within him, and it burst out along the deserted streets of the Queen City of the Plains.

He screamed.

"YEEEEAAAAAAAAGGGGGGHHHHHHHHH!"

The sound leapt from him and echoed off the glass canyon walls of the Sixteenth Street mall. He put his head down, blindly sprinting toward Broadway, ignoring lights, traffic and his own safety.

"Yaaaaaaaaaaaaaaaaaaaaaaaaaaaaaaaaaaaaaa!"

The magic was gone.

And yet, the course was clear.

Hell was coming.

Hell was coming.

And it was coming on two wheels.

Other Books in the Moody Cycling Murder Mystery Series

Two Wheels
American Will Ross attempts to fill the late world champion's shoes, but also discovers the death wasn't an accident.
1-884737-11-0 • P-MTW • $12.95

Perfect Circles
Drugs and murder at the Tour de France.
1-884737-44-7 • P-CIR • $12.95

Derailleur
Will Ross and Cheryl Crane leave European road racing for mountain bike racing in Colorado, but trouble follows.
1-884737-59-5 • P-DER • $12.95

VELO
press®

Tel: 800/234-8356
Fax: 303/444-6788
E-mail: velopress@7dogs.com
Web: velopress.com
VeloPress books are also available from your favorite bookstore or bike shop.